STRONG: SURVIVAL ROAD

CHRIS VITARELLI

Enjoy!

CHRIS VITARELLI BOOKS

✳ Created with Vellum

For Gabriel, "Stay ready, don't have to get ready!"

ACKNOWLEDGMENTS

Jody, the tireless sounding board and idea generator
Angelina, Landon and Sofia
Sara for unrelenting competition

All my friends who love a good adventure story

PART ONE

ONE

David Zabad pulled his tie through to finish the half Windsor. He looked into the mirror one last time to make sure he hadn't forgotten to comb his hair. With the pace of his job and a wife and toddler at home, David occasionally forgot those basics. Sure enough, the disheveled mop of black hair required him to open the vanity drawer to grab a comb. As he swiped the comb through his hair, he assessed his reflection. Dark eyes with thick heavy eyebrows. A large but inoffensive nose, which belied his Jewish descent. A strong jawline, covered with yesterday's growth, reminding David that he'd also forgotten to shave. In his face he saw his father. In his eyes he saw his mother, a woman he never met but knew from his father's pictures and stories. He thought of his father for a moment; where was he today? Sometimes David knew and could even do a video call, Elizabeth holding Hannah in her lap so his dad could see how much his granddaughter had grown. Most of the time, Ethan

3

Zabad's destinations were classified. Occasionally David would hear a news report of some foreign affair he felt sure his dad was involved in. But today, David didn't know his father's location. They hadn't talked for a while. David's last grandparent died five years ago leaving his dad as his only family, unless you counted Robbie who was more like an uncle than Ethan's partner.

He put away the comb and glanced at the clock. He needed to be out the door in five minutes. I-75 would be jammed as usual. He stepped to the bedside and gently kissed Elizabeth on the cheek. She barely stirred. Chasing their daughter Hannah around all day was an exhausting full-time job. David grabbed a granola bar from the pantry and filled his travel mug with coffee. With keys and satchel he headed for the car, unaware of the day ahead and how it would change his world.

June 29 – 6:29PM Gulf of Thailand

No matter how many times he'd traveled to Southeast Asia, he could not get used to one hundred ten degrees and high humidity. Even on the water, the air seemed to surround him like a wool cloak, stifling and steaming him into dehydrated weakness. The boat he was on had been skimming the coast, darting in and out of small bays and inlets, allowing Ethan to check in with friends and informants. The small fishing boat, chosen because it drew almost no attention, puttered toward the dock. Ethan was relieved to be heading home. This latest tour was long and the years of fighting for justice, resisting oppression and freeing modern-day slaves was taking its toll. His family and home called to him through the exhaustion. He needed a rest.

He looked down at his scarred hands, opening and closing them, listening to the cracks the joints made. So many scars representing so many battles. Tales from the last fifteen years of globetrotting could fill numerous volumes. Ethan lost track of some events and the faces of dead or jailed warlords ran together in his mind. He was a warrior and had waged war ever since his first battle with the cult leader, Rolf Gallinger. The boat bumped against the dock, stirring Ethan from his memories. Voices shouted as ropes were thrown and tied down to hold the boat in place. He reached down to begin tossing gear from the boat to the dock.

"You look terrible," a voice said behind him. Ethan turned to see his best friend Robbie Charles standing on the dock, arms crossed, smiling at him. Robbie was several inches over six feet, broad in the chest, with powerful arms. He had a wide smile that when fully employed revealed a row of even white teeth that showed in bright contrast to his dark brown skin. Robbie had partnered with Ethan ever since they met on their first mission.

"You don't look so great yourself," Ethan replied, knowing the words were hollow and that he was the one who looked as if he'd been used hard and put away wet. 'Are we ready to head home?" he asked hopefully.

"Plane's ready." Robbie gestured indistinctly inland. After a moment, Robbie asked, "Are you okay?"

"Just weary. I need to get home and see my kids. My grandkid." He threw a duffel onto the dock and grabbed a plastic weapon case from a hatch in the deck.

"When's the last time you saw David?" Robbie grabbed the offloaded gear, walked to the end of the dock and tossed it into the back of a waiting truck.

"At least six weeks. No," he corrected himself as he

leapt off the boat and followed Robbie to the truck. "It's been more than that. I spent Easter with them and then left for Africa. My granddaughter has probably grown five inches by now." Ethan shook his head, disbelieving the thought. He had not learned he had a son until David was eight. Ethan was in prison for those years while his first and true love, Sarah, gave birth. The ache over her loss crept up on him again like a shadow. He took a deep breath and fought off the feelings.

"You've given up a lot to do this. It hasn't been easy." Robbie motioned to Ethan to get in the passenger seat. Ethan had been born after his parents received a vision from God. They were told their son would be like the Biblical figure Samson, blessed with incredible, God-given strength. He was given a mandate to protect and help people find their way to the one true God. Ethan spent most of his life rejecting the account as a fairy tale. After his time in prison and coming face to face with his past he finally accepted who he was.

"I think when I head home this time I'm gonna stay for awhile." He got in, put his head back and closed his eyes in preparation for the ride to the airport.

"Just 22 hours and we're home. I guess if you get a break I do too. It'll be nice to spend some time with my family. We can talk about exactly how long a break once we get home right Ethan?" Not hearing a response, Robbie glanced over at his friend. Ethan was already asleep.

June 29 – 7:23AM Southeast Michigan

David flicked his turn signal and slipped between an SUV and a semi as he prepared to exit southbound I-75. The traffic this time of the morning was ridiculous and it didn't take much to turn the four lanes into a parking lot. He hoped he could make it the next mile and a half without a major slowdown. The radio announcer reported that it was going to be a beautiful June day, with highs in the low 80's, no chance of rain. This was good news, though it mattered little for David since he would be indoors all day, with the exception of a half hour lunch where he could take a quick walk around his building. He was the youngest engineer, and one of the few who didn't spend their lunch doing even more problem solving.

David blazed through school in less than three years. His senior project blew away his professors who had never seen a student with such an incredible grasp of integrated systems. He had an intuitive understanding of how things worked together. When his senior thesis was published in a trade journal, he had job offers rolling in from everywhere and in every area of industry. He'd had offers from the United States Military, computer developers, and automotive companies. He decided to get the best of both worlds and took a job with an automotive tech company. Detroit outpaced Silicon Valley in the last couple years with the number of tech jobs available and more foreign tech companies were moving to the Detroit area. It was a good fit for David and there was room for him to advance within his division. The only drawback was the commute. A drive that took almost forty minutes without traffic on I-75 usually grew much longer. Rarely did a day go by without some kind of slowdown or outright traffic jam.

As he aimed for the exit ramp, he could see a line of cars at the top of the exit. Not the worst backup he'd ever seen. *I might still be able to get into the office by 7:30,* he thought as he glanced at the bright green clock on his dash. He looked back at the line of cars waiting at the exit and realized the traffic signal was dark. Must have lost power somehow.

June 29 – 7:23PM Suvarnabhumi Airport, Bangkok, Thailand

Ethan stumbled into the airport ticketing area with his duffel and a small bag containing his laptop computer slung over his shoulder. Robbie set up a flight for them that would stop over briefly in Shanghai and then complete the flight across the Pacific. He stood in front of the monitors listing the departing flights and found his gate. Recognizing that it was a long walk for he and Robbie, he headed toward the tram that would take them farther down the terminal to the gate. The partners in combat didn't talk much as they walked. Many years cemented their relationship to the point that they were like an old married couple; not much needed to be said. Years of communicating in silence, simply with gestures or eyes while on a job helped them operate as one.

Upon arriving at their gate, Ethan spotted a television airing the news in and around Bangkok. They sat in two chairs facing it and tried to hear the news over the din of the crowd. Nothing seemed interesting until a bold red band appeared at the bottom of the screen which Ethan recognized as "Breaking News". Languages were never his strength but years of travel enabled him to pick up a few words in almost every country. A stock photo of the White House appeared as well as an aerial shot of the United States capital. Ethan and Robbie both leaned in to try and hear the report and interpret what words they could. As the shots flitted between the anchor and pictures of dams and power plants Ethan and Robbie stood up, each trying to make sense of what they were seeing.

June 29 – 7:43AM Southeast Michigan

The power outage appeared to affect not just the traffic light at the top of the exit but every traffic light and office building David could see from where he sat on the exit ramp. At this rate he wouldn't get to work until after nine. His cell phone beeped and flashed so he snatched it off of his hip.

"David Zabad, talk to me."

"David, it's Paul. There's no power in our building. They're saying it's widespread. This whole part of town. I wouldn't bother coming in."

"What happened?"

"Not sure, but – "

The call cut off and David looked at his phone. It was scanning for service which would only mean one thing: Cell towers in the area were losing power and were now unable to connect calls. There was no means to carry the cellular signal. He tried calling his wife, but the phone wouldn't even dial. Realizing that the best place for him to be was home, David eased his Civic into the left lane of the exit ramp in preparation to get back on the expressway toward home. He turned on the radio hoping to hear what was causing the power outage but every station was static. It was faint, but a flicker of panic appeared at the edge of David's consciousness. He remembered the East Coast blackout of 2003. This felt eerily similar.

Fifteen minutes later, after fighting his way across the traffic-choked intersection, he finally merged onto I-75 north. He prayed for Elizabeth, hoping that everything was okay at home. Traffic picked up and allowed him to reach 65 miles per hour which was not bad for this time of day. The faster he drove the better he felt about a possible power outage. He started reviewing what food stores they had in their basement and how much water was stocked. It wouldn't be a bad idea to stop before home and grab a few things. The power outage might not reach as far as Fenton though. He may be worried for no reason at all.

Fenton was situated south and a little east of Flint, Michigan. It was a comfortable little city – one that was working hard to go from country town to mini-city by building up its downtown and sprucing up its streets. It was known for its restaurants and lakes. People came from the surrounding communities to play on the water, shop, and eat. David and Elizabeth moved there because of its proximity to work and the reputation of its schools. They found a gorgeous nineteenth century Victorian downtown that they'd been fixing up for a few years now. It was a great place to raise a family. It also made a good place for David's dad to come back to.

As David thought of getting home, he was interrupted by a massive shadow overhead. David looked up through his windshield to see a 747 gliding by but not thousands of feet in the air. This plane looked like it was about to land. David was confused, being far from a major airport. Something about the plane seemed out of place and that's when he realized he hadn't heard it. The plane was silent, the engines disengaged – or disabled. David watched, hoping, praying that the plane would pull up, would surge to the right or the left and gain altitude. Perhaps there was an airstrip nearby he didn't know about. All hopes were demolished as he realized the landing gear was not engaged. This plane was trying to land on the expressway. It was a myth that one of every five interstate miles had to be built straight and flat so it could be used as an airstrip in times of war. Though this stretch of highway was fairly flat, it was not straight. Was the nation in a time of war?

David watched, sickened as the jetliner dropped sharply just beyond an overpass and tried to touch down. There simply wasn't enough room. Cars on the expressway were veering off into ditches, either applying the brakes and causing multiple pileups or increasing their speed so as to avoid the unstoppable flight of the jet plane. A southbound car swerved to avoid a car whose driver stopped and exited the vehicle to watch the attempted landing. The driver overcorrected his maneuver and careened across the grassy median. David watched helplessly as the errant driver plowed head-on into a vehicle several hundred feet ahead of him. The oncoming car flipped end over end as glass and metal exploded across the roadway. David performed a maneuver of his own to avoid the debris and spinning vehicles. The jet was still very low but distant now. If the plane landed on the road it would block traffic for miles in both directions. David gunned the little 4-cylinder Civic and raced forward as fast as he could while dodging the surrounding cars. One thought dominated his mind: "*I have to get home.*"

June 29 – 7:43PM Suvarnabhumi Airport Bangkok, Thailand

Ethan lowered the cell phone and stared out the window onto the busy tarmac.

"How bad is it?" Robbie asked tentatively.

"Bad enough that they still don't have a complete picture of what happened." Ethan turned back toward the television he and Robbie were watching minutes ago, before the call came from Colonel Reynolds. His satellite phone enabled him to make the call. More images were being displayed and it was clear that these were not stock photos but more recent pictures and video coming in from all over the Eastern half of the United States.

"So what *did* happen?"

Ethan ignored the question as he used the phone to dial David's cell number. Direct to voicemail. He handed the phone to Robbie. "Try calling your family."

Robbie did so and had the same result.

"Colonel Reynolds believes it was a coordinated attack on the power grid. Country's blacked out from Maine to Miami and St. Paul to New Orleans. There have been explosions as well. Several major cities are completely dark so they think it was some kind of electrical weapon."

"Electromagnetic pulses?" Robbie asked.

"They're not seeing any sign of radioactivity . . . yet. Along with the attacks on power stations and dams and . . . " Ethan trailed off as he stared at the screen. An aerial shot showed hundreds of people standing in the streets of a city. No landmark in the picture gave any indication of which city.

"Ethan? Any idea who? It's not easy to generate an electromagnetic pulse without a nuclear blast. Has there been . . ." Robbie trailed off too as they both were absorbed by the continuously flashing images of burning buildings, plane wreckage in nondescript fields, and gridlock surrounding every major metropolitan area. People in the terminal gathered around to watch the images as well.

The question Robbie asked was momentarily forgotten as a feeling of dread rolled through Ethan's chest. He pulled his eyes from the monitor and finally answered. "No idea.

And no, no one is claiming responsibility. The worst part is that he said you and I aren't going anywhere. They've declared a state of emergency." Ethan sighed and rubbed a hand over his eyes and down his face. "Robbie, I'm not staying here. Not when our kids are in the middle of that mess."

"National emergency means closing America's borders. Especially if over half the country is in a blackout."

Ethan didn't respond but glowered back at his friend.

"Ethan. You've got that look in your eye."

"What look?" Ethan asked defensively.

"The one that says you don't think closed borders mean closed to *you*."

"Robbie, I'm going home. I don't care if they cancel every flight going into the states. I'll swim if I have to. I'm not leaving my family to fend for themselves. And you shouldn't either. If the power is really out from the Atlantic to the Mississippi it means mass panic, food shortages, looting. Total shutdown of shipping and transportation. It's going to get ugly."

"I have family there too. You don't think I want to be there?"

"I *know* you want to be there, Robbie. That's why I don't understand why you would want to get in my way. I've been crossing closed borders for fifteen years now."

"What I want is to wait and see if this is something that can be resolved in a week – or two. Let's not jump to conclusions. I'm sure Reynolds will let us know when the borders reopen and it will be a lot sooner than you think."

"And if it's not?"

Robbie took his time responding. He knew Ethan had grown in his faith over the last few years, especially as they worked together but a trite answer, no matter how true, would not ease Ethan's fear. "I trust God with my family," Robbie finally answered hoping it didn't come across as simply a platitude.

"I trust God with my family," Ethan shot back angrily. "It's the thieves, opportunists and terrorists I don't trust, and if you think for one second they won't take advantage of an opportunity like this, you're crazy."

Robbie knew he needed to keep his friend calm. He learned long ago that he didn't have the strength to go toe to toe with him. "You're right. There are bad people who will take advantage of a situation like this. But how soon do you think you could even get there? A week? Two weeks? Longer, if the blackout spreads. David is strong and he's resourceful. I know you taught him to prepare. He'll be okay."

Ethan shook his head. "Do you remember the hurricane that hit Florida last year? Do you remember how long it took people to loot local stores and steal water and food? Take to the streets? Three days! I know David is strong. I know he's resourceful. But he's no soldier. And he shouldn't have to be." Ethan turned and walked away from the gate of the now delayed and probably canceled flight.

"Where are you going?" Robbie called after him.

"For a walk." Ethan took two more steps and then realizing he left his duffel on the airport floor, turned and snatched at it. His temper got the best of him and as he jerked the bag off the floor one of the handles gave way, tearing the side of the bag open. Clothes and personal items spilled onto the floor making Ethan even angrier. Hastily grabbing everything off the floor and tucking it back into the bag, he stormed off again, not looking back.

"God, help my friend to trust you," Robbie prayed.

"And watch over our families. Help us get back to them. Soon."

June 29 – 7:52 AM Northbound I-75, just north of Detroit

David stood up on his brakes as his Civic slid to a stop behind another mid-size. A tower of smoke rose high over the roadway in front of him. He hadn't seen the crash first-hand but the fireball was hard to miss. The attempted jet landing was disastrous. If a plane attempted to land on an expressway, it meant there was no communication between the planes and air traffic control. Or the runways were clogged. Or planes were circling so long they were out of fuel. Or all of the above. Those were the only explanations David could come up with. There were people all around him exiting their vehicles. The crash blocked the next exit from the expressway so there was no way off the road.

The panic that was just under the surface earlier when he couldn't reach Elizabeth was now finding its fulfilment. *I have to leave my car here. I have to walk home - around this aircraft wreckage. What if there are bodies? I have no food, no water. I'm fifteen, twenty, no twenty-five miles from home. Elizabeth doesn't even know what's going on.* David knew he needed to get himself under control.

Something unprecedented was happening. He knew little to nothing about how electricity powered his house. He knew there were power plants but didn't know where. He knew there were hundreds of windmills and windfarms all over Michigan. Why weren't they providing power to Metro Detroit? Why hadn't he seen a cop since this started? Why could he not make a single call with his phone? The unanswered questions kept coming like a flood and finally David slammed the steering wheel with his hand in frustration. David glanced up and saw people streaming past his car toward the smoke in the distance. He wasn't the only one in this predicament. Realizing it was time to act, he pulled himself together. He made a mental note of the mile marker in case he needed to find his car again. He opened the trunk and pulled out his umbrella, the jumper cables, and the stroller he kept for when the family rode in his car. He also grabbed the jack. There was a sweatshirt and a towel he kept in the trunk for if he ever needed to lay on the ground to fix a flat. Throwing his work satchel over his shoulder and loading all these items into the stroller he fell into the thin but steady flow of people heading toward the wreckage.

He mentally reviewed what it would take to get home safely. Water was essential and so as he passed stopped cars he checked inside each to see if there were any water bottles he could scavenge. None of these drivers would miss them. In just the first twenty cars he gathered three full half-liter bottles of drinking water and a fourth half full of what would probably be stale, backwashed water. He tucked them into the stroller, covering them with the sweatshirt. Feeling a little more confident, he continued checking cars for water and food but not as diligently. The smoke of the fated aircraft loomed ahead and every eye in the line of stumbling, awestruck, former drivers was glued to its thick, billowing darkness.

As he walked with other stunned business execs, pencil-pushers, factory workers and retail clerks, he thought of his dad. What would his dad do? It had been some time since he'd seen him. He knew he was somewhere in Asia but was never privy to the details of his missions. He always thought of himself as a Zabad, having been raised by his grandparents but once he met his father he had redefined his identity. He had a father - a man who loved him unconditionally and held no bitterness about not knowing he even had a son during the eight years he was imprisoned. If there was ever a time he needed his dad's wisdom and leadership it was now. How would his dad get home? What could he do to help David and his family now?

The beautiful June morning David was enjoying less than an hour ago was now a nightmare. He stared at the bridge ahead. The wreckage of the jet was not far away now. The bridge was damaged where the tail of the plane clipped it on its way down. The first signs of debris were now appearing. The cars closest to the bridge evidently slammed on their brakes causing a twenty-five car pileup. David passed a mini-van whose front end was buried under the back of a tractor trailer. If there was someone inside the van, David didn't see them. It became difficult to push the stroller on the shoulder of the expressway. So many cars abandoned the roadway to avoid collisions that there were as many cars in the median as there were in the road. Most of these cars were abandoned already and as David looked ahead, he saw a long stream of people winding their way through the abandoned cars and smoking wreckage. Some of the wreckage was from the cars but most of it was from the plane, the remains of which were now fully visible. As he continued to weave through the vehicles in the median he glanced into various cars hoping to find anything of value that he could carry. Though twenty-five miles could be covered in a day he wasn't sure about his stamina for such a walk nor was he confident that he could make it home before night fell. In spite of the very real need for additional food or water, David knew deep down he was stalling, holding off the inevitable walk of horror through the scattered debris.

The wind shifted and now the acrid smell of burning rubber and fuel assaulted David's senses. The sour, choking smoke brought tears to his eyes and he pulled his shirt up over his nose and mouth to block it out. The eeriest thing about what happened was that no one he walked with spoke – not one word was uttered. There were some shouts for help from the roadway where people were assisting those caught in their vehicles but no one was discussing the situation. It was as if the entire population went into shock and were unable to speak.

There was a commotion ahead of him. David heard, "Oh my God!" repeated over and over by the people in front of him and though he hated the casual use of God's name, he couldn't blame them. He uttered the words himself, as a prayer. They came upon the first dead body.

Based on the build and clothing it was a woman but she was badly burned. Her shirt was torn exposing her undergarments and a bloody gash laid open her abdomen. Several people in the shell-shocked caravan turned aside to vomit at the gruesome sight. The frequency of this response caused the group and those following behind to give an even wider berth to the body lying in the median. As David approached he carefully pulled out the sweatshirt stashed in the stroller. He'd never smelled burned human flesh. His own gag reflex momentarily choked him as he unfolded the sweatshirt and gently, slowly laid it over the victim's face and chest. He said a whispered prayer and then stood to continue moving. He caught the eye of man standing opposite the body who appeared to have been praying as well. He gave the stranger a gentle nod and then turned back to the stroller.

"Thank you for doing that." The stranger fell in beside David, speaking quietly.

"It wasn't right – for people to just walk by like that and not show any respect," David whispered back.

"No. It wasn't," the stranger replied. "Most of these people are seeing things live in color that they've only seen in movies. It's too much."

"How are you so calm?"

"Probably the same reason you are." They split for a moment as each chose different ways around a piece of debris.

David raised his eyebrows and gave a skeptical smirk. "I wouldn't say I'm calm."

"You don't have that look in your eyes. The one that reads 'terror'. Every one of these people have it. You don't." The stranger was quiet for a moment as they continued to walk. "I'm Nathan." He extended his hand and to shake it, David had to stop pushing the stroller for a moment.

"Nice to meet you Nathan, considering the circumstances. I'm David." He put his hand back to the stroller and pushed on, silently wondering how the terror and panic he'd felt back at his vehicle simmered down to rest beneath his calm exterior.

"Nice to meet you too. Where are you headed?"

"Fenton. You?"

"Fenton? You've got a ways to go. I'm headed for Brandon Township. I live just south of the high school."

"That's a hike too."

Nathan was about to speak again when another commotion stirred the group ahead of them. As they approached they could see there were more bodies on the ground. This time people wept and cried aloud. Several women up on the shoulder of the road simply broke down. David, with Nathan beside him, was cautious, unmoved, until he realized what was causing the extreme reactions. They climbed from the lower part of the median up to road level and were struck with the same shock and devastation as those around them. The roadway was littered with bodies. For the next hundred yards, debris and wreckage were strewn every-where but unmistakably scattered throughout were human bodies. David tried to imagine what must have happened. The plane had to have tumbled upon impact. Rather than a smooth but destructive landing the plane spun and rolled as it broke apart with the gruesome result being that every passenger aboard was flung from the aircraft and scattered, some still in their seats. There were no more cars. The grisly results of the crash created a dividing line between the vehicle pileup and the plane rubble. David hoped that as they got beyond the main body of the plane it would be easier traveling.

"You know we can't just walk by. We need to see if there are survivors." Nathan didn't wait for David to answer and walked amidst the shattered remains of the jet. David closed his eyes, steeling himself for the ordeal he was forcing himself to undergo. Thirty minutes later not one of the victims they checked had a pulse. They did all they could. David was fighting back tears as he made his way to where Nathan was standing, surveying the scene.

David looked at his recent acquaintance. "Still calm?"

Nathan broke David's stare and turned away from him toward the trees lining the highway. "Let's keep moving."

TWO

Ethan was not well. Since he'd stomped off away from Robbie he was wrestling with his options – and his emotions. He was a warrior. He had been in some desperate situations. Under fire, out of ammo, trapped in burning buildings. He had quite a list of worst case scenarios, all of which he'd lived through. But in each one, his own life was on the line; they didn't involve his kids. David was Ethan's only son, but he married Elizabeth, a beautiful young woman, whom Ethan looked at like his own daughter. They were only married four years but already, David and Elizabeth had one child and Ethan hoped another was on the way soon. Ethan loved being a grandpa. Just the thought of his grandkid threatened to make him wild with panic. He was a half a world away with no clear path to get home. The instinct to protect and the dread it caused were so strong, it endangered his ability to think coherently.

"Ethan! Ethan Zabad! C'mon man, I know you're in here somewhere." Dozens of people in the airport turned at the sound of this voice to see an enormous black man stalking through the terminal. If the situation wasn't so serious it might be comical to see Robbie walking through a crowd of locals, each a full foot shorter than him.

Ethan heard the voice too. *Why couldn't Robbie ever just let him sulk?* He bent over and grabbed his duffel from under the seat and slowly stood.

"There you are! I've been looking for you for the last forty-five minutes. I've got good news. And really, really bad news." Robbie made his way to the corner Ethan was hiding in and reached out to him. "We've got to get to gate G5."

"Why? I thought we couldn't go anywhere."

"Colonel Reynolds just called me. Well, actually he called *you* but you left your phone behind when you – well, you know what you did."

Ethan acknowledged the jab at his temper with a nod and asked impatiently, "What is it?"

"He said if we can catch a flight leaving here in the next 15 minutes, it's heading to Spain. From there we might be able to catch a flight to Mexico. He says the eastern half of Canada is experiencing the same thing as the U.S."

"Any more details?"

"I'll tell you on the way. Let's get walking." They stepped away from the bank of seats and into the flow of foot traffic leading to the "G" gates. "So the information is starting to come in from around the country," Robbie continued. "Most of it from low frequency radio operators. They know there were attacks on several nuclear power stations. For example, Three Mile Island, Beaver Valley and Fermi II were all hit. That brought down the I-80 corridor from south Jersey to Detroit."

"What about the wind farms in the thumb?" Ethan asked, referring to the massive wind turbines in the eponymous part of Michigan's mitten. David and Elizabeth lived not far from the thumb.

"Those, along with the coal and oil plants are all computer linked and susceptible to cyberattack. Most likely *have* been cyberattacked. Colonel Reynolds said that's the theory they're working with at the moment. The good news is that the electromagnetic pulses were *not* nuclear. The EMP's were generated by something built right under Homeland Security's nose. They're not clear on exactly what that 'something' was but whatever it was, it was used in Miami, Charleston, Nashville and Chicago – to name a few."

"But there would have to be an explosion to generate an EMP right?" Ethan stepped onto the moving walkway and continued to walk at a rapid pace.

"Reynolds thinks whoever did it used airplanes. They got their devices or explosives aboard flights preparing to land in each of those cities and who knows how many more and they all detonated simultaneously. They were circling to land above some of the most populous cities in the eastern U.S. It's bad, Ethan."

Robbie watched his friend's face fall and wanted to comfort him but his own family was on his mind. They were living in Kentucky and Robbie had no idea how they were faring.

They stepped off the moving walkway and made a beeline for gate G5. The flight was leaving for Barcelona in seven minutes. Both Ethan and Robbie prayed silently that they could find something from there to the North American continent. At this point, anywhere would do.

. . .

June 29 – 10:30AM I-75, North of Detroit

There was no easy path through the horror that lay before them. Who would bury these bodies? How would loved ones learn of their deaths? What about the wounded and dying piled up behind them? No sirens were audible. Southbound I-75 was empty since the wreckage blocked all traffic. Beyond the wreck it was identical to the northbound lanes – a parking lot. If help was on the way it would need to come quickly and in large numbers. What about the hundreds of other accidents that must have happened? The more David thought about these questions the faster he walked. His recent acquaintance, Nathan, noted the increased pace and stepped his up as well.

"There's nothing we can do for anyone here. Best to just keep moving, right?"

David glanced at Nathan, unsure if the words were sarcastic or for his own benefit. Not discerning the motive, he simply continued to walk, carefully pushing the stroller and not looking down at any of the bodies scattered across three lanes. It was surreal to be walking in the middle of a major expressway – a road he drove every day for work, never really looking at what he was passing at seventy miles an hour.

Nathan nudged him, pointing ahead. "The main wreckage is spread across the whole road. We'll have to head into the woods."

David looked ahead and saw a steady stream of people moving to the roadside and off into the low plant growth leading into the trees. "Better to stay with the majority I suppose." He cautiously steered the stroller across the road, being careful not to disturb any of the deceased. He couldn't bring himself to even look at them. The slow, careful walk to the roadside was eerily quiet. Strip away the smoke and debris and the victims could have been laying on a beach somewhere. They were not horribly contorted or grimacing in death. They looked at peace. Resting. Most of them were not cut or burned. They were simply ripped from the plane and died on impact. David tried not to imagine the terror they must have felt in their final moments.

He and Nathan finally reached the side of the road and made their way down off the shoulder and into the trees. A thin wire fence was trampled so people could get far enough away from the burning wreckage. Every few minutes the wind would shift bringing the repulsive smell back to the line of people snaking their way through the trees.

"So what were you doing down this way?" Nathan asked, breaking the silence.

"I was headed to work but got a call from my friend who said to just go home. Power was out everywhere. And then my phone died. Where were you headed?"

"Meeting with a friend. My phone died too. I figured he would understand if I didn't show. Seemed like things were getting crazy."

"Do you have family?"

"I do. A wife and a daughter. I'm glad this wasn't a school day. Trying to get her from school would be chaotic on a day like this." Nathan paused and glanced back at the roadway. "Of course getting my daughter from school seems like a small problem compared to what we just walked through."

"Well, let's just get home to our families. We've got a long walk ahead of us."

"David, you know, you might want to consider ditching that stroller. It draws some attention and I think it might slow you down."

"Maybe. I'm just trying to plan ahead."

"For what?"

"For anything. Any one of these things," he gestured to the stroller, "might prove useful. If the power doesn't come back soon it could be days we have to get through. If it's worse than that, it could be months." Longer alternatives came to mind but David was afraid to speak them aloud.

David was amazed there wasn't more panic or running. Most of the people leaving the roadway were walking quietly and simply minding their own business. He considered that shock might be a factor. Nathan and David were just two of the very small number of people actually talking.

"Water! Does anyone have any water?" The shout came from somewhere ahead of them. "Water? Anyone?"

"Yeah I've got some water," David called. He almost grabbed the tepid, half-full bottle but realized now was not the time for selfishness. "Here you go," David offered, handing the man who approached him one of the fresh, unopened bottles. He wore a filthy t-shirt, ripped jeans and what looked like steel-toed work boots. His disheveled hair matched his unshaved face. His pants were wet at the crotch.

"Thanks dude," the man replied as he greedily unscrewed the cap and chugged the water bottle empty while standing there. He swiped a short-sleeved upper arm across his mouth and asked David, "Got any more?"

The smoke, a hot June day, and another twenty plus miles until home all played on David's fears. "I'm sorry man, I can't. I've got a long ways to go and I really can't spare any. I'm sorry." David turned to move on.

"So you have some? You keepin' it in the baby stroller? Huh? C'mon man, just give me some water!"

The once quiet and orderly line of people sped up as they sensed a coming conflict.

Nathan spoke quietly and calmly. "Look, I know you must be thirsty. A lot of these people are too. We're all just trying to get home."

"Just give me water and I'll be on my way." The man pushed his face up into Nathan's and he and David recognized that the water the man chugged did nothing to wash away the smell of alcohol on his breath. They also both smelled urine; he evidently soiled himself. The scent of his unwashed body mixed with the already pungent odor of burning jet fuel.

David handed the man a second bottle. "C'mon Nathan, let's go. We have to keep moving," David suggested firmly.

"You're not going anywhere! Give me all of that water!" The man pushed Nathan backward. "We're all gonna die out here anyway! Did you see what just happened?" he shouted, pointing to the road. "Give me that water!" He lunged for the stroller, knocking it over. The few items David scavenged spilled into the brush. The man leaped when he saw a water bottle roll free. "Mine!"

"David, leave it, let's go!" Nathan helped David scramble to pick up the remaining things and shove them into the stroller.

Let the guy have another bottle. Escape was more important.

"No you don't!" The frightened, drunken thief grabbed David and threw him to the ground, again going for the stroller containing the last two bottles of water. Nathan saw David hit the ground and escape was no longer the objective. Nathan feared for David's life. He didn't hesitate but reached for the man's arm, grabbed it and spun him around. He reared back to punch the man but was doubled over by a blow to his stomach.

Nathan grunted and fell to his knees.

"No!" David watched as the drunken man pulled a knife from Nathan's abdomen, covered in blood. Then he turned and pointed the weapon at David.

"You stay there or you'll get the same." The thief-turned-murderer glared at David.

David glanced around looking for help of any kind. The people who were walking by just a moment before disappeared into the trees. The man still had the knife in one hand a bottle of water in the other.

"My water?" David threw a panicked glance at the assailant and realized he was demanding this from David. "My water! Now!" the man screamed again. David found the last two bottles, one full and one half full, and threw them to the man. He looked past him to check on Nathan. He wasn't moving.

The man looked at the bottles, reading their labels. "This one's drinking water. You know they bottle this from a tap and then sell it to you? This stuff sucks." He opened it and poured it out onto the grass, then looked at the half full bottle. "Someone drank out of this. Backwash. I don't want to get sick. Here, you can keep that one." He dropped the second bottle and staggered off in the direction David came from. "I'll keep this one. It's spring water", he slurred as he patted the third and final bottle tucked into his waistband. There wasn't even time to express rage. Only disbelief.

"Nathan!" David crawled across the grass and brush to his new friend's side. "Are you okay? Nathan?" He heard a groan as he lifted his shoulder and rolled him onto his back.

Nathan was clutching his abdomen and David had to work hard to get him to move his hands so he could assess the damage. There was so much blood. The knife had not gone straight in but up and under Nathan's ribs, to the center of his chest. David had no idea what to do. "I'm sorry, I should've given him all the water. I'm so sorry."

"It's not your fault," Nathan said softly.

"What?"

"It's not your fault."

David's eyes welled up.

"At least he left you a couple bottles of water."

"I don't care about that. I should have given it all to him. I was stupid."

"You're not stupid," Nathan whispered. His breathing sounded raspy and his voice weakened. "You were being – both generous – and wise."

"Let's just focus on getting you help."

"It's okay, David. I know where I'm going if I die."

"You're not going to die," David said forcefully. "I said, 'let's get you some help.'"

"Let's not kid around, there's no way I'll make it home. I already feel weaker."

"Stop talking like that. I'll rig up a travois to move you. I can carry one end and drag the other or use the wheels off the stroller. We can get you help."

"Don't bother. But I do – need something."

David wanted to get to work on a solution – anything that would ease Nathan's pain and his own conscience. He forced himself to stop and listen. "Anything. Name it."

"David, I need you - to go to my house. Tell my wife - what – happened." The words came hard as he struggled to breathe.

"I – I don't know where you live, your wife, what do I . .

. I'll take you to a clinic. You can tell her yourself." David was scrambling to avoid what seemed inevitable.

"Please. Tell her what – happened. She knows - I'm going - to see – Jesus – and our – our – son." Nathan's eyes closed and he tried to form more words but nothing came from his lips.

"Nathan don't!" David looked around frantically, "Help! Someone help me! He's dying!" He stared at this man he'd met just a couple hours ago, praying silently, willing him to get up off the grass and be okay. Knowing no one would be coming to help, he leaned close to Nathan's ear. "I'll do it. I'll go to your house. I promise. I will."

Nathan uttered a groan that ended in a gasp and David could no longer see the rising and falling of his chest as he struggled for breath. He felt for his pulse but could find nothing. David was stunned. Just a minute ago he'd been walking with a new friend. In the midst of this chaos, he had met a genuine human being only to watch him be killed by another human. No. No, not a human. An animal.

People came through the trees again, from the roadway, totally unaware of what just happened. The slight control David once gained over his emotions was beginning to crack and his mind started spinning. *I have to stay focused,* he told himself over and over. He walked through the trees and found several long, straight fallen limbs. Carrying them back to Nathan's body, he laid them down and tore the fabric from the umbrella he brought along into strips. He used these to bind the limbs together in a triangle shape. He then took the towel and tied its corners to the triangle making a small sling that would hold Nathan's body.

Once Nathan's body was on the makeshift travois, David dragged it through the trees until the line of people made their way back to the road. It was backbreaking labor to move Nathan's body through the tall grass and brush along the highway. Two compassionate people came to his aid - one to help pull the travois and the other to bring the stroller. At the road, David gently laid Nathan down and set about rigging his stroller to serve as a set of wheels. He used another long straight limb he picked up along the way and laid it across the stroller. He and his helpers lifted the back end of their travois and laid it across the limb to distribute Nathan's weight over the wheels. David, using his tie, his button down shirt, and Nathan's jacket, tied himself straps he could lay over his shoulders to more comfortably carry his friend's corpse. With this set up he became a pack animal, bearing part of Nathan's weight with the stroller behind carrying the rest. He was sweating liberally and already downed the half bottle of water. He set out at the fastest pace he could manage under the weight of his load and cried tears of grief for the first mile.

He had a long walk ahead.

THREE

"There are over forty flights heading west from this airport."

"Then book me on whatever flight will get me close to the United States." Ethan demanded.

"I'm sorry sir but many of these are showing cancelled because they have connections in the US." The ticket agent was staring at her screen with a furrowed brow. "I can get you to Mexico City midday July 2?"

Ethan almost leapt across the counter. "That's in two days!" he erupted.

The ticket agent stepped back, startled at Ethan's angry response. "I'm sorry sir, that's the best I can do."

"Book it," Ethan said angrily. Colonel Reynolds called them when they landed to inform them that there would be no military transport for them out of Europe. All assets were being focused on the task within the US.

"This is a nineteen-hour flight, Robbie. Think of what

32

could happen during that time. I don't even know if my kids are alive."

"I don't know about my own kids, Ethan. But we have to stay focused on just getting home to them."

The televisions all over the terminal were playing stories coming out of the eastern United States. The panic and chaos Ethan feared were widespread. Very little progress was being made in bringing aid to those affected by the power outage.

One story summed up the damage being done across the country. A hospital in Chicago went dark when the power went out and the EMP disabled the backup generators. Every person in the hospital on life support died before anything could be done. As the hospital workers tried to move the most critical patients to a more central location, throngs of injured Chicago residents swarmed the hospital's emergency room begging for assistance. While nurses and doctors tried to triage the wounded, others raced past medical personnel and stole bandages and medicine. The hospital pharmacist was fatally stabbed as a gang rushed the pharmacy and took everything they could carry.

June 30 – 4AM, Fenton, Michigan

A light fog hung over the streets. The city was completely dark. David shivered a little as he stumbled toward his street. He hadn't eaten since breakfast the day before and he finished his last water bottle before he arrived at Nathan's house. He was completely spent, emotionally and physically. All he wanted was to see Elizabeth and his daughter.

He was in a daze as he made his way up the footpath to the house's side entrance. He couldn't see his keys and so fumbled with them, trying each one until he got it right. When he was able to open the door he slowly pushed it open, expecting there to be furniture piled on the other side. He was not wrong.

He pushed the door open just enough to squeeze through. "Elizabeth?" He whispered her name, not sure if she tried to wait up for him on the couch. He was amazed at how dark it was in the house without the ambient light from ubiquitous electronic devices and carefully placed night lights. He turned on his cellphone flashlight to guide his way. "Elizabeth, it's me. It's David." He knew Elizabeth would be terrified to hear things go bump in the night, especially after the last twenty-four hours, so he kept whispering her name as he made his way up their back stairway. She never really liked the shotgun but he also knew she wouldn't hesitate to use it on an intruder.

He reached the top of the stairs and looked left toward his bedroom. He could make out the silhouette of his wife – and the shape of something long and narrow in front of her. He kept the light low so as not to blind her.

"It's okay, Elizabeth – it's me, David."

"David!" She ran toward him and dissolved into tears. "I thought you were dead. My phone wouldn't work. Our neighbor said she hadn't heard from her husband either. What happened?" They fell into each other's arms and just held one another close for a full minute while Elizabeth cried.

"Take a breath, Elizabeth. I'm here now." He touched her arm and ran his hand along it until he reached the gun. She released it and he stood it against the hallway wall. "It's okay. It's okay, Lizzie. You did good." He held her and stroked her long gently waved brown hair.

"Daddy? What's wrong?"

"Hannah!" David stepped back from Elizabeth just enough to bend and scoop his daughter up into his arms. They held Hannah between them for a moment as the relief washed over them like a warm rain.

"Hannah, go back to bed. It's still very early. Daddy needs to rest, ok?"

"Where did you go?"

"Daddy had a long trip to make. It's ok. I'll come tuck you back in." Hannah trudged back to her bed reluctantly but sleepily.

"What happened, David? What's going on?" Elizabeth grabbed his hand and pulled him toward the bedroom. "I know you need to sleep but I have to know first."

David quickly tucked Hannah in and kissed her on the forehead. He walked Liz back to their room.

"I don't know that much. I know the power is out in most of this area – at least from my office up to here." They sat on the bed together.

"Why did it take you so long to get home? And where's the car?"

There were things he didn't want to tell Liz. The images from the crashed plane, about Nathan. The darkness hid the fact that he was covered in blood not his own. She would see it eventually. If this was as serious as David was beginning to believe, she needed to know. He started with his screeching halt on the expressway, the plane crash and the search for survivors, ending with the shocking murder of Nathan in the grassy shoulder along I-75.

"No one stopped to help? Where were the police?"

"Lizzie, you don't understand. It was chaos. What happened today – I mean, yesterday was surreal – like living in a movie. People said their cars just died. One minute they were driving and the next their cars just –

stopped. People were acting normal one minute and the next all hell would break loose. It made no sense."

Elizabeth tried to let this sink in for a moment then asked, "Did he have a family?"

"Yes Liz, he had a family." David closed his eyes trying to clear his head of the image forever burned into his memory. Watching Nathan's wife emerge from her house, first out of curiosity, then out of fear, running to the travois that held her husband, was more than he could bear to think about. Her cries and then the wails of his daughter flooded his thoughts. He couldn't stop the tears from rolling down his cheeks.

"Oh David, I'm so sorry." She stroked his back gently. "You went to his house didn't you?"

"I had to. It took me almost six hours to walk to his house with his body. But I was not going to leave him on the side of the road."

"How did you know where he lived?"

"He told me the general area. I at least had his address from his wallet. I just asked around for specifics when I got there. People I did see out of their homes were scared. I let them assume Nathan was just injured. No one even got close enough to discover the truth."

"And his body?"

"I stopped at two different funeral homes along the way but no one was at either one. I passed two clinics but they were packed, lines out the door. Not that they could have done anything for him. I think I was just avoiding the inevitable. I had to go to his house." David stood up from the bed and took a few steps from Liz. "It was late afternoon when I finally got there. When she saw he was dead, she hit me. I think she thought I had done it and was trying to soothe my conscience by bringing him home. I can't blame her. After all, I'm covered in his blood. But after I explained what happened and she calmed down some, she helped me lay him out in her living room. I was going to leave but she asked if I would dig a grave."

"A grave? What about a police report? An investigation? Didn't she want to have a funeral service?"

"Lizzie, I don't know how to say this." David stood and turned his back to her, afraid that even in the darkness of morning she would see the fear on his face – the reality of what was happening.

"Say what? David, what is it?"

"Based on what I saw today, I don't think things are going to be normal for a long time." He turned back to her. "I buried him, Liz. Right in her backyard."

"You can't do that!"

"I did. It was in the eighties today. If she couldn't get him to a funeral home in the next twenty-four hours do you know what would happen?" He shook his head to dislodge the grotesque thought. "If this . . . crisis . . . passes in the next day or so she can always exhume his body, but for now she has closure. And he's where he belongs."

"But David – "

"Lizzie, I need to sleep. After I dug Nathan's grave I *walked* here from Ortonville. I've been on my feet for almost twenty-four hours. We can discuss this later."

Elizabeth stood and stepped close to him. "I'm sorry, I'm just scared."

"I am too." David kissed her and started to lower himself onto the bed before he realized he was still covered in grime and blood. He quickly stripped off the filthy clothes and stretched out his body on the cool sheets. He was asleep almost instantly.

FOUR

HE NORMALLY WOKE UP TO AN ALARM BUT IT WAS THE sun and the temperature that brought him to awareness. By the light outside, David guessed it was close to noon. It was the worst night of sleep he'd had in recent memory. Images from the plane crash and his encounter in the woods were vividly replaying in his mind all night. He kept smelling the water thief's breath in his dream. As he slowly awoke, he realized he was sticky with sweat and without connecting his dreams to the widespread tragedies of the previous day immediately wondered why the air conditioning wasn't working. He threw back the sheet that covered him and twisted his body until his feet slipped out of bed and hit the floor. He put his hands to his face but winced as the blisters on his palms contacted his facial stubble. Then the rest of yesterday came rushing back to him. He quickly grabbed a pair of shorts out of his nearby dresser and just slipped them on when he heard, "Daddy!" David looked up to see his daughter run from the doorway. She threw herself into his arms. Elizabeth was right behind her.

"How did you sleep?"

"Fine," David lied, his voice muffled by Hannah's hair. "Is there any news?"

"There's nothing, David. I've seen cars go by but there's no power. A few people have their generators going."

"I'm going to take a shower and try to feel human again," David groaned as shifted Hannah in his arms.

"There's no water, David."

"No water? You don't lose water during a power outage," David reasoned aloud.

"There's no power. No TV, Wi-Fi, radio. The emergency hand crank radio works but it's all static. There's not even an emergency broadcast message or signal."

David let go of Hannah and looked Elizabeth in the eyes. "You mean the 'This is an emergency' thing? Isn't that the whole point?" The same feeling of panic he had felt yesterday watching Nathan die was creeping up on David again. *Don't lose it! You have to stay focused,* he told himself again.

"What do we have in the house right now?"

"As in, food?"

"Yeah! And water? Do we have enough to eat and drink for the next few days?

"I think so but I was actually planning to go shopping yesterday when everything stopped." Elizabeth didn't like where David was going with these questions. "You're scaring me, David."

David was scaring himself. Looting, panic and fear were all he could think about. "Maybe we should go shopping," David declared. "Right now."

"Now?"

"Now," he repeated grimly. "Get your best walking shoes on and grab Hannah's wagon."

Things seemed fairy normal in Fenton as they made their way down the main street leading to the expressway. There were cars on the road and people were outside their houses. David relaxed; maybe his fears were unfounded. The plane crash, Nathan, his exhausting day yesterday were the worst parts of this and the power would be back on soon. No one they waved at as they walked seemed worried. They must not know about the plane that came down or any of the horrific things he'd seen. But why would they? They had no television or radio – no one to tell them what was happening.

They made their way past the high school and David almost completely relaxed until he saw the flashing lights and some groups of onlookers.

"What is it, David?" Elizabeth asked, seeing not only the lights but also the change on her husband's face.

"Something's not right, Lizzie." Four squad cars were parked at the entrance to the Target store. "Why are there cops here?"

"David, let's not go up there. If there's an accident or something crazy happening, I'd rather not get involved."

"Lizzie, we need some food and water and whatever else we can get here. I'll go up and see if it's anything we need to worry about."

Elizabeth put her hand on David's arm, pleading, "Don't go! Let's just head home."

"Lizzie, it's okay. I'll be right back." David put his hand on hers and squeezed. "I love you." He turned and purposefully walked toward the police cars. Nothing seemed out of place and he heard no commotion. It was quiet and felt like business as usual. Further relaxing his guard, he followed the sidewalk around a high grassy hill flanking the driveway and was then stopped in his tracks. The squad cars pulled up to provide cover for several officers huddled behind open doors. Down in the Target parking lot he could see hundreds of cars but between the main lot and the entrance was a man holding a gun to a woman's head.

"This is it! This is the end of the world as we know it! We're all gonna die!" The hostage taker was staggering around as he yelled, flinging the woman in his arms like a rag doll. She was crying and keeping her wide eyes on the gun in the man's hand.

One police officer was within fifty feet of the man with a bullhorn. "What do you want? We can help you if you tell us what you want."

"You can't help me," the man sputtered out as he sobbed. "I knew it would happen this way. No power, no food." He broke down and wept.

"Sir, the power will come back on. This is temporary. It's happened many times before. Why don't you let her go and we can talk some more?"

"You are going to let me into that store," he gestured wildly toward Target with the pistol, "and let me get what I need and then I will let her go. But you have to open the store."

"Sir, I can't do that. Target has no power and no emergency power. They can't let people in there. It isn't safe."

"You let me in or she dies!" He jammed the pistol into the woman's right cheek and backed his way toward the store, looking all around to make sure no one could sneak up behind him.

David drifted toward a small group of onlookers and spotted an older man who was dressed for a day on the lake. "How long has this been going on?"

"Eh, ten, fifteen minutes maybe. The guy's a nut job, but I do wish they'd open the store. No one else in town is opening either. The grocery stores, Wal-Mart, the restaurants."

"What do you think they'll do in a case like this?" David asked, gesturing toward the gun-wielder.

"Negotiate. But on a day like today when everybody's on edge, I wouldn't be surprised if they just shot him and ended this."

David shuddered at the thought of witnessing a second murder in as many days, and possibly a third death at the hands of police. He watched as the disturbed man made his way closer to the main doors. Then without warning, he turned and fired several shots into the automatic sliding glass doors. The glass shattered and fell out of the frame. The crazed gunman pushed his hostage to the ground and ran for the now-open doors but another single shot rang out and he fell just a few inches from the threshold. It was quiet across the parking lot. The former hostage was running up the parking lane toward police. David watched as heads popped up all over the parking lot. People who were under cover during the standoff now rose to see what happened. Several made their way toward the gunman, David presumed, to see if the perpetrator was dead. Instead, they grabbed hold of the shattered doorframes and pulled the automatic doors apart. With a shout and a roar of sound, an entire parking lot full of people rushed toward the store. David felt an icy block form in the pit of his stomach. He knew what he had to do. He jogged back to the corner so he could make eye contact with Liz.

"It's okay! I'll be right back," David lied for the second time that day.

Elizabeth tried to shout back but David already turned

and was running toward the open black mouth of the store as people continued to pour in before him. *I would be a fool not to go into that store right now and get whatever I can. Where else can I provide for my family right now?* In his panic and fear, David still couldn't believe he was choosing to steal. He was mentally reviewing the layout of the store so he would know where he was and could get to what he needed immediately.

As soon as he entered the store, he realized he waded into a mess. People were shoving and jockeying for position, some were ramming carts around while others were simply shoving things into pants pockets or pouches made from the shirts on their backs. These were otherwise law-abiding citizens, people he saw around town. It was surreal to think he was stealing from a store. He was a looter. Yesterday he was heading to work as an engineer – today he was robbing a Target store.

He managed to get a cart and immediately headed to the pharmacy. It seemed most people were headed toward the food aisles. He grabbed as many feminine hygiene products as he dared, knowing he had many other things to put in the cart. He also grabbed several bottles of cough medicine, fever reducer, dietary shakes, and food supplements. He was a good distance from the doors now and light was scarce. Some people found flashlights and were using them at various places in the store. David headed deeper into the store and by his nose knew he was near the pet food aisle. That meant he was close to the food aisles. His eyes were adjusting to the darkness but he still had difficulty seeing and the aisles were crowded with people. There wasn't much noise except some grunting and a few expletives as people argued over various items. He bypassed what he knew were snack food aisles and found what he was looking for. The baking aisle. He grabbed several huge bags of flour and sugar, several boxes of baking mix, and as much salt as he had room for in the cart. He had one last stop to make and he pushed his heavy load down a few more aisles, being led by memory more than eyesight and turned into what he hoped was the junk food aisle. He felt along the shelves until he found the packages of beef jerky and cheese. He filled the open spaces in the cart with these and made a beeline for the front door.

"Everyone stop right where you are! This is the Fenton Police. You are stealing! Everyone who leaves this store with unpaid merchandise will be placed under arrest." The bull-horn carried well through the unlit store with no AC running and no music playing over the speakers. David knew his only option was the back door. He made a U-turn and pushed his way toward the emergency exit he knew was at the southwest corner of the store.

If he could slip out the door and down the hill that led behind the nearby high school he might be able to stay out of sight. David strained to see in the blackness but it reminded him of the visit he'd once made to a cave in Pennsylvania. Halfway through the cave tour, they turned out the lights. The blackness was as complete then as it was now and David reached out with his right hand to feel the racks next to him. He felt the metal edge of the shelves and every few inches the small plastic tab that held the price tag. Slowly and steadily he made his way toward the back wall of the store. Strangely, there was no one around him. He heard shouts and screams from other parts of the store but there seemed to be no one nearby. He remembered the west wall of the store was lined with cases of bottled water. He threw three cases atop his already heavy cart and continued toward the exit.

The shelf beside him ended and David groped further to his right to feel the wall. He made contact but struggled to keep the cart rolling straight and feel the wall at the same time. And then he felt it. The cold steel of the door and the bar at the center that would release the latch. "C'mon David, you need to do this fast," he whispered to himself. He guessed at where to line up the cart with the doorway and rested his lower back against the crash bar. David pushed his hips against the bar and pulled the cart as quickly as he could. The door swung open and David was momentarily blinded by the midday sun. Not knowing what was behind he just pulled the cart through and started walking it past the back edge of the building.

His head was down and he was squinting, trying to adjust to the light. To his left was the loading dock and just past it a fence. Beyond the fence, the ground dropped away and led to a pair of little league baseball fields. David jogged behind the cart toward the fence hoping, praying there was a gap in it so he wouldn't have to carry everything around. He was counting on all the cops being out front dealing with the chaos of hundreds of looters. It was the only time David was thankful Fenton had a small police force.

I'm a looter, David thought to himself. *I'm no better than any of those people! But this is a matter of survival, right?* He continued to rationalize his crime as he made his way to the fence. In the corner there was a large section of fence pulled away from the fence post. It was big enough for a man to slip through but today it was going to have to let a cart through. He managed to wedge the cart through the opening but it was aimed downhill. The weight of the cart dragged him down the slope but David managed to keep it and himself upright. He struggled to get the cart behind a large oak tree flanking one of the ball fields. Satisfied that it was out of sight from the place he'd come through the fence, he jogged back up the hill and toward the last place he'd seen Liz and Hannah.

She was still there, on the sidewalk, holding Hannah's hand, as tears rolled down her face. David surprised her by coming from a different direction. "Lizzie, I was worried you wouldn't be here. C'mon, bring the wagon. We need it."

She threw her arms around him in relief and then pushed away. "You were in there this whole time?"

"Yes! We needed some things and they weren't opening. Probably weren't going to open – ever."

"You stole stuff from there? This is a power outage, David! What are you thinking? The power will be back on in a day or two and then what?"

The past hour's struggle of trying to calm himself and believe that all this tragedy was temporary ended in surrender to the truth. "The power won't be back on in a day or two."

"What?" Lizzie stepped toward him. People were walking past her on the sidewalk, either to watch the commotion at the store or to speed past with stolen packages of their own.

"The power," David moved closer so he wouldn't be overheard. "The power won't be back on soon."

"How do you know that? How do you know?" Lizzie was no longer just crying. Her face was white and her eyes wide.

"Planes don't just lose power. Entire sections of our state, metro areas don't just lose power. Cell phones are not just saying 'no signal'. Mine still has power but I heard people talking about it yesterday as I walked home. Their phones just went dead. This isn't an overloaded electrical grid. This is an attack of some kind. Some kind of electrical attack that doesn't just shut off the power, it destroys it completely."

"What does that mean?"

Gun fire erupted from the front of the store and the screaming reached a crescendo. "I will tell you more about it later. Right now just follow me." David grabbed the wagon and headed back toward the rear of the store, giving a wide berth to the commotion near the main doors. The police fired tear gas into the store and were subduing looters as they exited.

Once they reached the grocery cart behind the oak tree they unloaded its contents into the wagon and covered it all with a blanket that padded Hannah's seat. "We have to get home – now. David reached for Liz but she snatched her arm away.

"You're going to tell me everything you know on our way home. I want the truth. Don't try to make me feel better."

"What about Hannah?" David deflected.

Liz looked at Hannah who was standing quietly, looking up the hill toward the store. "You can talk quietly. But I need to hear what you're thinking."

"Fine, but you're going to hate most of what I say and you're not gonna want to believe it. I don't even want to believe it."

"Try me."

David sighed and pulled the wagon toward the high school parking lot several hundred yards away. "When I was walking home yesterday I talked to people whose cars just died. I mean they just shut off. Mine didn't. I had to stop because of the plane but people who were just a few miles behind me on the road lost power completely."

"What does that mean?" Liz asked as she scanned the field around them.

"I think it means that someone detonated some kind of device that ruins electronics."

"Like what?"

"Something that emitted an electromagnetic pulse. It's sometimes called an EMP. It destroys electronic circuits. Overwhelms them and causes them to burn out. I think it destroyed the electronics in the cars and brought the plane down. That plane was fifty miles from Metro Airport. It was probably circling to land when it lost power and tried to land on a glide." David was quiet as the magnitude of what had happened to him yesterday started to sink in. He witnessed murder – saw burned, broken bodies scattered across a highway. A lump formed in his throat but he shoved the thought away. He knew if he let the horror, the pain, penetrate his mind, his emotions then he would not be able to effectively lead his family.

"All those people," Liz whispered as she hung her head. Her eyes snapped back to David. "Does that mean that there's no one to come and take care of that crash site? Bury the bodies? Are there no ambulances? Police?"

"Liz, I don't know if I'm right. I think I am but I hope I'm not. If it was an EMP, there's no way to know how wide-spread its effects are. Maybe it hit harder near Detroit. But if I had to make a guess I would say no, there's probably no one coming to take care of the dead. If this was an EMP then there are probably disasters all over Southeast Michigan. How would the police and fire fighters get to the crash?"

"You don't think this was just some fluke – some strange power outage that will be over by tomorrow?"

"I don't. I didn't realize it until I went into that store. I became a criminal today, Liz. But I didn't comprehend until I was grabbing things off the shelf that this isn't going away. Everyone else in that store knew it too. I think even the cops know but they're trying to keep the peace. You watch – as soon as the police decide they need to be home with their families instead of doing their job – that's when we'll know this is going to last a while and it's not going to be peaceful."

They walked in silence the remaining mile home. Hannah happily walked with them, not realizing what was happening around her. David glanced at her, wishing he could feel the same.

FIVE

Ethan was pushing away panic again as he left the airport with Robbie. Their flight zigzagged across the Atlantic, first stopping briefly at Cape Verde, then landing for half a day in Sao Luis, a stopover in Caracas, and finally landing in Mexico City. The time that was wasted made it difficult for Ethan to sit still on the plane. This made things difficult for Robbie as well.

"So, are you done freaking out?" Robbie said this casually as he and Ethan left the baggage claim area.

"I'm fine, Robbie. I don't understand why you're so calm."

"I told you, God's got this under control. I'll get to my family when I get to them."

"You saw those reports. It's been four days and the power's still out. They haven't even gotten cameras to places in the center of that mess. No one even knows what's happening. Even Colonel Reynolds hasn't responded to any calls." Ethan walked toward an empty taxi.

"Ethan, you've been in worse situations than this."

Ethan spun to face Robbie. "Right. *I* have. Not my son, his wife, my granddaughter."

"Let's just get in this taxi and see if he can take us where we can catch a bus. We can talk about what we're going to do as we go." Robbie swung his bag into the back seat of the car.

"As long as we're doing something. I can't stand doing nothing."

The taxi driver took them to a local bus station and they booked two seats headed toward Brownsville, Texas. As they boarded the bus, which stank like old cheese and dusty attic, it creaked and groaned. Thankfully it was only half full, giving Ethan and Robbie a chance to stretch out.

"I'm surprised this bus isn't more full."

"The United States is the last place anyone wants to be right now, Robbie." Ethan adjusted to a more comfortable position then glanced over at Robbie across the narrow aisle. "Have you thought about crossing the border? The latest reports said they closed it due to the state of emergency. They'll let a couple old soldiers in, right?"

"I don't know. I think we better spend the next fifteen hours praying."

"Don't you worry, Robbie. I'll pray. But first let's figure out what we're going to do once we cross the border. We have a long way to go."

"That's easy. We'll do it the old-fashioned way," Robbie grinned, holding up a hitchhiker thumb.

"You're my best friend Robbie but sometimes . . ." Ethan shook his head slowly.

"What's that buddy? You kind of trailed off there." Robbie laughed and then settled his sizable frame over the two adjacent seats he had to work with. "Let's just look at this realistically. If the power is out from the east coast all the way to Texas there's no way we're getting a bus or a rental car. If it was EMPs that took out the power grid that means the highways will be parking lots, at least around the metropolitan areas. We can head to the nearest military base and hope they can get us part way. Otherwise, we're walking."

"Speak for yourself. I'm gonna find a Schwinn and beat you there by a month," Ethan challenged. The bus started loudly and pulled out of the run-down station, adding the smell of diesel fumes to the already strange odor of the bus.

"Ethan, all joking aside, I know we've got a huge task ahead of us. We're kidding about bikes and hitchhiking but I don't know how else we're going to get to our kids. If we head northwest of Laredo there's the Laughlin Air Force Base. Or closer to Brownsville there's the Texas Army National Guard. Those are the border installations. But they're not really our tribe."

"Whichever is closer, Robbie. Let's get into the states first and see if they can help."

July 2 – 12:20PM Fenton, Michigan

Sweat dripped from his nose and tears rolled from his eyes as a wave of smoke washed over his face once more. The smell of the smoke was welcome and familiar though the circumstances were not. Piled next to the charcoal grill were Styrofoam trays and crumpled plastic wrap from several packages of meat that, until that morning, had been in the deep freeze in David and Liz's basement. Steaks, chicken breast, sausage, and hot dogs had all fallen victim to the freezer purge. David hovered over the smoking grill, baking in its waves of heat while trying to cook every scrap of meat in the house before it went bad. Just after noon, the mercury lingered at 91 but threatened to peak five degrees higher.

"I can't believe how hot it is without the fans and the AC. How did people do this two hundred years ago?" Elizabeth asked no one in particular. She and Hannah were sitting on the back porch trying to catch a breeze. She fanned herself with a months old copy of Midwest Living.

"You want all this meat cooked, Liz?" David called from the yard.

"Every bit. It'll go bad otherwise."

David was wondering to himself if making jerky would have been a better plan. The meat would have lasted longer but without knowing for certain how to do it he opted instead to cook it all and eat it as quickly as possible. "You know it's lot harder to do stuff when you can't just look up how to do it on the smart phone," he said.

"Yeah or I'd be telling you to look up how to make a homemade fan," Liz offered.

"If I could look it up on my smart phone you wouldn't need the fan in the first place!" David shot back. He had already grown weary of her comments about the heat.

"No need to get snippy, David."

"Just pointing out the obvious, dear," he replied with resignation.

Two full days passed with no word from any authorities or even anyone with any news of what was happening outside of Fenton. David and Liz carefully rationed their water and been cautious with the food but there was no way to know how long they would have to do so.

"Makes me wish we had bought that used car last month."

"What does?" Liz answered, assuming David wasn't talking to himself.

"The fact that we don't know anything. I would have driven around, asked for news. Someone has to know something, right?"

"Maybe. Have you been over to see any of our neighbors? See if they've heard anything?" Liz suggested. David hated the idea of asking up and down the street. News would have traveled within their street by now if there had been any. Liz sat up in the wicker chair where she was slouched and offered, "Why don't you take a bike?"

"What, ride a bike all over town asking if anyone knows anything?" David said dismissively.

Undeterred, Liz persisted. "You could bike to Flint. It's the county seat, maybe they know something?"

"Flint is twenty miles away. And it's Flint," David added as if that explained everything. "Besides, the only thing worse than being around panicky people is being around them in Flint. And if someone wanted the bike there wouldn't be anything I could do to stop them. I'm not really a biker – or a fast one."

"Couldn't you make it go faster?"

"What, like make a motorbike?"

"I don't know. You're the engineer," Liz teased.

"I'm not that kind of engineer," David teased back. But it was not a bad idea. There might be some way to make a motorized vehicle with just the things in the garage. He had just enough gas to be able to . . .

"David? Hey!" Liz's voice broke through the plotting

going in his head as David realized he had totally zoned out considering the possibilities. He started removing meat from the grill. "I might have a few things in the garage that could be . . . reassigned."

"Since you're not going to Flint, where *do* you plan on going?"

"I can ask around for news," David assured her, "But it might be better if I find some things that will help us in the long run." David's mind was racing now as he thought about the possibility of some mobility.

"David, I trust you. Whatever you need to do just do it. Just promise me you won't put yourself in dangerous situations. If it looks bad, just walk away, okay?"

"Liz, if this keeps going we'll be in a dangerous situation every day. I'll be careful. But this isn't going to get better."

As David continued cooking, he had a sudden flash of inspiration. He put the lid on the grill so the meat could finish cooking and headed to the garage. He dragged Liz's garden cart out of the garage and removed the four pneumatic tires and their axles. He also removed the mower deck from the riding lawn tractor. He knew there was a way to swap out the pulleys for the mower blades and shorten the drive belts so the tractor would go much faster. He spent a few hours playing around in the yard adjusting the throttle and the pulleys on the engine until he could get what he estimated was better than 30 miles per hour.

Then he turned his attention to creating a small trailer. Using the four tires from the garden cart, he bolted the axles to a wheel base he constructed from some scrap two-by-fours. It had been a long time since David had to rely on a handsaw alone to make precise cuts. He was out of practice but managed to cobble together an adequate support system for his makeshift trailer. He still had a four-by-six piece of plywood from a project he completed last year. Their house was a fixer-upper and a portion of the second floor needed to be replaced. Several sheets of plywood later it was repaired. David never dreamed he would he appropriating that same plywood to make a trailer with which to scavenge.

What other scrap wood he found in the garage he cut and pieced together into a low railing. David's cordless drill still had power so he used it to screw the short rail around the edge of the plywood bed of the trailer. If he came upon any other scrap wood he could always raise the rail to hold more and larger items. A piece of chain and a padlock became the hitch for his homemade trailer. He proudly drove it from in front of the garage to the front yard where Liz met him, smiling.

"You're like a little kid who just built his first fort," Liz said admiringly.

"Oh yeah, I'm pretty proud of myself."

"What else are you going to make? I know I suggested a motorbike but don't get carried away making weird stuff."

"What if we need other weird stuff? Liz, I am the master of building nonsense. You've seen my Lego collection."

"My husband, the Lego nerd. By the way, I took the meat off the grill. If you wanted jerky, you've got it."

"Thanks. And hey, you knew when you married me that I still played with Legos." David laughed and Liz's eyes sparkled at him. There was no one else he would rather be with, especially in the middle of what was now happening. She knew him like no one else.

"So, what's your first destination?" Liz kept the question light, knowing that something was going on behind David's deep brown eyes. She knew the laughter and lightness at creating something was to be cherished. If David was right about the near future, there would soon not be much to laugh about.

"The number one need is water, right? I'll see if any stores have bottled water left. Even if I can find a case or two we can make it last awhile." The water David took from Target was laid out in their living room, carefully rationed to last several weeks. "I think I'll start right here in Fenton, maybe a gas station or two and then see if the hardware store has opened their doors. I'm taking some cash. I don't know if they'll take it but it's worth a try."

"It's getting late," Liz said glancing around at the lengthening shadows.

"At the speed I'll be going, I shouldn't be gone any longer than an hour. It won't get completely dark until almost ten." David looked into Liz's eyes. "I'll be okay. Nothing dangerous right?"

"Right." Liz bit her bottom lip as she stared back at David. "I'll be right here on the porch."

———

David's job was to focus on how to design and manage complex engineering systems. Sometimes in manufacturing, the tools, the methods, and product itself could undergo no further evolution to do something better or faster. A systems engineer would evaluate the process itself, try to optimize how something was done. David's job was to make sure that all aspects of a project or system were considered, and integrated into a whole. He did not care about manufacturing itself. David was tasked with looking at the big picture of how everything was done and make sure it was done efficiently with a minimal amount of failure.

David was currently applying all his job know-how to his

present situation. In his mind he had one job: Keep his family safe. That meant healthy, fed and sheltered. To do that successfully meant that many moving parts had to work together. There was the issue of water and food supply. Their food, if carefully rationed, might last until autumn but then there was the issue of warmth and food through the winter. If the power came on tomorrow, David would laugh about the close call and take steps immediately to be prepared if this ever happened again. Something deep down told him that was wishful thinking. Everything he did from this day forward would be for the preservation of his life and that of Liz and Hannah.

His modified lawn tractor was out of place on the streets of Fenton. He received a few unintelligible shouts as well as some smiles and laughs. His first stop was the gas station next to the highway. A hand-lettered sign was placed at each entrance. "NO POWER. NO GAS". Thankfully, David came prepared.

"Hey. Can I talk to you for a sec?" David asked the sweaty man behind the counter. He was leaning back on a stool against the cigarette rack slowly fanning himself with the latest issue of Hot Rod Magazine. He could not have been older than thirty.

"Nothing to talk about." The man stood up, put down the magazine and bellied right up to the counter.

"I was hoping I could get some gas. I have cash." David remembered this gas station was owned by two Pakistani brothers. This must be the younger one.

"You can't read?"

David extended a hand toward the clerk. "David Zabad. I live here in Fenton. I think I can help you get gas out of your tanks." The man cautiously took David's hand and then without warning strengthened his grip and jerked

David forward across the counter. The clerk's other hand came over David's neck and held him down.

"You think I'm an idiot?" the man shouted. "You've come to steal my food!"

"I'm not here to steal anything. I need gas! But I'll pay! I promise I'll pay!" David felt a small, cold, heavy circle pressed against his cheek and realized the clerk had let go of his right hand and grabbed a weapon. "I will show you how to get the gas out. You can make money. I promise. I don't even have a weapon." David closed his eyes and prayed silently. A moment passed and then the gun was lifted from his face.

David threw himself backward off the counter and stumbled to get some distance between him and the clerk. Looking up, the clerk was standing next to the register with the gun pointed at David.

With hands raised David calmly said, "I am not here to hurt you. What's your name?"

"Sadiq. This is my gas station. I've been guarding it since the power went out."

"Don't you have a brother?" David asked, testing the waters.

"I do. But he was in Detroit with the rest of our family when this," he gestured to the street, "happened."

"So, you've been here this whole time by yourself? Hasn't anyone else come in?"

"I put up the signs and no one has asked – until you." Sadiq's eyes closed, his head lolled forward and he sighed deeply. "I've been awake for the last three days. I'm more worried about my merchandise than the gas."

"I just need gas. If you'll sell me some of your snack food I'll buy it but, really, just gas would be fine." David's heart finally settled to normal beats per minute. "Do you have gas cans?"

Sadiq gestured to the left rear of the store. David obeyed the directions and gathered as many plastic five gallon cans as would fit on the trailer. He pulled the trailer over to the tank cover on the north side of the gas station parking lot.

Sadiq cautiously exited his building, still holding the pistol he had used to threaten David, and met him near his makeshift trailer. "What is your plan for this?" he asked as he gestured at the repurposed vehicle.

"The plan is to pump as much gas out of this underground tank as my little trailer will hold," David replied as he opened and arranged the plastic gas cans. I have a hand pump and this plastic tubing. It'll take a while but – I have time. Any ice left?" Sadiq shook his head. "Bottled water?"

Sadiq nodded. He was standing nearby, leaning against one of the powerless pumps closest to the ground tanks. His eyes closed again and as David watched Sadiq try to stay awake, he felt an urge to help him somehow. He did not have to try hard to imagine being miles from his family with no information about their well-being and no way of reaching them. The first twenty-four hours of this crisis gave David a robust dose of reality and experience with that level of uncertainty. After filling the gas cans, David determined he would find a way to aid Sadiq.

Ten minutes and ten gallons later David approached Sadiq who fell asleep on his feet. "Sadiq?" David reached out and touched the gas station owner on the shoulder who responded by leaping away from the post and swinging his gun around wildly.

"Get back! Get back! I have a gun!"

"Whoa, it's me, Sadiq. Easy!" David backed away, almost seeking refuge behind his revved up lawn mower.

"That's the second time in thirty minutes you've pointed a gun in my general direction. I'm starting to take it personally."

"I'm sorry. I just don't know who to trust. And I'm so tired."

"I have a proposition for you. I have ten gallons here. And I'd like as many cases of water as you're willing to spare. I have cash for all of it." David held out fifty dollars. "This should cover it."

"And your proposition?"

"I take this home and get my family situated. Then I come back and guard your place so you can sleep tonight."

"So you can empty my store while I sleep? You think I'm stupid?"

"No, I think that you can't keep trying to stay awake all night for much longer without doing serious harm to yourself. I will guard your store in exchange for some more merchandise."

"How much more?"

David smiled. This might work.

———

"You agreed to guard his gas station? David, what about your family? I don't want to be here by myself again. I won't sleep a minute!"

"Liz, if I do this it means more water, more food. I won't do it every night but you should have seen this guy. He has no one. He has no idea where his family is and no way to contact them. He needs help."

Liz stared into David's eyes. "You really think you should help him?"

"I do. If we weren't in this situation, I would be calling

people from our church to set up a rotation to help this guy."

Liz was quiet for a few seconds. "Show me again how to use the gun. If you're not in bed with me tonight, I at least want something I can protect us with."

SIX

of the United States border at Brownsville, Texas

By the time Ethan and Robbie reached the northern border of Mexico, they were the only passengers on the bus. The trip took less time because at each stop more passengers exited and none got on the bus. They grabbed their packs and hiked to the Rio Grande.

The Fort Brown border patrol was deployed in force at the Veterans Bridge. Robbie and Ethan showed their military identification and were admitted across the bridge. The moment their feet touched American soil they were escorted to the border patrol station and detained for three hours in a sweltering interior room. After a review of their recent travels and where they were heading next, the border station chief, who looked like he had not slept in days, released them with a warning about the danger of traveling into what he called the Dark Zone.

"You've already got a name for it?" Robbie asked.

"From here to – well, as far as we have information, there is no power and no communication. Haven't heard from Corpus Christi, San Antonio, or Houston."

"We've been on a bus since yesterday. Do you have any information at all? From the east coast? The central states?" Ethan was eager to hear anything that might offer some hope.

"I wish I could say yes, but I've heard nothing except the last command from the Texas border patrol chief."

"Which was?"

"Do your job. After that, the radios went off. I've been here since the things went dark trying to convince my staff to stay in shift rotation and so far they've hung in, but some of the guys with families are getting antsy. I can't say I blame them. I can't fault you guys for traveling north either. Wish I had more to tell you."

"We understand," Robbie offered. "We'll get info as we go. It's not our first time going into a bad situation. Thanks for not making this difficult. We just want to get to our families." Robbie turned to go but stopped short. "Anyone in town with a vehicle?"

The station chief reached a hand up and rubbed the back of his neck wearily and then ran the same hand through his disheveled hair. "Not that they'd be willing to part with. Even if they did, you'd have a hell of a time gettin' gas north of here. Even the stations here are on rations and that's when their generators are running the pumps. But you're sure welcome to try and ask around. I don't know everyone."

"Thanks just the same." Robbie and Ethan slung their packs over their shoulders and walked toward downtown Brownsville. "Ethan, have you calculated the distance to your family?" Robbie's question sounded skeptical.

"Have you calculated the distance to yours?" Ethan replied quickly. He did not mean to sound provocative but the stress of the last five days was beginning to show.

"I have," Robbie responded calmly. "I figure if we walk about twelve hours a day we can be to Louisville in a month. To David, another two weeks maybe? And it's possible we'll find some transportation along the way."

"Do you think my kids can hold out that long? What do they have in the house?"

"Are you asking or just thinking out loud?"

"Sorry Robbie. I guess a little of both." Ethan paused and looked ahead on the road. "Do you think we should stop here at all or just head north? No one here has a vehicle anyway."

"Let's stop at the Sunoco there," Robbie gestured to the gas station just east of I-69. "See if we can get some supplies and then head out."

"That's fine. I just need to keep moving. Other than you, big guy, David and Lizzie and that baby girl are the only family I have."

———

Three hours later, Ethan squeezed his eyes shut and blinked away beads of sweat that ran down his forehead and blurred his sight. He and Robbie were swapping the binoculars to look at a house sitting about 200 yards off the main road. He took them back from Robbie.

"See anyone?" Ethan raised the binoculars to his face and scanned.

"No but that doesn't mean anything. This is Texas and I don't want to surprise anyone. I also don't want to get ambushed."

"Robbie, we've passed hundreds of houses. Why are you fixated on this one?"

"See that garage behind the house?" He was pointing to a large steel pole barn that was covered with vintage road-side signs for gas stations and diners. "That's not a shed for collecting junk. There are valuable items in there. Maybe cars."

"No one has been willing to give or sell a car to us so far." They had stopped at dozens of homes on their way north with no success. "What makes you think this house is any different?"

"Those other people we asked had one or two cars. This place might have seven or eight."

Robbie had a point. The house itself was immense and the gate at the head of the driveway might as well have had dollar signs all over it. "You're right. Let's go. Keep your pistol handy." Ethan breathed a quick prayer. First, a prayer of thanks that they'd been able to bring their weapons all the way from Thailand and then a prayer for protection as they made their way down the driveway. There was every reason to believe that someone would be inside the house with a gun just waiting for the first looter or thief stupid enough to try and take something.

Halfway down the driveway Robbie called out, "Stop! Second floor, first window on the left, curtain moved."

Ethan dropped to one knee, lifted the binoculars, and had to wipe the sweat from his eyes again. He had just been in Southeast Asia dealing with the heat but there was something particularly scorching about the south Texas tempera-ture. He looked at the window, waited for it to move again, but nothing. "Clear!"

They crept forward , eyes glued to the front of the house, scanning side to side for any movement at the windows or behind the house. A tense minute later they mounted the porch steps. Robbie gestured to Ethan who knew immediately what to do. The long years of practiced communication came easily. Ethan positioned himself to the right of the door and Robbie knocked and then stepped back almost six feet from the door, hands hanging loosely at his side.

"Who are you?" a young voice called from inside.

"My name is Robbie Charles. I'm a Sergeant Major in the U.S. Army."

"And your friend?"

"That's Ethan Zabad. He's a Master Sergeant in the Army. We are heading north to find our families."

"I can't help you. Go away!"

"We were wondering if you had a vehicle we could buy from you. We're trying to get all the way to Kentucky and then on to Michigan."

"Keep movin'!"

"Ethan," Robbie whispered. "That voice sound like it belongs to an adult?"

"What are you doin' out there?" the voice called again.

"How old are you?" Robbie ventured. There were frantic whispers, then silence for a moment. Then more whispering. "Not a hard question," Robbie called out.

"Old enough to do this!" With that brief warning, a shot boomed from inside the house and the center of the front door exploded in splinters and dust.

Ethan, from outside the line of fire, looked to where Robbie was standing. His friend was now on the ground, prone. He crouched at his side to assess the damage. "Robbie, are you okay? Where are you hit?"

Robbie turned to look up at Ethan and whispered, "I'm fine! I dropped as soon as I heard her start talking."

"Her?"

"It's a girl. I bet she's barely a teenager. Play along with me." Robbie adjusted his position slightly and moaned. "Oh, Ethan! I'm bleeding out! This is the end for me. All I wanted was a drink of water. I see a bright light buddy! The light is getting brighter!"

Ethan almost laughed at his friend and whispered, "You are the worst actor I've ever seen." Robbie's eyes went wide, urging Ethan to continue the ruse. "Oh, right. Don't leave me Robbie. No! What about your kids, your wife! How will they ever find out what happened to you? Don't die on me, bro!"

Robbie was about to start act two of his impromptu drama when the shattered front door opened slightly to reveal a girl, shoulder-length brown hair, green eyes, a small upturned nose and round chin. "I didn't want to kill him," she whispered to Ethan as they made eye contact. "I was just tryin' to scare him. Promise." Her lip quivered and tears rolled down her face. "I'm no killer." The door swung open all the way and she made her way on to the porch dragging a shotgun behind her. "I was just tryin' to protect me and my brother." The tears were flowing freely now. "I'm so sorry."

"I'm okay, kid," Robbie said as he sat up.

The girl uttered a scream that would wake the dead and started to raise the shotgun at him. Ethan moved quickly to snatch the gun and yank it away before she could pull the trigger. She screamed again and flew at Ethan, arms flailing, nails lashing.

"It's okay!" Ethan attempted. "We're not here to hurt you. Calm down!" Her flailing slowed as Ethan's strength gently subdued her. "We're the good guys. We were telling the truth. We're both Army, just crossed the border in

Brownsville and we're trying to get north to our families. Now," Ethan slowly released her arms and backed away holding the shotgun. "Who are you and why are you here all by yourself?"

"My name is Audrey Pelham. I'm here with my brother 'cause my parents went to Corpus Christi."

"Today?"

"No. Five days ago. I haven't heard from them since the power went out and the cell phones stopped workin'."

"Do you have food?" Robbie asked as he got to his feet.

Audrey backed away, still not sure about the dead coming back to life. "We have some. No runnin' water though. Just some bottled in the basement."

"What were your parents doing in Corpus Christi?" Robbie was always better at handling the kids he and Ethan met throughout their career together. He moved toward Audrey with his hands out. When he got within a foot he knelt his six-foot four-inch frame down in front of her.

"They were signin' some papers for a vacation house they bought there. We were supposed to go there for July fourth. They never came back." Audrey was sniffling again. Another face peered out from within the house, this one a small brown-eyed face with tousled wavy brown hair framing it.

Robbie glanced at the boy and then nodded to him, "Come on out, it's okay." He turned back to Audrey. "What's your brother's name?"

"That's Peyton. He's nine." She paused and looked Robbie in the eye. "He has a zero three eight and he knows how to use it."

Robbie and Ethan both suppressed smiles as they realized she was stating the caliber of the pistol Peyton must have been holding behind the door. "A zero three eight, eh?"

Robbie said grimly. "He won't have to use it, we are not here to hurt anyone or do anything bad. We stopped to see if there were any cars here that we could borrow or buy. If you say no, we'll keep walking and leave you and your brother alone. Okay?"

Audrey seemed to consider this for a moment and turned back to look at her brother who moved out from behind the door. He was in fact holding a thirty-eight caliber pistol at his side that looked oversized in his small palm. "You'll just leave?" Robbie nodded. "There's no cars here," she said hesitantly.

Robbie and Ethan waited, expecting her to say something else. "You're sure?" Ethan pressed. "Not even in that big garage back there?"

"Nope. Now you said you would go."

Ethan glanced at Robbie trying to read his friends thoughts. He suspected Robbie was thinking the same thing. Audrey was trying to be brave and protective but was truly terrified and a dreadful liar. "Alright. We'll go. I hope your parents show up soon."

"Yeah, it's too bad you don't have a way to head toward Corpus Christi and try to find them. They're probably as worried about you as you are about them," Robbie added knowing exactly where Ethan was going with his comments.

Ethan handed the shotgun back to Audrey and then reached out to tousle Peyton's hair. "See ya, kid." Peyton did not say a word but fear and desperation were written on his face. Ethan noted this and turned with Robbie toward the porch steps and the driveway beyond. Thirty yards from the porch Ethan heard footsteps behind them. They swiveled to see Peyton dashing from the porch with Audrey close on his heels.

"There's cars in the stable! Lots of 'em! Take us to my mom. Please?" Peyton's wall was crumbling now too and tears started pouring down his cheeks.

"I told you we would be fine, Peyton!" Audrey lifted the shotgun at Ethan and looked down the barrel. "You said you would leave. Don't listen to him. He's just scared and wants our mom. There's no cars."

Robbie spoke sternly. "Young lady, we are doing exactly what we said we would do. We're leaving. We're willing to help you both but only if you let us. This is your last chance."

Peyton walked between the shotgun and Ethan and looked directly at his big sister. "Audrey, I want to see mom and dad. Please let 'em help. Please." Slowly, Audrey lowered the gun.

"You'll help us find our parents?" Audrey confirmed.

"I've spent the last fifteen years helping people all over the world. It's what we do."

Audrey looked at both men for a moment longer, still unsure if she could trust them. Finally, she lowered the weapon all the way. "Follow me." She led them back down the driveway, past the house and into the backyard where another paved drive ended at the door of the barn.

"This is the stable?" Robbie asked Peyton.

"My dad has a few Mustangs so he calls it a stable. But there's other cars too."

Audrey punched in a code on the cargo door keypad twice before remembering there was no electricity. She fished a hand into her pocket and pulled out a small ring of keys. After fumbling through them for a moment she found the one that opened a smaller side door. They entered the stable and waited a moment as their eyes adjusted to the dim lighting.

Ethan knew God led them to this place. He quickly scanned the barn which contained at least eight cars and perhaps more but they were bathed in darkness toward the back of the building. "So what should we take?"

"These are classics," she said pointing to her left. "These are the three mustangs. A sixty-six, a sixty-eight and a ninety." Ethan didn't think of a ninety Mustang as a classic but kept his thoughts to himself. "The one in the back is a fifty-seven somethin'." Audrey pointed straight ahead and to her right. "These first two are a BMW from eighty somethin' and a Cadillac that has wings on the back. That one is a Corvette. That's my favorite. And the one next to it is really old and I can't remember the name. My dad has driven it in parades."

"So is that it? Nothing newer than these?" Ethan inquired.

"We have an SUV in the garage."

"Extra gas?"

"Yeah there's a few drums in the back by the chop shop."

Ethan and Robbie said almost simultaneously, "The chop shop!"

Audrey shrugged. "That's what my dad calls it. It's where he works on the other cars he has. There's two back there that aren't finished yet."

"Got it." Ethan looked to Robbie. "Well, what do you want to do?"

"The corvette and the oldie are out. I don't trust the fifty-seven over a long distance. The Beemer takes diesel and an SUV is gonna have similar gas mileage to the mustangs." Robbie paused and grinned widely. "I've always wanted to drive a classic Cadillac."

. . .

After loading the colossal trunk with as many full gas cans as it could hold and manually opening the garage door, Robbie pulled out of the stable. Ethan rode shotgun while Audrey and Peyton sat in the back with gear and food piled between them. They emptied the house of its dry goods such as rice, beans, and pasta along with boxes of snack foods and crackers. They also grabbed a couple recent photos of Audrey and Peyton's parents, the Pelhams, so they could identify them. Ethan was glad to have a vehicle moving them ever closer to his own kids but was aware that any gains made by having the car would likely be lost due to the time it would take to help Audrey and Peyton find their parents. A twinge of regret made a brief appearance but Ethan suppressed it, realizing that his whole life was leading up to this type of mission.

SEVEN

A blanket of humidity lay over the city. Even at seven o'clock in the morning, the temperature was in the upper seventies. David, groggy from a long night holding vigil, stepped to the doorway of the Marathon station and scanned the gas pumps and the street beyond. Nothing was moving. No cars passed during the night and no one walked by or approached the gas station. The highway was quiet as well.

Sadiq was still sleeping soundly in the small storeroom behind the main counter. The deal they made was a good one. David would get several cases of water and some gas and Sadiq would get some company and some sleep. David felt he was getting the better end of things but not being in Sadiq's position it was difficult to say with certainty.

Sadiq woke by 8:30 and made the trade. David loaded his newly acquired items on his makeshift trailer and headed home. There had to be a way to make sure people were not in the same predicament as his new friend. The only way people would get through this crisis was if they banded together, shared their resources, and protected one another. A plan was forming in David's mind and by the time he reached home, he knew what he had to do.

"Liz, let's get our neighborhood together," he suggested once he parked and unloaded the trailer. He and Elizabeth sat on the front porch steps where it was just a few degrees cooler than the house. "Let's invite everyone to gather in the intersection and talk about how we can help each other. We can't be the only ones trying to figure this out."

"David, we hardly know these people. And I haven't even seen anyone out since the power went off. What makes you think they're going to want to 'band together'?"

"You make it sound like a bad thing."

Liz reached a hand to David's face. "You are such a sweet man. I love that about you. But not everyone is like you, David."

"I know."

"No, you don't. You have such a good heart and you really believe that you can unite this neighborhood. But this is the very situation that breeds an 'every man for himself' attitude."

"Are you saying you don't want to work with anyone either?"

"No, David. I'm saying that you're so optimistic and – well – idealistic. I just think you're going to be sadly disappointed."

"Look, I will write up an invite with a time and a place and I'll even stand out in the intersection so people know I'm serious. If no one shows, no one shows. But at least then we'll know where we stand."

After a couple hours of sleep on his hammock in the

shade of a giant maple tree, David went to work crafting the invite for his neighbors. Having only lived there a couple years they were still not as well acquainted with the neighbors as they would like. There were roughly thirteen homes in sight distance of his yard so after copying the message he started walking next door. The first five home deliveries were uneventful with the responses ranging from mildly interested to supportive though none were enthusiastic. David walked up the street that led away from downtown and into a heavily wooded portion of the neighborhood. There were two houses at the top of a hill that David could just see glimpses of in wintertime when the leaves were down. He knocked on the door of the first home, knowing an older man lived there alone. He was hoping some of the older, and perhaps wiser residents would come to the meeting. There was no answer after several aggressive knocks so David moved away from the door. The door swung open and the screen door was kicked wide.

"What do you want?" The old man of the house stood in his doorway with a rifle at his shoulder, dressed in Velcro-strapped sandals and swim trunks. He was shirtless and his pale chest was the stuff of beach trip nightmares. Like everyone else, he had not shaved in almost a week and his hair was badly disheveled. David guessed him to be somewhere around his mid-sixties.

"I'm here with an invite. Just wanted to let all the people in the neighborhood know we're going to try and work together, help each other."

"Help me? Do I look like I need help, boy?"

"That's not what I said. I'm talking about helping each other. I know we've met but I forgot. What's your name?" David quickly asked to cut off any retort that would result in an argument.

"I'm Roger. What do you mean 'work together'?"

"We're going to meet. Discuss what resources we have. See if there's anyone in the neighborhood that's in really bad shape. If this lasts a long time we're gonna need all the help we can get." David cautiously handed the paper with the details to Roger who lowered the rifle to his hip and snatched the message.

He scanned it quickly. "I'll be there. But I wouldn't bother with the folks up there," he said pointing with his chin toward the last house on the street. "They're a bunch of rats and thieves up there. Drugs all the time and when they're not high they're drunk. Wouldn't count on them for anything."

"I'll take it under advisement," David replied blandly. He was going next door anyway. He said good bye to Roger and made his way up the hill. Ever since he arrived home the first night of the crisis, he was reviewing his own situation and supplies. There were at least three twenty-five pound bags of rice in the basement. He knew he had bags of flour and sugar and a case of salt. With the water he had recently acquired, there was enough to last several months if carefully rationed but that was just for drinking. He needed another solution for washing and cooking. He thought about the rest of the food when a gunshot rang out causing him to jump and then stop as he looked for the source of the shot. Another shot kicked up dirt nearby and so he ran to the closest tree for protection.

"Why are you shooting?" David called hoping to convince his assailant he was harmless.

"I'm protecting what's mine!" a voice called back.

"I'm not here to take anything from you. I only want to invite you to a meeting with the neighborhood. We're going to try and work together."

"So you can take what's mine? I don't think so. You head back down this hill or I'll bury you on it."

David leaned around the tree he was hiding behind and scanned for the source of the voice. A window next to the front door was open and David could see the barrel of a rifle poking out. "I'm leaving now," he called. He waved the messages he was delivering out in the open. "Can I at least get your name before I go? In case you change your mind?"

"I'm Garrett. And I'm telling you so you'll know who shot you if you ever come up here again."

David backed slowly down the hill and as he passed Roger's house he saw the man looking at him from his front window slowly shaking his head. David finished his deliveries with varying degrees of success but no more bullets were fired at him. He scheduled the meeting for the following morning at ten. He did not know if anyone still had working clocks. Generators were running intermittently the last few days but fewer were heard now after six days. He and Lizzie still had some clocks running on battery power.

Though it was the Fourth of July, there was little cause to celebrate. Some fireworks sounded through the night but the party was subdued and short-lived. It appeared everyone was aware the situation was no simple matter of a downed power line. In power outages before there had always been someone nearby with access to local or national news. Now, for almost a week, no one in the area heard anything from any authority describing the situation and when or if it would be resolved.

David spent the rest of the ninety-two-degree day in the shade with Elizabeth and Hannah.

. . .

July 4 – 9:46AM Southbound I-37 West of Corpus Christi, Texas

What was normally a two-and-a-half-hour trip turned into two days. There were cars in the middle of the road along the way - stopped and without fuel. There were people walking on the highways. Some were scavenging among the stopped vehicles while others were carrying packs or pulling wagons, clearly heading somewhere else entirely. It was an up-close reminder of the last time a mass evacuation was ordered under the looming threat of an imposing hurricane. It was also a grim reminder of the ways in which a crisis either brings out the best or the worst of humanity.

Weaving between the vehicles and pedestrians added so much time to the trip that they pulled off the road last night for the second time and slept in the car. The other delay was checking every passerby to make sure it wasn't Peyton and Audrey's parents making their way back to Brownsville. There were a few stretches where they were able to go fifty to sixty miles per hour but these were rare.

Audrey and Peyton proved to be sweet kids. Smart and resourceful. They had had the sense to stay put and wait for their parents. They defended themselves. And Peyton wagered correctly on who was a trustworthy guardian to get he and Audrey back to their parents. Had he not stopped them, Ethan and Robbie would have stayed true to their word and left the kids on their own. They would have regretted it every step they took on the way back to their families but they would have done it.

Along the way, Robbie questioned the kids about where their parents may have gone. They went to Corpus Christi for a real estate deal but the kids had no idea which realtor or where the house was. Even a quick search through the house before they left yielded no leads. Corpus Christi was not the kind of city one could go to hoping to just run into someone – even less so under the current circumstances. They had two clues to their whereabouts. The vehicle their parents drove. It was a bright yellow Range Rover which Ethan and Robbie thought a strange choice for a classic car buff. But it was a providential choice, making the search easier than if they were driving a black SUV. The second clue was that Audrey heard her parents say something about island living.

Ethan and Robbie did not have time to meet privately since picking up the kids. The question in both of their minds was what they would do if they could not find their parents. Their extended family was not even living in Texas. They had addresses but the challenge of recon-necting them was as daunting as getting back to their own families. There was the question of the kids slowing them down along with putting a greater strain on what little supplies they had. They would be surviving on very little and could not expect to resupply anywhere along the way. The puzzle of getting them all safe would be more easily solved if they could reconnect Audrey and Peyton with their parents.

As they continued to roll slowly into Corpus, as it was called locally, the number of cars in the roadway increased. Ethan surmised that they ran out of gas rather than being damaged by an EMP. From the last bit of information they received from Reynolds, the EMPs detonated over cities east of the Mississippi. If power plants were attacked in the north along interstate 80 it stood to reason they were attacked in the south as well. They must have caused a ripple effect, destroying the electrical systems of East Texas. Indeed, most of the gas stations they passed displayed signs indicating they were out of fuel. Driving slowly enabled them to carefully look around for a bright yellow Range Rover, either on the west bound side or on an entrance or exit ramp.

They reached a point in the roadway where they could neither snake their way through or go around. Cars clogged the road completely, forcing the passengers to put the classic Cadillac in park and make some hard decisions. They sat in the car for a minute until Robbie broke the silence.

"We can't all walk around looking. We don't have enough water." It was a simple statement - to the point. It wasn't an exaggeration. The temperature soared to the high nineties. It was not wise to spend the day wandering around a city without proper supplies. "We can't sit in this car all day either," he added. The Cadillac did not have air conditioning and only the forward movement of the car creating airflow made things bearable.

"Robbie, why don't you take Audrey car hunting, or I can take her while you stay here with Peyton? We can back up the car so it's sitting under an overpass, out of the sun."

Robbie threw a quick glance to Ethan and said, "Can I talk to you outside for a minute? Kids, we'll be right over there," he reassured them, nodding toward the shade of a semi just ahead and to the left of the Cadillac. They stepped to the shade and instinctively put their backs to the trailer and positioned themselves to look over each other's shoulder.

"What's on your mind?"

"Ethan, look around. Man, there is no way we are going to find their parents. Don't you feel like we're giving them false hope?"

"We haven't even started looking. There's -"

"You know the supply situation," Robbie blurted, cutting him off. "What's your plan for water? What's your plan for travel? You know I will help anyone, anytime, anywhere. But we usually have a plan and right now I'm feeling like we're wandering."

"You're right. I don't have a plan for any of those things - yet. You know how this works. One problem at a time right?"

"Right, one problem at a time. But we need a deadline. A drop dead target where we don't spend the next month stranded in this city looking for people who aren't here."

"Just for kicks, I'll count and on three we both say how long we're willing to look."

Robbie rolled his eyes, accustomed by now to Ethan's oddities. "You're weird, you know that right? Half the country is in crisis and you want to do things for kicks."

"One—"

"I'm not doing this Ethan, it's stupid."

"Two—"

"Why do I even hang out with you?"

"Three. A week!"

"A day," Robbie uncontrollably spat out at the same time. "A week! We can't spend a week here."

"Okay, okay. Ninety-six hours," Ethan offered defensively.

"Thirty-six."

"Seventy-two?" Ethan said hopefully.

"Forty-eight."

"Alright, forty-eight it is."

"And if we can't find their parents?" Robbie asked.

"We can check in with the Corpus Police, see if they can help. Maybe the kids can stay with them but I bet they're already overwhelmed."

"We can't just leave them. They might have to go with us to Kentucky."

———

Robbie and Audrey loaded two backpacks with several water bottles each. Robbie put on his boonie hat he kept with him while Audrey tied a blue and white handkerchief around her face to block the sun. Robbie unholstered his pistol, dropped out the mag, checked his ammunition and then reloaded the gun, jamming it back into its holster.

As Robbie prepared, Ethan drove the Cadillac in reverse to an overpass less than a quarter mile from where they stopped. It was a tough piece of driving considering the number of stranded cars on the road. Ethan was constantly scanning, even as he guided the car into the shade, for the yellow SUV and for anything out of place. As close as they were to the city, there was very little visible activity. Though the attacks and the blackout happened just over a week ago, there was no telling what condition the city was in and how local residents were treating one another. Ethan didn't know if Robbie was heading into a ghost town or a war zone. He glanced over at Peyton who was quietly staring at his sister, a tiny figure standing next to Robbie up ahead of them. "She's gonna be okay. She's going out there with the best. I've worked with that man for over fifteen years and I trust him with my life."

Peyton responded so quietly Ethan leaned in to hear him. "I know she'll be okay. I just wish I knew for sure we were goin' to find my parents. I really miss them."

These were the conversations Ethan dreaded. Robbie was so much better at talking to kids and Ethan felt like he rarely knew the right thing to say. Robbie always told him to speak from the heart. "I know what it's like to miss someone. But I also know what it means to have hope."

"Who are you missin'?"

"My son. He lives in Michigan with his wife and my granddaughter. I haven't seen him in a long time and now with all the power out, I don't know if I'll be able to see him anytime soon."

"How far is Michigan?" Peyton seemed genuinely concerned.

"It took us a couple days to get here from your house right?" Peyton nodded so Ethan continued. "It would probably take a couple months to get to Michigan. Less with a car but I don't know if any places will have gas along the way. So I'll have to walk."

"You would walk for two months to see your son?"

"I would walk any distance, Peyton. That's what dads do. Dads do whatever they have to for their kids."

"Then why hasn't my dad come back to me and Audrey?"

His words twisted in Ethan's gut. He glanced at Peyton and then out the front windshield as Robbie and Audrey disappeared behind the abandoned cars ahead of them. Peyton's question lingered as Ethan wrestled with what he believed about the fate of that yellow Range Rover and its occupants. But he had to say something.

"Peyton, I don't know where your parents are. I know if there was any way they could get to you I'm sure they would. They might have no gas in their car or maybe no supplies like water and food to make the trip. But—" Ethan stopped because he was about to make a promise. The same promise Robbie would have made had he been sitting here with this scared little boy. "But if your parents are in this city we aren't leaving until we find them. How does that sound?" Ethan waited for Peyton to respond but instead his eyes went wide and he tried to speak. And then Ethan heard the click of a pistol hammer in his ear.

————

Robbie and Audrey continued along the expressway thinking the main roads were their best chance of spotting the distinctive vehicle. The silence was unnerving. The typical sounds of a city were absent and there was a ghostly feel to the highway as they passed car after empty car. The heat was cruel and relentless with little to no shade available for relief. Robbie glanced at Audrey several times in the first ten minutes of walking until she snapped at him.

"I'm okay! You don't have to keep checkin' on me. I'm stronger than I look."

"It's my job to find your parents and make sure you make it to see them in one piece."

"I know . . . I just . . ."

"You want me to think you're tough? That you can handle all this." Audrey walked on in silence. "You don't have to prove anything to me, Audrey. I know you're tough. You stayed in that house with your brother for almost a week. You handled yourself at the door extremely well. The only flaw in your plan was that Ethan and I are well-trained soldiers. We've been at it a long time. Anyone else approaching that house would have met their match with you." Robbie waited for her to reply. When she stayed quiet he went on. "Not many people, especially a kid, would have been able to pull the trigger. You did. You're a person who does what is necessary. I know you can handle yourself. What I want you to know right now is that you can rely on me and Ethan."

"I know. I do. I mean, I will." Her faint smile as she glanced sidewise at Robbie told him he had gotten through.

They walked on in silence for another few minutes. At each exit from the interstate they walked to the top of the ramp so they could get a better vantage point and see both on and off ramps and down the highway in both directions. It was several exits before Audrey voiced her fear that the search might prove fruitless.

"We're just getting started," Robbie encouraged. "This isn't the only highway that runs in and around this city. They could be on any one of them."

"I just wish I knew what they would've done. I think they would've come for me and Peyton but what if they didn't?"

"Audrey, do you believe in prayer?"

"You mean like, God and all that?"

Robbie opted not to comment on her tone or the barely disguised attitude of disregard behind her words. "Yeah, God and all that."

"I don't know. My parents took us to a couple kids things at a church back home. But we didn't really go on Sunday."

"You don't have to go to church to believe in prayer. But it helps you learn about who you're praying to."

"You think God cares about us findin' my parents?"

"I know he does. God's a parent too. The people who trust in Him He calls sons and daughters. How about this? I'll pray and you can listen in. If you agree with what I'm saying you just tell God."

"You mean, I just say - 'yes?'"

"Yep. Prayer is asking God for things. When someone prays so everyone can hear, everybody can ask God for the same thing at one time. That's what makes it so powerful. Peyton ever bug you to do something for him?"

"Yes, he can be so annoyin'."

"Imagine thirty Peyton's all asking you to do something. Could be convincing right?"

"So prayer is just annoyin' God so much he'll give you what you want?"

Robbie laughed aloud. "No, no, no. It's more like persistence. Sometimes God uses the prayers of His kids as a means to an end. The answer is already on the way but He wants us to ask Him for it and learn what it means to trust Him. Does that make sense?"

"Is that why my parents still want me to make a Christmas list?"

Robbie threw his head back and laughed again. "Sort of. They know what's best for you but they want to hear from you anyway. They want you to ask for what you want."

"Okay then, let's try it. But you do it. I'll just say yes to God while you talk."

"You got it."

EIGHT

"Nice ride. I saw you back it up a few minutes ago so I know it has gas. Now get out and I'll take it from here."

Ethan was facing Peyton and had not seen the man come down from above the overpass. He mouthed *it's okay* to Peyton and then addressed the stranger behind him.

"Is the gun you're carrying even loaded?"

"What?" The gun holder was a disheveled, maybe twenty-something, dark-brown hair, several days patchy growth on his face and clad in filthy plaid shorts and a salmon colored tank top.

"The gun - in your hand. Is it loaded?"

"Yeah, I -"

Ethan used the split second of disorientation to spin and snap open the Cadillac door sending it forcefully into the body of their assailant. He sailed back almost ten feet and the gun flew from his grasp. Ethan was out of the car in a flash and atop the young man subduing him. His yelps of pain would have been comical had the situation not been so serious. He struggled and whined until Ethan sharply smacked him in the back of the head.

"You're lucky I didn't just break the arm holding the gun." Ethan jerked him to his feet. Peyton gasped and stood at the hood of the car, staring. Back in the car, Peyton," Ethan ordered.

"What did you do?" the would-be car thief exclaimed looking down at his wrists.

"I used your shirt to bind your wrists."

"When did you take my shirt?"

"When I opened the car door I also grabbed the shirt. While you were learning to fly I was tearing the shirt off your body and getting it ready to tie you up. Any other questions? No? Good. My turn. What's your name?"

"Cael."

Ethan shook his head slowly. "What, like the leafy green stuff?"

"Yes. I mean no! It's spelled different."

"Okay green stuff. What are you doing trying to do, carjack me?" Cael looked away from Ethan and set his jaw. "I can leave you sitting here under this overpass tied up with your own clothes or you can start talking. I don't know where the cops are yet or how to contact them so it's just you and me."

"I gotta get out of here."

"You and half the city. What's so urgent?"

"It doesn't matter does it? There's nothin' here for me anymore."

"You don't strike me as the criminal type. Judging by what your hair used to look like and the brand name on those clothes, I'd say you're more Abercrombie and Fitch than Wal-Mart. Any parents, siblings?"

"What do you care?"

"Listen green stuff, I'm here looking for someone. So,

you answer my questions and then we can part ways which I am anxious to do."

"Yes, I have parents and a couple brothers. We lived on Padre Island."

"The spring break place?"

"That's South Padre Island and–"

"Wait, did you say *lived*?"

"My house – it burned. Everythin' is gone. A bunch of houses on the island burned." He turned away, fighting the emotional reaction to his loss.

"I'm sorry, Cael."

His composure regained he managed, "Yeah, whatever."

"And your parents? Your brothers?"

"They were inside. No one made it out." Cael's eyes filled with tears but he doggedly fought to keep them from falling. Ethan knew the look and understood well what kind of young man he was dealing with.

"And you weren't home because you were out doing something your family wouldn't be proud of?" Taking silence as an affirmative, Ethan continued. "I'm sorry, Cael. I'm sorry that happened to your family. I wish there was something we could do. But under the current circum-stances, you're going to help me and then I'm going to help you. You tried to rob me and you held a gun to my head with a kid in the seat next to me. So, I should just leave you here. But I'm all about redemption. I'll give you a shot at yours. Now, have you seen a yellow Range Rover in the last few days? I'm looking for these people." Ethan thrust the picture of the Pelhams in front of Cael.

"A yellow Range Rover? Bright yellow, like a canary?" he asked, directing his question at Peyton. Peyton nodded excitedly. "I'm pretty sure I have. That guy looks familiar but not her."

"Do you remember where you saw them?" Ethan demanded.

Cael thought for a minute. "I might remember if I retrace my steps from the last few days."

———

Robbie and Audrey stopped at the top of the interchange and scanned the roads leading in both directions. The interstate took them directly to downtown but Highway 358 led to Padre Island and through the more residential areas of the city.

"Audrey, can you think of anything your parents said that could help us know which way is best to look? 'Island living' is all you can think of?"

"They said it was a vacation home and somethin' about an island. That's all I know. They just didn't want somethin' on the water so close to Mexico. Down where we live, I mean."

"So, they wanted to be on the water here?"

"I guess. I never saw anythin' about it. They just talked a little."

"Audrey, if your parents were looking for a vacation home, there's a good chance they purchased something on Padre Island. It's a major vacation spot and it's only accessed by bridges. Bridges which could easily become clogged and impassable in an emergency situation. I think we should head that way."

Audrey just looked up at Robbie. He could see the fear and uncertainty in her eyes. But he could also feel her trust. He nodded at her and she gave a small nod back. They turned south and followed 358 toward the island. Immediately Robbie noticed a difference in the lay of the land.

They saw numerous hotels and restaurants. There were also more people out, walking along the highway, pulling wagons and makeshift carts. As they walked past an exit lined with fast food restaurants, they noticed several were burned down. What used to be La Quinta Inn was a smoking ruin. More cars lined the roadway than on the interstate. Their last intel said that EMPs went off over major eastern cities but by all the evidence it appeared that one detonated over Corpus Christi, much farther west than reported. All of these cars couldn't have run out of gas at the same time.

They were walking for close to three hours at a rapid pace which put them ten to twelve miles from the car. Robbie waved Audrey over to follow him off the roadway. They entered a gas station that was emptied of its snack foods and drinks but in the rack near the cash register were city and state maps. Robbie grabbed two of each and calculated their route and how far they would be able to get today. The farther they walked, the less he believed they would be able to find Audrey's parents in this mess of a city.

———

"You *think* they went west?" Ethan was ready to explode. The last hour started with the euphoria of possibly having a lead on Peyton's parents and ended with the despair of wandering city streets in extreme heat for an hour. They were sitting in the shade of a storefront awning.

"How would I know? They could have gone anywhere in the city!" Cael put his disgust and frustration on display for Ethan.

"Cael, I have no map, no access to a cell phone. I'm not

asking you to be a psychic. I need to know exactly where you saw the Pelhams and where they might have gone next."

Cael had told them that he ran into Peyton's dad and overheard him say they were walking home. That was all the information they had. Ethan was running scenarios where he backed the car out of the gridlock they were in and took back roads to where Peyton's parents might have stopped for help. He also considered just waiting it out knowing they could be heading out of the city a completely different direction on foot.

"Get up Cael. We're going for a walk," Ethan said decisively.

"To where?"

"First, we're going back to the last place you say you saw Mr. Pelham. And from there, wherever I say." Ethan's plan was to start again where Cael had seen the Pelhams and explore nearby, checking some of the back roads for the yellow SUV. There were thousands of possibilities for where the kids' parents might have gone - directions, options, possibilities. Ethan was just trying to think like a parent. *If I was in one city and my kids in another I would do everything I could to get to them.* But Ethan knew he wasn't just any parent. He'd had the training to survive almost any scenario. He'd battled criminals, human traffickers, warlords and drug cartels for over fifteen years. He was battle hardened and tougher than nails. He also had the supernatural advantage of God blessing him with incredible strength whenever he needed it.

To parents with a barn full of classic cars and a huge house in the country, survival instincts didn't come naturally. The possibility that they had simply started walking without any preparation was weighing on Ethan's mind. But he allowed for the possibility that they had the sense to stop for water and comfortable footwear first. Ethan had learned to hope for the best but prepare for the worst. The worst case scenario was death with the only variables being whether or not they were still with the car. He took Peyton by the hand and marched Cael out in front of them. He wanted to keep an eye on the young man. Ethan felt some sympathy for him but he wasn't taking any chances.

———

After another hour Robbie could tell that his young partner was starting to wear out. "You want to stop for the night?"

"I just want to go a little further. Can we just go past that next exit?" Audrey gestured down the road to an over-pass that looked clogged with the typical expressway fare of fast food and gas stations.

"Let's do it," Robbie said with feigned enthusiasm. Not because he couldn't handle the walk but because he was getting less sure by the minute that they'd chosen the right road. If Audrey's parents had tried to leave the city days ago surely they would have been seen on the road or their vehicle would have been spotted along the road by now.

They reached the exit and decided to hole up in an empty McDonald's, mainly because it had cushioned booth seats. Robbie didn't plan on sleeping much so he could keep an eye on his young charge. After an uneventful night, Audrey and an exhausted, bleary-eyed Robbie headed out into another sweltering morning. Thankfully it was still very early and there were no people visible yet. They walked quietly having already exchanged the typical morning greetings and questions about sleep quality. Robbie lied about sleeping well but decided it was better than adding to the girl's already worried state.

They crossed a short bridge and then passed a Wal-Mart on their right. It seemed they had only walked for half an hour before they came upon a wall. It was a pile of cars and debris stacked in the roadway completely blocking the road leading to the bridge to Padre Island. Next to the wall of debris was a sign that read, "John F Kennedy Memorial Causeway". Confused, they started picking their way over the pile to try and see what lay on the other side. The silence of the morning was broken by the distinct click of a gun being readied for use.

"You can go over there if you want but you won't be coming back."

Robbie looked up to see a scraggly, gray-bearded man with wire rim glasses and a dingy gray tank top holding a pistol. "Why is the road blocked? Is there something wrong on the island?"

"Nothing wrong. We just don't want all those folks coming over here and using up what little resources we've got left. That's where all the rich folks are anyway. They'll be fine. They can ride their fancy boats to some other port. Just not here."

"What gives you the right to make that decision? Where are the cops?"

"Haven't seen a cop in three days. Probably taking care o' their own."

Robbie had no idea what resources the man was talking about and what he had against the people on the island. "I see a huge problem with your plan. You're killing people. If the cars aren't working neither are the boats. You just stranded thousands of people out there and maybe have even killed some. You think you can justify that to protect what few resources you have? Have you even been down this road and looked at what's left of the restaurants and stores? What are you protecting?

"Ourselves. This is the kind of thing we stay ready for."

"By 'we' you mean militia folks?"

"Call 'em what you want. We're just protectin' what's ours."

Audrey stepped forward. "My parents might be over there! They need to get across that bridge!"

"Nobody's comin' over that bridge but you're welcome to go find em. I'll be waitin' for you when you come back." At this, he smiled and reached down for a rifle with a scope on it that Robbie had spotted while they talked. Robbie had waited for him to look down and used the opportunity to launch himself up the pile and grab hold of the gunman's hand. The old guard never had a chance to bring the pistol to bear on the seasoned soldier. Robbie wrenched the gun from him and kicked the rifle away. It skidded off the hood of a car and fell somewhere beneath the pile. Robbie restrained the older man and forcefully interrogated him. He had no patience for people like him. And though as a God-fearing man and firm believer in Jesus he knew he should show restraint, the stress of the last week had worn down his self-control.

After a few aptly applied pressure points and threats of broken bones Robbie learned that there were almost one hundred so-called militiamen who had thrown up the blockade just days after the power outage. They were on a rotating schedule of guard duty until the supposed threat from the island had subsided. The next guard was supposed to be there any minute so Robbie had dragged the now helpless old man off the barricade and behind the guardrail on the side of the road. Robbie hid Audrey well off the road behind some brush near the water, almost under the bridge itself. He tucked the pistol into his waistband and after finding the rifle he walked back up to the road to wait for the next guard. He didn't have to wait long. Robbie had just gotten to the middle of the roadway when a younger man, mid-forties, close cut brown but graying hair and wearing a pair of aviators strolled up, also carrying a rifle.

"You're not Ralph! Where's he at?"

"He had an emergency." Robbie moved quickly toward the newcomer and stretched out a hand like he was going to shake it. The man instinctively reached out to shake but at the last second understood Robbie's intentions. It was too late. Robbie grabbed his hand and pulled the man forcefully into choke hold. He shook him while commanding him to drop the weapon. When the rifle clattered to the ground he kept one hand around the militiaman's neck while the other hand snaked down his back to snatch the pistol he most surely had stuffed in his waist band. Now disarmed, the cocky replacement guard stepped back, doubled over and coughed, trying to regain his breath. Robbie offered no reprieve. He grabbed him again and bound his wrists with a strip of fabric he'd torn off of Ralph's shirt during his inter-rogation. Robbie was tired and angry that a small group of idiots was able to cut off access to a major city out of fear. His anger fueled his rough treatment of this second mili-tiaman and he dragged him off the roadway as well and dumped him about thirty feet from Ralph.

"You two can talk about all of your life mistakes. Maybe by the time I get back you'll have found a new path. Oh, and I almost forgot. Jesus loves you."

He walked down toward the water and retrieved

Audrey. "We've only got a few hours. We need to get across this bridge and see if we can find your parents. We also need to help the people on the island get to the mainland. That's a lot. Are you up to it?" Audrey nodded wearily and they hiked back up to the road.

———

Ethan and Peyton were following Cael for an hour and the longer they walked, the worse Cael's memory became. They passed a few places that seemed familiar to him but very few strong leads. Ethan was getting increasingly uneasy being this far from their only ride out of town and their only means of traveling farther north toward his son. He should have never left the vehicle since it was the rendezvous point with Robbie. But Ethan was not used to being the one staying behind while someone else did the work. He made the decision abruptly. "Cael, stop. We're going back. This was a mistake."

"Do I have to go with you?"

"If there was actually a way to punish you, I would say yes. Attempted robbery, armed assault. And I suspect lying. Normally, you'd be coming with me. But since the chances of our paths ever crossing again are slim to none I will leave you here."

"My weapon?"

Ethan looked at Cael in disbelief. "You must've hit your head when I disarmed you back at the car."

"How am I gonna protect myself?" Cael whined.

"Stay out of trouble. Don't do dumb things." The irony of his parting words wasn't lost on Ethan since the dumb thing he had done was to trust Cael at all. He knew deep down that Cael had lied to get them away from the vehicle.

That he had not seen Peyton's parents or the car. Ethan's discomfort grew as he turned and walked back the way they came, with Peyton in tow. He had traced their route and knew how to get back to the car but was now convinced that there would be little, if anything, to come back to. He tried to suppress the waves of negative thoughts crashing over him.

They spoke little as they walked. Peyton was increasingly silent throughout the previous day and was even quieter this morning. Ethan had no pep talk, no entertainment, no perks to offer him. It was simply a waiting game. He was contemplating what to do with the next few hours of daylight when they came up the grassy shoulder of the highway to where the car should have been. The Cadillac was gone.

Immediately, Ethan mentally flogged himself for being so stupid. He was a top military operative, skilled in every kind of fighting and weaponry, a strategist of the highest order and he was duped by his own eagerness to accomplish the mission. *Was Cael the distraction? Did a group of kids really outwit him?* Ethan knew even if it was a few kids trying to get a vehicle it was not really their doing. He was to blame. He had wanted to believe Cael's storytelling and used it as an excuse to go hunting on his own. In the process he lost the only motorized means of going farther north. He growled in frustration making Peyton look up at him.

"It's gone isn't it?"

"I messed up, Peyton. I thought maybe Cael could actually be a help to us but it was just me trying to be a hero. He lied to us. I'm sorry."

"Don't feel bad. I didn't want to sit under that overpass waitin'. I wanted to do somethin' too."

"You're a good kid, Peyton. You remind me of my son."

"Is that why you're anxious to go? You want to get to your son?"

Ethan nodded. Usually he could focus on the mission - the task at hand - and not worry about his family. But today he was distracted and it had cost them. "We have to stay nearby. Robbie and your sister are going to come back this way and we need to let them know we're okay." Ethan glanced down the road leading away from the city and caught a glint of light flashing off of something. Something moving. Thinking it might be the Cadillac still slowly backing away he ordered Peyton to hide behind a car. Ethan sprinted down the road toward where he had seen the flash. He saw it again and guessed the car was being maneuvered around the stopped traffic causing it to catch the light. It was at least one hundred yards away. He dodged around a Ford Focus and then heard the whine of a bullet, the report of a gunshot and the pop of a slug piercing metal almost simultaneously. He instinctively got lower with the Ford between himself and from where he thought the shot came.

Skirting the front bumper of the car he emerged on the opposite side to catch a glimpse of who might have fired at him. Another shot rang out and Ethan dove again to the pavement. This time he crawled forward past the Ford and scrambled to the front end of an SUV. After this vehicle it was quite a distance to any more cover. He unholstered his pistol and readied it, every muscle now ready. This scenario was nothing new. It had been a long time though since he fought battle on American soil. He didn't want to kill anyone but he also had multiple lives to protect. He said a silent prayer asking for strength and then with the Spirit of God filling him, he grabbed the front bumper of the SUV and pushed it backward toward the last place he had seen the Cadillac. The gunshots picked up in pace now and the back window shattered. A tire went flat but Ethan kept pushing. The more he pushed the stronger he felt and he gradually increased his pace. The SUV continued to skid along and eventually slammed into another car stopped in the road. The velocity of the crash sent the other vehicle skidding away and Ethan pressed on. He heard shouts on the other side of the car and gave one last shove. He had flipped it as he let go and the SUV spun upward, landing on its roof. Ethan glimpsed two or three young men scattering left and right.

One man stopped after leaping the guardrail and turned to fire at Ethan. Ethan raised his pistol and got off one perfectly aimed shot that looked as if it removed some fingers from the attacker's gun hand. The rest of the crew had scattered and Ethan ran forward to see if he was right. The Cadillac was there, intact. He glanced around quickly to make sure no enemies remained. Convinced all was clear he jumped into the driver's seat and carefully wove it back through the gauntlet of stopped cars, parking where he had left Peyton. The boy was standing on the concrete slope of the underpass, staring at Ethan with his jaw hanging open.

"That was amazin'! How did you flip that car?"

"There's a lot you don't know about me, Peyton. I can tell you first of all - that wasn't me. My strength comes from God." Ethan heard voices above him. "Get in the car. I'll tell you more later." They jumped into the Cadillac and Ethan backed it out from under the overpass and drove it backward, like the thieves had attempted to do, only more successfully. He could see several of the car thieves on the bridge watching him back away. None of them fired the weapons he knew they had, perhaps for fear of damaging the car.

Ethan's plan was to get the car off the main road and

hide it somewhere. He would have to watch for Robbie and Audrey somehow. He backed it far enough to get off two exits before the overpass, hoping the thieves would not be watching his every move. Finding his partner and Peyton's sister just got a lot more complicated.

NINE

Even with every window open, the house was so hot it was difficult to sleep. A meager breakfast of cooked rice sprinkled with sugar started the day. They used some bottled water to wash up and brush their teeth. Watching the water go down the drain reminded David that he had to figure out how to supply his family with clean water long-term.

At ten o'clock David walked into the intersection of Davis and Rockwell streets to await the arrival of the neighbors. The day felt similar to the previous one with temperatures again headed to typical July heights. As David slowly scanned the neighborhood, he occasionally glimpsed someone at a window or a child peeking out from behind a backyard fence. The minutes crawled by until finally a neighbor opened her door and made her way to the intersection. It was Martha.

She lived two doors to the east of David and kept mainly to herself. Widowed several years ago, she had one son who stopped by occasionally to cut her grass or do some handyman work.

"Good morning, Martha. Thanks for coming."

Martha scanned the two streets and then turned back to David. "You've got a scared bunch here."

"We're all scared. No one really knows what's happening. That's why we need to communicate." David's peripheral vision caught Roger coming down the hill and behind him another man carrying a rifle. A screen door slammed and David turned, looking south, to see another family, the Lavins, coming toward the intersection. The Lavins had been in the neighborhood for thirteen years. They had three teenagers – two sons and a daughter. Joining them in the street were Manny and Rochelle who lived directly across from the Lavins. David knew their names but nothing more. It seemed once a few neighbors had displayed the bravery to join David in the street, the rest joined. Soon there were more than thirty people standing in the intersection. David cleared his throat. "Thanks for meeting me out here. Just to remind you, my name is David Zabad and I live right here on the corner. I thought it would be good to talk about a plan going forward. We have no idea how long this power outage will last. We have to think about food, water, transportation and if it lasts long enough, staying warm."

"You think this is gonna last until winter?" This was Mark from next door.

"I don't know. But we should plan as if it is."

"It is." Garrett stepped around a few neighbors and planted himself in the center of the group.

Ted Lavin stepped forward too and stood directly in front of Garrett. "How would you know?"

"I own and operate a short-wave radio. I've been talking to guys all over Michigan and hearing things from all over the country. It's bad. Power outage ranges from here all the way up to the upper peninsula and Toledo, Cincinnati, Louisville, Pittsburgh – all have no power. Only people I've talked to with power are west of Texas. We'll all be dead of starvation in a few months anyway so I wouldn't worry about staying warm." Garrett directed this last comment toward David.

This confirmed David's worst fear but with the neighborhood looking on, he quickly shook off the worry and proceeded. "That's why we're here. We can help each other. If Garrett is right then we need to"

"If?" Garrett snorted. "If I'm right? You all just need to figure out how to take care of yourselves. Forget everyone else and get what you need."

"Garrett, if you don't want to be a part of this no one's making you. But you and that radio could be a huge help to our neighborhood."

"You come anywhere near me and my radio and I'll make good on that promise I made yesterday." Garrett hefted his gun, then stepped back from David and addressed the whole group. "And that goes for all of you. Stay out of my yard, stay out of my way. I only came down here to see what I was dealing with."

"So you won't help us at all?" David pleaded.

"If you have nothing to offer me – I have nothing to offer you."

Thoughts of violence flooded David's mind but instead he deliberately turned away from Garrett and addressed the rest of the group. "Alright, let's start by taking an inventory."

As the meeting went on David kept an eye on Garrett as he slunk away from the gathering and made his way back up the hill.

After an hour of tossing out ideas it was decided that the

neighborhood would together plant a garden. The two largest pieces of open land were next to David and Elizabeth and across the street from their house though there were several other plots that could be farmed as well. And though it was late in the season to start planting, there was nothing to be lost by trying.

July 5 - Padre Island, Corpus Christi, Texas

The four-mile bridge was clear except for two bodies from which Robbie steered Audrey away. The idea that Americans would shoot their countrymen just to selfishly hoard their resources made Robbie wonder what he was fighting for all these years. Was this really the land of the free and the home of the brave?

They reached the island and called out to see if anyone was around. Cars were lined up at the bridge for a long way, clogging the road as far as they could see. The cars first in line had bullet holes in the windshield. The strangest thing was that so few people were outside. With the temperature soaring into the nineties, Robbie assumed people would not want to be cooped up inside with no air conditioning. And yet, the streets were relatively clear and few people were on their porches. The stores and restaurants that lined the usually busy island shopping district were looted, broken glass scattered across the sidewalks, debris littering the street. They walked on until, finally, Robbie spotted a man being walked by his dog toward the Padre beaches.

"Excuse me! Sir, can I talk to you?" The man pulled hard on the leash, slowed and turned to greet Robbie. "I just came from the mainland. I wanted to"

"You came from the mainland? How did you get

through? Those animals over there are guardin' the road. People on the island are losin' their minds."

"I made sure the guard took a long break. Look, I need you to help me get the word out. If people want to leave the island, this is their chance. They probably only have a few hours before Beavis and Butthead get relieved and there's a new guard over there."

"Yeah, I can help."

"Great. Just start knocking on doors and spread the word. On foot only and only what people can carry." Robbie turned to keep walking and then remembered. "One other thing. Have you seen this couple?" he asked, pulling out a picture of the Pelhams they had taken from the house.

"I don't think so. Hard to say though. This place is always so busy."

"What about a bright yellow SUV?" Robbie pressed.

"Now that I have seen. A couple of them actually. Seen them go by before the power outage. Speakin' of that - do you know what happened? There was an explosion and everyone is talkin' terrorism but we haven't heard anythin'. A bunch of houses burned down further out on the island too. I've got kids up in Oklahoma but I don't know how to contact them, let alone get to them. Got any info?"

"I'm Sergeant Robbie Charles. U.S. Army. My last contact with my commanding officer was a few days ago and all he knew is it was a possible terrorist attack. He did say the power was out from the east coast all the way to west Texas." The clock was ticking. Robbie backed away while talking. "Start telling people if they want to go, to go now. Nice meeting you." The man nodded and continued on.

Mentioning his last contact with Reynolds made Robbie think about the satellite phone that was tucked into his bag. The last few calls he tried were unanswered. Colonel

Reynolds was most likely overwhelmed with coordinating the recovery effort that was surely underway. More information would be incredibly helpful now.

Audrey was about to burst. They took less than ten steps away from the man before Audrey said, "He said he saw a yellow SUV! That means they're here."

"Audrey, we don't know if he saw their vehicle. He might have just remembered a car similar to theirs or he did see a yellow car but it wasn't theirs. Don't get your hopes too high, kiddo."

Audrey's face did not change. She turned from Robbie and with increased speed headed down the main road in the center of the island. Aware that they were running out of time, he shook his head and jogged to get next to her.

"A couple miles, Audrey. That's all we can do. I gave Ethan a deadline. There's still a lot of city to explore."

"I know they're here," she said without looking at Robbie. Her face was fixed forward, scanning everywhere for her parents.

The day grew hotter as the sun approached its zenith. Robbie could only hope that the man they had talked to was getting the word out that the bridge was clear. That bridge needed to stay clear permanently for them to continue their journey. He and Ethan didn't come halfway around the world to get stranded in Texas on the Gulf coast.

Another half hour dragged by and as they walked they told anyone they saw that now was their chance to leave the island if they desired. Some seemed excited and ran back to their homes or hotel rooms while others shrugged and walked away, either unaware of what was happening several miles away or content to wait out the power outage. Robbie was carefully rationing his water and was giving as much to Audrey as he could. The lack of fluids was beginning to wear on him. It was not long ago he was in a much hotter place than this. The difference was the amount of stress he was currently experiencing. He put his head down, concentrating on pushing his body forward with each step but his head snapped upright when he heard Audrey squeal.

"It's them! It's them!" And she was running.

Robbie saw the yellow vehicle they'd been looking for and found his energy renewed enough to jog behind Audrey, making sure she didn't come upon anything she would regret seeing. She bounded up the steps to the house behind where the Range Rover was parked. She banged on the door and it opened cautiously. Then it was flung open wide as her parents burst through and hugged their daughter.

"How did you get here, sweetheart?" Mr. Pelham was amazed. "And where's your brother?"

"Robbie and Ethan brought me and Peyton all the way here. We drove your Cadillac!"

"You drove my—" Robbie detected instant anger both in Mr. Pelham's voice and face.

Mrs. Pelham cut him off before he said something foolish. "We're so glad you made it. We've been here since the power went out tryin' to figure out what to do. We heard the bridge was closed and—" Mrs. Pelham seemed to notice Robbie for the first time. "I'm so sorry. I'm Erin Pelham. This is my husband Todd. Thank you so much for bringin' our daughter to us."

"It was my pleasure, ma'am."

"It was probably your idea to bring the Cadillac, right?" Todd asked accusingly.

Robbie turned to Todd. "No, sir. It was purely a tactical decision. Gas mileage and plenty of storage."

"It had better be in pristine condition when I get it back."

"I can assure you, there's no way we would do anything harmful to it - on purpose. And, you're welcome."

———

Ethan parked the car on a quiet alley several blocks from both the freeway and the airport. It was out of the way and the only buildings around were warehouses or light industrial businesses. It wasn't until he stopped that he noticed the bullet hole in the upper passenger side of the windshield. He got out of the car and did a walk around just to make sure nothing else was damaged. It appeared that everything was in working order. After a quick recon of the alley, the street behind them, and the nearest intersection, he went back to the car. Peyton had stretched out in the back seat to sleep. The windows were down and the alley was shaded so it wasn't quite as hot. All they could do was wait. Ethan determined to check every few minutes to make sure no one crept up on them. But with so many streets and only one set of eyes, he couldn't watch everywhere at once.

One by one, silently, the car thieves made their way down streets and alleys, looking for the Cadillac and the man who had thrown a car at them.

———

The store was locked and strangely, not yet looted but Robbie made short work of the back door. They gathered four bikes from the store and after making sure they were in good working order and the tires were aired they rode toward the bridge. Robbie hated to ride off with the bikes but if the crisis was as bad as their info revealed, they would need every advantage. He felt silly on the bike since he couldn't remember the last time he'd been on one. But it was like he'd never stopped.

The bridge was no longer being guarded though they were forced to carry the bikes a short distance over some debris. As they passed over onto the mainland surrounded by other island dwellers making their way, they caught a glimpse of the two men Robbie had subdued, still tied up but now with bloodied faces. It was clear someone other than Robbie had taken out their anger and frustration on the bridge guards.

The trip back to where they had left Ethan took just a fraction of the time it had taken to walk. The only problem was that he wasn't where they had left him.

"Where's my car?"

"Mr. Pelham, this is where we left it. If it's not here there's a very good reason. Ethan is deliberate."

Mr. Pelham started a reply but the sharp report of gunfire startled him and shattered the peaceful afternoon. The Pelhams stepped off their bikes and simply looked around. Audrey rode up next to where Robbie had stopped and looked expectantly at him, having learned over the last few days that he was the person to look to in a crisis. More shots rang out but they sounded distant.

"It's coming from there," Robbie said, pointing south of the expressway. "Better get some cover. When bullets are flying you never know where they'll end up. Right there." Robbie pointed to a brick building with Grayson Plumbing Supply painted on it. "Get inside there. At least you'll have brick between you and anything or anyone that might be out there." Robbie walked his bike toward the building but Mr. Pelham's voice pulled him up short.

"And where are you goin'?"

"To find my best friend and your son. Stay hidden. This might not end well." He started through the service drive for "Authorized Vehicles Only" that spanned the median and saw Audrey behind him. "Audrey, you can't come with me."

"Audrey, get back here! Where do you think you're goin'?" Mrs. Pelham was trying desperately to keep herself together but the shrieks in her voice said she was failing.

"Go on kiddo. It's okay. I'll bring your brother back, I promise." Audrey slowly turned the bike around as her mother continued to beg her to come back.

Minutes later, Robbie was standing as he pedaled, moving as fast as he could on the stolen bike. As long as there were multiple gunshots, he knew Ethan was returning fire. He could not have had much ammunition. But the gunfire had not been going for long. Sensing he was near the heat of the battle, Robbie braked hard, leaped off the bike and leaned it against the wall of a warehouse. He flung his bag off his shoulder and slid out his Sig Sauer P220, making sure it was fully loaded and he had an extra mag with him. He carefully checked around the corner of the building where he'd parked the bike and looked for any sign of Ethan and the shooters. The street looked empty and so he made his way down along the building, weapon ready.

———

Peyton's eyes were wide with fear as Ethan quietly told him what to do. He did as he was told and then Ethan carefully exited the car from the passenger side. With Peyton laying on the floor in the back seat he would be safe from the gunfire, although it wasn't a guarantee. Ethan desperately wanted to take the fight to his attackers - a tactic he had relied on for most of his career. It was the one move in his arsenal that his enemies never saw coming. After all, what could one man do? The answer was, make a huge mess and do serious damage. One problem now was that he couldn't leave Peyton in a vulnerable position, exposed to danger, gunfire and possible kidnapping if his attackers were able to get the car. Another problem was that Ethan didn't even know who he was up against. The distance was too great to know if these were young men, teenagers, a bunch of punk kids or an organized gang. If he saw a gun, he would have no choice but to stop the threat. He prayed a silent prayer asking God to make his aim true and his hand steady. He also asked for good judgment. Ethan was not anxious to kill anyone so his goal was shoot to wound, disarm, and subdue. It didn't always work that way but he did his best.

He crept along the alley wall waiting for another shot to ring out. He did not have to wait long as the wooden wall exploded from a bullet, sending splinters flying. Ethan crouched even lower, scanning the street for where the shot came from. Nothing. And then Ethan heard the footsteps pounding behind him. He raised his gun to fire but stopped when he saw Cael.

"What are you doing here? I told you to get lost." He kept his gun trained on the young man.

"I came to help."

"Do you really think I would trust you after what you did to us?" Ethan approached Cael and quickly patted him down just in case he had found another weapon in the last few hours and then directed him with his pistol. "Over there. Next to the car."

He obeyed and slumped down next to the Cadillac. "All they want is the car. You know that right? They don't care about you or the kid in the back seat. They just want the car."

"So, you've been watching me? Look, this isn't my car to give away. And if someone comes at me with a gun I'm not going to assume they only want my possessions. I'll assume they're dangerous. You've come at me once with a gun which is why I can't turn my back on you."

"I promise you man, I'm here to help."

"And I promise you - shut up or I will make you unconscious."

Cael crossed his arms and scowled. His face abruptly changed however as something over Ethan's shoulder caught his eye. It was Robbie. Several gunshots rang out as he slipped around the corner toward the Cadillac.

"Cavalry is here!" He called out.

"Man, am I glad to see you." Ethan reached out and fist bumped him. "Where's Audrey?" He asked, looking behind him. Robbie grinned widely. "With her mom and dad! Found them on Padre Island at the home they'd bought."

"Robbie, that's a miracle! There's no way that could happen unless-"

"Unless God got involved? Yeah, hunches and common sense are great and all but – man, ain't nothing like a miracle. We borrowed a few bikes from a store on the island and here we are." Glancing at Cael, he asked, "Who's this?"

"He's the reason we're holed up here. He tried to carjack us and then lied about seeing the kids' parents. It was just to lure us away from the vehicle so his friends could steal it. I don't know why they're pushing so hard to get it but it forced us to move."

"I told you, I came to help," Cael protested.

"And I told you I'd knock you out. It's bad enough you tried to rob me but then you intentionally raised that boy's hope for the sake of a car. It's a very good thing we found them or I would have another reason to make you walk with a limp."

"What are you gonna do with him?" Robbie asked as he eyed Cael with suspicion.

"Leave him behind when it's time to go. We have places to be. Right now we have to get out of this alley and get Peyton reunited with his parents."

"Right. Then let's form a plan and move."

———

Robbie got behind the wheel while Ethan went down to the opposite end of the alley so he could circle around behind his attackers. The fact that they had not moved in toward him told him they were unsure who they were dealing with. The car being pushed and then flipped in the road must've been frightening. They obviously didn't want to die to get their hands on the car. But their motivation may have gone much deeper than a vehicle. It might have meant money, finding a family member or trading for food or water. Their reasons did not matter at the moment.

Ethan's goal was to neutralize each of his attackers by non-lethal means so they could get the Pelhams on their way. He had narrowed down the location of at least two gunmen. There was no way to know how many were out there looking for them. He turned left at the end of the alley and sprinted to the intersection two blocks from where he had parked the car. He worked his way up the street so he was looking back toward where he had parked. He pressed himself close against the wall of a brick office building and looked across the street.

He spotted someone lurking behind a dumpster at the

back of a parking lot, looking in the direction of the alley. He sprinted across the street toward the lurker and almost made it to him before he noticed. He turned at the last second to see Ethan bearing down on him. The lookout was a scrawny, twenty-something with a thin chin strap beard, close cropped hair, an earring and a gold chain around his neck. Unfortunately, he screamed like a little girl.

Ethan quickly struck him, knocking him out, but it was too late. His scream had drawn the whole gang. Before he had a chance to run for cover, Ethan counted at least eight guys, some looking as young as sixteen, all running toward him with guns drawn and aimed. "Okay, okay. You got me."

One of the older men stepped forward, snatched Ethan's gun off his hip and demanded, "The car. Take us to it. Now."

"Yeah. Sure. Of course." Ethan had no choice but to comply. He noticed his captors kept their physical distance but never took their guns off him for a moment. He had less than two blocks to get some kind of warning to Robbie that things didn't go as planned. He mind was running every possible scenario when the screeching of tires interrupted his thoughts. The Cadillac came screaming into the street backwards with Robbie at the wheel. Robbie quickly spun the car around and headed for the group standing around Ethan.

The gang shot at the vehicle and Ethan saw several more men come out of hiding on the far side of the alley. He went to the man who had confiscated his pistol and in one fluid motion snatched his wrist and spun the man around landing him on his back, gun hand straight up in the air. "Thanks for holding on to this for me."

He gripped the gun tightly and kept his eye on Robbie. With the car heading their way, the men around him no longer cared what Ethan was doing. Robbie drove past him even as the group of attackers continued to fire at the car. The trunk opened and Cael popped up. He dumped gasoline out of a can onto the road and then threw a lighter along with the can, into the road. The gas ignited and then exploded as it caught the fumes within. Ethan ran across the street, past where the gas was burning and was rewarded with a clear view of the car's rear. He saw the right indicator blinking. Robbie was doing what he could to direct him. With the gas burning and the men trying to decide their next move, he used the opportunity to sprint toward a street that paralleled the alley where he'd been hiding. When he reached the next intersection he found he'd been correct. Robbie pulled up to the corner, Ethan got in and they raced one more block to turn around and head back to the expressway where they'd left Audrey and her parents.

————

"I'm not goin' anywhere but home and this Cadillac is goin' with me." Mr. Pelham was visibly shaken.

"Mr. Pelham, listen, we're not interested in your car. We're interested in your safety. What will happen if you get halfway home and breakdown? We used up some of the gas we brought. Do you know how you'll get your whole family safely home? We have very little water as it is. The trip here took a couple days and probably wouldn't be much different going back. I just want you to consider all the possibilities."

"I have and you sayin' I don't know how to take care of my own family seals the deal. I won't stand here and be insulted by you."

Ethan could feel his blood pressure rise and he was sure

his face turned red. "I think you're forgetting we brought you your kids."

"And I appreciate that. I do. Without you . . . I . . . Uh, thank you. Yes, that was amazing. But I still have to get back to my own home."

Ethan ignored the halfhearted thank you. "There's one other thing." He gestured to the south side of the expressway to point out that several of the men were making their way from the streets out to the highway service drive. "We need to go." A gunshot from the assailants startled them all and Ethan and Robbie went into protective mode. "Everyone in the car, now!"

"I'm drivin'," Todd shouted but was physically placed in the passenger seat by Ethan.

"No, you're not. Not until we are clear of this mess."

The kids piled into the back with Mrs. Pelham and Ethan, while Cael, who was sitting in the trunk with the lid open, got out and started crawling over Todd to sit in the center of the front seat. Todd swore and Robbie looked in the rear view mirror at Ethan.

"Just drive," Ethan said. "Wait! I forgot something! Go and I'll catch up in a few minutes."

Robbie knew his best friend well enough to know not to argue. He dropped the car into reverse and wove around cars again until he could get to a clear enough space to turn around. Ethan grabbed the sturdiest bike Robbie had taken from the store, jumped on and rode. He wasn't the best bike rider but he was strong. His aggressive pedaling put him a good distance from the shooters and not too far behind Robbie. After a few more minutes he caught the car and Robbie, seeing him in the mirror stopped long enough for him to wedge the bike into the trunk and get back inside. "Now we can go."

. . .

After thirty minutes of steady driving Robbie stopped the car and turned to Todd. "It's your turn." He exited the driver's seat and walked to the trunk. Ethan got out as well, with a heavy heart. He couldn't agree with the Pelham's decision to go home. Robbie grabbed the bike from the trunk along with the bags they had carried over the border.

"It's time for us to go. We have a long way to travel," Ethan said to the Pelhams.

Audrey and Peyton hugged Ethan, and then Robbie, on one knee, put his arms around the little group. "Thank you for helpin' us," Audrey choked out. "I guess prayin' helped."

"It always does, Audrey."

"Thanks," Peyton's little voice chimed in. "You should take the bike, Ethan. You'll get to your son faster."

"That's a great idea, Peyton. Thanks for suggesting it."

"It was our joy to help you both. We had an adventure, didn't we?" Robbie pulled back from hugging the kids and Ethan could see he too, was struggling to let the kids go. He threw a glance at the Pelhams but Todd was determined.

"Thanks again for everythin'," Todd said as he approached Ethan with his hand extended. Ethan shook it and then Todd guided his kids to the back seat.

Bending over at the driver side window, Robbie said, "Uh, Cael? You have to get out."

"I'd rather not."

"They're not taking you with them. Now get out. You can come with me and Ethan."

Ethan glared at Robbie from where he'd been talking to the kids as they got settled in the back seat. They didn't have to bring him along. They could get him to the east side of Corpus so the car thieves couldn't find him. After all, he had helped them escape and with his family and home gone there was really nowhere else for him to go. Ethan's practical side immediately focused on the lack of supplies going forward. Water was number one, followed closely by food. Shelter wouldn't be an issue until they got further north.

If Cael was disappointed at the idea of tagging along, it did not show. The concern was all Ethan's as he considered babysitting this millennial all the way to Michigan.

Robbie wheeled the bike to Ethan and Cael as they watched the Pelhams drive back toward their home. The kids turned and waved out the back window as they drove away. They could see Audrey, no longer holding back the tears as she waved. "I can't help feeling like they're making a huge tactical error."

"If they were with us it would make our task a lot more difficult."

"But at least I would be able to keep an eye on those kids," Robbie pointed out.

"We still have a kid to keep an eye on," Ethan said as he lightly punched Cael in the arm.

Cael rubbed his upper arm. "I'm not a kid, I'm nineteen."

Ethan was appalled. "If that hurt we're gonna have to do a lot more than keep an eye on you. We're gonna have to toughen you up. And for the record, nineteen is like a kid to me. If you come with us, you have to pull your weight. I'm not carting your sorry butt all the way to Michigan."

"Mr. uh, Ethan is it? I don't actually know who you guys are. But I wanted to say I'm sorry. I know you're being nice to me, letting me come with you. So, I guess - sorry and thank you."

"Cael, my name is Ethan Zabad, this is my best friend and business partner, Robbie Charles. I know you've been through a bad time. I also know you tried to rob me and then lied to me. So, don't mistake my kindness for trust. Because I don't trust you. You came back and helped us. I admire that. But don't mistake my appreciation for trust either. You're gonna have to earn that."

Cael nodded during Ethan's speech and then spoke. "I understand. I know I screwed up." His lip trembled but he took a deep breath, blinked hard and shook off the wave of emotion Ethan suspected had more to do with the loss of his family than any regret or gratitude he felt.

"It helps to hear you acknowledge what you did. We can work with that. Now let's figure out where we're going from here."

"Who gets the bike?" Cael wanted to know.

Ethan had a few ideas. "For now we take turns walking it. When I find what I'm looking for we'll make you and that bike work for us."

TEN

It was only a bottle of water but the man lunged at David who could do nothing but step back against the tree. There was no escape. David blocked a right-handed thrust with his arm but the man produced another wicked-looking blade with his left. It slipped under David's right arm and pierced the cartilage between his ribs. The pain was excruciating and David could feel the steel penetrate all the way into his lung. He gasped and coughed a spray of blood onto the face of his assailant who gleefully looked David in the eye and calmly twisted the knife.

David sat upright in bed, sweat pouring down his chest. He dreamed the same scenario several nights now. The first dream involved Nate but subsequent dreams featured David as the victim. Had there not been a power outage, Elizabeth would have been telling him to call a therapist by now. The stress and trauma of the first few days of the crisis had passed but their effects had not.

It was eleven days since the power went out and an eerie silence settled on the city. Most home generators were out of gas. Mail delivery ceased just one day after the attacks. Fewer and fewer cars drove by on the main road. Vehicles in Fenton were not impacted by the EMP in Metro Detroit but there was no gas available. No sirens were heard for days. Garbage pickup was missed twice now and the result caused a stench to permeate the city. The sound that at one time was foreign to Fenton but increased a hundred-fold in the last week was gunfire. David calmly chose to believe it was the sound of people shooting squirrels or rabbits for food but faint screams told him his hopes were false.

He went to the river several times with garbage cans arranged on his trailer so he could bring back water. Most of his neighbors were out and were making their own treks to the river. Morning and evening the river was becoming a gathering time and place to visit and find out what was happening around town. It only took one day to realize the river water could not be drunk without treatment. Several people got sick after drinking directly from the river. Gathering water and boiling it was David's project whenever he took a break from preparing the ground for the garden.

The half-acre plot next door and another large lot across the street was torn up over the last few days and rows of vegetables were planted. Several neighbors discovered seed packets in their homes while others planted their own garden but had leftover seeds.

Whenever he was not working in the dirt or collecting water, he was trying to MacGyver a water distillation system with what was on hand. Black plastic and the summer sun worked well for now but eventually they would need something that produced more reliable and voluminous results. The goal was to figure out something he could easily duplicate so he could share the design with everyone in the neighborhood.

He was grateful to have a project every day to keep his mind busy. The alternative was sitting on his porch worrying. Two nights ago, he and Liz went to their basement and laid out every scrap of food in the house. After doing the math and carefully rationing everything, they realized it would be impossible to make the food last until the end of the year. The gardens would help but they would need a source of protein as well. There was still bottled water in their basement but they were trying to rely exclusively on water retrieved from the river. No matter how they approached their situation, there was no scenario that enabled them to live past the new year. They would be out of food and out of time. The power could come back on but David was resigning himself more each day to the fact that they were on their own. No representative from the city, state or federal government made an announcement, an appearance or an effort to reach out to the afflicted citizens. He at least expected National Guard troops to roll through but their equipment must have been damaged as well.

David sat back from his distillation contraption to wipe sweat from his brow. The heat hadn't let up. At least his trips to the river allowed him to cool off. Liz refused to accompany him to the river, preferring to sponge bathe with a single bottle of water. It was frustrating to see the water used that way but it was a small concession given the stress Liz was feeling. It was also the first time since they were married that either went more than a day without bathing and there were new smells to which they were adjusting.

Glancing at the sky, David noted the sun's position. His skill at being able to guess the approximate time based on the sun was growing. He guessed seven o'clock and was proved correct within ten minutes when he went inside and glanced at the battery-operated clock in the dining room.

David accepted their situation but he still held on to some hope that the power would come back on or that the military would roll into town with supplies and word of what was happening across the rest of the country.

A few days later David decided to go see Sadiq. He was placing sandwich bags full of rice and dried meat into a backpack. "I'm bringing him some real food. I don't know how he can stand to live on that junk food in the gas station."

"Don't you think at some point he'll just abandon the gas and come stay with us?" Liz carried two cans of soup up the basement stairs and set them on the counter so David could add them to the backpack.

"Not as long as there's gas in those tanks. It's becoming more valuable by the day. I'm not the only one who figured out how to pump it out. People are trading with him like I have but the deals are less appealing every day."

"I'm worried if they're desperate enough they'll just take it?"

Hearing the fear in her voice, David put his hands on Liz's shoulders and gently turned her to face him. "I will talk to Sadiq about leaving and staying with us. I'm worried about him too. Especially after what I heard at the river yesterday."

"What? Did we finally hear something from outside the city?"

"I don't know where it came from but a group of men were talking about the grid failure and the explosions over the cities being caused by Islamic terrorists. Maybe they heard something before the phones stopped getting a signal.

Garrett up the hill said he has a short wave radio so maybe he heard something. Or maybe it's all just talk. I don't really know." David looked down for a moment, fighting to clear his face of the surprising emotion he was feeling. He raised his head to face her again. "I'm afraid the people in this city are going to turn against anyone of Arab descent – anyone who looks even close to Middle Eastern. I'm worried about Sadiq. I'll try to convince him."

"You're worried about Sadiq? David, your parents are Jewish. You look as Middle Eastern as he does!"

"It's different with me."

"How is it different? Tell me," she pleaded.

"Liz, I'm going to be fine. Please trust me."

"You just be careful. I would love to have Sadiq here if only it meant that you weren't leaving us overnight anymore." He nodded to her then grabbed the backpack off the counter and headed for the door. "David?"

"What, love?"

"Please be careful."

David locked the door and pulled it shut behind him. The windows were open for airflow which would not stop an intruder but if they chose the door, it might slow them down. He had no direct information about home invasions but as readily available supplies dwindled, the crime and violence would increase. The random gunshots of the last few nights told him that things were happening around him but until the problems knocked on his door he would ignore them. Whether that attitude was right or wrong was not something David had the energy to think about.

He mounted the seat of his rigged riding lawn mower and started the engine. The makeshift tractor and trailer served him well. He went to the river several times and drove back and forth to Sadiq's gas station for supplies. This morning he had the road to himself. No one walking anywhere with grocery carts from Target, Wal-Mart or the local grocery store. No cars. No bikes. No cops. David decided to take advantage of the quiet and head to the grocery store and see if anything was still on the shelves. After struggling so hard the first day of the crisis with stealing supplies, the last few weeks resolved his moral dilemma. He would do whatever it took to survive. He doubted there would be anything left at the store but it was worth a try.

The rattle of the mower engine was a blemish on the morning soundscape of bird songs but David rolled along at close to forty miles per hour. He continued to tinker with the engine and coaxed more speed out of it. He passed Target and then as he passed Sadiq's gas station, he glanced to make sure everything was in its place. He would stop there next. Without stop lights and traffic, he arrived at the grocery store in less than ten minutes. As he pulled from the main road into the parking lot, he noticed just a few cars still parked there. The motion-activated sliding glass doors were standing open revealing the store's black interior. David pulled up onto the sidewalk that ran the length of the storefront and beyond to the other stores in the shopping plaza. He made a mental note to stop at some of them to see what might be useful.

After retrieving a high-powered flashlight from the bag he carried on the trailer, he made his way through the door to the first section of the store, the produce aisles. Swinging the high beam around revealed that most of the produce shelves were empty. Several sections had produce but upon closer inspection, he discovered they were covered in mold and rotting. The bakery was the same. The meat market floor was wet from melted ice. The smell of rotted fish assaulted David's nostrils and he pulled his t-shirt up over his nose so he could breathe without choking.

Continuing through the store uncovered only empty shelves. He was too late. He did well in the first days of the crisis to gather supplies and makeshift some helpful tools but he was too late to gather any more long term supplies. He was almost to the other side of the store when he noticed a main shelf was moved to sit perpendicular to the rest of the main aisles. It could've been looters pushing the shelf out of their way but it looked more purposeful than haphazard. He walked toward the front of the store where the deli counter was and realized that another section of shelving was turned perpendicular as well, closing off a section of the store for some reason. Like a barricade, to keep people out. Or a fortress to protect something or someone inside. David moved to the portion of shelving that faced the front of the store and the windows that looked out on the parking lot. It was somewhat lighter here. He climbed the shelves like a ladder and at the top shone his flashlight down into the pen created by the shelving.

Someone thought ahead. Inside the pen was a stockpile of hundreds of products from the grocery shelves. Cans were stacked to the height of the completely full shelves. Six-by-six foot stacks of breakfast cereal. Bags of flour, sugar, and rice piled high nearby. David's heart jumped in his chest and he backed down off the shelves to the floor, hardly able to believe his good fortune. "Thank you Jesus for providing for me and my family," he whispered. He clicked off his light and headed for the tractor. He had some loading to do. He never saw the carefully-aimed can which glanced off the back of his head, rendering him unconscious before he even hit the floor.

David opened his eyes and saw only darkness. He tried

to remember how he got there but couldn't remember where 'there' was. Then he felt the pain on his head. He tried to reach up to feel if he was bleeding and how big the lump was but found that his hands were restrained. He fought the rising panic and slowly tried to roll over. He was laying on his right side so he shifted his hips so he could turn. He thought he might be able to at least stand and make his way to daylight. He found that his feet were bound as well.

"Hello? Is someone there?" David's voice echoed which eased his mind for a moment, realizing that wherever he was, it was big enough to send his voice back to him. His worst fear was one he shared with his dad: waking up in a chest freezer, a tiny closet or a box. He sat up, wincing, as the pain on his scalp blossomed in to a full blown headache.

Blinding sunlight appeared and then disappeared about forty feet from where David lay. A door opened and as David blinked trying to help his eyes adjust to the flash, another flash burst onto David's face, this time from his own flashlight.

"You walked into the wrong store today." The voice was thin, reedy. It was not a voice of confidence. David wasn't even sure if it belonged to a boy or a girl.

"Are you trying to sound tough?" David replied while squinting against the high beam light.

"I'm just telling you, I did all that work. I brought all that food to the corner. It's mine."

"What makes it yours? You know there's a lot of hungry people who could use that," David argued, hoping he could appeal to his captor's sense of justice or compassion.

"I didn't buy it. I found it. You find it, it's yours."

The beam of light was relentless. "Could you lower the flashlight? And I did find it."

"But I found it first. You're going to have to find your own stash of food."

"Why - flashlight please?"

"Oh, sorry." The beam was lowered.

"Why," David continued, "don't you just let me go and I'll stay away from this place. I won't tell anyone about it."

"There's no way I could trust you. I – I just have to keep you here."

"What, and starve me to death? Why don't you just hit me on the head again with – what did you hit me with anyway?"

"Soup. It was a good shot," the voice bragged. "I was behind the deli counter."

"You've got a good arm, I'll give you that. But you can't just leave me to rot in here. Why don't you let me help you? There's no way your little grocery shelf barricade is going to fool everyone."

"You were the first one to figure it out and there've been lots of people in here. If anyone else sees it I'll hit them like I did you."

David sensed his captor was not malicious. Scared and desperate but not cruel. "So, what's your plan?"

"What do you mean, what's my plan? I have food and water. I'm going to stay alive until this is over."

"How do you plan to stay warm? What about the foods that need to be cooked? How can you guard it every minute - by yourself? I think a crisis should bring people together, not tear them apart." David's captor was quiet, evidently not knowing what to say. "What's your name?" David asked gently.

"Keith."

"And how old are you, Keith?"

"I'm – it doesn't matter how old I am."

David heard a thud and the flashlight clattered to the floor. The room was thrown into blackness again.

"David? Are you okay?"

David recognized the voice. "Sadiq! How did you know I was here?"

"I heard you go by my place a few hours ago. When you didn't come I thought I would come looking for you."

"What about the station?"

"It'll be fine for ten minutes," Sadiq said as he knelt next to David.

"What did you do to the kid?" David asked as Sadiq snipped the plastic binding his hands and feet.

Sadiq picked up the flashlight and shone it on the object in his hand. "Progresso soup, why?"

Just then Keith moaned and tried to stand up.

"Hey, take it easy," David cautioned as he knelt next to his former captor. "You just got hit pretty hard."

"You're gonna steal all my food," Keith said.

"Nobody's stealing your food. Okay, well, maybe that's why I came here. But I'm not going to just take it."

"What are you going to do to me?" Keith asked.

"I'm not sure yet. Why don't we get to a place where we can actually see each other and we'll talk about it?"

The three men picked their way through receiving and the storage area at the rear of the store. Sadiq led the way while David brought up the rear to keep an eye on Keith. They entered the store near the meat counter and turned right to get to Keith's barricade.

"You know this was a great idea, Keith." David said. Keith grunted. "I mean it," David persisted. "I only found it because I was dumb enough to walk in here with just this flashlight. But even with the light I almost walked right past this." Keith was silent, continuing to stare at David. He was probably no more than 17, shorter than David with dark brown hair, a pimpled face and a t-shirt that said "I make stuff up". He had sparse, unshaved hairs on his lip and chin.

"What gave you the idea? What made you come here when you could have just stayed home?"

"I worked here. I stocked the shelves. My dad lives up north and my mom," he paused, reluctantly, "my mom isn't good to live with."

"Sorry to hear that. Didn't people loot this place? How did you manage to save all this?"

"After the first day, I stayed up all night moving what was left. When people came in it was dark so they just grabbed the first thing they put their hands on. No one brought flashlights. After the first night, a few more people came but all they saw were empty shelves so word must've got out that we were cleaned out."

"Keith, you're smart. I don't like that you hit me on the head with a can of soup," David said as he felt the raised, bloody gash, "but you're smart. I think we can help each other."

"You should listen to him," Sadiq spoke up. "He's been helping me."

Keith looked warily from Sadiq to David and back again. David wondered if the young former employee would just run. Instead he simply said, "Okay."

ELEVEN

After poring over the maps Robbie brought from the gas station, they decided to follow Route 77 north toward Victoria. The stopover in Corpus Christi hadn't changed the mission: get to Kentucky to see if Robbie's family was okay and then press on toward Michigan to check in on Ethan's family.

Along the way they looked for pieces and parts they could use to create a faster means of travel. At a junk yard not far off the road, they were able to find a small plastic cart with solid rubber tires. It was the kind of cart that hitched to a small lawn tractor. They also found enough scrap to attach a piece of metal to lengthen the tongue of the cart that also connected the cart to the bike. Now, one of them would be able to ride the bike and pull the others much faster than they could walk. The only drawback was the extra drain on resources in the form of water and calories required. They stopped at every gas station, convenience store, and fast food restaurant they saw and each place yielded varying amounts of food or water. Every scrap of food, every drop of clean water was important.

With around two-hundred fifty miles to Houston, they didn't rush the trip but stopped frequently along the way to add to their growing stockpile of supplies. They now took turns riding in the little trailer because it was so full of bottled water, gas station food and odds and ends from their journey. The bike was helpful for scouting the road ahead. The biggest concern was the heat. After two days of walking on asphalt roads in ninety-five degree heat, Ethan and Robbie decided they would travel at night. Along the road, they found some out of the way places they could camp for the day. They needed shade and cover from passersby. They took turns keeping watch throughout the day as a precaution. The discipline was good for Cael who was not given much structure growing up. Late one night, in an effort to stay awake, he told them about his life before the fire that destroyed his family and home.

"My parents owned a souvenir store and made pretty good money."

"Must've been nice," Robbie commented.

"Yeah, it was good. We had nice stuff."

"So you spent a lot of time with your parents?"

"Oh, hell no. I mean heck no. Sorry!" Cael corrected himself. Ethan and Robbie had both asked him to watch his language since their journey began. "My mom and dad were busy at the store and hired someone to clean the house, do the laundry. We saw them more on days in the middle of the week. Tourism schedule, you know? But even then, they weren't really there." He realized how this sounded and backtracked. "Don't get me wrong, I love them. Loved – them. It's just that we didn't do much as a family."

"Every family has its own way of relating," Robbie suggested.

"I guess."

"Do you have a girlfriend, green stuff?" Robbie overheard Ethan use the nickname and liked it. It stuck.

"I've had too many to count. That's what was so great about living down there. The girls came to me from all over the country. And they came to party. A party, plus a few drinks means girls with no boundaries."

"Cael, it sounds like you treat girls with very little respect."

"I never did anything they didn't ask for."

"Stop talkin' right now," Robbie demanded.

"What? Why?"

"'Cause if you don't I'm gonna hurt you." The three travelers continued in silence.

The days were boring and frustrated Cael. The nights were long but he soon found out that complaining would not be tolerated. After eleven days and nights of walking, the trio reached the outskirts of Houston. It was close to dawn and they were actively looking for a place to stop to sleep.

Robbie slowed the bike and dismounted. They just across the Brazos River outside Richmond. "It's getting more populated here. It'll only get busier toward the city. What do you think, boss?"

"I think I'd rather stay out of downtown Houston. Who knows what's going on down there with the lack of food and clean water. I'm all for heading north and taking the loop around it."

Cael was draped over the contents of the trailer. "That'll be longer. Let's just go straight through."

"You'll be glad to walk a few extra days once you've considered the alternative. Tell him, Robbie."

Robbie stretched his back, twisted a few times and did several toe touches. The hard walking and bike riding was rough on his body.

"Are you gonna talk or start doin' jumpin' jacks next?"

"I'll talk when I'm good and ready, Green Stuff."

"It's not spelled that way."

"Doesn't matter. You'll always be Green Stuff to me now. And yes, you'll be glad to walk an extra couple days when you understand what could be down there."

"Like what?"

"You were in Corpus Christi for what, four, five days after the power went out?"

"Yeah, you showed up like, a week after or somethin'. I don't know."

"Yeah, it's hard to keep track of the days. But see, Ethan and I, we've been to countries where the people have been without water and power for months. Have you ever seen desperation? I mean true desperation?" Cael shrugged and slightly shook his head. "Desperate people will do anything to eat – to drink. They will maim and kill. They'll even attack the people who are trying to help them. Starvation is a terrible way to die."

"You think that's what's goin' on in downtown Houston?"

"Think about it, Greenie. You're in a city. It's all concrete. Your only food is trucked in. Your water comes from the pipes. You have no place for emergency supplies and no one is coming to your rescue. What do you do?"

"Leave!"

"Where do you go and how far would you get? You have to walk because your car is dead and you have no supplies. Plus you have a family to take care of."

"No stores, right?"

"Right. Completely cleaned out. The river water is contaminated and so are the bayous. Any other ideas?"

"Ask for help I guess. Friends could maybe get together and help each other."

"Okay, so your family has spent years stockpiling supplies for just this type of crisis. And the second it happens you have thirty or forty 'friends' at your door looking for a handout. What do you do? If you let everyone have something, you and your family die and you just prolong everyone's life by a little bit. But if you refuse, your family might live. As long as the 'friends' don't turn on you and rip you to pieces."

"You're saying everyone in Houston is screwed?"

"I'm saying if you were so desperate five days into a crisis, you were willing to kill for a car with gas in it, then what do you think people will do now? They will not hesitate to kill you for whatever food or water you might have and ask questions later."

"I see your point."

"Good, because I'm describing every city in the eastern United States. And the chances of us making it through Houston with any supplies, let alone our lives, are not good. About as good as getting a pig to fly."

Cael pondered a moment. "So, how are we gonna get to where we're going? I mean if everyone everywhere is freakin' out, how are we gonna keep findin' supplies and water? How are we gonna stay alive in these cities? Geez, why did I even come with you guys?" He got out of the trailer and paced in the road. "I knew it was bad but I kept thinkin' the power would come back on soon and now it's been almost three weeks. My family is dead, I have no home and now you're tellin' me we're gonna die somewhere down the road!" He fought to keep his emotions in check, even though his outburst said it all.

Robbie walked to Cael and put his arm on his shoulder. "You see that man right there?" he asked, pointing to Ethan. "That man is my hero. I've seen him do things you can't even imagine. Never, never has he ever given up. You know a building collapsed on him once and he managed to find a way out. We've been attacked, pursued over miles of terrain, shot at, had boats sunk from under us, jumped out of airplanes that were crashing, been tortured, deprived of food and water. But Ethan and I have come through it all. I trust him with my life. We'll get through this too but you've got to believe there's something in this for you."

"I don't have anything. My life used to be somethin'. Now I'm walkin' to who knows where with you two." Cael turned away from Robbie with his hands clasped behind his head.

"Your life *is* something. But not because of you. It has meaning and purpose because you were created with meaning and purpose."

"Robbie, are you gonna give me a God speech?"

"No, I'm going to give you a truth bomb. God loves you, Green Stuff, and He doesn't want you to waste your life. You've taken some hard shots in the last three weeks but you're still standing. And your life is going to change a lot in the next few months, years. But you can trust one thing to never change."

"What's that?"

"God will be with you wherever you go."

Cael shook his head. "I don't believe in God. God

wouldn't have done this to someone. Destroyed their life and taken everything away."

"Oh, He would. He's done it to a guy named Job. That's something I wish I had: A copy of the Bible. I had it on my phone for so long that I quit carrying a paper one. Ethan, first chance we get, man, I'm gonna get a Bible."

Ethan, who quietly listened to the conversation from where he was crouched down on the side of the road, stood and walked to Cael. "We've got a lot to teach you – if you're willing to learn. And don't worry about where we're going and how we'll get there. Believe it or not, Robbie is telling the truth and I think we've been in worse situations. I might change my mind about that three months from now. But at the moment, I'm confident. And I'm trusting God too."

Cael looked down at the road for a moment, shifting his weight from one foot to the other. "I guess I never had to make decisions like this – tried to figure out my life. Almost everything was decided for me." Cael paused and looked up at Ethan. "If you're as good as Robbie says you are – that's cool. But I still don't believe in God."

Ethan shrugged. "That's okay, He's patient. It took me awhile too but now I trust God in everything."

"No, I mean I don't and won't ever believe in God. Not after what he did to me. Now let's just go."

They found a place to sleep not far from where they crossed the river. When they woke, they decided to continue north around Houston, hoping to avoid whatever chaos was coming the next few weeks.

July 17 – 12:30AM Fenton, Michigan,

"Aren't you spreading yourself thin? If you make arrangements with every person in town, you're not going to be here – with me and Hannah." Elizabeth and David sat in their living room, a single candle in front of them on the coffee table. She just finished tending to the nasty cut on the back of his head from where the can of beans struck him.

"These arrangements are helping us. Water and snack foods from Sadiq and now dry goods from Keith? We need this."

"*We* need you – I need you. I need to know you're okay."

"Liz, I *am* okay. It's only a couple trips to the other side of town. And all Keith needed was some bedding and a little help protecting his stash. It couldn't be a better deal for us."

"But you're gone half the day. Two days in a row! How much longer can you ride around on that tractor before someone wonders where you got the gas? Before someone decides they want a tractor to ride on? Sandy Lavin was down here earlier today and she said she heard of a family of five driving out of Fenton. They were stopped in the middle of the road and the husband was shot because he wouldn't give up the car."

Nathan's face flashed through David's mind. "Well, I'm sorry that happened but he's an idiot! And I should know. Cars, food, bottled water."

"David!"

"When your family is on the line, you give whatever material possessions you have to keep your family safe. If someone really wants my tractor, they can have it. After all, they could break into the garage and snap the padlock if they really wanted to. I'm doing what I'm doing to help us and keep us alive."

"So was that father! He was taking them out of here to family across the state."

"Liz, I don't need this. From day one of this thing, I have felt the weight – do you hear me? I have felt the full weight of responsibility for keeping you and Hannah alive. It's not like driving to an office every day. I need you to support me -" David stopped mid-sentence to listen.

"What is it?" Liz tried to whisper but it came out much louder.

"I heard something at the side door. Get the shotgun."

Liz jumped from the couch and ran upstairs while David carefully stepped toward the side door. There were three entries to the house on the main floor. The side door was the one they used almost exclusively. He leaned through the living room doorway to peek at the side door. As he turned, he heard the knock again. David reasoned it out. If he ignored the knock, someone may think no one is home and be emboldened to enter. But anyone knocking in the middle of the night was either in desperate need or up to no good. He was not ready to open the door but perhaps he could learn more about this knocker.

"Who is it? What do you want?" David asked calmly.

"Do you have anything to eat? I've got three kids at home and they're hungry."

"What's your name?" The voice outside was silent. "Hello?"

Finally, a response. "Yeah, yeah. What was that? It's hard to hear with the door closed."

"I understand it's hard to hear but I don't know you. I asked your name." Elizabeth returned from the front stairway with the shotgun. "Fully loaded?" David whispered. Elizabeth nodded. "Hey out there. I still didn't get your name. Why don't you come back in the morning? I'd be a lot more comfortable with that."

"Can you just pass some food out the window or something? My kids haven't eaten in almost a week."

David heard a noise at the back door: Someone trying to turn the doorknob. "Is someone here with you?"

"What was that?"

"I asked if someone was here with you."

"No I'm all by my—"

David heard a clash of glass and the splintering of wood. He stepped into the living room so he could look toward the back door. Before he had a chance to identify the shape coming at him, it hit him with incredible force, knocking him back onto the couch, narrowly missing the candle. His wind completely knocked out of him, David struggled to breathe. A fist struck him, then another. In the flickering candlelight, he saw a glint of metal which he assumed was a blade. He reached out to deflect the arm holding it, all the while thinking only of staying alive long enough to protect Liz and Hannah. Hot breath seethed at him through rotted teeth. He smelled marijuana, alcohol, body odor.

In the midst of the onslaught, he heard more glass breaking. Elizabeth screamed. Someone was trying to come in the side door. David had his assailant's wrist in an iron grip, keeping the knife at bay. He managed to raise his right leg, no small feat with a man in his face, pinning him with his weight to the couch. He planted the leg against his attacker's upper thigh and pushed with all his might. His thrust moved the attacker back a few feet but it did not stop him. David did not even know who he was fighting. He was faceless, angry – David imagined him as a wolf, ravenous, stalking.

While the invader was on his heels for a moment, David

launched himself from the couch and hit him in the gut with a shoulder, driving him back another few feet, almost into the kitchen. His assailant pounded David on the back but before the knife could be brought to bear, they locked arms again. David was beginning to weaken. He'd been struck unconscious just one day ago and now punched several times. His attacker was stronger and more aggressive than he was and even the burst of adrenaline was already fading.

"David, move!" Liz called from the side door. The man at the side door reached through the broken panes several times only to have his hand smashed by the butt of the shotgun.

David heard Liz but he could not unwind himself from his attacker's arms. They were locked in a death grip. Another force drove David back into the living room and onto the floor. It was the second man from the side door; he came around the house to the back door to help his friend. All three tumbled onto the floor. The candle was knocked aside and went out, ending the eerie flickering glow that illuminated the close-quarter battle.

All was quiet except for the grunting and struggling on the floor of the living room and Liz's stifled sobs. He heard a sharp crack and a thud as one of the men pinning him down crashed to the floor. Elizabeth must have connected with the butt of the shotgun. The odds had now shifted in his favor but then David heard something that made his blood run cold.

"Mommy?"

He could not see Hannah but her little voice came from the kitchen stairway. Another surge of adrenaline coursed through him and he roared, pushing against the smelly bulk that was holding him down. He was able to roll over and get above his attacker. The knife was still gripped tightly in his attacker's hand. David put both hands on the knife and pushed it to the floor. He pounded the knife hand on the floor to make it release the weapon. The hand opened and David quickly swatted it away. But the victory was short lived as his attacker roared and pushed David back. The invader stood and though David still couldn't make out the man's features, he knew he was outmatched. Adrenalin alone protected him thus far but the man was five or six inches taller and broader across the shoulders. He moved toward David, this time clutching him around the neck and pushing him against the doorway to the kitchen. David could not speak, his wind completely cut off. He saw stars and could not think anymore. A bright blast to his left accompanied by a thunderclap of sound were the last things he remembered until he was aware of Liz crouched over him.

"What happened?" he managed to croak out. "Is Hannah okay?"

"She's here. Please don't go – don't ever go." Liz, cradling Hannah, leaned over David, rocking back and forth. David felt her tears falling onto his face.

"Daddy are you okay?"

David started to sit up but his head swirled and he laid back down.

"I shot him, David. I shot him." Her tears collapsed into shoulder-shaking sobs. "I've tried to be so strong, I've tried." Her sobs swelled into gut-wrenching wails.

"Liz, it's okay. It's okay. You did what you had to do. You did what you had to. He would've killed me."

"Is everything okay? I heard gunshots." The voice came from the side door.

David leapt to his feet, ignoring the dizziness. "Where's

the gun, Liz?" Instinctively, David reached next to Liz's hand where the shotgun lay on the floor. He stumbled against the door jamb.

"Whoa, it's me – Mark. Don't shoot!"

David let go of the gun. "You don't walk into someone's house in the middle of the night when you've heard gunshots! What's the matter with you? Put your hands down."

"I'm sorry, I just thought I could help."

After relighting the candle, David realized both intruders were still on the floor of his living room. One was dead but the other was unconscious. Angrily aware how close he and his family came to death, he snapped at Mark. "You wanna help? Help me drag their bodies outside," David demanded. There was no time to coddle Mark or his feelings and still wasn't sure if the danger was truly past. David let out a long sigh. "I'm sorry, Mark. I just – I almost lost my life five minutes ago. My wife just killed a man protecting me and my daughter almost got in the middle of it all."

David was thankful for Mark's silence. He grabbed the dead man's arms while Mark took his feet and they dragged his body out to the roadside. "I'll bury him in daylight," David said to no one in particular and Mark, sensing this directionless comment, remained silent. David stumbled back up the walkway to his side door expecting Mark to follow. Together they dragged the smaller, lighter, and still unconscious intruder outside and laid him next to his dead friend.

"You're just gonna leave him here?"

"What else am I going to do? Call the police? Imprison him? Kill him myself? When he wakes up he will see his dead friend and he will leave. I doubt he'll ever come back."

Without waiting for him to respond to these questions or thanking him for his help, David mounted the porch steps, went inside and shut the door. David went to the living room where Liz and Hannah still sat and silently put his arms around them. They quietly cried together. "Daddy's okay," David whispered to Hannah. "And thank you," he whispered in Liz's ear. "I love you so much".

"I love you too," Liz whispered back. After a few more minutes of holding one another and quietly thanking God for protecting them they rose from the floor. They slowly stacked dining room chairs against the side door and pushed the refrigerator in front of the back door. Satisfied they were safe for the night, the Zabad family went to bed.

———

David was tired of being sweaty. Tired of being hungry and tired of being tired. His shirt was sweat-soaked for the second time today. The first was digging the grave for the nameless attacker of early that morning. He took a break to eat their meager ration of rice and canned beans. The second was dragging the corpse to the hole and covering it up. He was correct; the surviving attacker disappeared by morning, slunk back into whatever hole he came from.

He slept last night only because he was so exhausted from the attack on their home. The trauma of fighting the two men in his living room left him shaken and mentally weak. All the determination and stamina that strongly flowed a few days ago was reduced to a feeble trickle. On top of the exhaustion was the fact that he now had to convince his wife that pulling the trigger on the intruder was the right thing to do. Elizabeth slept hard from exhaustion as well but woke to conflicting feelings and a swirl of emotional confusion.

David stopped shoveling several times throughout the morning to still his shaking hands. They would tremble, making it difficult to hold the shovel. He swung between wanting to cry and wanting to punch something. It was unlike anything he had ever felt before. He was throwing the last shovelfuls of dirt on the mound when Mark came to the fence.

"You okay?" Mark ventured, unsure if he would talk to the David of last night or the David he came to know over the last few years.

David planted the shovel and leaned on top of the handle, chin on his hand. He surveyed his yard which needed mowing but could've been worse if the weather wasn't so hot. He kept his eyes focused on the dry, uncut grass. "I'm not doing great, Mark."

"Is there anything I can do?"

David closed his eyes and all he saw was Nathan being stabbed for bottled water. Then Elizabeth, sobbing as she knelt over him last night. Food and water. Simple things, really. Things people were willing to kill for. "Mark, does your family have food? Are you all okay?"

"We have canned goods. That's about it. Why?"

David stared at the mound he just created. "This man came into my house looking for food. He can't be the only one who's hungry."

"Lots of people are probably hungry but don't you think help is coming soon? This is America, David. Help will come before we starve."

"Mark, it's been nineteen days. People are already starving. The cops have stopped patrolling, the grocery stores are empty. We haven't heard from anyone in authority. You should go home, really think this through. Start rationing."

"You're serious, eh?" David said nothing in reply to this noncommittal response. "Well . . . okay." Mark backed away from the fence to head home and then remembered why he stopped in the first place. "I just stopped to see how you guys were doing. Like I said, if you need anything, let me know."

David nodded. He was okay, barely. Liz was a wreck. Hannah. He would have to talk with Hannah and help her understand what she experienced last night. He knew deep down that he couldn't leave his family at night anymore. He was naïve to think that the people of his city, his neighbors, would respect one another, think rationally, not panic, help one another. He knew he must make preparations for the long term and improve the security of his family.

"See ya, David." Mark gave a small wave as he walked away.

David's mind was spinning already and it was merely reflexive habit that caused him to lift a hand toward Mark to wave goodbye.

He started with the broken back door glass and door jamb. The one broken window, of the nine, would have to be replaced with wood. There was simply no way to procure the right materials to do the door justice and so David turned back to his recently used handsaw and cut a piece of scrap plywood just large enough to cover the hole. Another small piece of scrap was laid across this and laboriously screwed into the door itself and the frame to hold it in place. As he was finishing this task, he sensed Liz watching him from the living room. She scrubbed the floor while David was digging. Most of the blood came off the floor but the area rug was ruined. She rolled it up and dragged it to the curb with the rest of the accumulated garbage.

Hannah was playing in the living room with a doll while Liz sat nearby, staring alternately at the floor she had just cleaned and David at the back door.

He glanced at her over his shoulder. "Let me finish this, Liz. And then we need to talk."

"I don't want to talk about it."

David stopped turning the screw and faced her. "We're not going to talk about that. We're not going to review it or think about it anymore."

"How can I not think about it? He's buried in the yard!" Tears were running down her cheeks.

He crossed into the living room to her. "We're not going to talk about it. You did the right thing. If you hadn't, we'd both be dead. And Hannah . . ." Emotion welled up as he imagined the worst case scenario. He couldn't – wouldn't finish his sentence. Hannah had perked up at hearing her name so David moved to her, put his hands on Liz's arms and spoke quietly. "That's not what I want to talk about. We're gonna talk about being safe. We're gonna talk about turning this house into a place we can live, not just survive. I'm not leaving anymore. No more nights helping Sadiq. No more guarding Keith's stash."

"But how will you get those supplies? What about your... arrangements?"

"I'll find a way. Things are going to get more dangerous. We have to be ready."

"David, what happened last night was the worst thing I've ever been through. I know you fought hard for us, but I don't know if you can keep us safe."

"What? Why would you say that, Liz? I will do whatever it takes to protect you."

"In the last two weeks you've been gone from us day after day, all over the city. We need you here."

"I've been all over the city for you! To find things that will help us. Water, food, batteries, whatever I can find."

"None of those things matter if someone comes into this house and kills us while you're gone. You told me how hard you fought to get to us the day all this started. I need to feel that from you: every day."

"I'm giving it everything I've got."

Liz had started now and there was no turning back. Her outward show of strength and courage over the last couple weeks was beginning to crumble and she needed to get this off her chest. "I'm sure you're giving it everything you've got. And I am so grateful for how hard you've worked. But maybe we should talk about going to my parents house."

"Your parent's house? Liz, that's a one day drive from here. And on foot it would be weeks." David knew deep down that Elizabeth's parents house, in Wisconsin, might actually be a better place to ride out the crisis. Though without a way of knowing their status, traveling that far posed a huge risk.

"I have no way of knowing if they're okay. I don't even know if I'll ever see them again. In the last two weeks I haven't even mentioned them because it hurts too much. And I - I know we can't go to them. I know it's too far. But you're talking about your dad coming to find us. You have hope. I need you to share that with me."

"I didn't know. I'm sorry Lizzie, I didn't know. I meant what I said. No more nights away. I'll stay closer to home. And I guess I thought you *did* share hope with me."

"I do. But David, you are in work mode. You've seen this as a task to be completed from the first day. Me and

Hannah are not a task. We can't just be on your to do list. Stop doing all this *for* us and do this *with* us."

David let her words sink in. "You are the strongest, most amazing woman I've ever known."

Liz wiped the tears from her face and nodded quickly. "Right. While I'm freaking out here."

"I'm freaking out on the inside." David smiled at her wishing he could think of something to lighten the mood. "You're right. Some things need to change. Let me finish the back door and then we can talk some more." He kissed her gently on the lips. "I love you, Liz."

"I love you too."

David walked back to the door, amazed at the woman God put in his life. He was tempted to be offended by what Liz said but he was able to see past the words to what she was asking for. It would not be easy to deliver.

TWELVE

They stayed on secondary roads, only walking at night and trying in vain to avoid more populated areas. Houston was a sprawling city of over two million people and its suburbs seemed to go on for miles. Running into locals, no matter how friendly they seemed, always held potential danger. Even though it was a long shot they still stopped at every store along the way hoping to find some left behind food item. Occasionally it paid off in a stray can of vegetables or tuna that had rolled under a shelf or cooler. It wasn't much but every can they found was an additional day of travel. Their biggest haul of the trip so far came when they broke into a sporting goods store on the north side of Houston. The camping section yielded a tent and filter straws which enabled them to drink directly from standing water. The food in the camping section also proved valuable. They also took two additional bikes, spare bike tires and a pump for the tires. It was a big day because with their new equipment, they were able to cover forty to fifty miles a night instead of twenty. This would speed their trip north, closer to Robbie and Ethan's families. This also made them bigger targets.

The traveling at night allowed the men to move quickly and not have to deal with other travelers. Ethan was aware that some lurkers passed by their daytime camps but he and Robbie maintained a guard and traveling as a trio aided in deterring would be thieves. Along with thieves there were scavengers and beggars about. The threesome kept their distance whenever possible. As compassionate as Ethan was and as much as he wanted to help anyone he encountered that was in trouble, he really didn't want to take another detour like the Pelhams.

They were near I-69 but heading north on parallel back roads. It was close to three in the morning when Ethan, who was riding lead, came upon the bodies in the road. The moon was low in the sky but still bright, illuminating the scene before them. There were four bodies in the road laying in various poses. All looked like they were dumped without care. Ethan slowed, sensing a trap. He halted Cael and Robbie almost fifty feet away and stayed quiet in case someone was lurking just off the road. He got off the bike and crept toward the closest body. It was face down so he pulled it toward him. It was a woman. Her face was peaceful. And beautiful. But she showed no marks of injury. The face didn't have the look of death. Her eyes opened and she uttered an inhuman scream, flying at Ethan with punches and once on her feet, kicks. Ethan screamed back at her, surprising himself. He hadn't screamed like that in years. He was more startled than scared as it was the last thing he expected. He assumed the bodies were dead or injured. He assumed if it was a trap, the attack would come from the side of the road, not the decoys themselves. And that was the problem. He assumed too much.

As Ethan retreated from the wild attack, the other bodies came to life in response to the scream and came at him as well. He was thankful he kept Robbie and Cael back. He didn't have a chance to look for them or even worry about them. He was too busy avoiding a beat down by a wild woman. He wasn't worried he couldn't defend himself. He was more worried that in the process he would harm the woman without knowing her motives. So far, all she did was chase him with flailing arms, screaming the whole time. The other decoys were trying to grab his arms and pin him down. He offered a silent prayer for wisdom and in that moment, felt he should surrender. It went against all his instincts but he decided to yield to what God was telling him – to let them win. He relaxed his arms and they pulled them behind his back, binding them with a plastic zip tie. He was relieved. Zip ties were easy for him to snap if he needed to escape in a hurry. He had no idea why God would want him to submit himself to capture but he had learned to trust Him.

He was marched to a neighborhood not far from where the group had staged their ambush. They walked him into a cul-de-sac ringed with modest two-story homes, most likely built in a nineties building boom. A small fire was burning in the center of the cul-de-sac. Ethan glanced around, hoping Robbie and Cael had followed him. There were a few lawn chairs scattered around and from the glow of the fire, Ethan could see there were a few toys strewn about.

The four who had led him walked right up to the fire and flanked him, two on each side. Ethan continued his internal conversation with God about what he was doing here. His son's face kept coming to his mind. He had a place to be and standing in this cul-de-sac was not it. Elizabeth and Hannah were on his heart as well. What possible reason could God have for him to stop here? Ethan stopped his mental rundown when he saw someone else approaching the fire. He was medium height, broad shouldered, and sported a goatee that filled in on his cheeks. He probably hadn't shaved since the crisis began. His head was also shaved at one time but Ethan could see a faint peach fuzz of hair growing and a very distinct place on his head that was still shiny.

"So do you head up the neighborhood watch?"

The man ignored the question and demanded, "Who are you?"

"My name is Ethan Zabad."

"Where do you live?"

"Right now, on the back of a bike for 10 hours a night."

"Where do you live?"

"When I'm not halfway across the world, I live with my son."

"I'm going to ask you one more time. Where do you live?"

"If you didn't like the first two answers you're gonna hate the third one."

"Which is?"

"On a prayer. Get it? Livin' on a prayer?"

The man didn't react to Ethan's wise-cracking routine. "What were you doing on the road tonight?"

Ethan dropped the jokes and decided to try a more direct approach. "Trying to get to my kid who lives in Michigan. I've been on my way since the power first went out in June. You're slowing me down. And by the way, do you make people lay in the road every night?"

"Yes, I do. Someone always stops. Sometimes several

times a night. It's a simple way to provide for ourselves. We capture them, they take us to their home, we empty it of anything useful and then let them go. No one gets hurt – unless they resist – and me and my neighbors can survive a little longer." Ethan was glad to hear no one was being murdered. But this wasn't exactly a group of people looking out for everyone's best interests. "So, the sooner you tell us where you really live, the sooner we can get what we need and you can go."

Ethan was beginning to understand why God may have led him here. They were simple thieves but they were cleaning out everyone within a few miles. A plan which would eventually backfire. Either the pipeline would dry up or the victims of these crimes would rise up against the thieves and simple theft would be avenged by murder. Not to mention it was plain wrong.

"This may be surprising to you but I'm actually telling the truth. I don't live around here. I'm not a Texan. I'm passing through. And what you're doing is wrong. Ambushing people with the whole, dead-people-in-the-road thing is just a slightly more sophisticated shakedown. My suggestion is you find some other ways to provide for yourselves. Ways that the whole community can benefit from. Your little scheme isn't gonna go the distance." Ethan said this loud enough so anyone outside the firelight would be sure to hear.

"*My* suggestion is drop the act and tell us what we want to know or else."

"Or else what?" Ethan used this statement to highlight his movement of breaking the zip ties. They snapped off and he brought his arms around in front of him. The people flanking him took a step back, unsure what he might do. "I'm not looking to hurt anyone. My whole life is about helping people who are being taken advantage of. I think that's why I'm here."

The leader was nervous but attempted to mask it with a question. "You think you're some kind of superhero?"

"No, I'm no hero. I just go where God tells me and do what He asks. What you're doing needs to stop. I mean it. No more ambushing people and taking their stuff. You're taking the lazy man's way. Let me guess, you've never laid in the road. Never gone to these houses and hauled stuff out."

These factual statements caused some murmuring around the fire. "Someone has to lead. Has to think for the group."

Ethan stepped slowly toward the man. "And you're just the guy to do it right? You needed to survive so you mobilized everyone and got them to work right? While you sat here and reaped all the benefits. What if someone you ambushed pulled a gun on your crew? Killed one of them. What if you went into a house someone was protecting with a weapon and people died?" Ethan was nose to nose with the man, who was wavering. "Are you prepared to be responsible for the deaths of all of your neighbors?"

The question hung there, demanding an answer and Ethan was hoping the rest of the man's crew were within earshot.

"No," The leader spoke it plainly but firmly. "I'm not prepared to be responsible for their deaths. You, on the other hand, I'm happy to accept responsibility for."

Ethan heard the metallic click of pistols being readied and his peripheral vision made out at least two men flanking their leader with the guns aimed his way. All over the world, Ethan saw crisis bring out the best and the worst in people. The people who responded with their best almost always saw crisis as their moment of truth – their call to action. It was their opportunity to affect change and resolve the crisis. They saw an emergency as their occasion to rise for the good of others.

For those who responded with their worst, they approached crisis with fear and panic. For them, it was a scramble for the nearest escape route and anyone who was trampled in the way a collateral expense. There was nothing noble about their actions. Merely a desperate bid for survival regardless of who got hurt. This man was the latter.

———

From outside the firelight, between two houses, Robbie and Cael looked on. They heard most of the conversation.

"Do we really have to go in there and rescue him?"

"Ethan doesn't need rescuing. He got himself captured, remember? He's got something in that mind of his. The trick is trying to anticipate what it is so when it hits the fan, we're in the right place at the right time."

"Does he do this a lot?"

"All the time." Robbie was about to move closer to the fire where Ethan was standing but heard something behind him. Something or someone was coming through the hedges at the back of the yard. He grabbed Cael and they pushed themselves deeper into the rhododendron they were standing behind. They watched as a group of people crept toward the house. Some were carrying guns and a few held garden implements. Glimpsing the faces of the group told Robbie all he needed to know of their intentions. He got a sick feeling in his gut but knew what he had to do. He followed his hunch and stepped out of the bush with his hands in the air.

"Hold it right there!" hissed the man in the lead. He aimed a shotgun at Robbie's chest. "Are you one of them?" The shotgun was raised so Robbie was looking right down the barrel.

Robbie whispered back, "I am not with them. My friend was captured by these people and we're trying to figure out how to free him – without anyone getting hurt." He emphasized this last part, hoping to get the message across. With limited light, it was hard to tell who he was talking to but Robbie could make out several bearded faces and a few women. He estimated a dozen in the whole group. "Something tells me you're here for them. And preventing anyone from getting hurt is not on your agenda."

One of the men spoke up, but still in a whisper. "These people robbed every one of us. We all live in a neighborhood a few miles away. They took everythin' of value and then just left us to die. We came to get justice."

Robbie's fears were confirmed. "Please don't do this. Let me and my friend handle it. We're working on a plan right now and—"

"We don't have time for your plan. We came to take back what's ours and if you stand in our way, you're as bad as one of them."

Robbie moved through the group to one of the women, hoping she would be able to listen to reason. She was toward the back of the group and in the dark, the only thing Robbie knew was that she seemed nervous. "Are you sure you want to do this?"

"Absolutely."

She was dressed in all black and carried what looked like a hunting rifle. Robbie tried again. "What's your name?"

"I don't know you. I don't care to know you. I am here

for one reason. These people took everything from me and my husband. Because of them, he hung himself three days ago. I'm here to make them pay." Her voice cracked and she raised a sleeve to wipe her nose. Hers was a fierce but fragile determination. "I have to do this for my daughter."

The rest of the avengers moved forward and spread out between the buildings. "You have a daughter? Why would you want to put your life at risk? Risk leaving her without parents by doing this? She needs you."

"Out of my way. I have a job to do." She pushed past Robbie and moved into position with the rest of her neighbors.

Cael, who was standing by during all this came alongside Robbie. "We need to warn him right?"

"Yeah, he needs to be prepared for a bunch of people to come running in there with guns blazing. I can't stop them. Not without getting shot."

"We have to try. At least one more time."

Robbie was about to agree when a gunshot blew apart the quiet night.

Ethan heard the gunshot and immediately got low. The leader of the thieves ducked as well and pulled a gun from his waistband. Screams erupted from outside the ring of firelight as more shots rang out. It seemed like the bullets were coming from all directions. He knew it wasn't Robbie. The caliber and the sound of the guns didn't match what was in their meager arsenal.

"Ethan! This way." It was Robbie's voice and Ethan moved toward it. He stayed low as bullets continued to whip around, some exploding in the fire. The boom of a shotgun got their attention as Ethan looked back toward the fire. The thief leader was returning fire with his pistol. If he'd been any kind of fighter, he would have known to get out of the firelight and return fire from a covered position. Even if Ethan told him to do so at that moment, it would not have mattered. He watched as he was hit with multiple bullets and knocked to the ground. He turned and dashed a few more steps and found himself almost running into Robbie.

"We wanted to warn you but there were about twelve angry people out there who would have added us to their hit list."

"It's okay. I had a plan too but never got around to pulling the trigger. Sorry, bad choice of words." Ethan noticed Cael standing slightly behind Robbie as the gunshots continued. "Hey, Green Stuff, you came with. I see you're staying behind cover."

"I've been shot at before. It's not on my list of favorite activities." He glanced around Robbie's shoulder. "I think we should go."

"I agree. I thought God wanted me here to stop what was going on but He seems to have other plans." He moved down the road away from the firefight.

"Ethan, wait. I need to stay here for a minute. I think you were right about being here but I don't think it was to stop what these people were doing."

"Okay. So who are these people and what are we really doing here?"

"They're all victims of these thieves. They came to kill."

"What does that have to do with us hanging around?"

Robbie waved Ethan and Cael over to a house several doors down from the chaos unfolding nearby. They slipped between the houses and crouched in the dark. "I want to wait until things settle down. These people aren't soldiers.

There's no medics here. This is a huge mess now but it's gonna be a much bigger one come daylight. Who's going to help them clean up this mess?"

"Robbie, you're starting to sound like me. Why didn't I give that speech?"

"Because you are already in Michigan – up here," Robbie pointed to Ethan's head. "And here." Robbie pointed to his heart. "And I get it because my heart and head are in Kentucky. But everything that's going on right now for you is just going through the motions. And it's okay, I understand. I know you're the Ethan I've spent the last fifteen years traveling the world with."

"If I wasn't invested I wouldn't have let myself get dragged into this mess. I'm not just going through the motions."

"Okay, okay. My imagination, I guess. Let's just lay low for an hour."

As soon as the first streaks of light appeared in the sky they made their way back to the cul-de-sac. No gunshots were heard for about 15 minutes and all that remained were bodies lying in the street and a fire turned to ash. Nothing was stirring in or around the homes at the end of the street. They moved from body to body checking for anyone still alive. There was no way of knowing who was on what side in the conflict but at the moment, it didn't matter.

Ethan kept Cael with him to make sure he was okay. He wasn't new to gun violence but Cael was usually running from it rather than walking through its aftermath. His previous experience didn't prevent Cael from vomiting when he saw three bodies on the asphalt, one who clearly took a shotgun blast to the face. There was little that could be done. It was a bloodbath and there was no winner but the devil.

Robbie saw a body lying near the front door of one house, propped up against the pillar of a small portico over the entry. It was a woman. He put a hand on her neck and felt for a pulse. Her hand reached up and clasped Robbie's. Robbie realized he was looking into the face of the woman he tried to warn just over an hour ago.

She fought to breathe out the words. "You were right."

"I didn't want to be right. Let's take a look."

She winced in pain and tried to hold steady while Robbie tried to find the entry wound. It was near the bottom of her rib cage. With a nod of permission, he pulled up her shirt just far enough to see where the bullet entered. Her breathing was shallow and every time she tried to take a deep breath, bloody bubbles formed at the bullet hole. She coughed, the sudden eruption spraying a bloody mist across the porch. It was gruesome and Robbie fought to keep his expression neutral to not further alarm the woman. The coughing continued as the woman could not catch her breath. Her lungs were filling with blood and she would soon be unable to breathe at all. Then Robbie remembered what she told him last night. She had a daughter who would soon be alone.

"I don't know your name but I know you have a daughter. Where is she? I can help her," Robbie pleaded. "My friend and I can take care of her."

The woman looked at him with tears running from her face. She tried to speak but every time she took a breath, she would only cough. Slowly, she reached up to her lips, swiped her finger in the blood on her lips and wrote a street address on the patio floor. It was a number and a street 652 Caven. No town or zip code. But it was enough to start. The woman coughed again, more blood bubbling from her lips. And then, the coughing stopped. Mercifully, she stilled and then slid over, her eyes fixed. Robbie gently lowered her so she would not hit her head. He checked her pockets for some kind of identification but she carried nothing except a school portrait of a girl. It was a typical school picture, blue background. The girl in the picture had brown hair that fell past her shoulders. Brown-eyed and apple-cheeked, she had a wide smile and braces. Robbie turned the portrait over and read, "Lauren – 9th Grade". At least he knew who he was looking for.

"Robbie, you okay?"

Robbie turned to see Ethan and Cael, both with blood on their hands and shirts. "Yeah, I'm okay."

"We cleaned up best we could. Didn't find anyone alive. This was probably a nice neighborhood at one time. All it takes is one person – one evil person to bring death and destruction raining down. I thought we came here to save these people – stop them from destroying each other. It was a waste."

"No, it wasn't." Robbie held up the picture of Lauren. "We have a new objective."

THIRTEEN

"Okay, keep your eyes closed."

"David, why do we have to close our eyes? C'mon."

"Liz, this is so cool. You're gonna love it. I just want it to be a surprise."

Rain was pouring outside and the water was rushing down the street in the way Liz's grandpa called a gully washer. It came and went in intensity with accompanying wind gusts whipping the trees across the street back and forth, threatening to snap them in half.

David stopped in the kitchen and turned Liz and Hannah to face the staircase. "Okay, open!"

"I see the stairs?"

"You *think* you see the stairs. But watch." David reached for the sixth stair and pulled it forward. It tipped out revealing an opening just big enough for someone to wiggle through.

"What did you do? What's under there?" Liz exclaimed as she stepped forward to peer inside the secret door.

"You could call it a panic room. If someone wanted to get in and do harm or take something, we just hide out in here and someone thinks the house it empty. We're safe, they can't find anything to steal so they just leave."

"But our food? They would take everything." Liz instinctively went to the pantry and threw open the doors. "It's empty! What did you do?"

"Watch this," David replied with a gleam in his eye. He bent over and opened a lower cupboard near the fridge containing the pots and pans. He removed the stack of pots from the upper shelf inside and slid the pans off their shelf. Then the shelf itself was removed. He reached to the back of the cupboard and pushed on the upper right corner. The back panel of the cupboard popped out to reveal cans of food stacked six high and four across. "I did this all over the house. None of our food is just sitting on a shelf. If anyone wants our food, they're going to have to tear the house apart!" Liz just stared, eyebrows raised.

"Can I go in it?" Hannah was standing on the step just below the opening.

"Not right now, honey. Let's follow daddy!"

"Come with me." David quickly replaced the open stair tread so they could ascend and headed upstairs. "See this bookcase?" David gestured to the built-in bookcase at the top of the front stairs. He bent quickly and removed all the books from the bottom shelf and then lifted the shelf off revealing a six-by-twenty-four inch by eight-inch deep box capable of holding valuables, food or whatever they deemed worth of hiding.

"When did you do all this?"

"Mostly in the early morning when you and Hannah

were sleeping." Hannah was sleeping with Liz in the master bedroom while David slept downstairs on the couch or a pallet on the floor next to Liz. It was a small price to pay for Liz and Hannah to be able to sleep without fear.

"So, what do you think is going to happen?"

"What?" David asked reflexively, knowing exactly what she meant by the question.

"You've done all this work. You're expecting something."

A bit too defensively David shot back, "I'm preparing. My job is to keep you safe. To keep us alive."

Liz blurted out, "I talked to Sandy Lavin, up the street, yesterday. She walked with her husband north of the railroad tracks, through the neighborhood behind the laundromat. She said ours isn't the only yard with a grave in it." This all came out quickly, as if she did not want to say it but had to. She was also aware that Hannah was listening to everything they said. "Hannah, that's all of Daddy's surprises. Why don't you go play in your room?"

"Why?" Hannah asked.

"So me and mommy can talk."

"Why?"

"Because we have important things to say."

"Why?"

"Hannah, just go play, okay?"

Hannah seemed to think this over and then turned and walked to her room.

Once she was in her room, David turned back to Liz. "The only graves we will dig in this yard will be for people who try to hurt us."

"I don't want to dig *any* graves David! That's not a comfort to me. I *hate* that gun. I never want to touch it again!"

"I understand but Liz, I want us to survive! I want my daughter to see adulthood. I will do whatever it takes to make that happen."

"I'm scared, David. I'm tired of being scared all the time. It's been just over three weeks and already people are dying. Everything feels like it's about to come apart. It's already happening. You didn't even tell me about what happened at the river."

David winced as he recalled the incident. He purposely shielded Liz from it, knowing she would forbid his trips to the river. "How did you know about that?"

"Rochelle and Manny were outside yesterday. They told me. You need to tell me these things."

A group of men assaulted families and individuals as they made their way to the river, hoping to take whatever supplies or food they may have brought with them. Even scarier was one group of scavengers followed a family home at gunpoint to take whatever was in their house.

"That won't happen to us, Liz."

"You can't guarantee that!"

"Okay, you're right, I can't guarantee that so let's make a plan. Let's lay out every possibility we can think of and decide how we're going to respond."

"That's your logical engineer brain trying to make sense of this."

"I'm sorry Liz, it's the only brain I have," David said with a smirk. "It's how I operate. I can make all the plans in the world but if you're not with me on them, it's useless."

"I hate when you think you're funny and I'm trying to be serious."

"I'm not trying to be funny. Well, not entirely. But I do need your help Liz."

"But what can we do? When people all around us are

getting desperate. They have no food! They'll do anything to survive. Just like us . . ." Liz trailed off and David knew she was holding the gun again, four nights ago, trying to decide whether or not to pull the trigger on their intruders.

"Liz, our trust is in God. He's not going to drop food and supplies from the sky into our yard. But He's given us a mind to think and a body to work. And ultimately we have to trust His plan for us."

"I know, I know. I trust God. I just don't trust everyone else."

David stepped close and put his arms around Liz. "We've made plans for our food supply. We've made plans for our water supply so let's make some plans for our protection and anything else we haven't worked on yet."

Liz nestled her head under David's chin. "It *is* raining. We can't do anything outside anyway."

David ran his hands down Liz's back and realized how long it was since they were intimate. There was always something to work on, prepare for. It felt like luxury to do anything purely for enjoyment and yet closeness was what they both craved. They needed one another. David reached for her hand and intertwined his fingers with hers and gently led her from the hallway toward the bedroom.

July 22 – North of Houston, Texas

After searching multiple gas stations, they were able to find maps of the surrounding suburbs. It's rare to find a phone book anymore so they couldn't search for the street name. They had no last name to work with so all they could do was scan local maps hoping to find the name of the street. The woman said she was from a nearby neighborhood but they searched all around and came up empty. No one else survived the attack on the band of thieves four nights ago and so there was no other information to work with. There was no Caven Road, Caven Street, Caven Avenue, Court or Alley. They checked for Caver as well just in case Robbie misread her message. It was, after all, written by a dying woman, in blood, with her finger. Surprisingly, Cael was the one to unlock the mystery. Not far from where they started their search, he found a Cavendish Road. She simply wasn't able to finish her message. It was the best option they found in four days so they reversed course and came to 652 Cavendish Road.

There was nothing distinct about the neighborhood. It was a typical development. The sign at the entrance read "Desert Oaks". The 'biker gang' as Cael sarcastically called their group, rolled through the neighborhood, past two blocks and then to the right. Cavendish.

Ethan calmly laid out the plan. "I'll go to the door. After what happened back at the border with the Pelham kids, I think all three of us on the porch would scare her more than she is already."

"We've got your back, Ethan," Robbie reassured him.

Ethan had his doubts about this whole mission. None of them had shaved or bathed in over a month. They were ragged, dirty and smelled awful. Why would this girl be willing to accept their help or possible come with them – three guys she didn't even know? He agreed with Robbie's promise and the spirit behind it. He just wasn't sure it was going to play out the way he hoped.

He carefully approached the small porch. The garage was built out in front of the house so Ethan kept the wall to his back as he moved toward the front door. He knocked on the door and took a few steps back. He was being extra cautious, especially when he considered how this girl's mother recently died. To his surprise, the door slowly opened. Ethan expected to see the little ninth grader from the picture. Instead he saw a young woman, definitely not a high school freshman. She had the brown hair from the picture and the eyes were the same. But Lauren was not a little girl. Behind her Ethan could see the house was a mess.

"Are you Lauren?"

"Yeah. Who are you?"

"My name is Ethan Zabad. I have some bad news for you."

"My mom's dead, isn't she?"

Ethan was speechless for a moment but recovered. "Uh – yes. We . . . encountered her in a neighborhood not far from here. She was with —"

"She was with my neighbors to kill those people. They took everything. I haven't eaten anything in days. Well, I *have* eaten stuff but not real food. I've been drinking water out of the toilet tanks. I told her not to go. I told her we would figure out a way to survive. But she couldn't let it go. Not after my dad—" She broke off and just sobbed. Ethan stepped closer to her and put a hesitant hand on her shoulder. Then as quickly as it started, the crying stopped. Lauren knocked Ethan's hand away and wiped her face with the sleeve of her t-shirt and asked, "So who are you again? Why are you here?"

He took one step back before answering. "I'm Ethan. I was captured by the same people who robbed you. My friends were getting ready to help me when your mom showed up with the rest of your neighbors. They started shooting and – and everyone was killed. Including your mom. My friend Robbie talked to your mom before she died and she asked him to find you – take care of you. Only . . ."

"Only what?"

"The picture your mom had was of you at a younger age. Ninth grade. So, we expected, assumed that you were—"

"You thought I was a kid who needed rescuing." Ethan nodded and she continued. "I'm not a kid. I'm twenty years old. I've done fine for the last few days. And do you really think I would leave my house and just go with total strangers to – where are you going?"

"I have family in Michigan and Robbie has family in Kentucky."

"I don't know anybody in those places. Or on the way to those places."

Ethan could understand her fears. "We have someone else with us too. His name is Green Stu— I mean Cael. His family was killed in a fire shortly after the power went out. We travel together, scavenge for what we need and if there's a way we can help anyone along the journey we do it."

"The power could come back on at any time right? Shouldn't I stay here just in case?"

"Just out of curiosity, what were you eating the last four days?"

Lauren lowered her head. "Worms, cicadas. I think I tried some ants too. They were nasty."

Ethan smiled. "Lauren! You're a born survivalist! That's exactly what we eat at least one meal a day! We save our canned goods and camping meals for special occasions."

For the first time since they started talking, Lauren smiled. "Listen, Lauren, why don't I introduce you to my friends? Robbie was the last person to talk with your mom. You are under no obligation to go with us and we won't pressure you. But would you mind if we camped out in your yard for a night or two? We've been on the move for about a month with very few breaks."

Lauren seemed hesitant and so Ethan quickly backpedaled. "You know what, never mind. I don't want to make you uncomfortable. You just take the time you need. We'll check in on you in a day or so."

"No! It's okay. I just don't know you. I have no way of knowing who you are. You might be a —"

"A weirdo? A sicko? Yeah, I realize that. I can show you my army identification. It's with my things. I also have pictures of my own family that I'm trying to get to. But you are under no obligation to do anything you don't want to. We are here to honor a promise we made to your mom. We've held up our end."

She looked at Ethan, her eyes pouring out pain. "I'm trying to decide what to do and I keep wanting to ask my parents." She cried again. "Nothing is the same but I can't leave – and I'm so hungry!" She laughed through her tears as she realized the incongruity of her thoughts.

"Come on, let's get you some real food and then we can talk about what to do."

"We're not leaving my house right?"

"No, we'll camp out in your front yard."

July 26 – 9:30AM Fenton, Michigan,

He threw another cardboard box atop the growing stack of paper and wood filling the small trailer. It was David's third load of the day and it wasn't even noon. Half of the garage was becoming a storage area for anything that could be burned as fuel for heat or cooking. The latest project was to find a way to efficiently heat at least one room in the house for the winter. The actual mechanism was still taking shape in his mind but it wouldn't mean anything if he didn't have fuel. He started with as many downed limbs and sticks as he could find. The cemetery near the house was a great source of firewood but as the garage filled up David decided to go for some of the easier pickings: scrap paper and cardboard.

The last three nights he, Liz, and Hannah spent the evening tearing the cardboard and paper into tiny scraps and throwing them into buckets of river water. David mixed the wet, pulpy mixture until it was somewhat uniform in consistency. He made a mold out of some scrap wood from his project castoff pile and used it to shape the pulp into a brick. Using his benchtop vice, he squeezed a smaller block of wood onto the top of the mold forcing out any remaining water and compressing the pulp into a neat rectangle roughly four by ten inches. The product of this process was then placed on the driveway to dry. After just two days, David amassed a sizable collection of these paper bricks. He tried one and found it didn't burn as long as wood but much longer than paper itself. Due to their shape and size, they would store easily and plentifully.

Keith and Sadiq would want to know about this and David realized it'd been a week since he'd seen either one. The last time they talked, Keith and Sadiq agreed to help one another and knew David would be available on a limited basis. They were both making plans to move their remaining supplies to David's house realizing that heating three separate places was a waste of resources, especially since there was no efficient way for Keith to heat the former grocery store.

Outside of the immediate neighborhood, fewer people were seen on the streets or outside at all. Those that were outside no longer waved or said hello. They looked on with hungry suspicion, hair-triggered to both defend their meager resources or to take what looked useful. As David went from house to house, most people tended toward the former and he was chased away from several garbage piles. He also encountered several houses that were abandoned, front door standing wide open, possessions scattered inside and in the yard. David threw some wet newspaper and cardboard from the bottom of a trash pile onto the trailer and determined it was full enough to return home.

After a month the smell of garbage peaked and infected every part of town. Another smell was growing too – human waste. With no water service, toilets were unused, and some residents were digging their own outhouses. Whether it was optimism that the power and water would soon return, laziness, or lack of common sense, most outhouse holes were not dug nearly deep enough, allowing the smell to rise and waft across neighborhoods. At least

As if the garbage and human waste smells were not enough, another problem was growing. Animals previously unseen in town were now walking the streets. There wasn't much additional garbage but the waste of the first few weeks was now rotting along every curb attracting skunks, raccoons and possums along with coyotes. None of this mattered to David at the moment. His focus was on getting home with this load of paper and making more winter fuel. He was so intent on getting home, he didn't notice the eyes sizing him up from behind a window curtain in a nearby house.

———

David slowly made his way home with his load. He kept his speed down to avoid having to stop and reload papers as they blew off. He was always cautious when out with his mower-trailer combo but as fewer people were walking the streets, he became less so. As the crisis wore on people retreated, hiding their resources, conserving their strength. Fewer people were at the river too, at least when David was there. The reduction was likely due to the increase in crime but could also have been due to the fact that there were simply fewer people needing to get water. It was a grim thought partly bolstered by the fact that his neighbor was right about the number of graves appearing in yards.

David noticed a few mounds here and there and guessed these were elderly folks, the usual first victims of a heat wave or of any loss of basic medical care. Lack of medicine, emergency services, and hospital care all contributed to these fatalities. Thirst would be next followed closely by hunger and then disease. The idea of providing long term care for his family under these conditions was a crushing weight. It reminded him of when he remodeled Hannah's bedroom and he carried in the drywall by himself. He didn't realize thicker wasn't necessarily better and so he laid each four-by-eight sheet on his back and carried it from his garage to the door, slid it through and pushed, pulled, carried the sheet up the stairs. Eleven sheets in all. His current task felt like much more than eleven sheets. It was an impossible task that never ended. Working an eight to five job was viewed as "providing for one's family." David would never view it that way again. That life was a luxury he might never experience again. True provision was what he lived for now.

Other than Keith and Sadiq, David largely kept to himself and didn't develop any other friendships or "strategic partnerships" as Keith liked to call them. At times, he wished he'd been more aggressive early on but Sadiq and Keith were excellent partners, providing his family enough to ration their way through the next few months, possibly beyond. Winter hung heavily in his mind, never leaving his thoughts for more than a few minutes. How would they get through the winter? His water distillation system was finished and knew they would have plenty to drink through the cold months, especially if it snowed but feeding three mouths would be an enormous challenge.

The scream came from his right followed by a shattering blow to his midsection. David was knocked, sprawling, from his tractor which, without a driver, turned hard to the left and ran into a telephone pole. David, his wind knocked out of him, tried to stand and face his attacker. He looked at his right side, not sure if he'd been tackled, punched or shot. There appeared to be no visible wound of any kind. His labored and panicked breathing was slowly returning to normal and he took in his surroundings. He went down this street many times and never saw anything suspicious.

"Still tryin' to figure it out?"

The voice came from behind and David spun to face it. He was looking at a filthy man. Five feet and six or seven inches, black greasy hair and a small selection of remaining teeth. He was wearing a Black Sabbath t-shirt with several holes in it, jeans that looked as if they could walk away under their own power and tennis shoes that might have at one time been white but were now covered in grime.

"You know how I got you off that thing?" He gestured to David's tractor whose motor was still running.

David shook his head, wondering how fast this guy was and if he had a weapon with him. The man's voice betrayed his life-long love of cigarettes and his teeth spoke of his love for chew.

"I spent a week rigging this up. Glad it didn't kill ya."

"Me too," David managed to say as his wind was still

gaining full strength, but having no idea what the man rigged up.

"See this is my street now. A toll road kinda. I started renting that place there," he said gesturing to a two-story farmhouse style house that was a constant project of renovators and house flippers but was never actually completed or restored to whatever glory it may have once had. "But now that it's my street I think I'll just live wherever on this street I want."

"Why does this get to be your street?" David gasped.

"Cause I'm the only one on it!" He said with glee and laughed a hacking, wheezy laugh that David, despite his condition, could not help but laugh with.

"Where is everyone else?"

"Dead, mostly – or gone away. I buried Glen and them two days ago." He said this as if David should know 'Glen and them'.

"How did they die?"

"Diarrhea. Worst thing I've ever seen. Whole family too. Even the kids. My neighbor back there—" he waved vaguely across the street. "Said it was probably cholera." He pronounced the 'ch' as one would pronounce it in the word 'champ'.

"Do you mean cholera?"

"I don't know nothin' about that. But my neighbor said 'don't drink their water'! I got no taste for water anyhow. I like to mix gin with mine. My Phyllis used to say, 'geez Lenny, you want a little gin with your water?' And I would say, nope, I want a lot!" He laughed again, tickled by his own storytelling.

"Where's Phyllis now?" David tried to keep his eyes from darting toward his tractor, which if he could get to, he might be able to get back on the road and away from Lenny.

"I ate her."

"What? You, you what?" David stuttered.

"Naw, I'm just kidding. She died two years ago. Had you going though, didn't I?" He laughed that wheezy laugh again that degenerated into a coughing fit. David used the distraction to start moving toward his tractor. "Don't do that – I mean it. Don't do that." There was no humor in the command.

"What do you want?"

"I want to take whatever you've got and then send you on your way." There was a long pause as the man stared David up and down.

"And if I just run away?"

"You won't get far." He lifted his tattered shirt to reveal a black handgrip protruding from the beltless waist of his pants. David assumed the rest of the gun was a nine-millimeter pistol.

David continued to stare at Lenny, trying to decide what to do. He had nothing of value with him which meant Lenny would come up empty, possibly making him angry and willing to hurt someone. Or it could cause Lenny to walk David back to his house to gather whatever supplies he had and possibly hurt Liz and Hannah. Lenny simply stared back at him and David thought about watching the old westerns Robbie introduced him to after they met. At nine years old, he and 'uncle' Robbie would act out the stare down, the squinty-eyed concentration followed by the lightning-quick draw of the pistol. It occurred to David that Lenny hadn't drawn the pistol and only showed it as a threat. David had a hunch and backed toward his tractor.

"Don't move!" Lenny shouted. He didn't draw the gun. David continued to inch toward the tractor.

"I mean it! Don't move. I don't want to shoot you. I don't. Let's talk some more!"

"I believe you, Lenny. I know you don't want to shoot anyone. Why else would you rig something up to knock people over?" For the first time, David looked around for what knocked him off the tractor. It looked like a punching bag laid on its side but hung by ropes to swing like a battering ram. Lenny's timing was spot on as his trap dismounted David and incapacitated him long enough to gain an advantage.

"Then stop walking," Lenny said this unconvincingly and the gun remained tucked at his waist.

"I want you to pull that gun out. Pull it out, Lenny." David turned his back on Lenny and stepped purposefully to the tractor. He leapt onto the machine and swung his leg over the seat, half expecting a gun to fire at any moment and half expecting his hunch to prove correct. The latter expectation proved to be true as a he heard a clatter and saw a black handgun with a bright orange tip sail past him and land in the road beyond the tractor. David glanced back.

Lenny's head was down, he kicked at the ground with a dirty shoe. "Alright, you got me. I don't have a gun."

David wrestled the tractor back a few feet and turned the wheel so it was facing into the road again. "And you don't have a tractor either. See you, Lenny."

"Just stay for a while! I got a lot more stories. I think I've got some cans of tuna! C'mon! Let's get a fire goin', whatta ya say?"

David revved the tractor and put it into gear. He yelled back over his shoulder. "I'm just starting to breathe normally again after you knocked me to the ground and you want me to stay for dinner?"

"I meant it. I'm alone on this street. There's nobody

here." David started rolling away. The last thing he needed was a leech, a con man or a thief knowing who he was and where he lived. "Most of these houses have some food left in them!" Lenny shouted. David rolled on but glanced back to see Lenny trying to jog along behind. "I'll split it with ya. You can have any green beans you find too," he said breathlessly. He jogged fifty feet and was already winded. "I hate green beans. They're all yours."

"Why should I have anything to do with you after you hurt me and then threatened to kill me?"

"It wasn't a real gun!" Lenny protested.

"But that was a very real battering ram!" David spat back. "And it hurt!" he added.

Lenny was still trying to jog but a deep wheeze was overtaking the sounds of normal breathing and an explosive cough erupted from his chest and he stopped, doubled over to expel it. With choking gasps, he tried to catch a breath but the wracking barks contorted his body and he sounded as if he would never inhale again.

David wanted to ride away – just head home to his wife and daughter and have a story to tell. He stopped the tractor, shaking his head even as he stepped off and walked back to Lenny, putting a hand on his back. He could not believe he was reaching out to help this man who moments ago was threatening his life. "Lenny! Hey, are you okay?"

Lenny looked up at him with bleary eyes and mucus running from his nose into his mouth. "Do I look okay?" He used his bottom lip to reach up and wipe his top lip clean, making a gentle sucking sound that drew in more of the mucus before it could dry. It was a practiced motion, probably made easier by the small number of teeth in Lenny's mouth. "Every time I try to go anywhere or do anything my damn lungs hold me up. Damn allergies or somethin'. You got allergies? I swear I'm allergic to my own stink. But I can't shower 'cause I think I'm allergic to soap. See it don't matter what I do." His eyes wandered to a point in the distance, farther down the road.

"I had a feeling you were allergic to soap," David said drily.

Lenny looked back at David and smiled. "Aw, that was a joke wasn't it? You're already joking with old Lenny - ha!" His laugh turned into another brief coughing fit.

"Listen, I need to get home. I just came back to make sure you were okay. You take down that stupid trap back there. I mean it. If I come back this way and it's still there you're in trouble." David paused as Lenny stood there, shifting from one foot to the other, receiving his reprimand. "Do you need anything? I mean you said these houses still have food in them. Are you looking for company or what? You rig up a potential death trap and all you want is someone to stay for dinner? Why didn't you just ask?"

"Everybody's angry and scared. If I talk to them, they want to hurt me so I decided to do the same. I'm just no good at it." Lenny scuffed at the asphalt with his shoe.

"That's a good thing, Lenny. I personally am very glad you're a terrible criminal." Lenny smiled and coughed a few more wheezy wet coughs. "Those aren't allergies are they?"

"Naw. Mostly from smoking for forty years. Everybody smoked in Tennessee. Some is from something I inhaled in Iraq and the rest – I guess I just been used hard all my life."

"You were in Iraq? The Gulf War?"

"Yup. Fought there and then got stationed there for a while." David must have had the question on his face because Lenny answered it for him. "I went in young and dumb and the military couldn't fix it. So there you go.

You're looking at one long string of mistakes. Except for Phyllis. No mistake there, boy."

"Tell you what Lenny, let's go through these houses and get what we can. We'll split it even and I'll get going home. If you promise not to bash me in the side again, I'll come back and check on you from time to time. And I won't take any food out of these houses without your say so. Sound good?"

Lenny ran his tongue around a single lonely tooth on the right side of his mouth while he contemplated the deal. "Alright. Let's go get some food." And with that he turned and walked back the way he came. David jumped back on the tractor and did a U-turn to follow him not knowing whether or not he'd made friends with the devil. Lenny seemed harmless enough but he was cagey and smarter than he let on. David knew he needed to stay alert. As he learned just minutes ago, anything could happen.

FOURTEEN

Lauren came along the last six days. The reality of her situation sealed the deal. She had nothing and her future was assured. Ethan and Robbie were her best chance of survival and she knew it. They didn't have a bike for her but she rotated with the guys, taking turns riding in one of the little trailers they made for the bikes. There were three ways to haul whatever they found on their journey. Ethan's ever growing concern was that they would not make it to Kentucky or Michigan before the weather became treacherous. The bikes were greatly improving the distance they could travel each day but they were also starting to break down. They would have been in Lufkin two days earlier but one of the bikes kept throwing its chain and another kept losing air in a tire. The heat and the constant riding also left the men saddle sore and constantly dehydrated. They could not find enough water each day to slake their thirst and replenish what they were losing through exertion. It felt like a puzzle. Keep riding and risk physical harm and exhaustion but get home faster, or walk and maybe not get home this year but at least they would live to see next year. Neither choice was appealing and was the topic of conversation since their last breakdown two days ago.

They rode all night and decided to enter the city of Lufkin. It was a city of about 35,000 but fairly isolated in east Texas. East of the city was a large reservoir filled by the Angelina River. Ethan was hoping they could score another supply haul and find a way to carry more water with them. They had little in the way of containers and the short supply left them doing more searching for water than actually moving forward.

Cael and Lauren formed a friendship over the last seven days. There was little else to do except talk and the two chatted as the miles rolled by while Ethan and Robbie listened, occasionally throwing amused glances at each other. They started the journey with Peyton and Audrey and were continuing it with two more kids, older ones but kids still. It was never their intention to pick people up along the way but Ethan and Robbie had a commanding presence. Lauren and Cael felt more secure traveling with Ethan and Robbie – that there was safety next to these men.

Lufkin appeared very similar to Corpus Christi in that there were very few people on the streets. There were not as many cars blocking the road way here and Ethan guessed it was because many cars were still running. Perhaps they were not directly hit with whatever killed the electrical power. As they progressed through the city, they realized that there were few cars anywhere. And even fewer people. They were able to bike all the way to the center of town without anyone waving them down or inquiring about who they were or where they were from. The downtown had some storefronts that looked operational, which surprised Ethan. Their doors were propped open, presumably to allow some airflow into the building. They stopped at a corner to survey downtown and perhaps find a place to rest and resupply. Ethan checked with Robbie who nodded toward a storefront across the street. It looked like it had general merchandise but still had a soda fountain counter as well, complete with chrome edged, leather topped stools. No doubt a holdover from days gone by.

"Cael, you're with me," Ethan ordered. They entered the store, leaving Robbie to look after Lauren and their bikes. If it was a store at one time, it didn't appear to be one now. The shelves were empty but there was an older man sitting behind the register at one end of the counter.

"Do you have anything for sale?" Ethan inquired.

"Wanna buy the building?" He said in a Texas drawl and chuckled to himself. He was close to sixty, with a close cut head of gray hair. Thin, but rugged looking, he sported at least a week's worth of growth on his chin.

"We just rode in from Houston. Seems pretty quiet here."

"It is. Most of the people pulled out a while ago. No power, no water. Stores emptied out pretty quick."

"How are you hanging on?"

"Had me a pretty good supply stashed. Been eatin' pretty good too. Helps to not be married no more. Ain't got little ones to worry about either."

"What's it like north of here?"

"Same as everywhere else from what I've heard. But I got something they don't have." The proprietor reached under the counter and Ethan tensed expecting a weapon to appear. Instead, he pulled up two Coke bottles that looked like they'd been on ice. "You want 'em?" he asked, holding them out.

"Sure," Cael answered, stepping forward to grab one.

"Ah ah ah," the man scolded. "We gotta trade."

Ethan held Cael back. "I don't think we're interested in Coke. We're looking for information."

"I don't know what I could tell you."

"You could start with how you have an ice cold Coke back there."

The man eyed Ethan for a moment, considering what little information he had about him so far. "I can show you a few things. But if for one second I feel like your questions are less than friendly, I'll let you know." And before Ethan could do anything he was looking at the dangerous end of a sawed-off shotgun.

"I can assure you I mean no harm, Mr.—"

"Mr. Abbott. Luke Abbott. And everybody says that when they're lookin' at a shotgun. Of course you mean no harm. Otherwise you'd be the first to die. Now, I've got a pretty good feeling about you so I'm gonna help you out and get you on your way. Where did you say you were headed?"

"We didn't."

"Smart man. You're right. You didn't say. Introduce yourselves and I'll let you have the cokes."

"This is Cael. I'm Ethan. Out in the street are Robbie and Lauren. We're heading north. Kentucky and then Michigan. We've got family up there."

"Long ways to go. Most of the people who left here were just trying to get to someplace there was still electricity. Didn't hear of too many people trying to get to their families. I admire that."

"My son, daughter-in-law, and granddaughter are there.

I can only hope they're still alive. My son is resourceful though. If anyone can find a way, he can."

"We all want to believe the best about our kids, don't we?" Luke appraised Ethan one more time as if adding to a mental database on him. "Why don't you get your friends out in the street and I'll show you my setup."

———

"Most people around here thought I was a few cows short of a herd. I spent years prepping for a time like this. It's paying off." Luke was leading Ethan's small troupe down an alley behind his store and into a public parking lot. "I bought this lot almost thirteen years ago. I tore up the existing lot and dug it out. Everyone thought I was going to build here but I actually went down about thirty feet and had two shipping containers brought in and buried. Did it late one night. Had a crew from out of town bring 'em in."

"You have a shelter under this parking lot?" Cael was fascinated. "How do you get in?"

Luke walked them over to an inconspicuous manhole cover in the middle of the lot. "This doesn't lead you to a sewer system. It's a shaft leading directly to the containers."

"How do you power it?" Cael was already trying to pull up the manhole cover to see inside.

"See that building there," Luke asked, pointing to the east end of the parking lot. "The roof and the south facing side are covered in solar panels, but not those bulky ones. These are top of the line, high efficiency panels, sourcing my cozy little hideout with enough juice to run the lights, the fridge, my TV, and play some tunes."

"You must have done pretty well for yourself to be able to pay for all this. How did you do it?" Cael asked.

Luke turned to Cael and cocked his head to one side. "Now son, some questions just aren't meant to be asked. I'm proud of what I've got here and you're the first to ask me about it. I'll decide what I show off and what I don't. So, tell me your plans. How are you gonna make it from little ol' Lufkin, Texas to Kentucky and Michigan?"

Ethan and Robbie glanced at each other. Robbie spoke first. "Ride the bikes 'til they're completely used up and then walk. Unless we can find some other means of transport."

"Okay, that's transportation. What about food?"

"Grab canned goods wherever we can find them. Eat a lot of dehydrated camping meals. Everywhere we go, people are hungry. They've eaten most of the ready-to-eat foods. We've tried to hunt along the way but we don't have the right weapons for that. Just handguns."

"Okay, that's food. And you answered my question about weapons. Tell you what, I'm gonna help you. I gathered all this stuff to survive a crisis and not one person in this town thought to ask old Luke for anything. I can be a little gruff sometimes but I'm no ogre. I *want* to help."

Ethan clapped a hand onto Luke's shoulder. "We welcome the help! Whatever you can give us would be great." Robbie stood grinning ear to ear.

Luke grinned at the two grown men trying to contain their excitement over the prospect of getting a little help for their journey. "I don't know what brought you here and how you found me but someone was looking out for you. Let's go down and see what's in storage." He turned toward the manhole cover, nudging Cael, who was still pulling up on the manhole cover, out of the way. He stepped on one side of it and then stepped off. A spring latch engaged and popped up one side of the cover, making it possible for Luke to grab the edge and lift it up. All five of them made their way down the ladder and were amazed to find a spacious, comfortable living space below. The temperature was close to thirty degrees cooler underground and they could feel the air moving.

"Air system is pulling fresh air from topside and by the time it gets here it's cooled down naturally. Fan draws just a couple amps."

There was a couch, a recliner, a small dining table and kitchenette, a television, a twin bed in one corner, and the rest of the space was filled with shelving for storage. Each shelf was full with bags, bins and boxes. "Make yourself at home while I figure out what I'm gonna do here. I designed this place to keep one person alive for six years. So let's see, if I gave you . . ." Luke started doing calculations in his head but Cael couldn't resist asking another question.

"How did you get the furniture down that little hole we just crawled down?"

"Tell you a little secret. I moved everything in before I buried the containers. Wasn't all set up. I just ordered everything I needed, put in the shipping container and then brought it here. The hardest part was getting them set in the right place and cutting out the side walls of each container so I could connect them."

"But how did you—"

"And if you interrupt me again while I'm countin', I'm gonna thump you one."

Ethan gave Cael a warning look. "Luke, I really appreciate you doing this, but are you sure you can part with any of this? I don't want you to jeopardize your plans on account of us. You don't even know us. Why would you help us like this?"

"Ethan – it's Ethan right? I just believe that folks ought

to help each other. That's all. What am I gonna do with all this?" Luke asked, waving at all the supplies. "You think this'll last six years? Five years? I don't know. There's just something about you that makes me want to help. You seem . . . different somehow. Can't put my finger on it."

"Luke, we've seen some bad stuff happen since this mess started. We were shot at and chased in Corpus Christi, kidnapped and then in another shootout north of Houston. It's nice to meet someone who isn't just out for themselves."

"Hmmph. Well, like I said. I like you. Don't know why. And I like what you're trying to do. Don't have any family but if I did I'd storm the gates of hell to get 'em back."

Because they hadn't yet slept after biking through the night, Cael and Lauren were exhausted and found the recliner and couch respectively. Cael turned on the TV hoping there would be something on. "No signal" displayed on the screen. Minutes later they were both asleep and lightly snoring.

As they slept Ethan and Robbie helped Luke gather things off the shelves. "Okay, so you've got your food," Luke said, pointing to the pile he'd started. "This will get you quite a ways. You have to balance supply with the amount of effort it takes to haul it."

He walked over to another pile he started. "Here's a couple hundred rounds of ammunition."

Robbie noticed right away. "Luke, that's for a rifle. We only have pistols."

"I know. That's why I'm giving you a rifle. It's over there in the corner. And then here I have these water purification straws. You put one end in a puddle or lake and start slurping. The water comes out the other end cleaner than the municipal water system."

"We had a couple of those. Could really use some new

ones. This is amazing, Luke. I still feel like we're taking advantage of you somehow."

"You can't be taking advantage of someone who's just givin' the stuff away."

"You've come quite a ways from pulling that shotgun on us in the store to now just giving us all of this."

"I was checking on you. Wanted to make sure you weren't gonna pull somethin' on me. Call it a character test."

Ethan nodded appreciatively. He might have done the same had the roles been reversed. They made small talk for the next half hour as Luke gathered things from every shelf, amassing quite a pile in the middle of the underground home.

"When you go you're gonna have to wake up those two youngsters. You'll need their help to haul all of this up out of here. And keep that Cael kid under your wing. He's hurtin' but he's got Texas-size potential. Might come a time he'll be the only one who can get you out of a scrape."

Robbie and Ethan exchanged glances each wondering what Luke could mean by that.

"I was just thinkin'. Why don't you stay here for a day or two and rest? Get a couple good meals in your belly and sleep in a real bed instead of on the ground."

———

Two days later Ethan and Robbie rose around 8AM, feeling better and more rested than any time in the last month. They each went to one of the teens and shook them awake.

It took some time to work it out but soon they had a system. Everyone grabbing something, lifting it up the ladder inside the shaft and then heading back down. As they went up and down the ladder several times, they were still looking at a deserted downtown. No one seemed to notice four people piling supplies in the middle of a downtown parking lot. Fifteen minutes later, Luke emerged from the shelter and gave the crew instructions on where to find three handcarts. "You can hitch 'em to the bikes for now but they'll be a lot more handy once the bikes play out. Lot easier than those little trailers you're using now."

Ethan held out a hand to Luke. Luke grasped it and shook it firmly. "Luke Abbott, we are so grateful. I still can't believe we ran into you. You know, when we met, you said you wanted to trade. I feel like you're getting shortchanged."

"I came out alright. And as for meetin' each other – sometimes you make the appointments and sometimes they get made for you," he replied with a smile. "Now get going. You'll want to bed down just outside town. The river and the reservoir are less than half a day's walk from there. Get yourselves all the water you can carry. Things get dry this time of year.

"Thanks Luke. Really appreciate it," Robbie added. Cael and Lauren said thank you as well and the group got to work unpacking and repacking the trailers with their new supplies. They made a pile of items that just wouldn't fit in the trailers they had. They decided to leave those things behind, most of which were canned goods. Once the packing was done they waved goodbye to Luke and followed his instructions to a warehouse several blocks from downtown. There, just as Luke described, were the three handcarts. After unloading the old trailers and filling the new, they found that the handcarts were more than adequate to hold everything they were given plus some of the other things they left behind.

"Robbie, we've got the room. Let's go back and get whatever else we can carry. I hated leaving behind some of those cans." Ethan said.

"Sure, we've still got lots of daylight. It feels like we're starting fresh." Cael and Lauren didn't say much; they were both wishing they could be asleep again.

They arrived in the parking lot where they waved goodbye to Luke and saw their pile of left behind goods. They were loading them up when Cael called out.

"What is it, Green Stuff?" Robbie asked.

"Where's the manhole cover?" Cael repeated.

They looked around trying to remember where in the parking lot it was located. "He probably has some kind of cover for it that makes it look like asphalt," Lauren suggested.

"Cael, why don't you go back to the storefront where we found him? I have a hunch."

"What kind of hunch?"

"Just go. Bring me back a Coke."

"What are you talking about?"

"Cael, just do what I'm asking you to do."

"All right," Cael huffed and headed back down the alley to the store.

As they watched Cael heading for the little store a voice behind them called out, "What are you all doin' here?" They turned to see a grizzled older man, bald on top wearing a sweat-marked button down and blue jeans. "You always just stand around in parking lots? You're not from here are you?"

"Just passing through Mr.—"

"Mr. Nichols. I live two blocks thataway," he gestured non-specifically. "So you came through Lufkin to stand in a parking lot?"

Robbie and Ethan exchanged glances and Ethan

suspected he and his best friend were thinking the same thing. "We were looking for Luke Abbott."

"Who?"

"Luke Abbott? He runs that little store downtown? He owns this parking lot?"

"There ain't no Luke Abbott I know of. And this here's a city lot. How do you know this feller?"

"We were just talking to him a couple hours ago. Waved goodbye to him on this very spot."

Mr. Nichols eyed the trio strangely and then shook his head. "If you're playing some game, I don't get it." He noticed the carts and their contents. "You got some nice looking stuff there. Where'd you get it?"

"Luke Abbott."

Mr. Nichols slowly licked his bottom lip as he stared down Lauren, Robbie and Ethan. He opened his mouth to speak, stopped, then tried again. Finally, he gave up. "I don't know what to say. I feel like you're making fun of me but you seem as confused as I am. Well, I was gonna help you if you needed directions or something but you seem to have what you need. Y'all have a good day now."

When he was out of earshot, Ethan exploded. "I knew it!"

"Knew what?" Lauren asked.

"Luke Abbott was not of this world."

"He was an alien?" Lauren was confused.

"No, Lauren he was an angel," Robbie clarified. He turned to Ethan. "When did you know?"

"I had a feeling from the moment he invited us over here but when he prophesied over Cael there was no doubt. And then the last two days he just seemed different. I couldn't put my finger on it."

"I knew when you looked at me you were thinking

something like that." Just then Cael approached the group holding two ice cold cokes in each hand.

"How did you know? These were sitting on the counter with a note. It says, 'Your families are okay. Enjoy the cokes. Blessings, Luke'. How does this guy know anything about your family?"

"Cael, the man we were talking to, I believe he was one of God's messengers – He—" Ethan could not go on. Overcome with emotion he turned from the group and walked a few steps away. He crouched and let the tears flow for a minute. Robbie, behind him, was reacting similarly, both overwhelmed that God would send a messenger to supply them for the journey and give them a message of hope regarding their families. It wasn't the first time Ethan's life was impacted by an angelic messenger. His birth was announced in a similar way to his parents years ago.

"What is going on?" Lauren was unnerved at the sight of her two protectors crying over something she didn't understand. "Was that guy a ghost or something?"

Ethan wiped some tears away and turned to face her. "Not a ghost. An angel."

"Aren't angels just people who have died?"

"No, angels are God's messengers, warriors and servants. They are completely different than human beings. We don't become angels and they don't become human. But to encounter one is a huge privilege. I don't know why God chose to do it now but we were blessed in an incredible way just now."

"How can you be sure it was really an angel?"

"Lauren," Ethan stepped toward her. "When the Spirit of God is living in you, He makes you sensitive to what He's doing. I can tell you, from the moment we met him I had a strange feeling that he wasn't what he seemed. His generosity, his demeanor, the way he talked to us. I had my suspicions but when he said something about Cael I knew it for sure."

"What did he say about me?"

"He said you had lots of potential and to keep you close under our wings because one day, you might be the only one able to rescue us."

"Whoa. That sounds kind of scary."

"Nah, it just means God has plans for you."

"You keep saying stuff like that but I don't even know God."

"You will Cael. I hope one day you will."

It was quiet for a moment as the group tried to take in what they just experienced. Robbie broke into the moment. "We should get going. We've got some ground to cover before we can sleep a little." Everyone grabbed a bike and a cart and moved out of the parking lot, headed northeast from Lufkin.

FIFTEEN

July 30 – 1 PM Fenton, Michigan

There was no breeze. The cicadas were buzzing all around and the shade offered little relief. The temperature all day had been around 90 degrees and hardly lessened at nightfall. The house was so hot the night before, David and the girls slept on the back porch, in spite of the danger. David and Liz each took a turn at keeping watch since there was always a possibility of thieves and hungry, desperate men. The heat was rough but it wasn't the worst thing they dealt with. The battle was psychological. The lack of information. The lack of any kind of authoritative word on what was happening beyond the city limits. Rumors flew around, especially each morning at the river. Even after several violent incidents, people were still going to the river out of necessity only now they were armed and families guarded one another while they collected what they needed for the day. The rumors ranged from the plausible to the outright ridiculous. Some speculated that the whole world was blacked out. Evidently there was some television show several years ago about a worldwide blackout. Others said it was a terrorist attack. Still others believed that west of the Mississippi people had power. Several families David knew of actually packed their belongings into the family car and bartered for gas, loading numerous cans onto and into the vehicle for fill ups along the way. Whether they made it or not no one knew. No word came from the government, state or national.

The only person who seemed to have any information at all from outside a ten mile radius was Garrett. Garrett shot at David several times when he tried to set up the neighborhood meeting and his attitude hadn't improved since the first week of the crisis. David assumed the man was a prepper. He had a ham radio, seemed to need no outside support and was wary, even paranoid that his neighbors would try to take what was his.

David didn't intend to speak to him but as fate, or God, as David believed, would have it, today was a divine appointment. The loose neighborhood group David assembled the first week of the crisis were working together on the garden and to keep an eye on each other's homes. They had yet to form a twenty-four hour watch cycle but as people around them grew more desperate, they would eventually need to protect the garden and their homes. David sometimes regretted not telling his neighbors about the partnerships he forged with Sadiq, Keith, and Lenny but every family made their own way of survival, helping others when they could and knowing when to keep information to themselves.

The people of the neighborhood gathered in the intersection in front of David and Liz's house to discuss the progress of the garden and see if anyone had gathered any news from around town. The Lavins, Ted and Sandy were there, along with Manny and Rochelle, Mark, Martha and even Roger from up the hill.

Mark spoke first. "So I went home like you said last week and rationed the rest of my food. It's worse than I realized. If nothing changes, I have food for a couple weeks. That's it."

The rest of the group looked down or up at the trees – anywhere but at Mark. They wanted to offer assistance, some kind of encouragement, but each one was thinking of their own plight, their own meager resources, their own desperation. And always looming – even if they survived the next few months – was the prospect of a winter with no furnaces and no steady food supplies. The awkward silence was made more so by the interjection of a voice no one expected to hear at their meeting: Garrett.

"I know I'm not really invited to these meetings but I thought I'd fill you in on what I know now."

"You're always welcome at these meetings, Garrett. We're just trying to help each other." These last words made David cringe as he thought of the awkwardness just seconds ago. He made a mental note to talk to Mark later. He could be an asset and perhaps trade work for food.

"Right. Everybody just helping everybody. One big happy family of mankind."

"Do you have something to say or can we get on with our meeting?" This was Manny, whom David was glad found the courage to confront Garrett's antagonism.

"I just came to tell you that there's power west of the Mississippi. People are heading that direction however they can. Walking, mostly. The government is trying to send relief and rescue operations from Kansas City, but having a hell of a time. Word is, most airports are unusable 'cause of the crashes and no working vehicles to clear the runways. Most of the highways are clogged too 'cause of the dead cars. Most of my contacts are saying that the power grid is demolished, take years to repair. The death toll is in the millions."

"We feel lots better now Garrett, thank you," Mark vented.

"You all want info right? So, I just gave it to you. Just trying to be neighborly."

"We should head west," Ted suggested. "Take whatever supplies we have and start walking."

"Do you know how far it is to Kansas City?" Garrett asked. "Close to eight hundred miles. You would have to carry with you everything you would need for the next two months. To make it there before October, you would need to average fifteen miles per day. You'd need enough food and water to sustain you for that distance and—"

Ted interrupted him. "But if we wait, it'll be even harder. We have enough supplies to get us there now. My kids are strong."

"I'm on my own. I have a cart I could bring along. I'll go with you," Roger offered.

Mark spoke next. "I have no choice but to go. I stay here, I'm a dead man."

Ted stepped into the center of the group. "Me and my family are going to start preparing to make the journey. If any of you are considering it, come over to our place so we can hammer out details."

"You'll never make it. Do you have any idea what's between here and Kansas City? You have your food stolen or spoiled or you have one medical emergency on the way and you're done," Garrett objected.

"Yeah, and you're the same one who seems to think if

we all stay here, we die too, so what's your point?" Ted spat back.

"We're all going to die so the only question is would you rather do it in your own home or out in the middle of an abandoned highway somewhere in Indiana?"

"You are not helping, Garrett." David was angry that Garrett had stepped in and thrown so much confusion into the group. "Everyone here needs to do what they think is best. My family and I are staying. I have my reasons. If you are staying, then let's keep discussing what we need to do to survive. If you are going, Ted has offered to discuss it with you and I think the sooner you go the better."

"Want to get rid of us?" Mark jokingly asked.

"No, I don't. In fact, I agree one hundred percent with Garrett. But I also think that if you're going to go, it's now or never. You have roughly two months to get to Kansas City before the weather really starts changing."

"Why are you staying?" Martha asked.

"We've already discussed going to west to Liz's parents. A trip like that would be difficult for Hannah. But mainly because my Dad is out there somewhere. I know he is and if I know him at all, he's headed this way. If I leave Fenton he'll never find me."

"That's touching," Garrett remarked. "You don't think he'll go to Kansas City first?"

"My dad knows how to survive. He said one of the first rules in an emergency is to stay near where you were last seen or where people know you are. That's right here in this house."

"Sorry, David. There's just no way we can stay." Ted backed away from the group. "Anyone who's interested, we'll meet at our place in about two hours to discuss travel plans."

Garrett stepped between Roger and Mark to face David. "Looks like your little neighborhood club is disbanding."

"What do you want from me, Garrett?"

"I don't want anything. I don't need anything. I was prepared for this. I think this," he waved a hand vaguely toward the neighborhood, "is pathetic. People laughed at preppers for years, said we were crazy. Now they're panicking and I'm not. Vindication feels good. That's all."

"We're gonna make it. God's been good to us and He's providing."

"Millions of people have died in the last five weeks but 'God's been good to us'? You're nuttier than I thought, Zabad."

David didn't like being mocked but what jarred him was the use of his last name. He barely knew Garrett, yet he used David's last name casually, familiarly. He was startled enough by it to make it the end of the conversation. "We'll see you around, Garrett," David said lamely as he backed away.

Garrett gave David a fake smile and said, "Good luck!"

SIXTEEN

August 7 – Near Shreveport, LA

It took almost seven days to reach Shreveport. They were trying to average twenty miles a day but continually stopping for water, rest, and repairs kept them from hitting the mark. There was no real reason to enter Shreveport. They had plenty of supplies from their encounter with Luke and water was available, especially since they had the means to purify it. Traveling at night was helpful as they avoided running into people on the roads.

When Ethan and Robbie were on guard during the days they always walked a long circle around where the rest of the group slept. Those walks revealed that some folks were handling the power outage well. They prepared for an emergency and had some impressive makeshift contraptions and tools. They also came upon quite a few graves and in some cases, decaying bodies. It'd been close to six weeks since the crisis began. Not long enough to starve to death, but without a steady water supply or drinking the wrong kind of water, death would arrive quickly and mercilessly. The heat continued unabated during their travels. Fortunately, they were able to avoid the worst of it by sleeping through the day. The biggest question on their minds now was which way to go next. Lauren had family somewhere in the south but couldn't remember exactly where. She didn't know them well and didn't want to derail Ethan and Robbie's plans by leading them on what could be a pointless search. Cael didn't know of any extended family he could run to so his decision to stay with Ethan and Robbie was made.

Sticking to the major highways would take them through every major city while sticking to the back roads might take them through some scary back-wood towns. Not that Ethan and Robbie couldn't handle the rough stuff. It was just that if they didn't have to, they would be okay with that.

The most difficult decision was getting rid of the bikes. They rode them from Corpus Christie, up past Houston, to Lufkin and now to Shreveport – several hundred miles. But the tires on two of the bikes would no longer hold air and the chain on the other slipped off continually. It was difficult to surrender the faster means of transport but at the rate they were actually traveling, it made the most sense. The handcarts, when disconnected from the bikes, proved easy to pull. With just three carts Lauren only pulled if one of the guys needed a break.

While the group took time to search a series of gas stations north of the city to find some maps, Ethan grabbed the satellite phone and with low expectations, tried contacting Colonel Reynolds again. The call was received.

"Colonel? It's Sergeant Zabad."

"Ethan, where are you?"

After summarizing their journey so far and detailing their current location Ethan got to the point. "Is there any way you can help us with transport? I'm sure military resources have been pushed to the limit but if there is any way - "

"Ethan, I'm sorry but I have to stop you right there. We are dealing with such a mess there is no way I can spare any resources."

Ethan was reluctant to let it go but he knew Reynolds well enough to know when it was a firm 'no'. "Can you give me some idea of what's going on? We haven't seen any responders in the areas we've been through."

"National Guard started in the coastal areas and the biggest cities. Our division was called in just days later. Western Command is pushing from St. Louis trying to get to the eastern central states but it's a shi- I mean, uh, crap storm from the coast to some parts west of the Mississippi."

Despite the grim news, Ethan smiled at the fact that his Colonel checked his language with a sergeant. It was a tiny moment of humor amidst a desperate and ugly situation. "Colonel, who did this? Has anyone taken responsibility?"

"Word from on high says they've ruled out ISIS and any other middle east backed terror group. I heard a rumor that this was home grown."

"Home grown? Why would anyone do this to their own country?"

"Like I said, it was a rumor. The investigation is above my paygrade. I'm mobilizing our guys on the ground and it's slow going. Death tolls are rising the further we get inland. This country tore itself apart. Whoever did this was highly organized and they were angry. They have a lot of blood on their hands."

"What exactly did they do?"

"The power grid is compromised. Power plants were bombed. Electromagnetic pulses were detonated in more places than we can count. It was like someone wanted us to go back to the stone age."

"Mission accomplished," Ethan said, without humor.

"Yeah, I never thought I'd see anything like this in the States."

"Colonel, I appreciate you taking the time." Ethan then detailed as best he could the approximate route they were taking. "If you can send help, we'll take it. And if at some point you need me and Robbie, you'll at least have an idea where to find us."

"Were gonna be at this for some time. But keep your phone close. Zabad, we'll see you when all this is done."

"Copy that, sir." Ethan ended the call and recounted it for Robbie. After an extra rest day in Shreveport, they pressed on, heading toward the Mississippi.

August 14 – 11 PM Fenton, Michigan

A week passed since the exodus from the neighborhood. The Lavins, Manny and Rochelle, Mark, and Roger all left. They told several friends in town what Garrett told them, so more people joined the caravan. In all, close to one hundred people joined together for the trek, with other groups following close behind and still others making plans to leave shortly.

Just days after they left, a helicopter landed downtown. David was not sure exactly where it touched down but he heard its engines and knew, after two months of silent skies, what it was. It flew overhead too quickly to be identified. David thought he caught a glimpse of a military marking but maybe he was just being optimistic. Before he had a chance to make it downtown to see what it was, it took off again and headed east, presumably to land in another town with whatever message it was carrying.

David was taking a shift guarding the community garden. Even though no vegetables were appearing yet, the seedlings could be easily dug up and transplanted. He and Martha, along with a few other elderly folks in the neighborhood, wanted to make sure no one stole their crop. Most of the families on their streets left which meant David was the youngest man in a two block radius. Most of the elderly folks stayed, knowing they couldn't walk eight hundred miles to Kansas City. Deep down, most of them knew they wouldn't survive the harsh winter either and so chose to stay where at least they had the comforts of home, such as they were, with the heat of summer upon them.

David already buried an elderly couple six doors down. He didn't know them but just under a week ago, he was walking around the block just to check on things and saw a dog at their door, pawing at it and whimpering. Evidently, the dog was outside when something happened to the residents. David went in the house and was greeted with the unbelievable stench of decomposition. He tied a kerchief over his nose to dampen the smell and reluctantly dragged both bodies outside into the yard. It was hot, brutal work digging graves but sadly, it was work at which David was becoming experienced. The dog sat at the graves for a couple days before trotting down the street to sit at the end of David and Elizabeth's walkway leading to their side door.

"I want him." Hannah was delighted at the prospect of having a pet.

"If we had some way of fattening him up I'd say let's save him for a special meal," David joked, making sure only Liz heard him.

"That's disgusting!" Liz exclaimed, giving him a gentle backhand to his upper arm. "We'll take him. He won't eat much."

That was true since the dog was so small. David wasn't entirely sure of the breed. He had shaggy, sandy blonde hair with a ruffled patch of off-white on his chest. He could have been a poodle except that his hair was not curly, but long and wavy. He wasn't groomed all summer which added to the mystery. He looked so shaggy that it reminded Liz of a cartoon she used to watch. They decided to call him Scooby.

Over the last two weeks, with fewer people in the neighborhood, David, Sadiq and Keith brought loads of food and bottled water from each of their respective stashes and lined David's basement with them. The secret storage compartments David built were not large enough to contain it all. Sadiq still had some gas in his underground tanks but no one was asking for it anymore. Many generators that worked early on died from constant use or people simply gave up trying to find gas. Keith was tired of living in the dark and the constant pressure to keep guard over his stash of groceries. With Sadiq and Keith in the neighborhood, they could share the guard duties along with the basic needs of survival like gathering water each day and storing supplies for winter.

They were still a week or so away from having everything moved. They were doing it slowly so as not to arouse suspicion and almost always made trips in the early morning when most people were likely still asleep.

All this spilled through David's mind as he watched over the garden. David was glad he could sit at the corner of the garden and still see his house. Ever since the attack, David feared the surviving assailant would return. He sometimes dreamed of the man's face – narrow, pinched with a long, hooked nose. His eyes slightly bulging. His hair was thin and brushed straight back. A lean, wiry build, he was tough to pin down when they wrestled in the living room. The whole encounter frequently replayed in David's mind.

It transitioned from dusk to dark during his shift and his mind snapped back to the present when he heard a rustle on the far side of the garden plot. He clicked on the LED flashlight he used when on guard and shined it toward the sound. Another swish to his left and he shined toward it. Nothing. He was used to seeing critters near the garden and the light typically scared them away. But this sounded different. Clicking off the flashlight, he reached beside his folding camp chair and picked up the shotgun. It was loaded with nine millimeter buckshot. He considered the slugs but preferred something with more certainty – something that spread as it went toward its target. He stood, and with the gun stock at his shoulder and the barrel pointed slightly downward, started a slow walk around the perimeter of the garden. His eyes were adjusted to the dark and so he kept the flashlight in his pocket in case he needed it again.

He made one loop around the garden but saw nothing. The exhaustion brought on by endless days of trying to provide were catching up with David. He was always up early gathering water. When he returned from the river, he would get to work heating the water and distilling it. Once that process was started, he often made the rounds to check on Sadiq, Keith, and some days Lenny. He tended the garden, collected whatever he could find around town, and prepared winter provisions. Life was a nonstop race for survival. He tried to catch a nap the days he was scheduled for guard duty but after most of the neighborhood left, David became responsible for every other night rather than just once a week. He was young, able-bodied and the older people in the neighborhood who stayed were relying heavily on him. He was thankful his friends would soon be living with him.

He heard the swishing noise again and this time he was quicker to flash the light toward the sound and caught a glimpse of something, someone running out of the garden toward the neighboring house.

"Hey!" David shouted. "Who are you?" The figure ran around the corner of the house and David was strongly tempted to follow but did not want to leave the garden unguarded. In these days, nothing was certain and it would be just like a couple wily scavengers to lure him away on a fool's errand while an accomplice cleaned out the garden. The house the dark figure ran to was owned by a single woman David did not know at all. She was something of a hermit and rarely spoke with anyone for any reason, not even attending the neighborhood meetings. David decided to wait until morning to knock on her door and follow any footsteps leading away from the garden. He still had hours of night watch left and needed to conserve strength. Meals lately were filling his stomach but not necessarily appetizing or nourishing. Mostly they consisted of rice - always rice and some kind of canned vegetable. Every few days, they would use some of their dried meat stores or open a can of chicken or tuna. Working with Keith was a big help in intro-ducing variety to their diet.

On one occasion, just over a week ago, David made the trip to their church to inspect the food pantry. No one had been in the building since the crisis began so there was plenty of non-perishable food. One food pantry item David never considered was beans. For some reason, people brought bags of dry beans to food pantries but no one ever took them. David was thankful for them now as they were nourishing, filling, and free. He was excited, however, by the prospect of having fresh vegetables. Even the canning they were planning to do would yield a better tasting product than factory canning and would be a welcome break in the monotony they would surely face through the long winter ahead.

Sitting near the garden, dwelling on food was making David hungry. He stood again to walk the perimeter of the garden and planned to walk across the street to the other large plot they cultivated and make sure things were quiet there too. The moment he stood to full height, he heard the breaking of glass. His first thought was his own house but he heard another clink of glass and it was from the house where he saw the shadowy figure run. He walked slowly but with determination toward the house, shotgun at the ready.

He made his way to the front walk and was able to see the front door standing ajar. He wished he knew the resident better so he could call out her name, warn her. Nor did he want to go rushing in if the person inside was armed. He stepped carefully to the porch and mounted the steps, thankful they were concrete rather than creaky wood. Silently he crept toward the open door, listening for clues as to where someone might be in the house. Near the door, he could feel under his feet the crunch of broken glass. Then he heard the scream. David's heart jumped in his chest and he felt the flood of adrenaline.

"Hello? Who's in there?" He stayed near the door until he could assess the situation. Someone in this house was in danger but all he could think about was his wife and daughter. "Hello!" David shouted again hoping victim or perpetrator would respond.

"Help me! Please! Help!"

The voice came from the stairway. David pulled out the flashlight and clicked it on so he could make his way through the house. Just inside the door – more glass. The stairway was on the opposite side of the house, through the dining room. He stepped quickly to the base of the stairs and looked up. "I don't know who you are but you better leave – now! I'm armed." David tried to sound convincing and unafraid. He was sure he failed on both counts.

Two people appeared in his flashlight beam at the top of the stairs – one in dark clothing and the other, a woman in sleep shorts and a tank top, being held around her neck by an assailant wielding a wicked-looking knife.

"Back off or I slit her throat!" This was aimed at David who involuntarily took two steps back from the base of the stairs anyway.

"You don't want to do that," David said carefully.

"You're right. I don't want to but I will if I have to. I want food."

The attacker's face was partially obscured by the woman's head and hair so David couldn't observe anything about him. "If you want food all you have to do is ask. We'll share but you can't just take."

"No one will share."

"So, why this house? Do you know this lady? Do you even know if she has food to give you?"

"She has it. She's still alive, ain't she?"

"Why don't you let her go and we can talk about getting you some food? But as long as I'm standing here with this gun and you're standing there with your knife no one is going anywhere." David silently wished now that he had loaded it with slugs instead of buckshot. He couldn't take a shot at this attacker without hitting the woman.

"You're not gonna talk about getting me food. As soon as I let her go, you'll shoot me down."

"That's not my intention, I promise you. But people I love live in this neighborhood. I can't have you terrorizing them."

"I'm coming down these stairs so you better back off."

"Let her go. You don't have to steal food. We can share." David raised the gun higher and pressed it more firmly to his shoulder. The flashlight was clamped in his left hand, held tightly to the grip under the barrel so he could look down it and light wherever he aimed. The woman was crying but said nothing other than her cry for help. "I'm warning you. Let her go."

The knife at her throat was raised higher and its blade menacingly twisted where she could see it. "Don't hurt her!"

"Back off!" He descended two steps. Paused. Then another two.

Each step he took, David backed off further and further toward the front door. "You don't have to steal. We will share. Just let her go." No response but an evil glare. He decided to try another approach. "What's your name?"

"Shut up!" The assailant reached the bottom of the stairs and forced his hostage toward her kitchen.

Lord, what am I supposed to do here? I can't walk away. But I don't know how to stop this man. David prayed silently, waiting for an answer. It came quickly, in the form of a tiny end table. The attacker knocked it over while moving to the kitchen and it got under his feet, tripping him. The stumble caused him to let go of the woman momentarily to right himself. David took advantage of the split-second distraction and casting the gun aside threw himself at the attacker. His flying tackle sent he and the man through the kitchen doorway and onto the floor in a heap.

David, aware of the knife, grabbed hold of the attacker's wrist and attempted to slam the knife hand against the floor to dislodge the weapon. Unsuccessful, he jumped up from the floor and snatched the shotgun from the dining room table where it landed. In one swift motion, he grabbed the gun and fired from the hip. The buckshot caught the attacker in the side of his chest, throwing his body back against the cupboards. He was unconscious the second he hit the floor.

David looked around for the flashlight and realized it was probably still on the dining room table. He found it and shined around at the scene. The first thing the light found was the assailant. Blood was pouring from his side. David knelt and examined the wound though there was little he could do. He could try to stop the bleeding but there were no first responders or emergency medical personnel. He felt for the man's pulse at his neck and just seconds after finding it, lost it. David frantically moved his fingers around on the injured man's neck trying to feel the gentle throb of a heartbeat. Feeling nothing, he accepted the truth. He shot and killed another human being. A swell of emotion rose in his chest and his breathing constricted. And then he remembered the victim. *Where was the woman?* He heard crying at the back door and there he found her, curled into a ball, cowering as if the attacker were still standing over her.

"It's okay. He's gone." David reached out a hand to help her up. "You're safe now." She whispered a thank you but didn't move. David heard at least two doors open and shut outside and moved to the front door to see who it was.

Martha appeared, with a flashlight, as did Garrett, though he came from much further away. David shined his light across the street and saw that Elizabeth was making her way over.

"What happened?" Garrett asked.

"Had a break-in while I was guarding the garden. He's in the kitchen." David gestured with his head toward the back of the house. Garrett swept past him to survey the scene.

"Is there anything I can do, David?" Martha asked.

"Yeah, see if you can help that woman in there. She went from a sound sleep to having a knife at her throat. She's badly shaken."

Elizabeth ran to meet David on the porch. "Did you fire that shot? Is everyone okay?"

"I did. Don't go in there." Though the full force of it hadn't hit him yet, he could now understand what his wife had been going through for several weeks. He killed another human being.

She looked lovingly at him. "Did you . . ."

David nodded slightly.

"Oh, David I'm so sorry." She wrapped her arms around his neck. "I wish you never had to do that."

He squeezed her back, but briefly. "I have to finish this. Go home. Make sure Hannah is okay."

"Okay. I love you." She gave him a peck on the lips and headed back.

David re-entered the house and learned that the resident's name was Melinda. He approached her in the dining room where she regrouped with Martha.

"Hi Melinda. I'm David." He extended a hand which she ignored. "I'm sorry we never had a chance to meet before tonight." He said this knowing that the lack of introduction was entirely Melinda's fault. She never answered her door or responded to any attempts to link her to the life of the neighborhood. She didn't help plant the garden or attend any meetings to date. "How have you been getting by all this time on your own?"

"I was prepared," she said simply.

"You knew this was coming or do you mean in general – like Garrett here – you're a prepper?"

She nodded but David had no idea which part of the question she was affirming. Her entire demeanor angered David and the fact that he risked his life, and taken another, in her defense without even a thank you made him wonder what she could be thinking. David never could understand why some people simply refused to be neighborly. To drive up to their garages, open them remotely, pull inside and never exit their homes seemed to David a foolish decision. Did these people not need the involvement of others in their life? Were they afraid of something? David knew he couldn't answer these questions at midnight so he put them aside in his mind and set upon a different task.

"Melinda, do you have any paper and a permanent marker?"

She nodded and pointed to a drawer next to the kitchen sink. David grabbed the items and neatly printed "We will share. You will not steal" on the paper and then with Garrett's help carried the body out to the corner where their side street connected with the main road. They propped up the dead man and tied the sign around his neck as a warning to those walking by. David felt a stab of conscience because they were not burying the man but those wanting to steal their next meal needed to know what would happen to them – at least in this neighborhood. He would bury him eventually – after he'd made their point. They walked back to the corner in front of David's house and Garrett started up the hill to his place.

"Thanks for your help, Garrett," David offered. It was not easy to show any gratitude to the man who, so far was nothing but antagonistic.

"Whatever. Try not to kill anyone else. That's two for the Zabad family so far," he added flippantly over his shoulder.

"It's not like I wanted to kill someone."

"You sound like your dad." Garrett let that sink in a moment. "Yeah. Well listen, I'd like to get some sleep tonight so, see you in the morning, Zabad."

"What do you know about my dad?"

"Goodnight!" Garrett shouted from halfway up the hill to his house. What could Garrett know about Ethan Zabad? David had the rest of the night to think it over as he guarded the gardens until dawn.

SEVENTEEN

"Why didn't we think about extra shoes?" Cael held up his foot, showing Ethan his shoe, the sole pulled away from the upper canvas part.

"You can live without shoes. Normally, I would say feet first. But without food and water - first things first."

The foursome sat on the westbound side of the I-20 bridge spanning the Mississippi. The sun was low in the sky casting long gold rimmed shadows across the road. The heat that assaulted them all day faded into a warm humid night. Lauren sat in Robbie's shadow, trying desperately to escape even the little bit of sun still shining. The river far below would have looked inviting if it wasn't so brown. A gentle breeze helped to move the air but it was still hot, humid air.

"I think walking in daylight was a bad idea," Lauren said to no one in particular.

"I think bringing you in the first place was a bad idea," Cael shot back at Lauren.

"Both of you stop. Your fighting the last week has been worse than the heat and the walking."

"Ethan, I think we should make these two do pull a cart together for the next week just to force them to get along."

"We aren't kids. You can't punish us like that."

"If you're not kids then —"

"Stop acting like one." Cael and Lauren glared at each other, both embarrassed that they spoke in unison.

"Great minds think alike. Isn't that what they say, Robbie?"

"Something like that. Listen, we've got a long trip ahead of us. Five hundred miles or so to Kentucky. Over a thousand miles to Michigan. Probably two months of walking. I can't handle fighting every step of the way."

"Did our angel throw in a roll of duct tape? I'm not above taping mouths shut," Ethan suggested.

"Ethan, don't give parenting advice." Robbie teased.

"What?" Ethan protested. "I'm a good parent. Sometimes you just have to stop the noise."

"So, where to from here?" Lauren loved looking at the maps with Robbie, helping to select routes and figure out how long each leg of the trip would take.

"I think it makes the most sense to go toward I-65. It's the most direct route to Louisville."

"Can't we just stop and camp for a few days? I need to find some new shoes and something to do while we walk."

"Cael, you should be fully detoxed from your electronic device addiction."

"I wasn't addicted."

"And every day that we're stopped is a day we're not getting closer to our families. I would love the rest but we just can't afford it. Robbie and I have been around the world together fighting side by side and we never won by stopping for a while. You go in rested and ready and when it's over you recoup. But when you're in it up to your neck and stuff keeps hitting the fan, you walk on. I need you to walk on, Cael."

"I get it man, but can't I at least get some shoes? And can we get some books or something? I think I can read and walk at the same time."

"Throw in gum chewing and you're a frickin' genius!" Lauren joked.

"Shut up! I'm so sick of your crap." Cael stomped off in the direction they came from.

"Cael, come back and sit down. Cael!"

"Let him go, Ethan. He'll be back. He knows where the food is."

Lauren stood and brushed bits of gravel off her pants. "I need a walk too. I won't leave the bridge. Promise."

"Okay, Lauren. We're here if you need us. And Lauren? Take it easy on him. He's hurting as bad as you are. You could be helping each other."

"I know. But I – I don't even know what I'm doing here. You guys are great and I know what you've done for me but – I just miss everything."

"We do too. Especially our families. We're pushing hard because we don't even know if they're still alive. We want to get to them. I really believe God put us in your path to help you – to get you out of your house before you starved to death there – alone. You're here for a reason."

She nodded solemnly and then turned to walk the length of the empty bridge.

The last stretch from Shreveport was uneventful aside from the two teens bickering but traffic greatly increased. More people were heading west on foot with the promise of government aid luring them on. Several people they talked to seemed to believe that west of the blackout zone were government supply stations set up for refugees. No one seemed to know where the information originated but they were all sharing it as fact. Their goal was Oklahoma City. Some heard rumors that there was electricity as close as the Oklahoma border.

"Do you think we should have turned back to get help?"

"What, to walk all the way back to Oklahoma and ask around to see if anyone could take us to our families? Along with everyone else in the country? If Reynolds couldn't help us . . . come on, Robbie."

"We might have had better intel on what's ahead. You heard those people talking about the nuclear power plant melting down." Some of the refugees heading west were telling stories about nuclear disasters accompanying the blackouts, EMPs, and power grid implosion.

"I think they were scared and were blowing things out of proportion. Reynolds did say that power plants had been attacked but he said nothing about nuclear fallout. I'm sure there were explosions but we're not having Chernobyl 2.0."

"We'll see. Speaking of meltdowns, what are we gonna do with those two? They're gettin' worse. I know they're hurting but why take it out on each other?"

"I don't know Robbie, but I'm getting ready to knock their heads together. Unless—"

"Unless what?"

"Unless – they like each other."

Robbie raised his eyebrows. "You might be on to something there. Hey, did you notice that?"

The golden light of the sunset was snuffed out. The men looked west toward the sunset and were disturbed to see a wall of black clouds making their way quickly toward them. But it did not look like an isolated storm. The clouds trailed down to the south and seemed to wrap around the sky almost all the way to the east.

"What is that?"

"Probably just a big thunderstorm."

Drops of rain spattered the pair as they stared southwest.

"Ethan, round up the kids. We need to get off this bridge and find cover. Now."

Cael was already heading back toward Ethan and Robbie, having been walking in the direction of the clouds. They grabbed their carts and raced to the east end of the bridge, overtaking Lauren and urging her forward.

"How much time do you think we have?" Cael asked breathlessly as rivulets of rain water streamed down his face.

"Hard to say but the sooner we can get shelter, the better I'll feel. We need a block building or someplace with a basement. It could just be a thunderstorm but that means a possibility of tornadoes."

"Maybe it's a hurricane." Cael offered.

"Hey, that's the spirit! Always the optimist." Lauren snarked.

"Shut up!"

"We're inland a ways so I have my doubts that it's a hurricane but that doesn't mean this can't be destructive or deadly."

"Shelter first. Talk later," urged Ethan.

"What about that place?" Lauren pointed to a hotel and casino just off the expressway.

"They might have stairways made of cinder block that would make great shelter. "Let's get there and wait it out. We need to sleep anyway."

· · ·

They made it to safety with minutes to spare. When the storm front arrived the howling wind was so loud and echoing in the stairway that Ethan and Robbie couldn't sleep. They sat with their backs to the interior wall while Cael and Lauren continued to sleep under the stairs as far back as they could crawl. The only door was metal with a small square window.

"No way we could've predicted this."

"No. I just wish we could move faster. Could find another car or even a boat. I'd take the river up to Louisville."

"Reynolds said they were working both ends of the country but I'm still surprised there's been no military presence? No national guard, no militia activity. I knew when we crossed the border everything was still unfolding but I thought by now . . ."

"This might be worse than their worst case scenario. Maybe there's no communication at all – nothing. Maybe some national guard units just melted away, went home. The police are supposed to be militarized too but how many of them have you seen out patrolling?"

"Just none."

"Exactly. We're on our own Ethan. Every step of the way we have to rely on our skills and the blessing and favor of God."

"He's already blessed us so much," Ethan said, thinking about Luke.

"No doubt," Robbie nodded.

"When this storm lifts, let's get Cael some shoes. There's got to be a place around here we can get some shoes. We scrounge for everything else, why not a decent pair of shoes? He also said he wanted to read. I wish we had a Bible to loan him."

"Why don't we go upstairs in this place and grab a Bible out of one of the rooms?" Robbie suggested. "It's a hotel after all. The Gideons are good at what they do. If there's no Bible up in one of those rooms, I'll buy you dinner."

"Sure, just lead me to the nearest Cracker Barrel." A barrage of thunder rattled the stairway and lightning illuminated it like a strobe. "Oooh, that was a good one!" Ethan exclaimed.

"You like this, don't you? I remember when we weathered that typhoon in Indonesia, you—"

"Sat at the window and watched the wind blow. It's fascinating, Robbie. The power of the wind, what God can do through the weather."

Another ear-splitting crash of thunder followed by the strobe-like lightning woke Cael up. "I'm trying to sleep," Cael mumbled.

"We'll see if we can turn down the storm volume for you," Robbie joked.

"Quit making fun of me."

"Cael, we're not making fun of you."

"That's how it feels."

"We're just making jokes. They're not at your expense."

"Pick on somebody else. I'm sick of it. Lauren and both of you."

"I know you're hurting bro, but we're on your side."

"You don't have to call me 'bro', Robbie. It's weird. And if you were on my side—"

Ethan angrily jumped into the conversation. "If we *weren't* on your side you'd still be running with a bunch of thieves in Corpus Christie, probably hungry and thirsty, and depending on where this storm came from, windblown and wet. I thought we'd been feeding you and protecting you for the last month. My mistake."

Robbie reached out and put a hand on Ethan's arm. Ethan knew what it meant. "I'm sorry, Cael. This is wearing on us too. We're tired, we're worried for our families. I'd like to think we're working together here – a common goal, you know?"

"I just feel out of place. I want to go home but—"

"Where's home?"

"I never even had a chance to say goodbye to my family. I don't actually *own* anything. Nothing but the clothes I'm wearing. That's weird you know?"

"We haven't known you very long but my guess is that before all this started, you were in a pretty good position – with your friends, your family, your school. Let me guess, you were well-liked, had a few girls chasing you and you had free run of the town?" Cael's silence confirmed Ethan's guess. "I know your type. Popular, wealthy, privileged. Sometimes feeling like you're above everyone else. I'm not saying that's you exactly but—"

"Nice to finally hear what you really think of me."

"I don't think that's who you are," Ethan clarified. "I think if you had continued the path you were on, you could have easily been that person. But the last six weeks have changed you."

Cael sat up, keeping his blanket around his shoulders. "Changed me how?"

"When I met you, it was at gunpoint and you were trying to steal my car. Then you lied about seeing Peyton's parents and led us into an ambush by that gang."

"I helped you out!"

"Yes, you showed up after an attack of conscience. But you were definitely in with them. And what were you doing when the power went out?"

Cael waited until another crash of thunder subsided. "I was selling."

"How old are you again?"

"I'll be twenty next May."

"Nineteen. And you were selling drugs?"

"Why are we talking about this?"

"Because you need to know that who you were six weeks, six months, even six years ago is not who you have to be. You can decide who you want to be. You can be mad at the world, hate everyone around you and you'll get back exactly what you give out. Or you can choose to forgive yourself, let go of the garbage in your past and do a new thing."

"I'll never forgive myself for not being there when my parents died. If I could go back -"

"If you could go back, chances are you would've died too. And you can't go back. Cael, I spent over seven years in prison for crimes I regret every day."

"What'd you do?"

"I was trying to help someone. I got cornered and with a wrench about that long," Ethan held up his fingers about seven inches apart, long enough for a flash of lightning to illuminate them for Cael. "I killed people. They were trying to hurt someone but I crossed the line. A lot of people died that night . . . because of me. I regret killing them, especially knowing what I know now. And I used to wish I could go back, rewrite history. But not anymore. If that hadn't happened I wouldn't have spent the last fifteen years doing what I do."

"And that is?"

"Most of it is classified. I can tell you that I help people. I was born to set people free."

"What you did with that car – back in Corpus – what was that?"

"A unique gift from God. Everyone gets at least one."

"Yeah? What's mine?"

"I don't know yet. You're young. Still figuring out who you are. And you don't know God. That's the biggest part of it. Besides, I can't tell you what your gift is. That's part of the adventure of life – discovering who you are."

"That's an adventure?"

"Don't knock it til you've tried it." Ethan glanced at the window. "Hey Robbie, I'm gonna take a look outside, see just how bad it is out there." Ethan got up and walked to the steel exit door and slowly opened it. Water was running past the door in a torrent toward the river. The sound of rushing water was so loud Lauren stirred. Thankfully Vicksburg sat high off the Mississippi River so there was no danger of flooding but they weren't going anywhere soon. "Speaking of adventure, check this out."

Robbie and Cael crowded into the doorway to see the torrential rain and the lightning. "We might be here awhile."

EIGHTEEN

THREE DAYS LATER, WITH WHAT MUST HAVE BEEN A hurricane finally past, they started north. "Good to be moving again." Ethan was out in front pulling one of the carts Luke gave them.

"But the break was nice." Cael brought up the rear, pulling a cart and enjoying the feel of his new shoes. A store with general merchandise near the casino where they rode out the storm was emptied of food but there was an aisle of shoes. Everyone picked up a couple pairs for when their shoes eventually wore out. They guessed correctly and found Gideon bibles in the hotel. They took one for each of them.

The hurricane's destructive power was evident as they walked east of the city. Downed trees, homes without roofs and debris everywhere told of how strong the winds were. From their hideout inside the casino they scouted the surrounding area and saw some residents out clearing their yards and talking to one another. The group stayed clear of the residents, fearful that what they pulled in the carts would be too tantalizing to resist for a hungry person. It was slow going as they wove their way around fallen limbs and debris.

"It's strange to see this mess but no first responders out to help clear it. The protocols for this type of crisis have been completely ignored. I don't understand it."

"Robbie, it's a crisis. You can run all the scenarios in the world, but when it happens, everything's up for grabs."

"Where were you when this started?" Lauren asked.

"We were in Southeast Asia. Myanmar, India. We ended in Thailand right, Robbie?"

"Man, it feels like it was years ago. I can't even remember. That sounds right."

Ethan quickly recounted their journey from Asia to Mexico and then to the border. "If we could have come into the country another way we would have but Mexico into Texas was the only option."

They all stopped to watch Ethan lift a tree limb out of the way and then continued on.

"You've talked about your son. I think it's amazing that you're going all this way to be with him."

"His wife Elizabeth – she's not a daughter-in-law. She's like a daughter. And I can't believe how perfect she is for my son." Ethan tossed another branch out of the way.

"What are you going to do when you find them?"

"I just assumed they would need my help. I don't know what they're facing. I don't even know what the country at large is facing. There's no face on this enemy yet. Other than the loss of electricity. So, whatever I can do to help – that's what I'll do."

"Ethan isn't one for extensive planning. He likes to make things up as he goes. Keep me on my toes."

"You like it that way and you know it, Robbie. If you

wanted boring and predictable, you'd have stayed with your old unit."

As they walked Cael eventually pulled up alongside Ethan. "You know how a while back you were saying what kind of kid I was back in Corpus?"

"Yeah, privileged, wealthy, scoring with the ladies," Ethan said with a smile.

"All you had to say was 'yes'. Anyway, do you know what's up with Lauren? I've been with her twenty-four seven for weeks now and I can't crack her code."

"You mean she's not interested?"

"That's a serious understatement. She could care less about me."

"Couldn't care less," Ethan corrected.

"Nice. I'm trying to get your advice and you're giving me a grammar lesson. It's like you could care less too."

Ethan ignored the opportunity to tease him again. "You're right. Listen, if she's not interested there's not a thing you can do about it. Maybe you're just not her type."

"She's gorgeous though."

"So? What do her looks have to do with her being interested in you?"

"She's hot. I want her to like me."

"Cael, listen. First off, I'm not the guy you ask for advice on love and dating. Never was good at it and second – in case you hadn't noticed, I'm not wearing a wedding ring. I've been too busy at my job to think about it."

"Okay but can you help me? Maybe I don't need advice. I just need – a little nudge."

"I don't think you need any more nudging."

"No, I mean nudging her toward me. Tell her what a good guy I am. She trusts you."

"Cael, if she isn't interested in you, there's not a thing I could say to change her mind. So, I'm not going to do that. What I can do for you is help you understand what it means to be a real man."

"I came to you for help and you're slamming me."

"I'm not slamming you, Cael. I want to tell you something helpful. I want to tell you the truth. Something too few people have done in your life. We are in a life and death situation and you want help with your love life. That tells me all I need to know about you and your priorities."

"So, I pretend like she's not there? I can't be attracted to her?"

"No, you treat her like a fellow human being and not an object you want to get your hands on. I'm saying you need to shut your hormones down for a minute and think about something more important – like staying alive. That's what a real man does."

"So now I'm not a real man?"

"You have all the building blocks, Cael. But you're nineteen and you still think you're smarter than everyone else. I wasn't a real man at nineteen. I didn't have the first clue about what that meant. I was selfish, prideful and motivated by fear. I had a lot to learn – I just didn't know it yet."

"I'm different."

Ethan ignored the boast. "Cael, I can help you. Tell you what I've learned. But you have to be willing to listen."

"You just told me you know nothing about women."

"I'm talking about more than just women, Cael. I'm talking about life. I've lived twice as much life as you have. I know a few things."

"And I've had more action with the ladies in the last two years than you've had in the last fifteen," Cael bragged.

"Yeah, you win that round. But do you think I haven't had chances to live that kind of life? I made a choice a long time ago to live for something more than my cravings. I have a higher calling than temporary satisfaction."

"I guess you just think you're better than everybody else."

"No. I know I'm not. I know what kind of person I am. I faced myself in the mirror years ago and measured what I saw. I came up short in every category. You can ask Robbie. He was there for most of it. The first step in maturing is recognizing you're not who you're supposed to be in the first place."

"I like myself just fine."

"Then be prepared to be who you are right now for the rest of your life."

"Up yours, Ethan. You suck as a friend – and a wingman."

"I'm sorry, it's the best I can do."

"I'll walk by myself for a while." Cael dropped back behind Lauren and fell to almost fifty feet behind the rest of the group.

"Okay, Cael," Ethan called back to him. "Your choice. Nice talking to you."

Ethan drifted back toward Robbie. "Overheard some of your conversation. Sometimes he seems like he's grown up a bit and then he reminds us he's still a drug dealer who just got orphaned."

"I feel bad for him. I wish I knew how to help him."

"Ethan, you were doing better than you think. He needed to hear all of that. Truth hurts but it's the best fixer too."

"I've gotten my share of truth from you over the years."

"That you have my friend," Robbie said, slapping Ethan on the back. He turned to check on Lauren who was walking just behind them but she was no longer there.

"Ethan, where's Lauren?" They stopped in the road and quickly scanned both sides for any sign of movement or the cart she was pulling.

"Cael!" Ethan called out but heard nothing in response. "Lauren!" The night remained silent. "Robbie, we need to find them now."

"Do you remember when we were in the Philippines and we had to rescue those hostages that were being marched into the jungle?"

"You mean when we followed the rebels and silently kept removing the last person in line? That's not what's happening . . . you think that's what's happening?"

"I don't know but if we don't figure this out quick we will lose both of them."

"Too late." The new voice made Ethan and Robbie whirl around and found they were under the gun of a heavily bearded camo-clad man. "Your young friend is in my custody. She's a pretty girl. What are you doing out here in the middle of the night?"

Ethan knew he could drop this man in an instant but he had no idea where Cael and Lauren were. *Did he say friend? She? What about Cael?* There could also be watchers along the road making sure the man holding the gun was not assaulted. He knew God was with him and could feel His strength already. But he waited. He turned to Robbie and nodded, knowing he would do a better job talking. When Ethan was ready for action, he was not a good conversationalist.

"We're on our way north. We have family we're trying to get to."

"You know where you are right now?"

"Somewhere in Mississippi."

"Nope. Not anymore. You're in my jurisdiction. "

"Oh, so we're in crazy town then?" Ethan blurted out.

Robbie put a hand on Ethan's shoulder. "Ethan, stop."

"Sorry, couldn't help it."

The man ran his fingers across and down his thick mustache. "You're funny. But I'm not crazy. Since you're on my property it's my responsibility to make sure you're not here to hurt me and mine. Sort of a local immigration policy."

"We're on a state road. How is this your property?"

"Given to me in a land deal. But we can talk more about that back at camp." He nodded to his men and they walked to Robbie and Ethan, stripping them of their guns. They watched as their carts were wheeled off the road and onto a grassy two-track. Flashlights illuminated the area just in front of them. They resisted the urge to talk knowing that every set of ears around them would be listening in. Besides Brock, there were at least six other men, all heavily bearded, carrying rifles and sidearms, and in green digital camouflage.

The two-track wound through several fields, skirted a tree line and then sharply turned left into a tree lined clearing with five large pole barns, all with their main sliding front doors facing each other in a huge semi-circle. The barns had exterior lighting and behind them Ethan could see a long, two story building that looked like a miniature hotel. Several windows in it were lit.

"How do you have electricity? No one we've seen in the last six weeks has had electricity." Robbie wondered.

Brock ignored the question. "Take them to building four. I'll be there shortly."

Four of Brock's soldiers flanked Robbie and Ethan while walking them to one of the pole barns. Once inside, they passed through an open area where several SUV's were parked. On the far side of the structure, there was an interior room with a plate glass window facing the vehicles. Inside was a small desk, a round table circled with chairs, a bookcase, and two filing cabinets. Ethan and Robbie were seated at the table and one of their escorts stepped out for a moment and came back holding two steaming cups of black coffee.

Brock stepped in behind the coffee and sat behind the desk. "How long has it been boys? How long since you had coffee?"

Robbie continued in his role as mouthpiece for the duo. "A couple months. There's been too much going on to even think about it though. I appreciate the coffee but nothing caffeinated is going to distract us from the fact that you have someone we care about in your custody and you walked us here at gunpoint. To my knowledge, we've violated no laws and haven't harmed anyone close to you. I'd appreciate it if you'd just let our friend go and we'll be on our way." Robbie ended his plea with a sip from the Styrofoam cup.

Brock stared at Robbie for a moment, irritation written on his face. "You think you're being treated unfairly?"

"Right now, you're a kidnapper. You have no more authority to arrest us and detain us than a self-proclaimed warlord or gang leader. I don't know you. What gives you the right to do any of this?"

Ethan agreed with everything Robbie was saying but was uneasy that it was too aggressive too soon, which was ironic coming from Ethan.

Brock stood and leaned over the desk. "I'd say I have the right given the fact I'm sittin' across from a nigger and what looks to me like a Jew. Two people who deserve everythin' this country just got."

Ethan and Robbie were too stunned to say anything.

"People like you destroyed this country and I helped fix it. Enjoy that coffee cause it's the last luxury you're gonna have."

Robbie found his voice again. "You did this? The blackout, the EMP's?"

"That's the beautiful thing. I made a deal. I got what I wanted while the people behind this mess got what they wanted."

"Who? Who's behind this?"

"I'll educate you on that later. Why don't you tell me who you are? I like to know my enemy." Brock stepped back, crossed his arms and leaned against the wall.

"I have nothing to say. I want our friend released and then we'll be on our way."

"You don't get it. If I don't like how this conversation goes, I can make your last days on earth hellish. So, let's try again. Who are you, where are you going?"

Robbie looked at Ethan hoping for some direction. He raised his eyebrows and shrugged. "Him knowing who we are or where we're going doesn't matter. Finding our friend does." As bad as the situation seemed it was still not the worst they'd ever been in.

"My name is Robbie Charles. US Army retired. I have family in Louisville, Kentucky I'm trying to reunite with."

"U.S. Army? Well, well. Still can't believe they let you knuckle draggers into the service."

Robbie stiffened, resisting every urge to tear this man apart.

"That's right. Control yourself. Prove me wrong. If I had a dollar for every black man who tried show me up." Brock came off the wall and walked around the desk to stand over Robbie, as if daring him to react. "So you have family in Kentucky. Hope you said your goodbyes. Cause you're never leaving here. If I could clean this whole state of your filth I would do it in a heartbeat." Brock let this linger for a moment and then nodded to two of the men standing nearby. "Get him out of here. Put him in a hole. That's where he belongs."

Brock watched as Robbie was guided from the chair and out the office door. "Let's talk about you. He was doing the talking but I'm guessing you're the leader."

"My name is Ethan Zabad. I am also retired from the U.S. Army. I have family in Michigan. That's my only business in this county. Just passing through."

"Two retired army grunts. Just happen to be passing through here? If you're both retired then what are you doing now?"

"We help people." It was all Ethan felt comfortable saying but he knew it wouldn't satisfy Brock.

"Help them how? What are you? Aid workers? 'Aid workers' are usually just spies in disguise."

"I don't know anything about that."

Brock settled himself on the desk right next to Ethan and put a foot on the chair Robbie had recently vacated. "Right. Two retired soldiers doing aid work. Do you believe a word of that?" Brock directed the question to two of his lieutenants standing near the door.

"No, sir."

"They don't buy it either. Come on. Give me the rest of the story."

"I already told you. We go to places around the world and help people. We solve problems. Mainly people problems."

"Now we're getting somewhere. People problems, eh? What does that mean?"

Ethan looked Brock directly in the eye. "Problems like you."

Brock didn't respond right away but stared at Ethan, which felt less like a natural pause and more like an attempt at intimidation. Finally, he broke his intense stare. "Zabad, is it? Sounds Jewish to me. That sounds like a name right out of the Holy Scriptures." Brock stood and walked back to the desk chair. "So, you were in the army. You solve people problems. You're just an agent working for . . . a military contractor? Private corporation? Or some bureaucrat who had his own private military service?" Ethan didn't react to any of these suggestions. He'd been interrogated before.

"You know, it doesn't really matter. To me you're just a dirty Jew who's about to get what he deserves."

"I'm not the enemy."

"Oh, maybe not you personally. But your people. You and your friend out there. You represent everything that was wrong with America."

"America has never been perfect but it enabled people to live in relative peace and security. You destroyed that."

"It was a mercy killing. But the crazy thing is, this mess wasn't even my idea. I was promised a free hand here to run things as I please as long as I stayed out of their way."

"Then who is responsible? Who would do this?"

"You wouldn't believe me if I told you. I'm done with you. Take him out and put him in hole one." The conversation ended so abruptly and Ethan was moved out of the room so quickly he had no time to respond. He knew there was no prison they could put him in that would hold him. But he had to hold back on using his strength until the time was right – until they could locate Lauren and Cael. In spite of his confidence in the abilities God gave him, he was still worried about their whereabouts. Finding them and getting off this compound would be complicated.

Hole one turned out to be just that. A hole in the ground with an oak grid laid over the top. The hole was just deep enough that Ethan had to jump to touch the lid. It appeared that he was the first ever guest in hole one. It was hastily dug and was not lined with anything. On his way to the hole, with the benefit of ambient light, he glimpsed several similar grids in the ground not far away. He assumed Robbie was in one of them.

Ethan didn't handle tight spaces well. Holding back his strength and not escaping were going to be much harder than he originally thought. Claustrophobia was rising up in him. Ethan had the self-control to stay in a six-by-eight cell. He lived in one for years in the state penitentiary. But he would have to summon greater discipline to stay in a three-foot diameter hole in the ground. He said a silent prayer asking for God's peace. As he prayed his mind drifted, as it often did, to the task in front of him. Sometimes the answer to a problem would come while he was praying. After quickly asking God if it was His idea or Ethan's, he would say a quick 'amen' and get busy. This night, no answers seemed forthcoming.

Coming up with an escape plan without communication with Robbie would be difficult, especially if the plan had too many moving parts. He decided to check if Robbie was nearby. He called Robbie's name three times before he heard his deep, rich voice. "They told me, 'hole three'. Hole three? Really?"

"Hey Robbie, I'm not the most creative guy in the world but even I could've come up with a better name than that."

"You down there, shut up," a guard spat at Ethan.

"Hey, Ethan, we're hole neighbors!"

"Yeah, it's exciting."

"Both of you shut up."

"I'd say it's still a free country, but I think I'd be wrong."

"Keep talking and see what happens," a guard hissed.

Robbie couldn't resist the threat and was dying to see what would happen, so he recited the constitution. Just a few sentences into article one, a five gallon bucket of water was emptied into his hole. Another bucket was poured into Ethan's.

"Ah, you know I haven't had a shower since this crisis began. It didn't affect me much until I got trapped down here with my own stink so thank you – thank you for the shower." Robbie was prepared to poke the proverbial bear all night.

A second bucket was dumped into each hole.

"Robbie, I can appreciate what you're trying to do here but small spaces and water are not a good combo for me."

As much as Robbie wanted to continue the game with his captors, he loved his friend more. He fell silent and the water stopped. The rest of the night passed uneventfully. They were only able to sleep in snatches since they couldn't lay down and even curling up in the bottom of the hole meant they were in a few inches of muddy water. The morning dawned hot and muggy. The camp above came alive and they could hear trucks moving around. Ethan jumped and carefully grabbed the oak lid of his cell. Too much effort and it would splinter, giving away his incredible strength. He pulled himself up trying to catch a glimpse of his surroundings. At ground level, there was little to see. So he devoted his attention to listening. He listened for any voices that might be Lauren or Cael. He tried to discern where most of the vehicle and foot traffic came and went. He also had the snapshot in his mind of the camp layout that he glimpsed on his way to hole one.

Hours in the hole allowed he and Robbie time to think. Ethan wanted more than anything to grab Brock and hurl him as far as his strength would allow. He was personally responsible for the deaths of countless thousands and participated in the deaths of millions more. He treated it casually as if it were the reorganization of a local civic group. To what end? Ethan knew so many men like this. Cruel nonchalance, limited awareness of the cost of their actions, flamboyant disregard for moral standards and any kind of accountability. Ethan always believed in the inherent sin nature of mankind but after the work he did around the world, he knew some men were not just involved with evil – they were possessed by it. Like a random attacker on a school or church, these men lacked conscience and soul. Most called them crazy or psycho-pathic. Ethan called them demon-possessed.

Demon-possessed or not, the question remained – who was behind the attacks that shut down half the country? Brock was not taking responsibility and he was clearly a white-supremacist. He led a militia in the deep South and was prepared for a catastrophic event. A doomsday prep-ping, conspiracy theorizing neo-Nazi? Perhaps. There were always militia groups wanting to destroy democracy in the name of saving it. States' rights fanatics who believed the federal government was corrupt and overreaching, putting their hands in the pockets of average Americans to steal their livelihood. But if Brock and his ilk didn't orchestrate this attack who did? Who hated America that much? He continued to work through the problem with little progress.

No food was brought during the day. Ethan didn't even hear anyone walk close to his cell. He called out a couple times to Robbie but with all the other sounds he was hearing, he couldn't make out a response. The quietness of the night allowed their voices to carry.

Night fell and Ethan tried whispering to Robbie. This time he was able to respond. They exchanged no more than asking each other if they were okay when another bucket of water was dumped in each hole. Another wet, sleepless night went by while Ethan and Robbie spent the day listening. The hardest part for Ethan was knowing that he could leave his cell at any time. The only thing preventing his escape was what might happen to Lauren if they didn't leave with her. And they still had not located Cael. They couldn't risk leaving without either of them and so the only way was to stay put and wait for something to change.

The third night came and Ethan gleaned little by listening throughout the second day. He contemplated freeing himself and running for the dorm building behind the pole barns. If he could get inside unseen, he might be able to start his search there and eventually locate Lauren. Perhaps he could free her and send her to hide in the woods until he could get Robbie out. Every plan he envisioned he ultimately scrapped because of one variable. Cael. Until he knew where that kid was, he couldn't make a run for it. One second he was walking with the group and the next he disappeared.

Ethan looked up through the grid to the sky above to observe the stars. He didn't know what time at night it was but there weren't any sounds from the camp for quite a while.

From outside his cell he heard a crack, like a bat to a ball, and then the thump of something hitting the ground. A moment later the rattle of a chain, the clatter of wood and metal and Robbie's voice in a hoarse whisper. Then two faces appeared above Ethan's hole. Cael and Robbie.

"Well boss, you coming?" Robbie whispered.

"Yeah." Ethan jumped and grabbed the oak grid that formed the cell door. Planting his feet against the sides of the hole he pushed up and broke the door off completely. A hand on each side of the hole, he lifted himself out neatly. He saw the source of the thud. One of the guards was lying face down between holes one and two. "I've been waiting to do that for three nights. Where did you come from Cael?"

He hefted a two-inch thick stick of maple and said, "I'll tell you in a minute but right now we need to move. The next guard comes this way in about ten minutes."

"Lead the way." Ethan stole a quick, surprised glance at Robbie as if to ask, "can you believe what you're seeing?"

Cael set out quickly toward the tree line while Robbie and Ethan limped along behind. "Cael, a little slower. We haven't eaten and standing and laying in muddy water for forty-eight hours made our feet really tender."

"Oh, sorry. I didn't know that." He slowed a bit and led them to a stand of trees and scrub brush just beyond the group of pole barns. They stopped and Ethan and Robbie took the opportunity to lie flat on the ground and stretch out.

"We just need to lie here a minute. what happened to you?" Ethan asked. "When we were captured, you just disappeared."

"After we talked, I started walking real slow, just to make you mad. But while I was walking I heard voices – not you guys and Lauren, but men talking. I stopped walking and pulled my cart off the road. After a few minutes, I started walking again and that's when I saw the flashlights."

"And you didn't want to warn us because they would catch you too?"

"I figured if at least one of us was loose, we had an advantage. I hid my cart by the road and followed them here."

"Did you see what they did with Lauren?"

"No. At first they took her to the hive but then they moved her and I couldn't see where."

"The hive?"

"That's what I heard the guys calling that building with all the windows. The one like a hotel?"

"You mean for the last two days you've been sneaking around this place spying and listening to these guys?"

"Yeah. I have a couple good hiding spots. I walked back to my cart to eat and sleep a little and then came back to spy at night too."

Ethan was dumbfounded. He was glad for the darkness so Cael couldn't see the amazement on his face. "You did good work, Cael. Really good work. Man's work." Ethan stood up again and Robbie followed. "Let's get some more distance between us and this place so we can figure out how to get Lauren. I didn't see any other women here and I'm afraid of what they might do to her."

"I found a trail from here to where I left the cart. At least we have some supplies. Your carts got pulled into one of the barns." Cael darted back further into the trees and then into a clearing. He skirted the edge of it and headed south to another stand of trees. And then they were back on the road. He led them across the road, through a gap in a wire fence and down a slope to a copse of flowering bushes. The cart was under the brush and was barely visible, even with the moon shining brightly. They pulled some food and water from the cart and with the bushes as a shield, built a small fire with the driest fuel they could find to minimize smoke.

They ate and drank slowly, knowing that to wolf the food down would make them sick after fasting for two days. When they'd eaten and started drying their clothes and feet, they discussed a plan to find Lauren and get off the compound before they were discovered.

Robbie was the first to speak. "Our weapons are no longer an option. They took them at the road and I never saw where they went."

Ethan looked at Cael hoping he had information on their weapons. Cael shrugged. "By the time I followed the flashlights, your weapons were gone."

Ethan swatted the ground with a small stick he picked up off the ground. "One of those pole barns is bound to have weapons inside. We just need a way to search the grounds without drawing attention."

"Has to be at night, Ethan," Robbie reminded him.

"Yeah, but by now they've found the guard he took out and they'll know we're on foot, running."

"What're you thinking?"

"There's no sense in all of us risking capture. I'll go in tomorrow night and look for weapons – anything we can use. If I'm successful we go back the next night and check the Hive first and then whatever other buildings are on the property."

"And if you get caught Ethan, we're back to square one. Let's all go. If we can help each other maybe we can do this all in one night."

"It would be nice to have a few sets of eyes. But Cael was our ace in the hole the first time. Don't you think we need to keep something or someone in reserve?"

Cael spoke up. "Don't I get a say in this?"

Ethan started shaking his head no but Robbie spoke. "I think you've earned it, coming to get us like that. What do you want to do?"

"I want to come with. I know the layout and they've never seen me. For all they know I'm just some hungry kid looking for food."

"He's got a point," Robbie offered.

"Okay, you can come but you do whatever I tell you. No going rogue or trying to be a hero."

"Yes, sir."

"Alright," said Ethan, suspicious that Cael was mocking him. "Let's get some sleep and we can plan our attack in the morning." They kicked dirt on the fire, laid down in the grass and slept like dead men.

NINETEEN

The mayor called the meeting. She recruited a dozen men and women to spread the word both at the river for several mornings and in some of the neighborhoods furthest from downtown. After almost two months of no word from any authority, David saw this as a feeble attempt to make some show of action. After all, if the power came back on tomorrow, the mayor wanted the residents to say that she did everything she could in a time of crisis. With the growing number of fresh graves being dug all over town and the increasing quantity of abandoned houses, David wasn't sure how many people would actually show up for a meeting. What could the city possibly offer now? He determined to go purely out of curiosity. He made sure he went armed. Traveling with protection was now possible after his last trip with Lenny.

Lenny biked to David's house a few days after the attack on Melinda and urged him to grab his tractor and follow along. David was using the tractor less, all the time trying to conserve what little fuel he had left. He rode his bike instead and determined that as soon as the weather turned, he would spend the winter converting bike parts into what David decided to call a "human pickup truck". The tractor was a wonderful tool for now but would eventually be useless without gas. David planned to convert the trailer into something he could easily tow behind his bike. It would work even better if he could fix it so Liz could provide leg power as well and let Hannah ride in the back. He hadn't quite worked that out in his mind yet. There was still too much to do each day simply to survive.

When Lenny arrived and told David to follow, he did not tell him they were biking almost ten miles. Had he known, he would have eaten more for breakfast than a handful of beans and some water. The trip proved to be worthwhile. Lenny led him to a house on a lakefront that had to be over six thousand square feet. It was well appointed inside with an almost three-story river-rock fireplace and chimney at its center. Lush furnishings and an immaculate sitting room and den made David want to sit and rest awhile. The den boasted three walls of bookshelves filled from floor to ceiling. David quickly perused the titles and on just one shelf spotted at least five books he would love to read. Unfortunately, space to carry things home was limited and he needed to reserve room for the essentials. Books would have to wait.

"Hey, do you wanna read or get something that's actually important?" Lenny urged.

"Sorry, I just haven't had time to read. I love books," David said slowly as he tore himself from the bookshelf, still reading titles to himself.

"Love moving faster, okay? That's what I want you to

love. I get in. I get out. Every time I show you a house, you slow me down."

David was used to Lenny's abrasive but somehow still humorous manner. It was true though. Lenny brought David to several houses since they met and each time David was fascinated with walking through another person's home. Things looked the way they had when the residents left. Like his own neighbors, people left with a few things but mostly just what they could carry with them. Homes all over the country were being left, fully furnished, some with food still in the cupboards. Some of the food left behind was not what you would make a meal of but still, it was nourishment. David filled one side of his garage with things like fifty cent corn muffin mixes, bags of uncooked, dry pinto beans, boxed milk and other charitable food pantry staples that people usually left behind. It was hard to fathom being picky during a crisis but to a nation of citizens who were used to having whatever they wanted, when they wanted it, some were slow to realize just how desperate their predicament was. Some never realized until it was too late and died with food still in their cupboards - not necessarily from starvation but from causes that a strong, healthy body would normally be able to defend against.

David was following Lenny through the vast mansion, glancing into the bedrooms and down each hallway. They stopped in the master bedroom which looked as big as David's entire second floor. Lenny led him over to the separate dressing room which was lined with men's and women's shoes and clothes. He reached behind a rack of shirts and grasped something and suddenly the trio of mirrors at the far end of the room rotated revealing a secret room. David heard of wealthy homeowners installing secret rooms to hide their treasures or simply for whimsy's sake but never saw one.

"There you go! Told ya I'd find ya somethin' good." Lenny stepped back, with his chest thrust out. It was a proud moment for him but David still didn't know why until he saw the gun safe tucked inside the wall of the secret room. It was open and lined with pistols. David picked three pistols, one a forty-five caliber M-1911, a .22 Sig Sauer and a Glock 34. The gun owner was clearly a person of means and a student of effective defensive firearms. He wondered what the homeowner took if these three were left behind. There were also some rifles in the hidden room but David did not have the capacity to carry them home. He decided to come back later with Lenny and his tractor so he could fully unload the contents. They closed the safe and the room so no one would find it before they came back.

That trip with Lenny was just a few days ago. David made his way the five blocks to downtown for the mayor's meeting armed with one of those pistols. Exploring abandoned homes became a pastime with Lenny but they had never came across such a jackpot. David looked forward to going back to retrieve the rest of the arsenal.

When he arrived at city hall, he was unimpressed with the turnout. In a city of roughly twelve thousand people, perhaps one hundred showed. It might have been due to the early hour of the meeting, but if people were leaving the city at the rate they left the neighborhood there just might not be that many around. With fewer residents, word of the meeting may not have been efficiently communicated.

The mayor, elected to office for the first time the previous November, emerged from the city building with several people, two of whom David recognized as council members. She mounted the steps of the gazebo that graced the center of the town's main park, overlooking the mill pond and river. She looked as tired and unwashed as the rest of the residents.

"Good morning everyone. As many of you know, a helicopter landed here in town over a week ago. Until hearing firsthand what was going on around the country, I was hesitant to call you together. But now I've been given a message from the United States government. The good news is that relief efforts have begun. The crisis has affected all of the United States from Maine to Florida and from the East Coast to just past the Mississippi River. Sections of the West are affected like Texas and the northwestern states. The southernmost parts of Canada's provinces have also been impacted. So the relief efforts have begun in the areas bordering unaffected territory. The bad news is that we are seven to eight hundred miles in either direction from relief zones. It will be some time before any authority arrives with help."

"How long?" A voice shouted from the small crowd.

"I wasn't told. The exact words of the officer I spoke with were, 'Do the best you can to hold on.' No timeline or even a hint of any kind. Just the promise that help would eventually come. I think as a community, we need to brace ourselves for at least this winter and perhaps another. As you know, our city council is typically made up of seven citizens but with the crisis, three have left to try and reconnect with family across the country while two have succumbed to deprivation and illness. Let's observe a moment of silence for them and for those in our city that have died since the crisis began."

David glanced around during the moment of silence to

see how people were responding to the mayor's speech. Few bowed their heads and many bore hardened, haggard faces reflecting the hardships of the last two months.

"Thank you," the mayor continued after twenty or so seconds. "We are certain that if we come together as a community we can survive the difficulties that are coming."

A voice called out, "Too little, too late, Mayor." Other voices echoed this cry and the crowd grew restless.

"I know that nothing has been organized yet but we knew as much as you did at the beginning. We were waiting for more information – confirmation that the crisis was as widespread as we feared."

"What do you know that we don't know?" The crowd approved of this anonymously shouted question and murmured their agreement.

"The officer I spoke to said it is believed that this crisis is the result of a coordinated terrorist attack. No one has claimed responsibility. The United States government is still functioning from an undisclosed location. I was asked to carry the message to smaller, nearby communities. We are responsible for organizing our own relief efforts to the best of our ability. This means we will need to consolidate our food supplies, coordinate water retrieval, preparation and usage and begin laying up what we will need to make it through a winter. I hope everyone here will tell their neighbors about our efforts and be willing to work together for the good of our city. Our first planning meeting will be held four days from now, right here in the park. That should be sufficient time to get the word out. Anyone is welcome and please, bring ideas for helping our community survive. That's all I can tell you at this time. As information becomes available I will be sure to let you know. Thanks for coming."

There was little conversation as the meeting broke up. Most of the people David saw looked like he knew he must look – weary, burdened and uncertain of their future. He shuffled home to Liz and Hannah, wondering how to break the bad news that their nightmare had only begun.

TWENTY

East of Vicksburg, Mississippi

"But if we split up we have no one watching each other's back."

"You have to admit, I know how to hide. I snuck up on you in Corpus," Cael argued.

"Cael, these are sound military tactics. We function in squads. We don't fight like Rambo."

"Who?"

"Rambo, the movie? Sylvester Stallone? One man army?"

"Sounds cool," he shrugged.

"I keep forgetting how young he is," Ethan said to Robbie.

"You mean how old *you* are."

"Whatever. So we start with the westernmost pole barn. It's the least guarded, correct?"

255

"I only saw a couple guys even go in there. Everyone was in the first two though."

"That's good work, Cael. I'm really impressed. We were inside the first one. We know there's vehicles in there. It wouldn't hurt to have one of those."

"One thing at a time, Ethan. Now, we check the unguarded pole barn and if we find firearms we move directly to the Hive. If not, we move to the next building. We continue until we find weapons or we're made. In that case, we'll have to fight our way out until we can try again. But we're not leaving without Lauren, right?"

"Right. I think we should pull our remaining supply cart to the north side of the compound. They'll expect us to go back toward the road. Maybe we can throw them off by heading north instead and trying to catch some back roads."

"They won't let her go without a fight."

"But that's what we're bringing. Let's get some more rest and we'll plan on moving after midnight."

———

The moon was not full but it was bright when it wasn't obscured by clouds. They moved carefully across the clearing and into the trees lining it. Cael concealed the cart behind a few closely growing trees and shielded it with some fallen branches. They took note of their surroundings so they would know how to find the cart again. They each found a sturdy stick to use as a weapon until they could get their guns back. Ethan hated going in at such a disadvantage but he knew that God was with them and would help. He'd never been in a situation yet where God didn't show up.

They crouched in the trees not far from where they hid the night before, during their escape. From the small stand of trees they had a good view of the pole barns. One variable they did not have sorted was how many people were actually on the compound. If they were identified and targeted, how many guns would be pointed at them?

Cael led them across a gap between the tree line and the first pole barn. They crept along the wall until they reached a single door in the back corner. Cael and Robbie went just around the corner out of sight while Ethan carefully opened the door. The inside was dimly lit. He walked along the outer wall and scanned the room. It appeared there was a single bulb hanging from the rafters. The barn contained dozens of 250-gallon watering troughs, a stack of baled straw, and a blue tractor. Nothing that would help. Ethan went out and shut the door behind him and found the others. He reported his findings and they moved on to the next building.

At the rear corner of this building, Ethan noticed a worn spot where boots stopped to unlock the door and the paint on the jamb was slightly chipped. Again, Ethan checked the door with the others behind him. This door was locked so Ethan bore down on the knob twisting it right off. The knob on the inside fell and clattered to the floor. He winced at the sound, hoping it wasn't as loud as it seemed. He waited ten seconds and hearing no response, pushed the door open all the way. This barn too, was lit by a single bulb. As Ethan skirted the edge of the room he saw a promising sign. On the wall opposite the door was a row of safes. He could not read the labels but he hoped they were gun safes. He crossed the room and grasped the handle of the first safe. Not bothering to try and crack the code he pulled on the three spindled handle and wrenched it from the door. Being able to perform such feats of strength never ceased to amaze him. It was a gift he never took for granted.

When you know what you're born to do, you simply do it. When you know what you're born to do and it comes from God, you never forget to be thankful.

After destroying the handle and manually pulling back the locking mechanism, Ethan opened the safe and found the jackpot. The safe was loaded with rifles across the back, seven pistols sat upright in stands on an upper shelf and the door itself sported several more. He ran back to the door and waved Cael and Robbie inside. They each grabbed two pistols. Ethan and Robbie also chose a rifle. Ammunition was in a smaller, locked box at the bottom of the safe. He made short work of the lock and they loaded up.

"Why don't I get a rifle?"

"Because you're not here to be a sharpshooter, Cael. You're here to provide cover fire and when the time comes, to get Lauren."

"I can aim and shoot."

"I'm sure you can. When you've got nothing but time and there's no pressure. I need you to shoot those pistols where I tell you and keep reloading until the ammo is gone."

"Robbie, don't you think I can shoot?"

"You've proven your worth beyond my expectations. Don't take a step backward by complaining. Ethan is the boss on this and if he says stick with the pistols and don't be a hero, then I suggest you do it."

"I've proven my worth?"

"Yeah, you did a great job getting us this far. Don't let it go to your head."

"Alright guys. Sorry to interrupt the conversation but let's get out of this building and see if we can make our way further north toward the hive."

"You're not gonna check the other buildings?" Cael asked.

"The longer we search these buildings, the greater the risk of discovery. One thing you'll learn Cael is that things can change in seconds. You never get comfortable and you never make assumptions about your enemy."

"What about the barn that has the cars in it? We could get one of those SUV's!"

"We could. After we found the keys, opened the barn doors, gathered up our supplies from each cart - that we still haven't found - loaded them up and drive off the compound. So yes, we could, but there are too many variables. If it becomes available, I'll consider it. Now let's get moving. I don't want to be out here at daybreak."

They left the building and entered the trees that surrounded the pole barn clearing. After a short walk through the trees, the Hive became visible. There were still lights on in the hive. A man was guarding the door closest to them. Up close, it looked like they copied the design and floor plan of a Hampton Inn. There were even square pillars out front with a roof over them and an automatic sliding glass door. The single guard was not at attention or doing much guarding.

"I bet we could distract him. Get him away from the door," Cael suggested.

"I'm sure we could. But what we need right now is information. Even if we got inside we'd have to check every room to see if Lauren was inside."

"So . . ."

"So," Robbie explained, "you get to distract him while we apprehend him – quietly. We get him someplace quiet and get him talking."

"And if he doesn't talk?"

"We go room to room."

Cael walked out of the trees toward the front door of

the Hive and the guard immediately noticed him. He lifted his rifle and aimed it at Cael. "Stop! Right there. Identify yourself."

"I'm just coming back to sleep."

"I've never seen you." He steadied the rifle with his trigger hand and used the other to reach up to the radio he clipped to his shoulder. His hand never made it as Ethan swiftly moved up behind him, bent his hand down behind his back and snatched the gun out of his other hand. The guard tried to turn around but a sharp knife-like blow from Ethan's open hand brought his to his knees.

"Don't fight me. I only have one question. We're looking for a girl named Lauren. Brown hair, blue eyes, about five-foot-three."

"Haven't seen her."

Ethan twisted the arm harder and higher behind his back. The guard cried out in pain and Ethan silenced him with another chop to the throat. "Can't have you getting any friends involved. Now where is Lauren?"

"Never heard of her," the guard managed to choke out.

"Wrong answer." Ethan lifted him off the ground by the back of his shirt. "This can get worse or it can stop. Where's Lauren?"

"I told you, I don't—" Ethan let go of him and the guard dropped and went to his knees. He yelled, "Help, I need—" But Ethan stopped him with a blow to the jaw. He spun the guard around, put a hand over his mouth and pulled him so close he could smell his stink.

"You're gonna tell me where Lauren is or the last scenic view you're going to see is what this compound looks like from forty feet in the air."

"You're bluffing."

Ethan tossed the man into the air. Not forty feet but

high enough that the man's feet were at Ethan's eye level. The second the guard hit the ground he spat out "one, four, seven" over and over. "Good, thank you. Robbie?"

Robbie walked over and bound the man's wrists and ankles and then gagged him, dragging him inside the Hive and placing him in a storage closet along the main hallway. The inside of the Hive was not decorated. It was bare walls and concrete floors but it was almost certainly a hotel floor plan. They moved toward the hall that led to their right and saw a door marked with numbers. Before stepping fully into the hall Robbie glanced around the corner and spotted a man standing guard four doors down. He gestured this to Ethan who, after nodding his understanding, backed up to the far side of the lobby. He sprinted across the lobby and entered the hallway at top speed.

Surprise, speed and sleepiness all worked for him and by the time the guard was aware of Ethan's attack there was no time for him to bring his weapon around or to utter a warning. The tackle sent him sprawling and before he could rise, Ethan struck the guard with a knockout blow. He dragged the unconscious man back in front of the door he was guarding and propped him against the wall. The belief he was sleeping might buy them precious seconds if anyone came looking. Standing in front of 147, Ethan knocked gently. Robbie and Cael flanked the doorway not knowing what to expect. Other doors in the Hive could open at any minute, exposing their intrusion. It was well after midnight but there was no way to know who was behind all these doors. The door to 147 slowly opened and Ethan saw Lauren's face peeking out. She squealed and came through the doorway to hug him.

"I can't believe you're here! I didn't know what happened to you guys." She stepped back through the door into the room and out of the way, waving for them to come inside.

"Long story, but we were stuck in the mud for a few days."

"Huh?"

"Never mind." Ethan entered and took a look around the room, seeing that it had a bed, a dresser, and a bathroom. One window in the room faced away from the main compound. "Have you been treated okay?"

"Yeah, I guess so. They mostly left me alone but I wasn't allowed to leave the room. There's no TV or books and I can't see much out the window. But I had my first hot shower in a couple months. I even washed my clothes in the sink."

"You need to gather whatever you've got in here and get ready to move. We escaped last night and they'll be looking for us." Lauren entered the bathroom to collect her things.

"Aren't you surprised we found her so easily? They had to know we'd be coming for her." Robbie, for the first time, seemed uneasy.

"You know how it is, Robbie. We think everything through, forwards, backwards, and upside down. We're always a step ahead of the enemy. That's how we've survived. Cael, help Lauren get – where's Cael?"

"I thought he followed us into the room."

"He was in the hall but I don't remember seeing him actually come in."

"We think it all through right? Do we have a plan for what to do if someone in our group goes rogue?"

"Not a good time, Robbie. Check the hall. Maybe he's standing guard."

"Nope," Robbie said after looking into the hall. "I think he must've slipped away when we came into the room."

"What is he thinking?" Ethan paced across the room.

Lauren emerged carrying the few items she came with. "I'm ready. What are we doing about Cael?"

"I think I know what he's doing. He wants a vehicle. He wouldn't stop talking about it last night or on the way over here."

"We could be on our way back to the cart and headed north again." Robbie was aggravated but trying to keep his cool.

"Robbie, I made myself very clear. He knows getting a vehicle is near impossible – not without risking our lives."

"We have to stop him. If he gets captured trying to steal a car, we're right back at square one. I really thought he had turned a corner."

"He turned three corners and ended up back where he started. I want to get moving. I don't have time to deal with this Brock character."

"I have family to see too, Ethan. I say we grab Cael and get out of here. Do you remember where the cars are?"

"They were in the barn we entered that first night," Ethan recalled.

"Alright, then let's send Lauren to where we hid the cart and we can get Cael." Robbie headed toward the door.

"I'm not walking out into the woods by myself! I'm staying with you guys."

"It'll be dangerous, Lauren. It's for your own safety."

"For my own safety I'm staying with you."

Ethan almost doubled down on his plan but realized his fight was with Brock and his crew. "We don't have time to argue. Stay behind us, especially him," Ethan ordered pointing at Robbie. "We're going to move fast so you need to keep up. Have you eaten anything?"

"They brought me two meals each day. Small, but it was something."

"Okay, we can't have you fainting while we're at a dead run. Everyone ready?" With nods from Robbie and Lauren they exited the room and headed for the main exit. As they came around the corner into the lobby, they saw a group of camo-clad men with automatic weapons leveled at them. Ethan turned and pushed Robbie and Lauren back into the hallway and they ran back toward Lauren's room just as gunfire exploded behind them. Ethan unholstered the pistol he'd selected earlier and fired a few shots back at the group but they were still concealed by the corner.

"That just ruined my day," Ethan spat.

"We just need another way out. No problem," Robbie said as he walked to the window and pulled the curtains. "Turn out the lights, Lauren."

She did this as Ethan reasoned things out. "They know we're in here. They'll have every exit covered. Do you think they found Cael? Maybe he talked, told them where we were."

"I doubt it, Ethan. I think they must've already known we were here. It's only been a couple minutes since we realized he was gone."

Ethan fought the urge to blame the current situation on Cael, even though he knew it was no one's fault. As he'd said many times over the years, *it is what it is*. He hated it when people said it to him because it sounded so flippant, yet it was the best description of reality and the fact that there was no way to deal with it other than go through. "Okay, so do we go to the end of the hall, out a window, fight our way out the front door?"

"The window won't work, they'll be outside. Front door is covered."

"You're not helping, Bob." Robbie hated when Ethan used that nickname.

"Come on, Ethan, we haven't lived this long by always thinking inside the box. What else?"

Robbie was a partner and friend for all these years and was always able to draw out the best in him. Ethan always wanted to answer the call, to be the person he knew he could be. Tonight, all he wanted was to run for it and get to his son, daughter-in-law, and granddaughter as fast as he could. Fifteen years, he did all he could to help. Answered every plea for aid. Walked into more dangerous situations than he could now count. He was tired, frustrated, and at the moment wanted Robbie to make the decision.

"Ethan! We have no time!" Robbie urged again.

A voice came from the lobby area of the Hive. "There's no way out. Just come out with your hands up. There's no use getting anyone hurt."

"Get down against that wall," Ethan ordered, gesturing to the corner behind the bed. In frustration, Ethan grabbed the dresser on the wall opposite the bed and heaved it through the window. The breaking glass and broken window frame flew out and scattered across the ground. They heard shouts and footsteps outside and then automatic weapons lit up the opening. Ethan grabbed the queen size mattress and leaned against the window, momentarily muffling the gunshots. He stepped to the wall where the bed was, pulled it away from the wall and punched a hole through the wall. He kicked away drywall on both sides of the hole and made it big enough to step through. Thankfully, no one was occupying the room next door.

"After you," he gestured to Robbie and Lauren. They squirmed through the hole he made and then Ethan stepped through, reached back and from the next room, pulled the bed back in front of the hole in the wall, the headboard just covering the damage. "That should buy us a few minutes." They exited the room just in time as they heard the door to Lauren's room slam open and shouted orders given to search the room and the area just outside.

Ethan waved them close so he could whisper. "It's a risk but I think we should go out the main entrance. Some of these guys are outside searching, some are next door. We might be able to get to the trees."

"What about Cael?" Lauren pleaded.

"If we can hit the trees it will buy us time to circle back to the barns under cover. But our first priority is getting out of here. Ready?" With a nod from Lauren, Ethan stepped to the door leading to the hallway. He gently opened it, expecting to see a weapon aimed at his head or a group of counterfeit-soldiers waiting for him. Instead, the hallway was empty except for a single man standing in the hallway. Ethan moved quickly, clamping one hand over the mouth of the hall guard and the other around his waist, as he picked the man up and carried him to the front entrance. Robbie and Lauren followed closely, with Robbie making sure she was right behind him at all times. They quietly made their way to the main entrance. Before Ethan checked around the corner to see the front door, he struck a sharp blow to the man's neck rendering him unconscious. There was one fake soldier at the door, a young one judging by the pimpled face and lack of stubble on his chin. Ethan dropped the unconscious man to the floor and boldly walked around the corner, immediately drawing the attention of the young man who brought his rifle to his shoulder. "Hold it right there or I'll shoot."

Ethan never broke his stride. He walked right up to the boy, reached up, and bent the tip of his rifle barrel into an

"L" shape. "Don't pull that trigger, son." Robbie and Lauren hurried out the front door behind Ethan, leaving the young man speechless. They only went a few steps however, before he found his voice again and yelled for help, screaming out the direction they fled.

They sprinted for the trees in the direction of the barns, every second hoping they would overtake Cael and be able to head for safety. Once into the trees northwest of the compound, they could hear semi-automatic weapon fire open up in their direction. Bullets whipped and slapped leaves and branches overhead. Several bullets smacked into trees, throwing splinters everywhere and forcing the trio to duck involuntarily. They pressed on through the trees, keeping the light from the barns visible to their right. Then, as quickly as they'd made their escape, the trees abruptly ended. Ethan thought the cover extended all the way to the east of the compound but now they were looking at a clearing. They trapped themselves in a small stand of trees that would be their grave by morning unless they could figure something out. Ethan thought about making a run for it and finding cover as they went but in the dark, not knowing the terrain as well as he'd like, was suicide. Gunfire opened up on them from the clearing, immediately ending that idea, bad as it was. They pushed back into the trees and crouched down to discuss options.

"Ethan, that first pole barn is not far. I can see the light from it. We could head that way and see if Cael is inside."

"We could. My fear is that there's a distance between these trees and the barn that leaves us vulnerable."

"Don't know unless we try."

"Alright, let's go." They moved away from the edge of the clearing and toward the barn.

More shouts and Ethan knew they were being

surrounded. But they heard a new sound too: An engine revving.

They weren't the only ones to hear it, as several of their pursuers headed in the direction of the sound, the first pole barn. "We're not out of danger yet. That might be Cael, but it might be Brock."

"Lord, let it be Cael," Robbie whispered.

They tried to see through the trees ahead, if headlights were visible or the red of tail lights. If a vehicle was moving, it was at the front of the barn and not visible from where Ethan was. But they received confirmation in the form of gunfire as the vehicle became a target for every fake soldier on the compound. They heard the engine rev hard and the spit of dirt and rocks hit the side of the metal building. The engine was loud at first and then faded telling them he was moving in the opposite direction.

"That's got to be Cael. He's probably headed to our rendezvous, Ethan."

"That means we need to get there too."

It seemed that a stolen vehicle was more important than three fugitives. Once they headed toward their rendezvous point where their remaining cart was hidden, their pursuers melted away and ran in the direction of the car. Whoever made up Brock's army were not well trained. There should have been squad leaders and someone giving orders which made Ethan wonder where Brock was. It looked to Ethan like a group of preschoolers playing soccer – a herd following the ball wherever it rolled. Not that he was complaining. It gave them the break they needed. Whatever this militia was supposed to be, it was not prepared to face an actual, well-trained military force. The break they needed was the ability to move without fear of getting shot at. That freedom lasted until they neared the vicinity of their cache.

They made their way west to the group of trees where they stashed the carts. Most of the way they stayed under cover, only occasionally having to cross openings in the trees or small two-track paths. It was getting close to sunrise. Ethan guessed it to be close to five. They would soon lose any help from the darkness.

As they neared the cache there was no sign of the vehicle but they could hear footsteps around them, cracking fallen branches and leaves and occasionally a whisper. With only two groups running around in the woods they knew they managed to run right into the perimeter Brock's men formed. Ethan pulled Robbie close and as quietly as possible, told him to go north around the men. Cael might have wrecked the car, grabbed the cart and left, or just stopped long enough to see if his friends were there before driving off again. He was so unpredictable Ethan could not guess where he might be.

Robbie moved silently through the trees, trying to keep Ethan to his left at about his six or seven o'clock. There were few landmarks Robbie recognized. Everything they did in preparation for finding Lauren was done quickly. The lack of rest and food were making he and Ethan sloppy.

He pressed on through the trees trying to be as quiet as possible. Occasionally he would hear a yell from his left or a gun would fire, probably one of the younger men under Brock's command shooting at shadows. The men who initially captured them must have been the best Brock had. It was early morning and Robbie could hear birds singing in the distance though they stopped momentarily whenever a gun went off.

He was tiring much more quickly than normal. His

steps were plodding and even in the early morning, was sweating heavily. His recovery time was not what it used to be. He stopped to lean against a tree to catch his breath and take another hard look around. He started his 360-degree scan at the tree he was using for a prop and before he could begin rotating his gaze, realized he was staring at the right rear quarter panel of an SUV. He turned to move around the tree to the front of the vehicle when the click of a pistol stopped him short.

"Hold it right there."

The dark prevented him from making out the face. But that voice. "Wait a minute. Is that you, Green Stuff?"

"Robbie? You found me! Where's Lauren? Where's Ethan?"

"Shh, shh. Back that way a couple hundred yards. I'll go get them. Nice job hiding the car by the way." Cael parked next to the tree and then using fallen branches and fresh leaves, completely camouflaged the back of the car. In the dark, at a distance it looked like a blob of vegetation. Robbie didn't have far to go since Ethan and Lauren already started making their way toward him.

Robbie was surprised to see them. "I was coming back. What happened?"

"More of them coming. They started filling in around us. We had to almost walk between a few of them to get here. Any longer they would have spotted us. Sun is starting to come up."

Robbie noticed that it had indeed gotten lighter and a foggy mist was rising to greet the morning. "Lauren, you okay?"

"I'm fine. Let's just go."

They arrived at the car where Cael was already loading the contents of the cart in along with the cart. Ethan noticed in the back of the SUV another of the carts that was confiscated.

"Cael, how did you get that other handcart and the supplies?"

"They were in the same barn as this vehicle." Cael tossed in a few packages of meals-ready-to-eat.

"But how did you get the vehicle? I mean, this is amazing."

"Didn't think I had it in me, eh?"

Ethan threw in a vacuum-sealed bag of beef jerky. "I'm gonna be honest and say, no – no I didn't think you had it in you. And I don't know whether to be upset that you ignored my direct wishes and smack you, or kiss you for getting us this car."

"Are those my only two choices?"

"How about I just shake your hand?" Ethan suggested. Cael jumped down out of the vehicle where he'd been arranging things and extended his hand to Ethan who shook it firmly. "Good work. Now let's get out of here. Everyone ready?" Ethan no sooner uttered these words when gunshots erupted from behind them. Shadowy shapes were coming through the trees. "Get in!" Ethan jumped in the driver's seat and turned the engine over. It smoothly hummed alive and Cael got shotgun. Lauren was in the back seat with her head down. "Robbie! Let's go."

"I just have to shut the hatch!" The rear door slammed shut, Robbie got in and Ethan put his foot to the floor. Dirt and grass spun from under the tires, clattering against the bottom of the car as it found traction and sped away from the tree. Sharp clangs and pops were heard all around them as the Brock's men opened fire on the vehicle.

"Turn off the headlights!"

"What?"

"Turn off the headlights," Cael demanded.

"I think they stay on automatically." Ethan was frantic, trying to steer the car through the trees to the clearing beyond. Cael reached across, pushed a button and the lights went out.

"I smashed out the tail lights so we could get away without them seeing."

"That's brilliant, Cael. Nicely done."

"Uh, Ethan, I need your help," Lauren said shakily from the backseat.

"What is it, Lauren?"

"Robbie's bleeding. Bad."

"What? From where?"

"I'm not sure, but there's a lot."

"Cael, take the wheel." Ethan gave the SUV some gas and then wiggled out from behind the wheel to crawl into the back seat while Cael squirmed into the driver's seat. It wasn't pretty but the car didn't slow down much at all, even as it bounced over the brush and undergrowth beneath the canopy. The gunshots were still audible but they were finally gaining some distance between themselves and Brock's army. Lauren slid over the backseat into the cargo area with the carts and supplies. It was uncomfortable but, under the circumstances, the only way she could give Ethan the space he needed.

Ethan landed in the back seat to find Robbie passed out, his head bouncing against the window. "Robbie! Robbie, wake up. I need you to talk to me! Cael, turn on the interior light, right now."

The interior dome light came on and Ethan was able to see the blood that was spilling from Robbie's leg from the time he entered the vehicle. He must have been hit when he closed the rear door but didn't want to distract from their getaway. "Lauren, grab the first aid kit." Ethan stripped off his shirt and tore a thin strip of it from around the bottom. With this makeshift tourniquet he wrapped Robbie's leg and tied it tight.

Cael spotted a gap in the trees and shot through it, bouncing out into a field. He turned the lights on for a moment just to get better visibility in the mist that coated the field. "Lauren, can you grab our maps too?"

"I'm trying!" She found the first aid kit, handed it to Ethan and went back to the pack she was digging in to find one of the maps they'd collected back in Shreveport.

"Map!" Cael yelled from the front seat.

"Give me a second!" Lauren slid over the back seat again and carefully crawled over Ethan and Robbie to flop into the front seat. She quickly opened the map and tried to figure out where they were as they bounced along.

"I need a road and I need it now. I can't do anything with this leg until we're not bouncing like a basketball."

"Found it!" Lauren shouted. "Keep going and veer a little to the left."

"Are you sure?"

"Yes, I'm sure," Lauren said as a rear tire slammed down into a rut, throwing her sideways.

"But how do you know?"

"Because." another bump tossed her the other way. "Cael, do you remember what road we were on when we got captured?"

"No."

"Well, I do. So I know where we are and where we need to go!"

"Cael I need that road now," Ethan urged.

"Almost there." They hit another massive dip which sent them all flying into the ceiling. Ethan made sure his hand was on Robbie so his head didn't slam into the window again. The back wheels dropped into the same hole and rocked them all again but they managed to get onto the road they sought.

"I thought you said to veer a little to the left!" Cael complained.

"You didn't even believe I knew where the road was and now you're mad because I didn't veer you properly?"

"Lauren, you navigate and Cael – just drive. Leave the light on. I have to see if I can find the bullet and the source of the bleeding."

"We've got a full tank so take all the time you need."

Ethan prayed while he worked on his best friend. "God, this is not how Robbie's story ends. It can't be. He has family waiting for him in Kentucky. Don't do this. Don't allow this. You can bring good out of any circumstance but I am asking you to change this circumstance. I am asking you for a miracle." Ethan worked and prayed for over thirty minutes. Robbie remained unconscious. As they drove, the sun rose to their right and as Cael adjusted their route it eventually was shining directly in their eyes. By midday, they were heading north by northeast. Other than Ethan praying and crying, no one spoke. The road was mostly clear, with Cael only occasionally switching lanes to avoid a stopped vehicle. This enabled them to drive at normal speeds. They rode for almost five hours in silence until Cael reported the gas situation. They all heard the chime indicating the car was low on fuel.

"Drive until it's dry Cael."

"How is he?"

"Still unconscious. The bleeding is stopped but he lost a lot of blood. And I'm not sure how we can move him."

"We just passed a sign. It said ninety miles to Chattanooga."

"Just get us as far as you can." Ethan adjusted Robbie so his head was toward the center of the car with his injured leg propped up. It did not look comfortable but lifesaving was rarely pretty. They continued to roll along as Ethan thought back over the last few weeks. He would have done nothing different. How could he approve of all his decisions and still find himself in this situation? He knew what Robbie would say: "No one is right all the time. Even when you do the right thing, it can be wrong. Your problem Ethan, is you think it's possible. You actually think it's possible to make the right decision every time and never have it go sideways. You're just gonna have to let go of that dream." Robbie had said it before – more than once. The quietness in the car forced Ethan to dwell on thoughts he fought hard to push aside. It was easy to focus on taking another step, providing for others' needs, getting to a destination with no regard for himself or his pain. But Robbie was not someone or something he could ignore. He was family – Ethan's connection to his past, the only one in his life who understood who he was before. With both his parents gone, he leaned on Robbie now in a way he hadn't just five years ago.

The car went silent after jerking slightly a few times. "That's all folks," Cael joked from the driver's seat. It coasted to a stop and Cael parked it neatly beside the expressway. "Now what?"

Ethan scanned Robbie to make sure he was still breathing. "I can get him into one of the carts. We make him comfortable and see if we can find a place to hole up for a few days. He needs time to recover. Do we have any maps of this part of Alabama?"

"None that I know of. The last sign was—" Cael trailed off as he looked through the few things he had in the front seat. "Chattanooga, ninety miles, I know. I can't think of anything between here and there worth talking about. Some small towns maybe."

"We only need one small town with a vacant house," Cael suggested, trying to be helpful.

"Should we even move him?" Lauren was on her knees in the passenger seat leaned over, watching Robbie.

"We can't live in this car. It's too small. And if Brock's army did decide we were worth it, they could follow this road and eventually find us. We're moving."

———

With Robbie barely tucked into one handcart, and Cael and Lauren teaming up on the other one, they made their way north on interstate 59. It was still relatively early in the morning. Ethan guessed close to ten. It was cloudy but the sun peeked through regularly. Warm, intermittent breezes hinted at the heat which was lined up for the afternoon. Shimmering heat waves danced on the asphalt ribbon that rolled ahead of them and into the ridges and valleys that marked this part of Alabama.

Ethan stopped to check Robbie's leg every few minutes to make sure the wound hadn't reopened. His stitching job in the back seat was primitive and wouldn't win him any awards but it had closed the wound and so far stopped the bleeding. Brock and his militia were on his mind. They must be in pursuit. Brock's conceit wouldn't allow him to simply let his captives go. The only question for Ethan was when would they show up. He tried Colonel Reynolds on the sat phone hoping for some assistance with Robbie and their pursuers but Reynolds didn't answer. There really wasn't anyone else Ethan could call.

When Ethan stopped again to look at the leg, Cael and Lauren plodded on not realizing they were leading the way. Lauren turned, saw Ethan far back and told Cael to hold up. They waited for Ethan to catch up and when he pulled abreast of them, they started walking again.

Cael glanced sidewise at Ethan. "So, are you guys, like, more than friends?"

"You're such an idiot, Cael!"

"Give me a break, Lauren, like you never thought it."

"They've talked non-stop about their families and you ask that!"

"You don't have to be straight to have a family."

Lauren let out an exasperated sigh.

"Are you two done?" Ethan asked quietly as he continued to walk.

"I just figured, you know, it's like the end of the world so just ask right? What could it hurt?"

"Cael, it's actually possible to love a man and not love him in the way you think. There is a love that goes beyond friendship – beyond romance. It's a love I heard a preacher talk about once. He called it agape love. It's in the Bible."

"Love is love."

"No, it's not. You loved your family?"

Cael stopped walking and gave Ethan a hard stare. "You know I did."

"You love pizza?"

"Yeah, but that's – not – the same thing." It slowly dawned on him. "Okay, I get what you're saying."

"Right, love is not just love. There are different kinds."

"So, what kind is that agape love?"

"It's not romantic. And it goes beyond friendship. It's

deeper. It's a love that doesn't depend on the person you love. It doesn't matter if the person is worthy or not. It's a love that gives even when it doesn't make sense. A self-sacrificing kind of love."

"It sounds beautiful," Lauren said.

"It is. Robbie is a happily married man with two of the most beautiful kids you ever saw. I've loved a few women, the first of whom made me a father. I would marry if the right *woman* came along. But make no mistake, me and Robbie are closer than brothers. There's nothing he could do to make me walk away."

Cael started walking again. "Sorry, Ethan. Sorry if I offended you."

"It's okay, Cael. No offense taken. But I appreciate the apology," Ethan replied as he too began walking.

"Well?"

"Well, what?"

"Aren't you going to apologize too?"

"Cael, please don't make this into something. What do I need to apologize for?"

"Underestimating me. You look down on me. You just won't admit it. You didn't even expect that apology."

Lauren wisely kept quiet as the conversation escalated.

"You're right. In this situation I underestimated you. I'm sorry."

"So I guess with Robbie out of it, you and I are in charge."

Ethan stopped pulling Robbie, looked directly at Cael and with too-fatherly-a-tone said, "You will never take his place. You get me? You are not in charge and the fact that you're even thinking that right now just," Ethan was too angry to finish.

"Okay, okay, I know I can't take his place but I think I've earned a little respect. You even said I did good."

"You got the car and I'm grateful. But you snuck off when we were finally all together and we needed you. We had to backtrack to find you because we didn't know where you went."

"If I had asked to go get that car you would have said no!"

"You are correct."

"Well. I wanted the car."

"And that's the problem, isn't it? Story of your life. Something you want, someone says you can't have it so you go crazy trying to get it anyway. That's the exact opposite of the kind of love I was just describing."

"That's a fairy tale. No one loves like that. There's always a catch."

"No Cael, there's not. God loves that way. And He wants His kids to love that way too."

"Don't get all religious on me. I told you I don't believe in any of that."

"Maybe you should. God has the power to change anyone and make them into the person He wants them to be."

"Maybe you should get a job as a preacher."

"I already have a job."

"Yeah, criticizing me non-stop! You won't let up on me."

"If I didn't see potential in you I would leave you alone! I would tolerate you. I would walk two thousand miserable miles and never say a word about your attitude or the way you treat others. But I *do* see it. It's there, humming below the surface, ready to emerge."

"I'm not your project, Ethan."

"You're right. My job is not to try to help you. If you want me to, I will back off. I'll just do my job."

"Yeah, okay. That would be good."

"But I need you to fall in line. You and I are not partners or co-leaders."

Cael put his hands on his hips and exhaled loudly, walking in a small circle. "So, if I want you off my back I just have to do everything you say? That sounds like a great deal – for you!"

"Look, I just want to get Robbie to his family and get myself back to my son. That's my mission right now. But I also have a job to do. One job," Ethan almost shouted, holding his index finger up in the air. "To keep all of us alive."

"That's not your job! You made it your job. Like those kids in Corpus! You just want to be everyone's hero." Cael stepped back from the cart he'd been pulling and summoned his courage. "I can take care of myself."

"So, you want to leave?"

"I don't know. I don't know if I like the way I'm being treated here."

"No one is making you stay, Cael. But if you go you will go empty-handed."

"I helped regather most of this stuff. I've earned it."

"I want you to stay, Cael. I think we can teach each other a lot. But this is not going to work if you won't listen to what I say. Every tribe needs a chief and right now that's me. Unless you want to fight me for it."

The image of Ethan flipping the SUV end-over-end on the expressway back in Corpus took center screen in Cael's mind. "No. But I at least want a vote when we decide stuff."

"This is all or nothing, Cael. You're either in or you're out and I'm not negotiating."

"I want respect," Cael said decisively.

"Respect is earned." Ethan let that sink in for a moment, then added, "you're on the right track."

Ethan couldn't explain the look on Cael's face. It was wonder, shock, loss and pain. He was visibly shaken and fought rising emotion. Lauren moved from her side of the cart where she was watching the argument unfold and put her arms around Cael's shoulders. Ethan walked to him and did the same.

"I'm fine you guys." Cael managed to say through the lump in his throat.

Something triggered this emotion in Cael. Ethan surmised it was his affirmation that Cael had grown and had earned respect. It was possible no one had ever said that to him or offered him a real shot, beyond a drug dealer or thug exploiting him.

"We've all been under incredible stress. We've had no chance to process anything that's happened to us. It's a lot to deal with."

Cael nodded his head but couldn't speak. They stood in the middle of the road, Lauren shedding some tears. Ethan glanced at his friend, still unconscious, and felt the weight of getting him healthy and home safely.

"We need to keep moving, guys." Ethan stepped back from the pair and asked, "Cael, what's it going to be?"

Cael cuffed his eyes clear and held out his hand to Ethan. "I'm not leaving."

Ethan gripped his hand and shook it firmly. "Good. Neither am I."

TWENTY-ONE

David woke and stoked Liz's cooking fire, while Scooby nosed around looking for any food scraps that might have fallen during the last meal. With no gas service and David's reluctance to have flame in their historic home, they constructed a brick enclosure near the back porch for Liz to boil water, cook whatever food they had, and heat water with which to wash. He was still thinking through how to safely move the makeshift oven and heating fire into the house. It was just one of almost a dozen projects David was trying to figure out. He'd given up on the bathroom issue and simply dug a hole in the backyard, currently surrounded by a sheet for privacy. A more permanent structure was also on his to do list before winter.

He and Liz's weeks found something of a rhythm. Though there were many tasks that filled their days, one day was a designated wash day, two days were wood gathering days. David designated one day of the week a scavenging day with Lenny. David devoted another day to winter preparations, which included the various problems associated with going from twenty-first century accommodations to nineteenth-century living. One day they devoted to rest and family worship. David was uncompromising on this. His father followed Jesus and though he hadn't met him until he was eight, instilled his faith in David. There was nothing fancy about their family worship. David picked a portion of the Bible to read, they sang some songs whose words they remembered, and spent time praying together. David even convinced Lenny, Keith, and Sadiq to join in though none of the three were comfortable.

David was convinced that in a crisis like the one they faced, surrounded by death and despair, it would be easy to let go of their faith so he was determined to do the exact opposite by clinging fiercely to it.

On the morning of the meeting the mayor scheduled, which for Liz was a wash day, David readied the fire, not knowing how soon he would return, and headed toward downtown. He told his neighbors about the meeting but they elected to send David as their representative. They offered few ideas anyway and were content to let David speak on their behalf. Sadiq was meeting him there, as were Keith and Lenny. He tried to invite Garrett but was shouted at from the hilltop to stay away. Garrett seemed to be doing well by himself and had surviving figured out, causing David to wonder why he wasn't willing to help anyone else.

David arrived at the gazebo park next to city hall expecting a larger crowd. He was not disappointed as the grassy slope leading to the river and the gazebo was teeming with people. He sought out Sadiq and Keith who were standing together near city hall. Lenny was walking toward the meeting from the opposite side of the river with two men David didn't recognize. There was a murmur of conversation across the hillside as everyone waited for the mayor and remaining city council members to appear.

"Good morning, guys. Got any bright ideas?" David asked with a smile.

"Good morning, David. I would love to help people but there isn't one person here who will volunteer their food reserves or weapons. If anyone here talks too much about how to do something, or how successful an idea has been, it would be easy for others to assume they have extra." Sadiq obviously would not be telling anyone about his convenience store even though over half of his inventory was now in David's basement. He did not want to make himself a target in any way.

"You're right, Sadiq, but there have to be some ways that our community can work together beyond just sharing. Ideas are what will help us – not just distribution of resources. We have to forge a brand new way of living."

"Don't you mean an old way?" Keith offered. "People have been living this way for thousands of years. If they could do it and do it well, so can we. We just have to remember how."

"You can't remember what you never learned," David replied. "But didn't you tell me about some books that taught all those skills? Firefox or something?"

"No, Fox Fire. It's a series of books that shows how people did stuff like, a hundred years ago. They're pretty cool."

David's interest was piqued. "Do you know where you can get them?"

Keith thought for a moment. "Maybe in a big bookstore or a library. My friend's grandma had the whole series but she lives like fifty miles from here. We could start here in the library," he suggested, gesturing vaguely toward the east.

"Let's do that. And we can even suggest that today. Maybe someone has those books already in their house."

Finally, the mayor emerged from the dark city hall, followed by the greatly reduced city council. She waved to the waiting crowd and made her way down the slope to the gazebo. The grassy area was always the site of summer concerts in the park with kids running around, smells from the nearby restaurants wafting over the spectators and the ice cream stand doing brisk business just across the river. Now, the flowers in the hanging baskets at the street lights were dead, the grass in the park overgrown, and a different and disgusting smell rested on the city.

The mayor stopped to talk to and shake hands with several smaller groupings of people. David had voted for her. She seemed genuine and even though she hadn't handled this crisis the way David would have, he believed in her now and hoped the meeting would be a success.

"Good morning, citizens of Fenton. Thank you for coming today. I know it's early but I know we all want to avoid traveling in the heat of the day. My hope for this meeting-"

"Could you speak up?" A voice shouted from the hillside.

"Yes. It would help too if you all moved down the hill a bit closer," she shouted back.

David, Sadiq and Keith moved down the slope. David watched as the crowd reluctantly shuffled forward a few steps. He glanced up at the mayor and in an instant, David saw the gazebo where she was standing completely disappear in a ball of fire. Wood splintered and flew in every direction and David felt the heat of the blast on his face.

The people closest to the gazebo were blown back by the force of the explosion. David staggered back and his ears rang from sound of the massive discharge. Bloodied people ran past David in all directions but he could not hear their screams. As his mind slowly cleared, he remembered that Sadiq and Keith were flanking him as they walked down the hill. He glanced around and saw Sadiq's back. He was moving slowly uphill toward Main Street. David stepped quickly toward him and put a hand on his shoulder to turn him around. Sadiq spun with a look of terror on his face and shrugged David's hand off frantically. When he realized who it was, he calmed and asked David where Keith was. David, whose ears were still ringing, regained enough hearing to discern the question and together they ran back toward where they were standing before the blast.

The former gazebo site was a scene of smoking ruin. The posts that held up the structure were now blackened stumps protruding from the ground, flaming bits of the cedar structure, still aflame, scattered about. Several bodies rested on the edge of the river, draped over the boulders lining its banks, like a macabre sunbathing scene. Some compassionate citizens ran toward the carnage hoping they could rescue an injured person but chaos ruled as the smoke and flame billowed, swirled around the grassy hill and brick-lined gazebo area. David turned in a tight circle trying to take it all in and decide what to do. The decision was made for him as he caught a glimpse of Keith lying flat on his back in the grass nearby. David called Sadiq's name and rushed to Keith's side. He lay unmoving and after looking him over, David discovered why: a splintered piece of wood that was turned into a weapon by the force of the blast was driven right through Keith's chest just below the collarbone. Keith was unconscious. The noise around him faded and

David punched the ground. After weeks of trying to survive and actually making it through the early stages of this crisis, a bomb was the last thing David expected. He was timid to remove the jagged chunk of wood not knowing how big it was or if it would do more damage coming out than going in. David remained crouched over Keith with one hand on his shoulder to staunch the bleeding as he thought through how to get him home.

Sadiq came and placed a hand on David and said calmly, "His struggle is over. He's at peace now."

"He's not dead Sadiq! We have to move him."

"I'm so sorry my friend. I didn't realize."

David glanced around. "We need to go – before another bomb goes off." Most of the crowd dissipated, many who were knocked down by the blast, now upright again, people moving to help others who were slower to get up, some who would never get up. Two people stopped where David and Sadiq knelt, offering their help, faces blackened by soot and smoke, hands still bloody from helping other victims. Sadiq shook his head, declining.

David barely noticed the offer of help. He was thinking about getting Keith home and treating the wound. Another thought occurred to him as he looked down at Keith's face. This teenager could have been killed. And even if he made it through the day his wounds might still mean death by infection. David had never taken the time to tell Keith about his faith in God. He wanted to pound the ground with both fists. "Sadiq, I made a huge mistake. I didn't tell Keith about my faith – and I haven't told you either."

"That can wait. Let's get him home," Sadiq said.

David agreed by standing and preparing to carry Keith the half-mile back to his house. He looked around the gazebo area where people were attending to the wounded.

Fires were still burning but a few individuals were carrying buckets up from the river to douse the flames. David estimated the death toll to be at least twenty. The mayor, three council members, the other city officials standing near the gazebo and the other collateral deaths. "No one had a chance to talk, to share anything of value. We were all lured here to be killed."

Sadiq was growing restless. "David? Come. We need to get Keith out of here."

David knew Sadiq was right and so he finally shook off the shock and began to apply his mind to the situation. "We need something to help us transport him. I don't think we can just carry him with the wound in his chest."

They quickly went to work piecing together a travois similar to what David created two months earlier for Nathan. David said a quiet prayer of thanks that he wasn't transporting Keith for burial. There was still a chance for him.

Once they were ready to move Sadiq, gesturing to the chaos still swirling about them, asked, "What about all this?"

"What about it? Keith doesn't have time for us to do anything. Could we do anything other than try to identify the dead? Try to comfort the dying? There's no medical care, no medicines that will make a difference." David fought the waves of sadness crashing down on him. In he and Lenny's abandoned home expeditions, they came upon more than one suicide: Bodies still sitting in driver seats inside garages that became tombs; bodies slumped over desks or backward in easy chairs, pistols nearby with dried blood and brain matter splattered on the wall or floor. David was beginning to understand. How much easier would that be than to keep fighting? To keep waiting, hoping his father would show up with help? If only he could worry about just himself.

As he and Sadiq dragged Keith toward home, David battled his own accusations. How he accepted help from these people, lived and worked with them, but never told them of his life's core belief - faith in God.

"You're quiet," Sadiq ventured as he adjusted his grip on the device carrying Keith.

David debated whether or not to tell Sadiq what was bothering him, beyond the fact they'd just witnessed a bombing. Survival kept everyone so busy that facing the looming shadow of death was ignored. Life was so fragile, so brief. What made life's brevity acceptable to David was the belief that there was a life after this one. A life that contained no bloodshed, pain or suffering. *How could I have forgotten to tell my friends about this?*

"Are you okay?" Sadiq tried again.

David answered immediately in his thoughts. *I'm not even close to okay.* But he decided to play it safe with Sadiq. "I'm fine. It's just that you and I need to talk. I need to say some things to you. You and Lenny both. And Keith – after he pulls through."

"Sure David. Whenever you want."

As soon as David and Sadiq got home they laid Keith down on the couch in the living room. Keith came to and began moaning with pain. Sadiq went to the basement and grabbed a bottle of whiskey out of a box he brought from his store. Once Keith had choked down a glassful of the burning liquid he calmed down.

With Elizabeth's help and armed with antiseptic, gauze and tweezers, they started the gritty work of removing the chunk of wood from Keith's upper chest. Almost an hour later they had it out and had removed dozens of splinters from the wound. As far as they could tell the flying splinter did not pierce a major artery, though there was certainly plenty of blood. It needed to be stitched up so David, using a needle from Elizabeth's sewing kit, bent it into a curve and tried suturing the hole closed. It was messy and reminded them all of Frankenstein but they were hopeful.

———

"You know what today is?" David asked sleepily as he rolled toward Elizabeth, her back toward him. She grunted in response.

"Labor Day."

"It's been Labor Day since all this started. Every day has been Labor Day," she quietly mumbled.

David smiled in the darkness. Liz was qualified to make that statement. She worked every bit as hard as he to survive. While David was roaming all over town collecting things to support the family, she was home figuring out how to wash their clothes, keep the house clean, and make their food stretch even further. The emergency food supplies that were supposed to last six months, David now estimated they would be able to stretch to nine. That would get them through most of the winter. Along with other things he collected, they should be okay going into spring. After that, he wasn't sure. Keith was healing nicely. He would have a terrible, puckered scar on his chest but he had miraculously avoided infection. It would be a couple weeks before he was able to do anything around the house.

As he laid there, he moved his face into Elizabeth's hair, splayed out on her pillow. It smelled of woodsmoke and the outdoors. Their bodies had taken on an earthiness that all the chemical soaps they used usually masked. It was not a foul odor but something natural that was probably closer to what God intended, rather than sandalwood and cloves, gardenia or cucumber lime verbena. When David found products like that in his scavenging, he would bring them home but Lizzie was too frugal to use them every day. Since the day of the blackout, they hadn't had a bath where they were fully submerged nor had they showered. They reverted to the language of an earlier era by asking Hannah or one another if they "washed up". A pitcher of boiled water stood just outside the back door with a bowl nearby for handwashing before entering the house.

The lack of showers and baths did not diminish David's appetite for Elizabeth. If anything, they were intimate more frequently since the blackout. There was a salving effect on their hearts to be together. Both were aware of the potential consequences but were trusting God with whatever happened. If Elizabeth got pregnant, they would do what they had to. Both simply knew they needed to be together. With nothing and no one to cling to but each other they regularly found their way into each other's arms.

Things that David thought would be a turn off to him physically actually had the opposite effect. Smooth legs were simply not a priority in a survival situation. David thought of the movies and television shows he watched in the past that focused on a post-apocalyptic world. All the actors and actresses appeared to have clear complexions, clean hair and groomed beards. Reality was much different. David's beard came in fiercely and was now starting to curl. Liz already trimmed the hair on his neck and over his ears. The constant work coupled with the sun, wind, and heat rendered their cheeks red and dry, and their hands rough and calloused. Both he and Elizabeth were leaner than at the start. The rationing of their food and the hard work had caused David to lose at least twenty pounds. He was a bit fleshy around the middle and could afford to lose the spare tire. Elizabeth lost weight as well but David was always encouraging her to eat more. He was worried about her not getting enough nourishment.

His goal was to remove that concern entirely, if possible. His plan on this Labor Day was to break into the city library and gather whatever books he could find related to survival. Several years ago, he downloaded a book on his tablet about urban survival. It would have been immensely helpful if he was able to charge the tablet and access it. Keith told him about a series of books that detailed how people in Appalachia made do in the mountains over the centuries. He would look for those but there were plenty of other related books explaining how to find food in the woods, field dress small game and many other techniques they would need to survive the winter.

David rolled away from Liz and stood up next to the bed, carefully stepping over where Scooby laid.

"Are you leaving now?" She asked as she turned toward him.

"Yeah, I want to get in under cover of darkness and out before people start waking up. It shouldn't take me long."

Liz sat up, her long brown hair falling over her face. She swept it back so she could look David in the eye. "Be careful."

"Liz, we go through this every time I leave the house," David replied, not mentioning the fact that the toss of her hair always seemed to rev him up.

"And I mean it every time you leave the house. Don't take any chances!"

"You know you're pretty sexy when you're fussing at me?"

"I'm serious, David! Don't try and change the subject."

"I probably still have a couple hours of darkness. Should I get back in bed?"

"Oh my gosh, David. Now?"

"Why not? You have something else to do?"

"Yes! Sleep! I'm going back to sleep." David grinned at her and moved back toward the bed. "I know that look. Ugh. I haven't even brushed my teeth. No." Liz flopped back down onto her pillow and pulled the quilt back up around her shoulders.

"What look? It's kind of dark in here." David peeled the quilt back on his side of the bed and slid underneath the cool top sheet to where the bottom sheet was still warm from his body. He slid toward Liz, placed a hand on her shoulder and leaned over, kissing her gently on the cheek. She turned toward him.

———

The darkness held and David was able to reach the library unseen. It was a cool morning, probably forty-eight to fifty degrees. He was glad he put on the hoodie along with the long sleeve shirt. He walked the perimeter of the building and didn't see any signs of anyone else breaking in. He chose the rear door. He opened the small bag of tools and removed a thin pry bar along with a small clamp. He had a few ideas about how to break in but his ideal method was to use the clamp to push the door frame away from the latch, which would simply allow the door to come open without breaking anything. The frame needed to be wood though and this was unlikely. The other method was the pry bar and the hammer. Much more forceful but highly effective.

The hammer proved to be the successful method but

David was skeptical that anyone in the homes near the library heard the banging. He was unsure if anyone was still living those homes. It was hard to tell if a home was occupied or not.

David moved quickly past the circulation desk, the movie shelves, and then past the fiction section. He knew what part of the library to look in but had no way to find it. The library did away with their card catalog years ago and went exclusively to the computer system. He pulled out a small flashlight and scanned the shelves for what he needed. Thirty minutes later, he had a small stack of books. Knife and ax skills for wilderness survival, a book on navigation based on stars and compasses, a US Army survival guide, and a wilderness survival guide from an outdoor magazine. He stashed the books in a separate bag he brought and headed home. A light fog hung in the air and a gray pall colored everything. Very few birds were singing this morning and David didn't see another soul the whole way home. Almost.

Turning onto his street, he thought he saw something or someone in front of his house. He sped up, almost running to try and see what it was. Arriving at the end of his walkway, he scanned the street and the neighboring yards. Nothing. He put down the bags of books and tools and walked slowly up the street toward Garrett's house. He was suspicious of him all summer and couldn't think of anyone else in the neighborhood who might be snooping around. There were few people left in the neighborhood.

He moved up the dirt and gravel road toward Garrett's house, listening for the sound of feet moving through the brush or across gravel. Silence blanketed the neighborhood and smothered David with apprehension. A few more steps and David realized he was holding his breath. He exhaled slowly and drew in another breath. He pressed forward. David did many things in the last few months he would have never dreamed of doing but necessity was the mother of courage. And invention, yes, but David was moved to a boldness he didn't know he possessed. A protective instinct developed in him, much like the abilities his father possessed, manifested in him years ago. David didn't possess the strength of his father but crisis revealed characteristics in him that before now were unknown. He reached the top of the hill and could see down the lane to the front porch of Garrett's house. David crouched low and scanned both sides of the lane and the area around the house. No movement.

David stood and moved closer, keeping his eyes glued to the front of Garrett's house, well aware that a moving curtain, a window opening or any movement at all could signal a weapon being aimed it him. David stopped beside a tree and again scanned the area. He was brave and cautious but not schooled in military tactics or jungle warfare. Otherwise, he might have seen the snare laid just beyond the tree. He stepped around his protective cover and placed a foot inside the snare, triggering the trap that snatched his foot and pulled him into the air. It happened so fast that his back slammed into the ground, knocking the wind out of him. He dangled by his ankle trying to catch his breath when Garrett walked up to him from about twenty feet away.

"I think I told you to stay away from my place."

David tried to speak, only uttering a long groan as his lungs fought to inhale.

"Trying to catch your breath? Yeah, I had to test this a couple times and they each had the same problem." Garrett walked past David and spun him gently as he hung like a pendulum. "What do I do with you, David? I don't like you,

you know? I'm annoyed by you. You're too kind. A 'holier than thou' kind of thing. Like you can save this neighborhood or this city. Or your friend Sadiq?"

David's eyes involuntarily went wide.

"Oh, you thought that was a secret arrangement? I know all about your deal with him. I probably have a better idea of your basement inventory than you do. Oh, and I noticed Keith is injured. I saw him go down at the city hall meeting but wasn't sure until I saw you walk him out to the porch the other day."

"How do you know all this?" David managed to gasp.

"I've been following you. And watching you. It's part of my job." Garrett continued to walk slowly in circles around David as hung upside down, swaying and spinning gently.

"Your job? Who are you working for?"

"I'll probably tell you before I kill you. Just so you go to your grave knowing the truth."

"Garrett, I have a family. I don't know what I did to you but I think we can talk about this. Maybe I can help you?" David gasped this out taking deep breaths between each phrase.

Garrett tied David's hands behind his back. "You wouldn't help me if you knew what I was doing. See, I'm against everything you stand for. That patriotism crap, the 'one nation under God' farce. The truth and justice bull that gets preached every election cycle. There is no justice in this country. Well, there wasn't, until recently."

"Garrett, that's not true. America isn't perfect but it's still better than most places in the world."

"See, that's the lie everyone wants Americans to believe. That we're this great country. That we're better than everyone else. They preach American exceptionalism. I preach American atrocity. American lies. American destruction." Garrett unexpectedly cut the rope holding David off the ground causing him to drop onto his shoulder and neck. David grunted on impact and then moaned as the pain set in from what was possibly a broken collarbone. "Oh, did that hurt? Should've warned you."

"I think I broke something."

"You won't need that bone anyway." Garrett leaned down and grabbed David's injured arm and pulled him to his feet causing him to scream in pain. "I'm just not doing a very good job of telling you what's next, am I? Hmm. I should probably apologize."

"What's your goal here, huh? Are you just talking big or do you have some kind of plan?" David's voice wavered as he spoke, giving away his fear and pain.

"Do I have some kind of plan? How do you think I know about Sadiq. About Keith. About Lenny? Oh yeah, I know about your little excursions with Lenny. Funny little guy. If I had a chance to talk to him, he'd probably be on my side in all this."

"Your *side*? What are you talking about?"

"What do you think you've been living through the last couple months? Hmm? C'mon, David Zabad. You're a pretty smart fellow. I know where you work. Engineers in your field are not idiots. I've seen all the little contraptions you've built at your place." Garrett was now marching David toward the house that for so long stood as a fearful, hilltop fortress. David knew if he entered that house, he would most likely never leave.

"Why am I so important to you? And what do you have to do with the last couple months?" David deliberately stopped walking, hoping to keep Garrett talking long enough for him to escape somehow.

Garrett laughed aloud. "You're not important to me. I

mean, you could be. Your ingenuity is actually what we all need right now. But my bosses just figured it was easier to kill you than to try and deal with you. "

"Your bosses? What is going on?"

"You've been so busy surviving you've never stopped to ask what this is all about."

"It's a terrorist attack. Islamic terrorists launched a coordinated attack and took out our power grid. It's been vulnerable for years."

"Who told you it was Islamic terrorists?"

David thought for a minute. No one who passed this information on was an original source. It was hearsay, rumor. Even Garrett's information was tainted because he clearly had ulterior motives.

"Isn't it depressing when you realize how much you've missed?" Garrett scoffed.

David was already flogging himself for not seeing the truth sooner. "Some of us have been busy trying to survive. We haven't had time to play detective. And anyway, it had to be terrorists. It had to be," David spat back, going from defensive to less certain.

"Oh, it was terrorists all right." Garrett stared right through David, grinning widely.

The truth dawned on David as he thought through everything Garrett said. This man was part of a larger conspiracy than David ever dreamed possible. Why was it so easy to believe Muslim terrorists concocted a plan to destroy the United States but so hard to believe that in reality it was her own citizens who took her down? But *why*? How did they do it and how extensive was the damage? And what could be done about it? How could America ever come back from this? The problem solving portion of David's brain was in overdrive. He knew he needed to regroup and get back to the present or he would not have to worry about solving anything. David quickly formed a plan for the immediate future. If he could get away from Garrett, he could form a longer term plan.

"Shocking isn't it? The best part is that no one saw it coming. The world has been so busy rooting out Islamic terror they never noticed the network growing right under their noses."

David slumped his shoulders and bent his knees slightly, giving Garrett the impression that he was defeated and discouraged.

"Yeah. It sucks." Garrett glanced around, checking for prying eyes. "C'mon, let's get inside before someone sees you."

David sprung up and aimed a drop kick with both legs at Garrett's chest. He never saw it coming. Garrett took both feet square in the chest and the wind was knocked out of him as he flew back almost ten feet into the brush lining the gravel drive. David knew his plan would result in him landing on the ground without being able to break his fall, and would probably send crippling pain through his shoulder again but desperation and near panic drove him to do what was necessary. He hit the ground and was able to prevent the wind being knocked out of him but he was nearly blinded by the raging pain coursing through his shoulder and radiating throughout his entire torso.

A wave of nausea swept over him and he was threatened with the possibility of losing consciousness. He fought through the pulsing menace of darkness and rolled onto his stomach. Hands still behind his back, he was able to get his knees under himself. He rose up, half stumbling, half running toward his home, down the hill, toward Liz, toward Hannah, toward safety.

. . .

David reached the side door of his house and banged on it with his knee. His key was unreachable in his pants pocket. "Liz!" He shouted. Scooby was barking on the other side of the door. He banged the door again and seconds later Liz opened it. "Liz!" David shouted again.

"David, why are you yelling? And why are you tied up?" She stepped quickly to him and untied the knots at his wrists. He knew Garrett would come. As soon as he caught his breath, he would come. He would bring his psychotic brand of terror to David's doorstep and put his family in jeopardy.

"David, say something!"

David spoke slowly, deliberately but with intensity. "Liz, I want you to go wake Hannah."

"But I want to—"

David cut her off harshly. "Wake Hannah. Go to the hiding place under the stairs. Keep her quiet. Go now."

She finished untying his wrists and protested. "But, David I—"

He spun to face her. "There's no time, Liz. He's probably already on his way."

"Who?"

David looked Liz in eyes, trying desperately to convey the seriousness of the situation "Garrett. Now do as I tell you. There's no time to explain everything." He kissed her gently on the lips and she used the moment to fiercely grab David and hug him, causing him to grunt in pain.

She released him and stepped back. "What? What did I do? What's the matter with you?"

"Liz, please." David cracked, the desperation bleeding

into his voice. "You have to do what I say. I will tell you everything when this is over. I promise."

She set her jaw, her eyes narrowing as she stared at her husband. "David Zabad. I love you."

"I love you too. Now go!"

David tested his arm's range of motion. He could not raise it above his head. He thought of the shotgun but wasn't sure if he would be able to hold it to his shoulder. And even if he could, would he be able to handle the recoil? It didn't kick much but if it further injured him, he would not get a second shot. He moved to the window and glanced up the street. It was quickly getting brighter outside.

What would dad do? David wished again that his dad was here to help him. He knew his dad used firearms but his greatest skill was in employing the unexpected. He knew how to use his environment to his advantage. Keith could not aid him at the moment and so he helped him hide under one of the beds upstairs. Sadiq left while David was at the library and he had no idea where Lenny was so there was no help from them. He was on his own.

David pulled aside the curtain again, hoping to see some movement up the street – some sign that Garrett was coming his way. If he was Garrett, he would have caught his breath and instead of barreling down the street after his prey, gone back to the house and retrieved a few key items needed to break in and kill. It was a deadly game of chess, with David trying to see several moves ahead and anticipate the strategy of his opponent.

He helped Liz and Hannah get in their hidey-hole under the stairs. He also handed them some water and a flashlight in case they needed to wait out their adversary until dark. David kept trying to put himself in Garrett's place. If he just revealed a secret that changed everything and wanted make sure that information stayed secret, he would have to eliminate anyone who might have heard. He found himself wishing he had worked on a secondary escape route from the house. He briefly considered making a run for it but at least in the house he had some kind of defensive advantage. If Garrett wanted him, he would have to come get him.

Hours passed and David stood guard. Twice he went to the stairs to check on Liz and Hannah to make sure they were okay. The tension and stress of being on guard were starting to take their toll. David was exhausted and still in pain from his injuries. He caught himself dozing but snapped awake when his chin touched his chest. The shotgun was loaded and ready but he had a feeling that whatever Garrett brought to the fight would be much more powerful.

Afternoon faded into twilight and finally darkness fell on the city. David let Liz and Hannah out of the stairwell hideout so they could stretch their legs. They had to do everything in the dark. There was no way David would give Garrett a target. Even with the curtains pulled, David was taking no chances. David finally had time to tell Liz what Garrett told him about the attacks.

"Can Hannah sleep in her bed?"

"Liz, I don't know what this guy is gonna do. He's—"

"He's crazy, that's what he is. If what he told you is true then he's a nut job."

"No Liz, I don't think he's crazy or insane. That's the problem. If he was insane, I think we could count on him acting wildly, irrationally, making a mistake. But he is very much in control and acting methodically, rationally."

"You're defending him?" Liz was aghast.

"Of course not! I'm just saying he isn't just running wild with a gun or a knife or blowing things up. Like the city park bombing. That was calculated to take out the last of the city leadership. He's here as part of some master plan to pave the way for something. I'm assuming it's a complete takeover but I don't know who is actually responsible. Garrett just said it was terrorists and that it was a network that sprung up while everyone was looking for Islamic terrorists. All I'm saying is that he's very much in control of his mind."

"That's even scarier."

"I know. At least if he was off his rocker I could dismiss what he was saying about this mess not being international terrorists." A clatter sounded outside the house. David stopped talking and listened.

"David? I can't see your face. What is it?"

"Shh. Grab Hannah." She was asleep at the foot of the stairs after being lifted out of the hideout.

"Ok but what—David—do you smell that? It's smoke! Is he setting our house on fire?"

"I don't know, Liz. Just—just give me a second." David's mind was racing. He felt fear since this crisis started but what he felt now was different. It was deeper. If his house was ablaze, he could stay inside and die, or he could run outside with his family and watch them die.

"David! What are we going to do?" Liz was on the verge of full blown panic.

"Stay here. I have to get Keith and find where he set the fire." David dashed up the stairs and helped Keith out of his hiding place. After sending Keith back down the stairs he went down the front staircase, through the entry hall at the front door but saw nothing bright and no evidence of a fire. He walked through the dining room and into the adjacent bathroom. The orange gleam through the windows was unmistakable. He couldn't be sure how much of the house was actually engulfed but he knew they couldn't stay. He returned to the kitchen, where Keith was leaning against the kitchen island, exhausted just from descending the stairs. For a 17 year old he was surprisingly strong, handling crisis and stress better than some adults. His resolve remained but the last few days of recovering had weakened his body. "Liz, it looks like there's flame outside the down-stairs bathroom window."

"Then let's go out the front door. We can't stay here, David."

"Liz, he didn't just set this fire and walk away. He's not trying to burn us to death. He's driving us out of the house toward him."

"That's just sick, David. I told you he was crazy."

"Not now, Lizzie! We're going out the back door."

"The back door? Where the flames are?" She broke into a violent coughing fit. The smoke in the kitchen was thicker.

"He's expecting us to go opposite of the flame. That's why he set the fire in the back of the house. I would bet a lot of money that he's standing out in the street waiting for us to come out that door." David's last word was choked off as the smoke stung his throat and he launched into a coughing fit.

Liz was struggling to talk without coughing but managed to say, "Actually, David, you're betting our lives."

David finished coughing and was able to guide Liz and Keith toward the back door. She held Hannah, while he held the shotgun.

There was simply no time to get anything else. They spilled out onto the porch expecting to be blasted by the heat of a house on fire. And they were. Only it wasn't their house that was burning. Mark's house, the one right next door, was completely engulfed and a southwesterly wind was carrying the smoke directly into the Zabad's house. Was this Garrett's doing? Was he trying to prove a point? Thankfully, Mark and his family left earlier in the summer and David was confident no one was inside. But the heat pouring off the house was searing and had the potential to set the houses around it ablaze including theirs. With so much uncertainty about how and why the blaze was started, David felt it was best to leave and come back later to check any damage.

David whispered to Liz, "Up the hill toward the cemetery."

They ran through the backyard and up the hill that led through several neighbors' backyards and into the city's cemetery. As they ran, they felt the heat of the fire fade and eventually they could no longer see the orange glow. Liz glanced back just once and saw that the fire engulfed the entire house. She said a silent prayer that the wind wouldn't carry the flames onto their house. It was all they had.

David ran with the gun in his good hand wrapped around Keith. He wanted to help Liz as she struggled to carry Hannah up the hill but couldn't leave Keith on his own. David felt bad that he was making her do the heavy lifting but the alternative was that Liz was holding their only means of protection – the shotgun. She still struggled with the first time she used it in self-defense and wasn't anxious to touch it again. They made it into the stand of trees that circled the cemetery and were able to slow their pace. They were out of breath and still wheezy from inhaling the smoke that so quickly penetrated the house.

"What now, David? We can't spend the night out here in the woods."

"We can head toward Sadiq's place. Though I think Garrett knows about him. Never mind. We can . . . we can go - Liz, I don't know. I have no idea what to do. This is unbelievable!"

"David, I don't need you to have all the answers. I just need you to be able to focus right now and get a plan because I am about to lose it! Do you understand me? My house might be burning down. We will have nothing! Nothing! We won't know until later. We can't figure all that out but right now I need my husband to make a decision."

"Lenny!"

Liz gave him a quizzical look.

"My buddy Lenny. He's the only one left on his street. We'll head over there. Garrett knows we've gone hunting together but doesn't know where he lives – I don't think. And there are several empty houses we can sleep in, at least for tonight."

"You don't *think* he knows where Lenny lives? But he knows about Lenny?"

"That's what he said."

"How far is it?" Liz was losing patience again.

"Less than a mile." David glanced around at the quiet night. "I think it's safe to switch now," David said as he leaned the shotgun against a tree and carefully cradled Hannah in his good arm. Liz picked up the gun and tried to smile at David.

"Lead the way."

TWENTY-TWO

Travel was excruciatingly slow. By the time they stopped the first day, they had been awake for over twenty-four hours. They were the walking dead. They hadn't come across a vacant home that was safe to sleep in so they camped just off the road for a couple nights. On this night, they found a nice grassy area just off the expressway under some trees. They hadn't seen any one since the car ran out of gas some thirty miles back. Robbie remained unconscious. Medically it probably would have been considered a coma. All Ethan knew was Robbie was still breathing and that was enough to make him work overtime to get him additional help.

Ethan gently laid him out in the grass and elevated his leg. He tried to get some water into him but couldn't make him swallow it. The conversation in the road and Cael finally letting himself feel emotion was good but it didn't

307

get Robbie any closer to health. They were not going to build a fire because of the heat but Ethan realized it would be a good idea to boil some water and bathe Robbie's leg to make sure there was no dirt in it or infection setting in. After a quick bite to eat, Cael and Lauren drifted off to sleep. Ethan hovered over Robbie, making sure he was comfortable. "I'll bring you all the way home my friend. Your family needs to see you again. No matter what, I'll get you home."

Ethan was growing increasingly frustrated the longer the journey became. He was regularly in situations that enabled him to use his strength, the main asset with which God blessed him. This journey was just nonstop walking. Sure, there were a few moments where strength was needed but it was the feeling of helplessness that Ethan couldn't abide – that there was nothing he was physically able to do to fix the situation.

The sun was down, the kids were sleeping, and Robbie was resting comfortably. Ethan smiled. He thought of them as kids even though Lauren was 20 and Cael was 19. They would not have thought of themselves as kids. But he needed to think of them that way. His protective nature was in overdrive and he was constantly looking over his shoulder or checking on them wherever they went.

He removed items from the carts and categorized them. The miracle of the angel back in Texas was still carrying them forward and providing. He laid out the food in one pile and the water purification supplies in another. He was removing an extra blanket from one cart when he saw a bright flash from the road. The flash became a steady shining light and then Ethan heard the rumble of a truck. He quickly swept up everything he had just removed and dumped it back in the cart. He turned to a nearby tree where earlier he leaned a rifle and grabbed it, walked to Cael and woke him up.

Lauren popped up from her wadded up sweatshirt she'd used to make a pillow and sleepily mumbled, "What's going on?"

"Someone in the road. Coming from the north." Ethan kicked dirt over the small fire and ordered Cael and Lauren to get behind the trees nearby. Ethan dragged the loaded carts over and established them as a barrier between Robbie and the road. Ethan planted himself behind them as well with the rifle in one hand and the pistol still on his hip.

The headlights he saw were still coming. *Just keep going. Lord, let them just keep going, right by us.* Ethan kept praying, willing the vehicle to keep moving. And then Ethan saw the second vehicle and the third. "Cael! Come here. I need you."

He cautiously peered out from behind the tree he was hiding behind with Lauren. "Really?"

"Really. Grab that rifle," Ethan ordered, "The one in the duffel."

"Are you sure?"

"Cael, we've got three vehicles up on the road coming from the north." Ethan watched as the lights stopped moving. "Okay, quick, take my position. I'm going to swing around to their rear. They'll never know I'm there."

"What am I supposed to do?"

"Stay down. Stay quiet."

"That's your plan?"

"I *have* a plan. Your part in it is to stay. Down. Stay. Quiet."

"Jeez, okay. I got it."

Doors were opened and the Ethan could hear the dinging of an interior car chime as the dome lights cast an aurora across the roadside. Then the doors were slammed shut and a group of bodies spread out and walked into the trees along the road. The piercing beams of their flashlights swept back and forth across the slope and illuminated the trees.

Ethan sprinted forty or fifty yards north from their camp and then cut left to head up to the road. He was now looking at tail lights. It didn't appear that they left anyone to guard the vehicles, which were still running.

"Hello down there! Anyone there?" One of the men in the group was hailing the camp but Ethan was not ready to reveal himself or anyone in his care. After Brock he wasn't taking any chances. They put some distance between them and Brock's militia but a short wave radio was all it would take to get word to a nearby, like-minded militia. But Ethan needed to do something before these came upon the carts and Cael. He ran to the first vehicle in line, opened the door and quickly ran around the front. The dinging from the open door soon caught the attention of the men.

"Mason, take the brothers and find out what that is. *Who* that is."

"Sure thing, sir." Three of the men headed back to the vehicles.

"Carter! We got something!" The lead searcher called out, almost on top of the hidden campsite.

"What have we here? A couple nice little carts."

Cael couldn't resist. "You better back off." He stood with the rifle to his shoulder and pointed the barrel squarely at the chest of the man they'd called Carter.

"Whoa, son," Carter said, taking a step back. "I didn't know you were back there. I'm not here to steal anything."

"You're right about that."

"Okay, okay. Why don't you put that gun down and we can get to know each other?"

Cael remained still. "Why don't you just head back up to your vehicles and keep moving? We've seen guys like you before."

"And I've seen plenty like you. And I think you just said 'we', didn't you?"

Cael realized his mistake but quickly denied the accusation.

"No, you said 'we'. I won't allow this area to be overrun with scavengers and thieves. If people want to work together to survive, give what they have to share, then me and that person will get along. How many are you?"

"We're not scavengers or thieves." The insinuation caused Cael to get emotionally defensive and momentarily drop his guard. One of Carter's men slowly flanked him and the moment the gun wavered he leaped and disarmed Cael, subduing him with one deft move.

"Nice work, Halverson. Alright," Carter shouted. "We've got your man. I don't who you are but you'd better come out with your hands in the air or we're taking this kid with us!"

Lauren burst from her hiding place wielding a tree branch and swung it at the nearest man. He dodged the wild swing and then stepped close and grabbed the branch out of her hands. Another man stepped close gripping a shotgun. "Darlin', you'd better quit struggling. I ain't never had to shoot a lady and I don't want to. Just settle yourself."

Carter shouted again. "Correction. If you don't come down here we're taking both of these young people with us."

"You're not taking them anywhere! I've got three of your men up here." Ethan worked so quickly and silently that none of his captives even had a chance to cry out. They were bound and gagged next to the truck.

"Some plan," Cael mumbled.

"What was that?" Carter inquired.

"Nothing."

"I don't know who you are but we're not your enemy. My name's Carter Mattson. I lead the Southwest Tennessee Freedom Militia. We got a report of a campfire in this location. Just here to check it out." Carter shouted all this into the dark, toward the road.

"We just escaped from another militia, east of Vicksburg. We just want to be left alone," Ethan responded.

"Escaped? Doesn't sound like our kind of militia. We're peacekeepers, trying to help people in this crisis. Who are you?"

The whole conversation so far was both men yelling into the darkness. Ethan decided to keep it that way. "My name is Ethan Zabad. I served in the United States Army and am now serving under a classified special ops unit. I'm trying to get to Louisville, Kentucky and then to Michigan where my family is. I just want to get there. I don't want any trouble."

"How about you let my men go and I'll release these young'uns I've got down here?"

Ethan looked to the passenger side of truck where the three men were bound with the jumper cables he'd found in the back seat. "I need some assurance. The last thing I want to do is hurt anyone."

"I don't want that either. I may be able to help you."

"I'm listening."

"We're based in Chattanooga. We're headed back that way tonight. I can get you that far. If you want to stay awhile you can. If you want to press on you can."

"That's quite an offer. What's in it for you?"

"If you're really a scoundrel and a thief, you'll be on your way out of my territory. If you're not then I've helped some travelers and I feel good about myself. Either way, it's a win."

Ethan decided to step forward just a little so the men in the trees could see his silhouette. He knew it was a risk but his crap detector was not going off. Something rang true about this man. "I'll let them go right now. And then I'm coming down." Ethan was true to his word. He untied Mason and the other two men and followed them down to where Carter waited by the stacked carts. Cael and Lauren were released as well but they withheld the gun. "Alright, here I am."

"Carter Mattson," he said, extending his hand.

"Ethan Zabad. This is Cael. I told him his role was to stay down and stay quiet. He didn't listen well but to his credit he had something with him that I wanted him to protect. My best friend and business partner Robbie Charles is there. He was shot two days ago and lost so much blood he's been unconscious ever since. We've been trying to find a place to hole up for a few days but had to camp roadside instead."

"Who shot him?"

"Some militia group led by a guy named Brock. He told us his militia and others like it all over the country played a role in the power outage. He didn't tell me who was ultimately responsible but if it turns out you're a part of something like that, I promise you I won't hold back."

Carter eyed Ethan suspiciously for a moment. "I'm not sure what that means but I don't plan on finding out. This group is made up of patriots. We love our country and wouldn't do anything to hurt it. We're trying to help it get back together. Law enforcement out this way has been spotty and disorganized. So we're trying to track down and get rid of any criminal elements moving in."

"This is Lauren. I told her to stay hidden too. Anyone lays a hand on her or so much as looks at her sideways will answer to me. Is that clear?"

Several men snorted derisively but Carter nodded. "My men will keep a respectful distance, won't we? I said, *won't we!*"

"Yessir!" the men shouted in ragged unison.

"They're not going to be a problem. They're just doubting you can follow through on your threats," Carter warned.

"They wouldn't be the first. And they would be wrong."

"Like I said, I don't really want to find out what that means. Meantime, let's get you and your people loaded up. We can take you back to Chattanooga tonight and get some medical care for your friend. We were able to get the hospital there running on generators. Lost a lot of people there in the first few days but we have a fella who figured out how to get electricity to it using water power. Darndest thing."

"Okay Lauren, grab your gear. You too, Cael. I'll take care of Robbie."

"I'll have my men help you."

"Thanks Carter. If we seemed aggressive, it's only because of what we've been through the last few days."

"I understand. It's hard to know who you can trust these days. Alright men, let's get these supplies loaded in the second truck. Ethan, you'll ride with me in the first truck and we'll put your buddy in the back seat. Your two kids can ride in the rear truck." Ethan couldn't help but laugh. "What's so funny?"

"Right before I saw your headlights, I was just wondering if I could get away with calling them kids." Ethan paused as he realized once again, God was providing in an unexpected way. "I really appreciate what you're doing here. It would've taken us days to get to Chattanooga."

"Glad to help."

Ethan watched as these men, all unknown to him, got busy carrying gear up to the trucks. Good men. Men willing to risk their lives to keep the peace – to keep some semblance of order alive. So different from the men they encountered just days ago. Cael climbed the slope to the trucks with Lauren next to him. Ethan was the last to head back to the trucks, along with the men helping him with Robbie. He wanted to believe that David was like these men – helping others – doing what was right. He hoped he raised a man like that. He would know one day. When he finally completed this journey, he would see firsthand the kind of man his son had become. He only hoped they both could survive long enough to reunite. After getting Robbie settled he entered the passenger side of the truck. They did a U-turn and headed north toward Chattanooga – north toward some rest. North toward hope.

TWENTY-THREE

It was one of the first mornings they noticed that the weather felt different. It was a little cooler but it wasn't the only thing that felt different. It was the second morning they awoke in a strange house, in a strange bed, in a strange neighborhood. Less than forty-eight hours ago a house in their neighborhood was burned down by their neighbor – an anti-government conspirator and a domestic terrorist. But they were alive. Whether or not their house survived the onslaught of the flames was still unknown. David hadn't yet gone back to check. He felt waiting a couple days would give things a chance to settle down a bit.

Lenny was gracious to let them in the night of the fire and give them lodging in his place. David was exhausted not only from the constant worry for his family but the stress of always being on guard. He laid next to Elizabeth as she dozed. Keith was in another bedroom. The flight from the house had worn him out as well.

Hannah padded from her pile of blankets in the corner and tried to climb into the bed with David and Elizabeth. David gave her a boost with his strong arm and flopped her over his body between he and Liz. She giggled at being tumbled onto the blankets. He looked at her wide brown eyes, her innocence. She didn't know what was happening around her. She only knew that she was with her mom and dad. There was a kind of bliss in being unaware of the current situation. Hannah may have wondered why they were hiding under the stairs, running through the woods late at night or sleeping in a strangers house but if it scared her, she didn't let it show. Maybe to her it was all an adventure. David looked from Hannah to Liz. They were his world. They stayed in bed together for another half hour and then rose to meet the day.

Lenny let them choose a house to make their own. In David's mind, it was temporary. He planned to go back to their house and see if it was intact. He would go either at dusk or just after dark. It made him sick to think about all the food they stored in the basement. If the house burned, they may be able to save some of it. The intensity of the fire made David believe the worst. If it burned down it would have fallen in on itself. He would know soon.

His shoulder was feeling a bit better than the first day but there was really no treatment for a broken collar bone. Lenny looked it over and felt it was in the best position to heal. It just meant David couldn't use that arm. The pain he did have was alleviated by Lenny's stockpile of pain meds, again, retrieved on one of his many excursions into the uninhabited house market.

Lenny did a good job of providing for himself and was also willing to share some of his food with the Zabads. "Did ya lose your tractor thing in the fire?"

"I haven't been over there yet, Lenny. And it was in the garage which sits back from the house. If the house burned, I don't think it would have touched the garage. Unless he torched that too."

"I'll go with ya. We'll get that tractor. I really like that little guy."

"Yeah it comes in pretty handy." David was thankful for Lenny's hospitality but he was getting to the point where he didn't really trust anyone fully. He thought of Sadiq and hoped he hadn't come by yesterday. It worried him that if Garrett was watching the house he might hurt whoever came by just to make a point. David's mind was running scenarios all the previous day, all night, and now was starting again today. Why would he burn Mark's house? Was it just a warning? David kicked him down, heard his secrets, and knew there was still more he was not told. Surely Garrett was looking for revenge or to silence him.

Then it hit him. Garrett knew about his basement stockpile, the gadgets he built to help his family. He knew about Sadiq, his trips with Lenny. There's no way he would have let the house burn. He would have wanted what was inside.

"Lenny, we're leaving for my place in ten minutes. Bring some water, food, and a weapon."

"Sure thing. Like my Phyllis used to say, never leave home without it."

"Did you always carry a weapon?" David was surprised as he recalled their first encounter where Lenny had a toy gun.

"Naw, Phyllis did. Biggest pistol you ever saw, jammed in her purse. Made me nervous. Threatened me with it more than once. Nope, she never left home without it."

"Grab whatever weapon you want to use and let's get

going. I have a feeling Garrett has been in my house and I'm short a few things."

Liz overheard the conversation from the next room and came to David's side. "Are you sure you want to go back there today? Feeling the way you do, your collarbone and all?"

"I think what you mean is, 'please don't go David. It's dangerous. Let's just wait until your shoulder heals.'"

"See, you still speak 'wife'. You translated that perfectly."

"I have to go, Liz. I have to make sure the house is intact, which I'm now almost positive it is. But even so, I want to get inside, grab a few things, and see how it feels to be back there. We can't live off the kindness of others forever. We've invested so much there."

"I know. I'm just doing my job. Being worried about you. Be safe. Don't take any chances."

"That's all we do anymore. See you later." David kissed her gently and headed for the door.

———

They approached the house from the cemetery hill so they would have a higher vantage point. They watched from a neighbor's yard, positioned just behind an air conditioning unit. The neighborhood was still and quiet. It was just mid-morning but it seemed earlier due to the cloud cover.

"I don't see anything, David."

David ignored the comment. "You ever had to kill someone Lenny?"

"Me? No. Wanted to. My ex-neighbor decided to raise chickens which was fine 'til he got that rooster. Worst alarm clock I never owned."

"So you wanted to kill him because his rooster woke you up every morning?"

"No! That's a stupid reason to want to kill someone. No, I killed that rooster and ate it and it was the worst piece of meat I ever put in my mouth. He sued me for it. *Then* I wanted to kill him."

David just shook his head. "Lenny, you are quite a character."

"I don't know what to say," Lenny answered, clearly taking the comment as a compliment.

"Tell me it's okay to kill this Garrett guy. He told me he was going to kill me. He implied that he was responsible for the mess Michigan is in. I'm afraid for my wife and kid. Tell me it's okay to kill him."

"Bible says it's wrong to murder."

"Says the guy who assaulted me and threatened me with a toy gun!"

"But I was never gonna murder you!"

"And what do you know about the Bible?"

"I know a lot. When they were still meeting, I went to two or three different churches in town. Got food from one, help with my rent at another one and there was another where I would just go talk to the pastor. Ask him all kinds of questions. I read the Bible all the time too. I know you're not supposed to kill anyone."

"I know that too, Lenny. I just – I don't see how I can go back to my house with my family and not address the guy up the street who wants me dead. It would be easier to just – you know, kill him."

"You shot that guy in the house down the street. Probably never wanted to either. Don't ask me how – at least not now – but one day I'll tell you. I know how you feel. You kill someone, it never lets you go. Every day you see their face, hear their voice. You think about it all the time. That something you're dealing with?"

"Some. I know God would forgive me if it were in self-defense, right?"

"God forgives us of all our sins, past, present and future. But that ain't the problem. It's forgiving yourself."

David knew deep down Lenny spoke truth. "C'mon. We need to get down to the house and see what's going on inside. They moved from their lookout spot and headed through two more backyards before sprinting across the backyard, tracing the same path they'd walked two nights ago. Mark's house was completely consumed, just a few black heaps of debris were all that was left. David could make out the shapes of what used to be the furnace, stove, and water heater. Other than a few other metal objects, the heat of the blaze melted or destroyed everything. At David's house, they could see a few plastic toys Hannah played with in the yard were melted. The end of the vinyl fence closest to Mark's house was completely gone.

"Check the back door," David suggested. Lenny stepped onto the porch, swung out the screen door and tested the knob. It turned easily and the door swung in. Lenny moved to step through the doorway but David had a hunch and stopped him with a gesture. "Check for traps. He laid a snare for me up by his house. It would be like him to rig a trap here."

After carefully looking at the doorway and the floor inside, they determined it was safe to enter. And that was the whole sweep of the house. Check the doorways, the floors, the closets, hinges, anything Garrett might have rigged to explode or cause harm. Nothing. They checked the basement. Everything there was intact. David was so sure Garrett's move was to get them out of the house so he could move in and grab everything. Or kill them as they left. But so far there wasn't one scrap of evidence to show he'd even been in the house. From the other room, David heard Lenny call out.

"Man, you should see this. This is creepy."

David walked into the dining room and Lenny was holding up a piece of paper. On it was a short note: *I'll be watching you. Through the scope of my sniper rifle. Or just from my front porch. You and your beautiful wife. And that little girl of yours. Your house would burn even faster than Mark's. See you around.*

"Where was this?" David demanded.

"Hanging on the front door. Didn't see it until I opened it up."

"He would know we never use that door. He knew we'd be looking for evidence of him having been here. He's playing games."

"You think you're okay here? He's writin' notes and struttin' around like he's in control. You oughta get your rag head buddy here and help you guard the place."

"Don't call him that, Lenny!"

"Your buddy? What's wrong with that? Ain't he your friend?" Lenny asked too innocently.

"You know what I'm talking about."

"Just teasin'."

"Uh huh," David said slowly and skeptically. "But you're right. I should get him over here, finally move him in and then we can work together to guard the place, watch out for the girls. I just can't leave when we've done so much to survive in this place. We have the gardens, the wood for our heat supply. We're close to what we need in town."

"Yup, you just live down the street from a psycho. Personally I'd pack up and go but hey, to each his own."

David chuckled at this and then offered, "Actually I was hoping you'd move in too."

"Hey buddy, I live down the street from a guy who sets houses on fire *for fun*. Come live with me! Yeah, no thanks."

"Lenny, there's strength in numbers. We can keep an eye on each other and on Garrett. What do you say?"

"I say I've got enough regrets already. But what's one more?" Lenny sighed deeply. "Yeah, I'll move in with ya."

"Thanks, Lenny. You won't regret it."

"Davey boy, that's what Phyllis said when she asked me to marry her."

"So you're all in?"

Lenny split his skinny face with a wide, almost toothless grin. "I'm in!"

TWENTY-FOUR

LENNY, SADIQ, DAVID, AND LIZ SPENT THE LAST
eleven days preparing the house for winter and securing it
against any advances from Garrett. Even Keith had begun
to move about and was helping any way he good. That
meant harvesting the garden David and a handful of neighbors so carefully guarded all summer. Some of the gourds
were not done yet. Neither were the onions and carrots. But
there were beans and more zucchini than they could count.
It also meant setting some traps around the house in case
there were any unwanted guests. David was confused as to
why Garrett backed off the night of the fire and not pursued
him back to his house. Especially knowing David was
injured. But he had some theories.

Garrett might have been injured worse than David first
thought. He kicked him fully in the chest with both feet.
Broken ribs and a concussion from hitting the ground were
both possible. David thought too, about all the supplies in
the basement. Garrett may not have wanted to risk losing all
the supplies David stockpiled. Or there was David's most
chilling theory. He didn't come after him that day because

he wanted to make David suffer. Maybe he was unable to do what he most wanted to do: repay David for what he did and use Elizabeth and Hannah to do it.

Whatever the reason, David needed to focus on what was in front of him and not dwell on his fears. Sadiq decided to sleep in the front of the house in a room that was used for a home office. Lenny moved in with Keith, into the room next to Hannah's, further down the hall from David and Liz, at the back of the house. They were closest to the rear stairs.

The days of preparation went quickly. September was typically just as warm as June but October was anyone's guess. Having a means of staying warm throughout the winter was essential. They had a limited supply of propane for the small space heater but David was extra cautious about using it; carbon monoxide was nothing to mess with. One of his trips with Lenny was a lesson in what not to do when you've lost power.

They broke into a home that looked deserted only to find an entire family scattered throughout the house, dead. Each looked as if they fell asleep doing various activities. It happened recently enough that the bodies were not decomposing. After searching the house, they discovered a generator in the basement that Lenny believed was running at one time. If the generator was running indoors, it would have produced enough carbon monoxide to kill everyone in the house before they even realized what was happening.

They also needed something to cook with indoors. There was no more natural gas. They hoped their heating solution could double as a cook top. David studied the books he brought back from the library, learning how to make snares for small game like rabbits, squirrels and groundhogs. Every animal they caught with a snare was one more bullet to use for their protection. David didn't look forward to killing, cleaning, and cooking a squirrel or a rabbit but knew that every scrap of food they could find for themselves stretched their resources further. David also studied from a book how to kill, gut, and butcher a deer. He wasn't sure what turned him off most – eating squirrels or carving up a deer carcass. What he was sure of was that he wanted to make his stockpile last as long as possible.

They never left the house alone. Each day, after their daily chores, David and one of the men would take a trip, leaving the others to guard the house with Liz. There was still much to be gathered around town.

After several hours of scavenging, David and Sadiq returned with another load of scrap wood and paper. They also carried a few personal hygiene items down to the basement. Finding razors, toothpaste, soap and new toothbrushes was always a blessing.

"Every time I look at all this stuff I think about finding Keith in that grocery store." David said.

Sadiq put down the box he carried down and sat on top of it. "I think of that too. It's amazing what he was able to do at just 17."

"If I hadn't gone into the grocery store that day, if you hadn't come looking for me, we might have never found Keith and all of this stuff." David sat as well and put his back to the basement's dusty stacked stone foundation.

"You never know what life will bring your way. The universe is smiling on us – for now."

"Sadiq, I thought you were Muslim. What do you mean the universe is smiling on us?"

"I grew up Muslim but I never practiced it. Perhaps the universe is the higher power?"

"The universe is a thing, not a person."

"Yes, but the universe is a force, like fate. Or luck." Sadiq said this more as a question than a statement.

"Sounds like you're mixing a few different religious ideas. Do you not believe in one ultimate power, one creator of the world, one being in charge of everything?"

"Not like I did when I was a child. There is too much hate and evil in the world for me to believe in an ultimate god. Like all of this," Sadiq said with his arms outstretched. "If there was a God, he wouldn't have allowed all these people to die. Or for you or Keith to be so badly injured. It's just the whim of the universe, the force or power that keeps the world turning. It's as arbitrary as the wind."

"But the day Keith was injured, when you thought he was dead you said he was at peace. What did you mean by that?"

"He would have ceased to exist. He would not be troubled with the things troubling us right now. So, he would be at peace. Besides, an ultimate, powerful and benevolent god would not have allowed any of this to happen."

"So, you've defined the conditions of God's existence?"

"Of course not. How could I do such a thing?"

David leaned forward and pressed the question. "You just said that if there was an all-powerful, benevolent God he wouldn't have allowed any of this but because it happened, there must be no God."

"Well . . . yes."

"So the only way for God to prove his existence is to create a perfect world?" David asked.

"Of course. Why would a good god allow such horror?"

"And you know what is good and what is bad?"

"That's pretty obvious, isn't it?" Sadiq said, annoyed with the question. "Good things benefit others and the world. Bad things hurt people and make life difficult." He shook his head with exasperation.

"But without bad things happening we wouldn't be able to recognize the good. We know what good is because we see its opposite. More importantly God tells us what is good and bad. Apart from that, we become the deciders of what is good and bad. And then life is just a big free-for-all."

"I don't know about that. What I do know is that a good god would prevent people from being hurt. I've been separated from my brother and the rest of my family since June. Why would a good God allow that? It's easier to believe that the universe is randomly handing out the good with the bad. Otherwise it feels . . . too personal."

"Sadiq, I gotta ask you a really personal question."

Sadiq shrugged. "Go ahead."

"Have you ever done anything wrong? Ever hurt someone with your words or actions?"

"Of course. The day we met I slammed your head onto the counter at the gas station." Sadiq laughed at the memory.

"Anything else?" David said, matching Sadiq's laughter with mock annoyance.

"Yes. I've said many things I wish I could take back. Why?"

"So, you admit that you've hurt people but a good God stops people from being hurt. Are you saying you want God to jump into your life and physically stop you from doing anything that might hurt another person?"

"What, and have god babysit me? Of course not. I should be able to make my own decisions."

"But that's your definition of an ultimate, benevolent God. One who always steps in and stops bad things from happening. If you wouldn't want God to do it for you, you can't expect him to do it for everyone else."

"Hurting someone's feelings and blowing up the city council or shutting off the power to half the country are vastly different."

"So, who decides which is worse or what's bad enough to earn God's attention? Maybe in your mind something is not so bad but God sees it as a terrible evil. See, human beings have the ability to make decisions about how they live. God honors those decisions. But they don't come without consequences. I think you're going to have to find some new criteria for deciding whether or not God exists."

"You're saying if there was an ultimate benevolent God, he would allow evil people to do evil things. Meaning, we should be saying, ultimate God and just leave off the benevolent part?"

"I think we need to let God be God. God might allow something bad to happen but use it to ultimately bring about something very good. Just because we see a bad thing happen doesn't mean God is stumped, trying to figure out what to next. He's like the ultimate chess player – always many moves ahead. Except in God's case he sees the whole game at once."

"This God you believe in sounds amazing."

"He truly is."

Sadiq slapped his hands to his knees and pushed himself up off the box he'd been perched on. "Ah, well I admire your faith. You certainly seem to know this God you speak about. I wish I could be that certain of anything."

"You can be." David walked to Sadiq and put a hand on his shoulder. "I've been praying for you. You can pray too. Ask God to help you see Him. As he really is."

"David! Can you come up here?" Lizzie called from the living room.

"Sadiq, let's talk about this again. You okay shelving all of this?"

"Of course. Thank you, my friend. For everything."

"My pleasure." David dashed up the stairs to find Lizzie in tears. She threw her arms around his neck.

"I'm so sorry. I'm so sorry, David, please forgive me."

"Forgive you for what? What's going on?"

"David, we need to talk. In private." She grabbed his hand and led him up to the second floor to their bedroom. The windows were open and a beautiful fall breeze was billowing the curtains. They sat on the bed.

"What is this all about, Liz? You seem terrified. What happened?"

It took some time for her to regain her composure. When she could speak without crying, she looked David in the eye and calmly said, "I'm pregnant."

"That's—that's—that's wonderful! I mean I—I know why you're crying, I think. I mean, we *are* happy about this right?"

The tears started again as Elizabeth tried to explain. "I am. I know I'm supposed to be. I don't understand. I was being so careful –*we* were being so careful."

"This is a God thing, Liz. Whoever this kid is, there's no stopping him – or her."

"But how can we bring a child into this world, the way it is now? How will I do the pregnancy without a doctor? What about the birth? David—"

"Lizzie, it's going to be okay." David was saying the words but deep down he was remembering the most terrifying moments of the last few months. The times when he had no idea what to do and could rely only on God. Those were the times when he had no idea if things would ever be okay again.

He held her as the tears flowed. He knew she felt real fear about the possibility of giving birth in the current environment. David suspected that she was weeping over the fact that she felt any regret at all. Children were such a blessing and to despair over being pregnant may have seemed to her like a terrible thing to do.

She wiped the tears away and took a few deep, calming breaths. "I am so sorry, David. I know how much you need me to keep it together."

"I know I expect a lot of you. You've worked harder than anyone I know these last few months. You're tougher than I ever gave you credit for. But keeping it together all the time is not one of the things I expect of you. This is hard. Life got way harder in June. And the thought of bringing a child into this mess is scary. Don't ever apologize for being real. I need that now more than ever."

"I'm tough. huh?"

David laughed. "Out of that whole speech, that's what you heard? How tough you are?"

She scrunched her nose and upper lip in an angry grimace and nodded at him. "Don't mess with me." She held up a misshapen fist to convey the idea.

David smiled at his wife's attempt to change the mood. "One second you're crying and the next you're playing tough guy? You really are pregnant."

She playfully smacked his uninjured arm and David laughed again. "So, when do you think he's due?"

"I'm not really sure. I think sometime in April. Maybe early May."

"Okay, we've got time to figure this out. Maybe we can

find a doctor who's still in town. Someone who can help us along the way."

"Yeah, I'm sure there's someone around."

"Come on, Liz. Let's go back downstairs. Everyone's probably wondering what happened to us. We need to tell them the news anyway. And let Hannah know she's going to be a big sister."

———

"David, wake up! There's someone outside." Elizabeth frantically threw back the quilt and headed for Hannah's room. She almost ran into Lenny coming out of his room, heading for the stairs.

"You heard it too, huh?" Lenny asked in his nasally rasp, accentuated by the lateness of the hour. "Gonna head down, see what I can find."

David stood sleepily at his doorway. "Keith? Stay with the girls. Lenny, you got the back door right?"

"Do bears poop in the woods?" he replied with a grin and headed down.

When David reached the front door he found Sadiq already waiting. "What is it?"

"Somebody knocking. Yelling for help. I hate to leave them out there but it's an old trick."

Several houses in town were robbed, their inhabitants beaten or killed after a person claiming to need help turned out to be a thief. David whispered, "You loaded?"

Sadiq nodded. "Safety off?"

"Orange means danger."

"I'm opening the door." David pulled open the front door from the side and cautiously looked around the jamb to see who was on the porch.

"David, please I need your help!"

"Martha?" David barely recognized his elderly neighbor. He hadn't seen much of her in the last month. He was so busy preparing the house for winter, guarding against a potential attack from Garrett and nursing his broken collarbone back to health that he wasn't checking on the neighbors. She looked gaunt and tired and that was just in the light of the lamp. Somehow, she survived this long. "What's going on?"

"Someone broke into my house but I got out the back door before they saw me. They'll take everything I have left."

"Sadiq, stay on guard here. Check the back and side door every few minutes. Lenny!"

"Yeah boss!" he called from the back of the house.

"You're coming with me." He and Lenny each carried a sidearm while Lenny had an additional shotgun and a candle burning inside a lantern box. David slung a rifle across his back. They exited the front door and followed Martha back toward her house. It was dark and quiet like most of the houses on the street. And then they heard a clang of metal.

"Lenny, go around, watch the back door just in case he or she takes off. They get away, they live to rob another day."

"A bullet a day keeps the thieves away."

David did not have time to appreciate Lenny's humor. "Martha, stay out here. In fact, it wouldn't be a bad idea for you to wait back at my house with Liz," David suggested. "If they have a gun they might want to use it." Martha quietly backed toward David's house, too terrified to argue.

David crept toward the front porch, listening for more sounds of movement, anything that would give a hint as to where the intruder was. Part of him wanted to just invite Martha in for the night, let the thief take what they wanted and figure things out in the morning. But there was another part of David that wouldn't allow someone to take what was not theirs. He was more like his father than he realized. A strong moral compass was one of Ethan Zabad's trademarks and David paid attention while growing up. Even though he didn't meet his father until he was eight, there was plenty of time to pick up many of his traits and habits. The moral fortitude to not only run off a thief in the middle of the night but enter the house he was in the process of robbing was a unique trait. Not many people would have done it.

David gripped the handle of his Glock, feeling his palms get moist and clammy. His heart pounded and for a moment he wished he had sent Lenny in to investigate. His last late-night encounter ended with him shooting an intruder at Melinda's house. He pointed the pistol out in front of him and tried to check around corners the same way. He cleared the living room and dining room and was about to enter the kitchen when he heard a new sound. A scuffling of feet and the muffled sound of someone trying to speak from behind a hand or thick fabric. The house was cloaked in darkness, a stick-built black hole, drawing David in while at the same time threatening to destroy him. The sound of a muffled voice came from the kitchen again and David was certain there was more than one person inside. Then, a person crying out in pain.

"Whoever you are, you need to come out right now! If you leave everything behind I will let you walk out of here but you need to go." He knew calling out would give away his position but he felt an urgency that demanded action.

There was another yelp of pain and then the sound of bodies crashing against cupboards. David called out to

Lenny to come to the back door and bring some light. The windows were open enough for him to hear and shortly David saw the glow of the candle lantern appear, eerily illuminating the kitchen. Sounds of a struggle persisted and the voice of the one being assaulted was young, female. It was dark enough that faces could not be recognized but light enough for David to see a man wrestling on the floor of the kitchen with that young female.

David plunged through the doorway and toward the struggling bodies on the floor. He grabbed the man by the shoulder to pull him off but he turned and took a swing at David which he managed to dodge. "Leave this woman alone!" David ordered but the command fell flat as he was still struggling to get his footing and get a gun aimed at the invader.

To regain control of the situation, David let go, stepped back and aimed his pistol at the man's back. "I said, leave this woman alone. Get up. Get your hands in the air." David moved around the kitchen island, keeping his gun trained on him and opened the back door of the house so Lenny could come in and help. His candlelight was stronger now and David could see the face of the intruder. It was dirty and covered with a short brown and gray beard but David recognized it. "Ted? Ted Lavin? What are you doing here? I thought you left with your family over a month ago."

The girl on the floor used the awkward silence to get up and run for the front door. Lenny started to follow but David reminded him that she'd just been terrified by Ted and didn't need another man following her outside.

"You know I can't just let you walk out of here Ted. Where's your wife? Your kids?"

Ted didn't answer for an achingly long time. He hung his head, shaking it slowly. "I wasn't gonna hurt her," he said. "She wouldn't tell me where the food was. I'm just so hungry, David."

"Ted. Your family?"

"We were almost to Kalamazoo. Walking with so many people heading west. It was almost eight at night. Still light out. We could see something building in the sky – a storm. The wind kicked up and before we could even get off the road, a tornado was touching down." His hands were shaking and it was then David noticed how emaciated he looked. In the candlelight, his normally healthy demeanor appeared skeletal and his eyes were sunken and dark.

"What did you do?"

"The only thing we could do. We ran. We ran off the road into some fields but the tornado shifted direction and came right at us. It was like a living thing – hunting us. We stopped in a stand of trees to try to figure out where to go next. It was so loud. Everyone says it sounds like a train. And it does. But not like the trains that roll through town. More like one going through town at a hundred miles an hour." Ted was lost in the traumatic memory for a moment and David gently encouraged him to go on. "There was a pole barn. We went inside and the tornado hit it. Everything just exploded around me. I don't remember anything after that. When I woke up, I was in a field not far from what was left of the pole barn. I couldn't find Sandy and the kids anywhere—" Ted broke into deep, heart wrenching sobs. "I searched for days. For days! I couldn't find them. They're gone—" Ted slumped against the kitchen counter where David halted his attack and slid down into a heap on the floor. "I came back here because I couldn't go on. I just couldn't. I had nothing to live for. Nothing."

David glanced at Lenny and nodded toward home where Martha was waiting. Lenny got the hint and walked through the house to the front door. "Ted, I'm so sorry about your family. I can't imagine how bad that hurts. How long ago did all this happen?

"Maybe four weeks ago. I'm not sure what day it is."

"It's September 19. You've been gone over six weeks. I can't believe it. Sandy and the kids."

"We should have stayed. I should have been stronger."

"Ted, don't. That kind of talk leads nowhere." Ted quietly cried, cuffing at his eyes and nose. David let him mourn but knew he had to sort out what just happened in Martha's kitchen. "I have to ask – why were you assaulting that woman?"

"I'm hungry, David! Look at me! Why do you think I'm here scrounging for food like a beggar?"

"Lots of people are hungry, Ted. Why didn't you just knock on my door?"

"Why do you think? You told us not to go. You warned us."

"I didn't want to be right, Ted. But why break in? And why Martha?"

"Look what you're holding David. I knew you'd be armed. Martha is alone. She knows me. I knew she wouldn't have a gun. I thought I could grab some food and slip back out without her knowing."

"That's a mountain of assumptions. And the girl? It didn't look like you were having a casual conversation."

"I asked her where the food was. She was so freaked out, she wouldn't answer. But the more I asked, the more she freaked out. I was just trying to keep her quiet."

"Do you know who she is?" David inquired.

"She's my granddaughter," Martha answered, surprising everyone as she walked back into the kitchen. "And I don't want you anywhere near me or my granddaughter."

David wanted to ask where her granddaughter came from and explain Ted's actions and try to defuse the situation but the moment passed him by as Martha continued her angry barrage of words.

"I don't care if you were my neighbor or where you've been. You don't break into my house and scare my grandchild half to death and try to steal from me. I ought to take you out in the street, hang you upside down and beat you like a piñata for just a minute."

"Martha, I'm so, so sorry." Ted was on his knees, lifting a pleading hand toward her.

"Yeah, me too. For ever being friends with a sicko like you. She's sixteen! David, can you please get him out of my house?"

David, deciding further discussion was useless, grabbed Ted's upper arm and guided him toward the front door. He met Lenny out front and they headed home.

"What are you going to do with me?" Ted whimpered.

"I don't know." David started to speak several times as he walked Ted down the street but each time he stopped before any words came out. The man was destroyed by the loss of his family. There was no punishment David could mete out that would even come close to that. But he couldn't excuse the fact that he broke into a friend's house with intent to steal and assaulted a girl. "Ted, do you have anything to eat in your house?"

"No, we took everything with us when we left."

"Do you have any way to keep you warm when the weather turns?"

"Maybe a couple blankets we left in the house."

"Do you at least have a weapon of some kind to protect yourself? Anything?"

Ted just shook his head sadly. David felt compassion

and frustration at the same time. It was a wonder Ted made it back from where he lost his family. He was always likable and seemed carefree. He played golf, rode bikes around town with his kids, and liked to fish on the weekends. But he didn't rise to the level of leadership this crisis demanded. He did not know how to turn his skills and abilities into assets for survival. The thought of taking in another mouth to feed frightened David. Looming in his mind, always, was a cold, ravaging winter that could still have its grip on the land into early April. Providing for his family was always on his mind. There would be no breaks all winter. Every day would be another scavenging trip, another log added to the woodpile, another can of green beans or corn to add to the stockpile. If Ted could be prodded into usefulness, he may be able to feed himself. With all the lakes around Fenton it was possible he could be helpful by putting his fishing skill to use.

David stopped in the middle of the road and turned to face Ted. "I can't punish you. I don't know what I can do to make you feel more remorse than you do already. But you can do penance. Pay for your crime – so to speak."

"I'll do anything. I can't believe I lost it on that poor kid! I broke into her house . . . What's wrong with me David?"

"You're not yourself, Ted. What you need is something to put your mind to. Something you can focus on that will help others." David almost added, *instead of just yourself* but refrained. "For now, you live at your place. Come each day, early. You can have breakfast and dinner with us. We only eat two meals right now. But you will earn those meals. Every day, you'll be collecting fuel for our winter heat. You'll also go scavenging with me, Lenny or Sadiq – every day we search for and collect anything that can help us survive. Or you'll stay at the house with Keith and Liz.

We're not looking at just making it until spring. We're looking at surviving long term. There's no helicopters coming to drop supplies. No truckloads of food and water. We are on our own. You will work or die."

"First it's penance and now it's work or die?"

"Ted," David said as calmly as he could. "It is literally work or die. You understand what I'm saying? That's not a threat. That's reality."

"Got it. By the way, did you say 'Sadiq'?"

"Yeah, why?" David could already guess the answer.

"Sounds like an Arab name."

"And?" David tried to keep his voice even but he saw Lenny in his peripheral vision move up close, looking ready to brawl.

"And – you know who caused all this right? Ay-rabs. And you're working with one?"

"You have no idea what you're talking about, Ted. And you should stop right now."

"I know exactly what I'm talking about. It's all we talked about walking out west. We have to take this country back from the people who ruined it."

"Ted, you are not in a position to talk this way. You don't even know who caused all this. I am trying to help you! I am offering you a way to stay alive."

Ted was defiant. "Not if it means working with the enemy."

"He's not an enemy. If it wasn't for Sadiq, we wouldn't even have half of our supplies. He's been nothing but generous and helpful from day one. He's become like family over the last three months."

"If it wasn't for Sadiq's kind, my family would still be alive!"

The fist flew from David's left. Lenny let loose with a

left hook Rocky would be proud of. Ted took it hard on the chin and crumpled to the asphalt. David wasn't sure whether to applaud or hold Lenny back. He'd almost done it himself. "Get up, Ted. You have two options. Help us survive or go it alone."

Ted pushed himself up off the ground and without saying a word staggered toward his house at the end of the street near the cemetery.

"Did you see that, David? Just like when I fought Artie Spencer." Lenny shadow-boxed a few jabs and hooks.

David didn't know who Artie Spencer was and was not in the mood for a Lenny story. "Come on, Balboa. Let's go check on everyone else." They were just one door down from David's house when Sadiq met them at the end of the walkway. "Did you hear any of that?" David asked.

"Yeah. Yelling in the road in the middle of the night when I'm on guard kind of gets my attention. So, I'm like family huh?"

"Don't let it go to your head. Let's get back to sleep. We've got another busy day tomorrow."

Sadiq took one last look around the house and nearby intersection. He did not know it, but he and the rest of the house were being watched – a silent observer in the dark tree line, waiting until the time was right.

TWENTY-FIVE

"I forgot how disgusting this is. Not having running water is so much worse."

"You'll be through the morning sickness by winter. That'll help a little."

"At least these mornings aren't freezing cold." Liz lifted her head from where she was bent over the porch railing and wiped her mouth with a rag. "The leaves are starting to show some color."

"Last day of September. Peak color week is just two weeks away. I've always loved fall but I don't think I can get as excited about it this year. It doesn't mean what it did last year. This year it means winter is one day closer."

"You said we'd be fine this winter. We have the food, we have the fuel for heat. You've worked so hard."

"*We've* worked so hard. And yes, we have a lot of supplies, but things could change in an instant. And there's the baby – and Garrett."

"There's no use worrying about the baby. She'll be fine."

"*She?*"

"Yes, David. I'm convinced it's a she."

"I would love to have a son but right now all I want is for you to be okay."

"We will be. And as for Garrett, you've prepared the best you could. We have to trust God for the rest."

"I do. I just hate being on edge all the time. Sadiq is okay but Lenny – and I can't believe I'm actually saying this, but, Lenny – is a lot like me. He's not good at sitting around. And not being able to go out every day is making him crazy. Not Garrett-crazy but still . . ."

"You are so funny."

"What? Why am I funny?"

"David, the men you've connected with and gathered here – they believe in you. They trust you. And each of them in their own way is a little like you. But you're leading them."

"No, that's my dad's department."

"David, you're his son. You may not have the supernatural strength but you have a strength of your own. Look at all you've done. How many men do you know just in this city that have worked as hard to provide for their families as you?"

"I'm sure there's some."

"Name one. In all of your searching around town for supplies and food and whatever we needed, how many people did you run into that shared a good idea with you? How many showed you a contraption they'd made? How many people did you see still riding a tractor with a trailer long after everyone ran out of gas? You don't even realize what you've done."

David surveyed the yard where his water collection system and distiller sat. A heavy dew covered everything – the makeshift outhouse, the tractor parked next to the shed, the pile of wood pulp blobs that were supposed to look like bricks. There was much more inside the house he did, some of which he hadn't even showed Liz.

"Liz, I've done what I felt I had to. God led me to Sadiq and Keith, and to Lenny, even though he almost killed me. I've done what I felt any man would do to protect his family."

"You're every bit the hero your father is. Maybe more."

"Ah, now you went too far. See you were doing well 'til you said that."

"David, I know he's your hero. But you're a good man. And yes, a lot of it is because of him but you've chosen to be the man you are. And I'm so proud of you."

"I'm proud of you too. I don't know any women who could have been as strong as you have. I'm so impressed by you."

"I've been a mess since this started. You must be talking about your other wife."

"Funny. You've faced every challenge with determination and always still encouraged me. Come on, let's go back inside. You need to upchuck again?"

"You're so sensitive, David," Liz teased. "No, I'm fine now."

"Glad to hear it. Ted should be here soon."

"It seems like Ted's been working hard," Liz said as she opened the rear screen door.

"He's doing the work. He has to do something – keep busy – or he'll go crazy with grief. He feels responsible for the death of his whole family. I can't blame him for not thinking straight."

"You could have been a lot harder on him," Liz said, putting a hand on David's arm.

"I almost was. I was so angry about what he did to

Martha and her granddaughter. And what he said about Sadiq."

"Are Martha and her granddaughter okay?"

"Shaken a bit but they're fine. I guess her granddaughter just showed up and Martha didn't want to advertise it. I was rattled because I almost killed Ted when I went in there. We'd be having a very different conversation right now if I had."

"So, what's on the agenda today?"

"I'm sending the guys out to the northwest side of town, across the expressway. We haven't done much scavenging over there. I'm still hoping we can find a wood stove instead of what we jerry-rigged in the basement."

"Sending the guys? All of them?"

"I'll keep Keith here. I can't go. I think my collarbone is almost healed but I wouldn't be much use if we found a stove. Those can weigh a couple hundred pounds. They'll be out and back by late afternoon. Another couple weeks and I'll be back to full strength."

"Alright. Let's go inside and get some breakfast."

When Ted arrived, Lenny and Sadiq were ready to go. "Got your list?" David asked.

"My list is up here," Sadiq boasted, pointing to his head.

"Yeah, mine too," Lenny added. "Like my Phyllis used to say, mind like a steel trap," he said pointing to his head, "And mine's rusted shut."

"Lenny, that's not a compliment."

"Sure it is. Means nothing gets out!"

"Right, Lenny. It also means nothing gets in. A rusted trap doesn't catch anything."

"Aw Davey, why you gotta go ruinin' good memories? It's a compliment to me!"

"Okay, Lenny. You keep those two out of trouble."

"You can count on me. See you later."

"I wish I could go along," Keith lamented.

"You'll get your chance. For now, I need you around here."

David watched the three men walk out to the main road and whispered a prayer of thanks that he was able to make some real friends, even during the crisis. Most of the people he worked with or went to church with lived far enough away that he hadn't seen them or heard from them in months. He was looking forward to a day with Liz and Hannah to just relax. He hadn't taken a day off to rest in a long time. Maybe the day after he broke his collarbone when he and his family ran to Lenny's place for a couple nights to escape the fire and Garett's retaliation. David continually looked over his shoulder, never fully relaxed or ever believing that Garrett had decided to let things go. He was convinced that if he had entered Garrett's house that morning, he would not be breathing air right now.

"Come on, let's go sit on the back porch," David said to Liz as he walked back into the living room. He grabbed a couple books he'd been wanting to read about sustainable farming techniques and urban farming. His second trip to the library was even more profitable than the first. He went in daylight, deciding that even if someone saw him, there was nothing they could do about it. And David was willing to share the books. He'd taken copious notes on the first books, returned them and gathered these new ones. It seemed silly to return them but there might be someone out there who needed them too.

They went out to the porch and enjoyed the mild

morning for half an hour. Hannah was playing on the outdoor carpet while Liz and David rocked slowly on the glider bench. Keith was sitting across from them, also reading a book. David felt it before he heard it. It felt like a whisper on his neck, like a fly landed on it, then moved on. But the whisper wasn't a fly. It was a bullet grazing his neck and the touch was followed by what sounded like the massive crack of a whip.

"David, your neck is bleeding!" Liz exclaimed.

"Holy -!" Keith didn't finish as he dropped to the floor.

"Liz, get down! Hannah, go inside!" Hannah cried in fear and didn't move. "Liz, go. Get her inside." The top of the wooden glider they were sitting on broke apart as it was hit by another bullet. Liz grabbed Hannah and got inside. David reached up to touch his neck and felt a warm trickle of blood. He was so angry all he wanted to do was run up the hill and put his hands around Garrett's neck. He lied on the porch floor and scanned the road that led to Garrett's house and the hill it sat on. No sign of the shooter but he was probably in camo. For all David knew, he was in his sights right now. "Keith, do you see anything?"

"No. But the bullets had to come from the hillside. He's probably already moved from his first position."

"We're going in. Come on." David moved to the wall of the house and slipped in the back door.

"I wish we could go back to throwing soup cans," Keith grumbled as he crawled toward the door.

"David, he's coming. I knew we shouldn't have sent all the guys away today." Liz said as he came inside with Keith close behind.

"I guarantee you, they heard those shots. They're already on their way back," David said it confidently but in his mind he was thinking of how many times over the last few months they'd heard gunshots but done nothing. Would Sadiq and Lenny know the difference? "Alright, I want you and Hannah in the stairwell again."

"You don't think he knows about that?" Liz asked.

"There was nothing disturbed on the stairs and no sign that he found it. What else are we going to do? You can't just sit in the living room. I don't care what happens to me. But he threatened to do very specific things to you and that's not going to happen. You understand me?"

Liz nodded, as Hannah clung to her legs. "David, I can help you."

David grasped Liz's arms. "I am not letting you anywhere near that man. I'm trying to do what's right. I am trying to protect my family. I have Keith here too. It will be okay."

Keith left the kitchen to look out the living room windows and let David and Elizabeth talk.

"You are always trying to protect us and I appreciate that so much. You are always trying to be *right*. Do right. But you can do right things or do things right. They're not always the same – what I'm trying to say is, the right thing is for me to hide and protect our daughters—" David smiled at Liz's confidence. "But," Liz continued. "If we are going to do this right, I need to help you. You need another set of eyes. And another gun."

"He could be on his way down that hill right now. Get hidden and whatever you do, do not come out."

"You didn't listen to a word I said."

"I heard you, I just don't agree."

"David —"

"Don't worry. I have everything I need." He kissed her fiercely on the lips. "I love you." He knelt and kissed Hannah on the check and squeezed her before nudging them both toward the stairs. He quickly helped them both into what they now called the hidey-hole. He went from there into the living room and grabbed the Sig Sauer he'd picked up on a scavenging trip and the shotgun that was used frequently since June. He loaded it with buckshot and grabbed another box of ammunition for each gun, tucking them into a hip pocket and a cargo pocket in his pants. Fully armed, he went to the front of the house and looked through the faux leaded glass door to see if he could spot Garrett.

"You see anything Keith?"

"Nope."

As David peered through the beveled glass trying to get a clearer view, a shotgun blast sounded behind him and he turned to see pieces of the side door flying across the dining room.

"Keith! Are you okay?"

"I'm fine. But he must have been up on the porch. I didn't see him."

David swiftly stepped into the doorway to Sadiq's room and trained his shotgun on the side entry, waiting for Garrett to step through it. Instead, he heard another blast at the back door. Keith ran to the kitchen doorway and carefully peeked at the back door but Garrett was not there either. The doorknob was shattered and the door was open a few inches. David had just reached the kitchen behind Keith when they heard another shotgun blast at the front of the house. They felt like they were chasing shadows. Every door was now blasted open but they had yet to actually see who was doing it. They knew it was Garrett. But now there were three entry doors, none now with functioning knobs or deadbolts. Garrett was playing with them, performing a physical shell game – which door is he coming in?

David didn't want to play. His mind went to his father

and everything he tried to teach him in the short times he was able to be at home. If only his dad could be here now. He would know how to handle this situation. David imagined him stranded in some foreign country, unable to fly into the US. Surely, he was worried about David, Liz and Hannah.

He had to make a decision. Liz was right. He was obsessed with always making the right decision. But in some circumstances, a decision had to be made and there was no time to weigh all the options and choose the perfect move. "Keith, go to the basement and keep a gun trained on the stairs. If he walks by, shoot him." David went upstairs to his bedroom and positioned himself so he could see the doorway. He also had a window behind him so he could check for Garrett outside. If he was coming to kill him and his family, he would have to find them first.

David listened for footsteps. Any movement at all. He had an advantage, since he'd lived in the house for some time. He knew every creaky floorboard and stair tread. He knew what each part of the house sounded like when Liz walked through it. Details, details. David's engineering mind was spinning with all of the details he could use in this scenario to impede the progress of his foe. He calmed his thoughts and reminded himself that he was doing what he needed to do. Wait and when the opportunity presented itself, ambush him.

Then he heard it. The back door swung open, pushing aside the debris from the gunshot that destroyed it. David heard his footsteps cross the kitchen and enter the living room. That meant he passed the basement stairs. *Why hadn't Keith fired?* The careful steps continued throughout the first floor and David was sweating and shaking. Finally, David heard the steps coming up the stairs and he knew he would see Garrett reach the top at any moment.

He heard the whisper, "I came to kill you. Pure and simple." It was so vivid and so close David thought he might be hallucinating or that Garrett entered the room without him seeing. He slid down behind the bed, shaking. He entered homes that were under attack, fought an intruder in his living room and surprised himself at his bravery. Why could he not even look over the edge of this bed to see if Garrett was standing there? "David, you're the kind of guy who will only get in my way. Get in the way of progress. You're good, moral, patriotic. But you're part of the problem. This country was destroying the world. Literally. Coal, crude oil, plastic. So much consumption. We just reduced that by more than half. We're not done. We have to give the world a fighting chance.

Garrett's footsteps moved away from the bedroom and down the hall. "I know you're in here somewhere, Davey. You and your pretty wife."

At the mention of Liz, David found something akin to courage. It was enough to get him off the floor and to the bedroom doorway. He continued to shake with nerves. But he could see Garrett at the other end of the hall, with his back to him, inspecting the spare bedroom where Lenny slept. David raised his shotgun and fought to keep it steady. Garrett must have sensed David behind him and he turned, trying to bring his 12 gauge shotgun to bear. David pulled the trigger and the buckshot ripped into Garrett's right arm and shoulder spinning him and throwing him into the bedroom door. He cried out in shock as the pain exploded through his arm and upper torso.

David was shaking before he took the shot but now, with adrenaline fully inundating his system, he could not relax. He knew he needed to finish the job. Eliminate the threat to his family. He racked another shell into the chamber and raised the shotgun but a drop of sweat ran into his eye momentarily blinding him. He tried to blink the sweat away and finally swiped at his eye with a sleeve. His eyes cleared enough to see Garrett growling in response to the pain in his arm. Garrett used his left arm to raise his shotgun and David realized what was coming. He leaped back into his bedroom as the gun went off, buckshot hitting the door and tearing a gash across it. Then David remembered the pistol. He jerked it out and crawled back to the door way to aim at Garrett. He was gone.

David jumped to his feet and walked toward the bloody puddle on the floor. He glanced in Lenny's bedroom and then walked back down the hall and checked Hannah's room. No sign of him. He was about to go back to his bedroom when Garrett sprang from the bathroom and tried to tackle David. They grappled and David tried to aim the pistol at him. Garrett grabbed David's wrist and spun it around forcing him to drop the weapon. A crushing left hook made David see stars and then another left to the solar plexus put David on his knees. Dizzily, David could see Garrett's right arm hanging limply at his side as he bent to pick up the pistol. Garrett stood to aim the weapon, but David launched himself from where he knelt and drove his fists into Garrett's chest. This move forced Garrett toward the top of the front staircase. He threw another fist into Garrett's right shoulder causing him to scream in agony. A left to the chin and right to the nose. Garrett tried to come at David but he sidestepped him and hit him again with a left. Garrett stumbled backward and tried to catch himself on the handrail but missed. He hit hard and his feet went up over his head and he rolled the rest of the way down the front staircase. David felt the bile rise in his throat as he watched Garrett tumble down like a pile of dirty laundry and stop hard at the bottom. He looked down the stairs at his attacker to see him in a heap.

"Why did you have to come after my family? Why? Who am I?" David cautiously made his way down the stairs, pistol in hand. He thought Garrett must have suffered a several broken bones, maybe even a broken back. And his arm was bleeding worse than before. But then David saw that his nemesis struck his head on something at the bottom of the stairs, evidenced by the growing pool of blood beneath him. "This didn't have to happen."

Garrett struggled to breathe and to speak. "You're a Zabad."

"What does that even mean? Why do you know anything about me?"

"Not you. Your father. When they started planning— they made lists—persons of interest. Your father—was one of them—I was assigned to you. Me and another neighbor."

"What possible difference would I have made in whatever you were planning? I'm a nobody but you came after me and now look at you."

Garrett coughed feebly and blood appeared at the corners of his mouth. "I can't feel my legs."

"I'm not sorry. But I'm sorry you think I'm such a threat that you would come after me. Or that this country is so bad that you have to do this to it. What is this all about? Why?"

"There's more of us. We were ready. More will come." He coughed again and tried to twist away from the shelving unit his head was resting against.

David knelt and spoke quietly but firmly into the face of this domestic terrorist. "More are coming? Then I wish I could take a picture of you – the way you are right now.

Then they would know what would happen to them if they came after my family."

"You can't stop us. No one can. If winter doesn't kill you, we will."

"There's no *we* anymore. You're done."

Garrett closed his eyes for the last time, succumbing to the blood loss and injuries.

Keith came up behind David to look at Garrett.

Just a few minutes later, Sadiq and Lenny ran into the house, guns at the ready, while Ted stayed just outside on the porch. Lenny went up the back kitchen stairs and Sadiq stood in the living room and scanned the house. "We heard shots. Almost didn't come back but Lenny insisted. What did we miss?"

David waved him to where he and Keith stood over Garrett just as Lenny was coming down the stairs.

"That your handiwork?" Sadiq asked.

"Yeah. I got the drop on him upstairs. But then I lost it. I couldn't take a second shot. I was shaking so bad. We fought and he landed here."

Sadiq put a hand on David's shoulder. "It's okay. You did good. You protected your family."

"My family!" David realized he hadn't told Liz and Hannah to come out. He ran from the front stairs to the kitchen stairs. "Liz! Hannah! I'm alright. You can come out." David yanked the false stair tread out of place and reached in to grasp Liz's hand.

Liz tearfully handed Hannah out to David. "I heard the shots. I thought—I didn't know."

David helped Liz out of the hidden stairway compartment and held her tight. "I'm okay. It's okay. He's not going to threaten us anymore." He chose to keep Garrett's last words to himself.

"I knew something wasn't right," Lenny was saying. "I could feel it. Like when there's gonna be rain and my knee starts acting up."

Ted came in from the porch "Lenny, you're so full of—"

"Hey!" David cut him off. "That's enough. I'm just glad everyone is okay. We'll take our little trip tomorrow instead."

Liz interjected, "Maybe we should all stay close to home for a little while. And David, we need another escape route. Another place to go. Every time there's a threat, you can't stick us in this little hole. We need a place we can all go and not be in the dark."

"What did you have in mind?"

"I'm not sure but I want it done soon. Whatever it is."

"Okay. I'm going to work on that through the winter. But we still have a lot to do. These doors need fixing now. The rest of the harvest needs to come in. I heard there's black walnuts all over Fenton we can collect and eat. So, one thing at a time."

They carried Garrett's body outside and buried him in the yard next to the first intruder that died in the house.

Sadiq and Ted, at David's insistence, spent the next few days sorting through everything in Garrett's house. David considered him an enemy of the state, if there was still a United States of America, and didn't have any qualms about ransacking the place. Garrett prepared well and there was plenty of food and weapons in his basement. They also found three generators and a cache of fifty-five gallon drums full of gasoline. He had a shortwave radio set up in his living room. David insisted on taking it even though he'd never used one. Another trip to the library would help him with that. Perhaps they could finally get some information about life outside of Fenton or better yet, contact his dad.

TWENTY-SIX

A WEEK AFTER GARRETT'S ATTACK, DAVID STARTED THE generator for a few hours so they could enjoy electrical lights and use their single serve coffee maker for the first time in over three months. There was a festive atmosphere in the Zabad's living room. Lenny and Sadiq each enjoyed a cup of the strongest coffee available while Keith and Hannah sipped hot chocolate. Ted tried to brood in the corner but in spite of everything he'd been through, was still able to smile. A cloud was lifted and fear and despair were replaced with hope.

"I wish we could do this every night. I'm so tired of the dark." Liz said.

"I know, Liz. We'll have lots of nights like this though." David replied.

Sadiq stood from the ottoman he'd been perched on and announced, "I'd like to propose a toast. To David, for uniting this group of misfits—"

"Speak for yourself. I ain't no misfit. Like—"

Sadiq cut him off. "If you say, 'like my Phyllis used to say' you will officially seal your misfit status."

"Uh, well, my Phyllis, she uh – aw dang it."

Sadiq raised his mug in triumph, "To all the misfits!" They all took a sip and then, looking around the room, Sadiq continued. "Without these circumstances we would never have known each other. We would never have worked together as we have. We have found friendships." He nodded to Lenny. "We have found family. And we have found shelter." He nodded to Ted. "We have experienced pain. But we have survived. In some ways, even thrived. It has not been easy but we are better for it. Thank you, David. You are the reason we are all here tonight. And please say a prayer of thanks also to your god who I think may have had something to do with all this."

"You can thank Him yourself."

"No, I wouldn't know what to say."

"I think you just said it."

Sadiq stared into his mug for a moment letting the steam rise around his face. "Perhaps one cold winter day we can discuss that next to the fire."

————

David switched off the generator on the back porch and stood listening to the sounds of the night. A breeze blew across the yard, scattering the first of the fallen leaves, their dry brown shapes whispering across the grass. A dog barked in the distance and David thought he could hear an owl high in the trees they ran to not long ago to escape the house. The screen door pushed open and David knew immediately it was Liz. He waited for her to come and put her arms around him. She did and squeezed David from behind before he turned and wrapped his arms around her.

"You have some true friends in there David. They feel indebted to you."

"They would be fine without me. I hardly did anything," David deflected.

Liz untangled herself from David's arms and stepped back to look at him. "Modesty is an attractive quality as long as it's plausible."

"What's that supposed to mean?"

"It means it's one thing to shift the praise to someone else. It's another to flat out lie."

"Liz, it's not a lie. I didn't really do anything."

"David, you are a leader. You inspire people. Sadiq is behind you one hundred percent. And Lenny *loves* you. He thinks you're the greatest thing since Phyllis!" David couldn't help laughing as he tried to imagine Phyllis and Lenny in the same room. "And Ted is still here because of you."

"Ted's here because he's hungry and lost and broken. The man lost his whole family. That has nothing to do with me."

"And he could be anywhere right now but you took him in. You gave him purpose. You kept him so busy this last month that he's not the same as when he showed up that night. He's healing."

David grudgingly saw her logic. "Okay, you're right about Ted but this guy you're describing just doesn't sound like me. It sounds more like my dad."

"Do you think this apple fell that far from the tree?" she asked as she lightly punched his upper arm.

"I'm not a leader, Liz."

"Maybe you never set out to be one but that's what you've become. Leaders aren't born, right? They're made.

Out of the fire of circumstance, the crucible of pain and trial."

"Listen to you. Are you turning into a poet?"

"I'm finally reading all the books on our shelf. I've been jotting down the parts that speak to me."

"And memorizing them?"

"It's a lot easier now with fewer distractions," she said with a smile. This crisis has made a leader of you. You always led our family well but you have become a leader of others – our neighborhood, these men in the house. Don't dismiss the ways you've changed. I'm proud of the leader you've become." She kissed him gently on the lips.

"Behind every good man is a great woman though, right?"

"Oh, that was cheesy."

"Come on, I thought that was good!"

"I said you were a good *leader*. Knowing the right things to say, make speeches – we have to work on that."

"Okay. In all my spare time. We actually have a lot to do, you know."

"I know," Liz said quietly as David pulled her close.

"We defeated one enemy so far. But we have another fight coming – against another enemy. One I'm afraid is much deadlier, relentless. All the leadership in the world won't make it quit."

"Who are you talking about?"

"Winter. It will be different than any winter we've ever been through. Even a mild winter will test us. We've always had instant hot water, instant heat in the house. Just staying warm will be a full time job."

"I'm ready, David. Ready for our daughter to come. Ready to stop being afraid. Ready for whatever's ahead."

"I'm ready too. As long as we're together." David broke off their hug and stepped to the porch rail. "A night like this makes me wonder where my dad is. I think about him every day."

"I think about my parents too. I do wish we could make the trip."

"We'll revisit the idea. It may become doable." David shivered against the air that grew cooler since they started talking. "Come on. Let's go inside." He took Liz's hand and led her through the screen door and into the kitchen. He lit an oil lamp and carried it into the darkness of the second floor.

to be continued . . .

ABOUT THE AUTHOR

Chris Vitarelli lives with his wife Jody and their four children in southeast Michigan. He is a pastor, author and conference organizer. He is sought after as a speaker for conferences and seminars. His other books include *Strong* and *Small Church BIG Deal: How to rethink size, success and significance in ministry.*

ALSO BY CHRIS VITARELLI

Strong: A Novel

Small Church BIG Deal

A NOVEL

STRONG

CHRIS VITARELLI

SMALL CHURCH

BIG DEAL

HOW TO RETHINK SIZE, SUCCESS AND SIGNIFICANCE
IN MINISTRY

CHRIS VITARELLI